Please feel free to send m
publisher filters these ema

Melissa Bender - melissa_bender@awesomeauthors.org

Sign up for my blog for updates and freebies!
http://melissa-bender.awesomeauthors.org/

About the Publisher

BLVNP Incorporated, A Nevada Corporation, 340 S. Lemon #6200, Walnut CA 91789, info@blvnp.com / legal@blvnp.com

DISCLAIMER

Forgotten Sweethearts

By: Melissa Bender

BLVNP

ISBN: 978-1-68030-814-3

Table of Contents

Bailey, Mason and Everly.
This is for you, to show you that dreams can come true.

FREE DOWNLOAD

Get these freebies and MORE when you
sign up for the author's mailing list!

melissa-bender.awesomeauthors.org

PROLOGUE

High school sweethearts as most would call us; I fell fiercely and violently when we first met at fifteen. He was leaning against the lockers in the school corridor when I laid eyes on him for the very first time. My heart raced at the sight of him, pounding against the inside of my chest so hard that I thought it would nearly explode. I walked past, blushing as my gaze dropped the second our eyes locked. Luckily for me, he felt the same way too.

I looked at him with love and complete devotion and always craving his deep blue eyes on me. Often, I'd look up to see him staring right back, gazing ever so lovingly towards me and sneaking hidden glances during classes. Even when we finished school and moved in together, he would always watch. At night, Brody would always hold me as if I were about to disappear, never wanting to let go.

Fast forward eleven years and two children later, the only thing exploding of late was my anger towards him. The fire of passion between us was no longer explosive. Lovemaking was a rare, occasional occurrence, and I had no clue what foreplay was involved of anymore. Was it spitting on my own fingers or giving him a quick grab? I didn't know. I just knew it wasn't what it should have been.

Every touch, lingering kiss and glance towards each other were just for show. Behind the large wooden door of our home, we were anything but happy. Living a lie, it was what we'd become accustomed to. This was our life.

To everyone else, we appeared the perfect couple. Deep down, I knew the divorce was near.

We spent most nights apart, sleeping in separate bedrooms. I hated it. I hated that we'd grown to loathe each other. The undeniable attraction was still here, just fizzled out. Neither of us was willing to try to keep the spark alive or to keep what we once had. Both of us had given up.

His personal life was suffering because work always came first. Brody worked hard all the time. I won't deny that. He had thrown himself into becoming the best he could, climbing the ladder to the top. I said nothing when I really should have spoken up the second I began feeling left out. My thoughts were kept hidden away and left unsaid.

His family never noticed, too busy engrossed with their own lives to notice just how bad things had become. Brody's mother loved her weekly family dinners and the yearly vacations. We would always manage to avoid those. Using work as the perfect excuse when in all honestly, we just couldn't stand to be in the same room with one another for two weeks, which was a sad but true harsh reality.

I was unable to complain too much as Brody had given me a wonderful life, a beautiful six-bedroom home, much bigger than we needed, but it was ours. Brody earned enough to keep the bills paid and then some. After Noah was born, I stayed home full time, taking the new job title as a housewife.

It was hard at first, as I had always loved my job, enjoying the daily interactions with other adults and feeling like I mattered. Now, I was used to being a stay-at-home mother, enjoying my children and living life through them.

Pathetic, I know. I just didn't know how miserable that would make me in the end.

CHAPTER ONE

Quietly, my knuckles rapped against the wood before I reached down and turned the knob. Pushing the door open, I began to walk inside his office. My husband sat behind his large wooden desk, a soft glow against his face from the dimly lit lamp close by. His office filled with bookcases and family photographs. A couch pushed against one side of the wall and a TV in the corner for the nights he spent in here.

This was his usual spot when home, working and away from everyone.

He looked so handsome with those blue eyes I wanted to lose myself in and dark brown hair. For a moment, it was easy to forget that we were in a war against each other most days.

"The kids are asleep. I'm going to bed now," I said, interrupting him with a heavy sigh as I crossed my arms over my chest and leaned against the white wall.

Brody didn't bother looking up. "Good night."

I lingered, wishing things were differently. How I wanted to go over there, walk across the timber flooring and pull his swivel chair around; to sit on his lap with my arms draped over his shoulders and kiss or just talk about our day; and, to be close to him once again.

Paperwork scattered all around, his eyes were narrowed as he concentrated hard on whatever was on the screen. His fingers typing furiously on the Mac keyboard stopped. His head stayed bowed as his dark eyes glanced upwards. "Yes?" His voice low yet still held authority over me.

I felt uncomfortable in here. Awkwardness filled the room as I stood by the door. "Did you need anything before I go?" I asked, swallowing the dry lump in my throat as he just stared.

"No." Short and curt came his reply, and just like that, he was back typing away.

We rarely spoke about anything else other than the children or what our week entailed. As I went to close the door, I heard a disgruntled sigh. There was no need to say anything else. I left the room, making my way down the hallway to the children.

Lila was fast asleep, clutching her doll against her cheek as I pulled the light pink bed cover up over her shoulders to keep her warm during the winter's night. Her dark brown hair curled and splayed out against her pillowcase as she mumbled something incoherent and rolled from her side to her back. I couldn't help but just smile, wanting to sit in here forever and watch her.

At seven, she was determined but stubborn at the best of times with a huge imagination. Her daddy was wrapped around her fingers, his little princess. Noah, who was a year older, was the opposite. He was very laid back and easy to keep happy. He'd gotten that from his father. The children were both often mistaken as twins with their age so close. Noah wasn't much of a talker, either reading a book or outside riding up and down the driveway on his bike. Lila loved to talk about anything and everything.

I kissed her good night and then made my way across the hallway to Noah's room. The second book of Harry Potter on his face as he had fallen asleep reading again, I laughed softly to myself, placing the bookmark on the open page and leaving it on his bedside table.

I couldn't deny it. Brody and I made beautiful children. Biased or not, they were my life.

Kissing his forehead as my fingers combed through his dark, almost black hair, I stood up straighter, leaving his bedroom and making my way back to ours. I paused momentarily and stared at his office door once more. I almost went in again. He was in there, shutting me out and blocking me away. Deciding against it, I left.

Slipping into the shower, I began to lather body wash into my olive skin and clean myself. I loathed the way my body looked after having children. Twenty-seven and I loathed my body. I could lie and say that I kept my figure or lost the weight, but I hadn't. I had leftovers from Lila, probably some from Noah too. It was too easy to eat and enjoy the sugary sweet cravings from being pregnant, convincing myself that I'd work hard to wear it off once they were born. It just never happened.

My hair hadn't been cut in years, just not bothering with it. It only went up in a ponytail, the way boring mum does. Even makeup went untouched, just a quick dab of blush and gloss. I really couldn't be bothered with it. The clothes that I used to wear, all those shorts and tight-fitting jeans were hiding in the back of my closet, hidden away for the day that I was finally able to wear them again without the embarrassing belly fat bulging over the top.

Brody never once complained or said anything, but my subconscious told me that it bothered him. He'd only gotten better looking with age, successful at work and grown into a strong man. It made sense for him to have a beautiful woman on his arm. However, I was never on his arm. I hadn't even been asked to join him at one of his work dinners since Noah was born. He would call up late, inform me last minute that he wouldn't be making it home until late.

I was convinced he was fucking his receptionist, the woman who took his business calls. He denied it, of course. What man wouldn't want to be sucked off by a gorgeous blonde when his wife wasn't doing it to him?

The last time we were consistent with being intimate was when we were trying to fall pregnant with our youngest, Lila. I'd become increasingly aroused during my pregnancy with her, craving his touch, his kisses… to feel his hands on my skin. He never seemed to mind, always up for a quick romp between the sheets before work, before dinner or when our eldest Noah was napping.

When Lila entered the world, sex and sleep were a distant memory of the past.

You could say our marriage began taking its toll when Noah entered our world. Brody had only just made it to the hospital. Another five minutes and he would have missed the first of his son, Noah. It was the same with Lila, another business meeting that he couldn't dash away from.

Sex was boring. Neither of us even really tried, and I had faked so many orgasms that I lost count.

As I stepped out of the shower, I quickly dried off in fear that Brody would already be in the room. I hated the thought of him seeing my body. Slipping into my flannel pyjamas, I sat down on the bed with my legs tucked up and put a braid in my half-dried hair. The bed felt cold and lonely as I slipped under the covers after brushing my teeth. It was too big, too empty.

We didn't have a TV in our room. When we first moved in, Brody said we didn't need one. The bedroom was for two things, sleeping and sexy time. Now, I wished there was a TV in here.

My eyes stared at the door, waiting, hoping he would come in and wanting to hold me. He didn't, and I fell asleep.

I could vaguely hear him undressing in our walk-in closet. Barely awake, I rolled over, picked my phone up and noticed the time, almost 2 AM, hours after I had said good night to him.

Putting the phone back down, I snuggled further beneath the covers as he joined me in the bedroom. "You awake?" his voice soft, half-heard.

"No," I replied.

I kept my eyes closed as I rolled to my back. This was his usual pickup line when he wanted some. They opened just as he walked around to his side of the bed, naked. Sitting down, I watched as he opened his side of the bedside table drawer and take out a condom. Tearing it open, he tossed the foil wrapped and began rolling down the condom down his thick length. I wasn't offended. Neither of us wanted any more children.

Raising my hips, I lowered my bottoms but still kept one leg in, easy to put back on afterwards.

There was no kissing, barely any moans, and he was quiet after from some shallow breathing. He'd always been silent, and it made me feel like shit. We weren't experienced with other people, only being with each other. I wasn't counting the bitch at his work until my proof was solid.

My hands gripped his strong arms, legs wrapping around his thighs as his body moved against mine. Closing my eyes, I laid here wishing... wishing for what wasn't. I couldn't have faked it anymore if I tried. This wasn't lovemaking. It was a job. As husband and wife, that's what we were meant to do — have sex.

Brody's hips began to move more forcefully, hurrying himself up. His breathing picked up slightly, and just when the actual pleasure began to sink into the pit of my stomach, he climaxed. I was too embarrassed to speak up, to tell him what I needed and wanted. It was okay, though. We'd have sex again in a month or so... whenever the urge came on.

His heart was racing, beating faster as his breathing slowed down. My arms draped around his neck, wanting to keep this closeness for just a moment longer before he pulled out and walked back to the bathroom. Knowing that the second he moved, it would be gone. At least this way, we could pretend. Well, I could.

He didn't pull away, letting me relish in this small connection for a moment more than he possibly wanted. He was doing this for my sake. I felt his fingertips tracing against the nape of my neck. My eyes opened to darkness. I inhaled his scent, a strong musk of the aftershave I'd bought him for Christmas. I tasted the sweat on his skin as I pressed my lips to his shoulder, kissing him softly.

I began to feel a mere comfort. That feeling went as soon as it came when he began to move off of my body.

I already rolled over and pretending to be asleep when he made his return from the bathroom. He was spending the night in here, always in here after we'd slept together. Otherwise, he'd be in the spare, and I would end up with Noah or Lila, whoever wanted to snuggle with their mama that night.

I didn't stop them from coming in. I liked that they still needed the comfort of me.

My parents had been furious that we weren't raising them with Italian traditions. Hell, they were still furious that I hadn't married an Italian boy. What did they expect, though? They had come home from a holiday and announced we were moving to an island called Tasmania. I had not ever heard of the place before. My papa quit his job, found work over here, and the next thing I knew, we were moving, and I was enrolled at the school. It was rushed. I barely spoke any English and was the only Italian in my school. How could they not think I would fall in love with an Australian boy? I was fifteen for crying out loud. My hormones were raging all over the place for him once I laid eyes on his cute face.

I knew it broke her heart when we had children even naming them Noah and Lila. My mama never mentioned it, but I knew she was disappointed with our choice of names for them. We didn't care. We loved them.

Waking early the next morning, I started my morning routine of getting ready, hair up, face washed and the usual baggy clothes on which involved a loose-fitting shirt paired with a pair of black mum jeans that sucked in my gut. Black was my choice of colour. It was more slimming.

Brody was still asleep when I entered back into the bedroom. His snores were the only sound filling the room of silence. I could have woken him up, but I didn't want to. He worked hard, providing for his family. I was just the housewife, not that it bothered me as I loved being able to take our children to school and clean our home, but still, he earned the right to sleep in more than I do.

Flipping the pancakes over, Noah was telling me about school when he brought up playing soccer. It caught me off guard as he's never shown any interest in playing school sports. "Really?" I asked, genuinely surprised. "That's great."

"What's great?" His voice deep, masculine voice startled me as he entered the room.

Lila was already jumping up to run over to him. "Daddy!" she beamed, hugging one of his legs tightly. "Good morning."

Brody smiled back at her, bending down to her level and kissing her cheek. "Good morning, princess. Did you sleep well?"

"I did," she replied, going back to her plate of pancakes. She poked her brother in the arm on her way, trying to provoke him. He ignored her.

"Eat your breakfast and leave your brother alone, Lila." He shook his head, lightly scolding. "Morning, Noah." He went over to the breakfast bar where the children both sat, kissing him on the head while they both kept eating.

He had a mouthful of food, mumbling back. "Morning, dad."

I set his coffee cup down on the white marble counter, pouring milk into the boiling hot caffeinated water and giving it a stir. Turning my back, I reached for the metal spatula and flipped another pancake. "Your breakfast won't be long." I pointed out, getting ready to plate them.

Clearing his throat as he sat with the kids, I glanced up and watched the three of them chatting away and laughing. It made me smile on the inside that our children were happy with no idea about their parents. I felt like I was failing them. My eyes crossed back over to Brody, and I couldn't deny that he wasn't extremely attractive in a suit because he is. We were a mismatched couple. He was handsome, and I, just bland. Quickly, I looked away when I noticed him watching me.

"I might be late home tonight," he started, coming over with his empty coffee mug. "I have dinner with a client. I only just received the email." Pulling out his phone, he raised a brow. "Want to check for yourself?"

It was to mock me for not believing him the last time he had mentioned a work dinner. I had called bullshit, accusing him of heading out to screw the blonde at work and proved me wrong as he dialled his boss's number to confirm the meeting was an actual work one.

Biting my tongue, I wouldn't fall for it. "Fine, are you going to eat your breakfast? I didn't make it for you to watch it go cold."

His jaw twitched as his blue eyes glanced over at the plate of pancakes covered in maple syrup. "No."

Rolling my eyes, I snatched the plate up. "Asshole," I muttered, walking over to the cupboard and pulling out the bin.

"Bit dramatic for eight in the morning, don't you think?"

I spun around, glaring. "I should have known better than to think that you're going to eat breakfast with your family for once."

Pushing up his black jacket and white sleeve, he looked down at his watch. "Gabriella, I need to leave. I'm running late."

"More like running to your whore," I muttered under my breath.

Judging by the scowl on his face, I knew he had heard me. He ignored it and walked to each of our children again, giving them a kiss goodbye. I began to stack the dishwasher, just wanting him to go and get out of my face.

"Don't forget to kiss mama, daddy," Lila pointed out.

I froze. "Daddy needs to go," I reminded, looking ahead out into the garden.

She was stubborn, not letting this go. "Kiss mama like in the movies, daddy."

Sometimes I thought they knew just how bad their parents hated each other. Was it hate? I didn't know. It wasn't what it used to be, though.

Brody was already walking towards me when I had turned around. My heart pounded as one hand curled around my hips and pushed my back against the sink with his strong top half and his leg between my thighs. I wanted to scream, "Get off of me," but the other part desperately wanted him to stay like this.

He was mad. I could tell by the way that he stared into my eyes. His breath was minty across my face as he spoke softly. "The kids want a kiss, Gabriella. Are you going to say no?" He was pushing me, knowing I wouldn't refuse in front of the kids.

"Go to work," I said, keeping my voice low and quiet from the kids who were watching us. "I have beds to make since I guess you didn't do ours."

"Why should I? That's your job." He shot back, cocking a brow.

I could just slap that smirk off his face. I wanted him out of my face. "Asshole." I pushed my hand against his chest, trying to make him move but he didn't budge.

"So I've already been called." He smirked again, fingers tightening against my hip to hold me in place as his other hand came up, cupping my cheek with a gentle caress. My eyes softly closed a moment as I felt his lips skimming against mine before he pushed them against, nothing open mouth, just a strong kiss. It was simple and enough to make Lila squeal with delight and Noah the opposite.

Pulling back, his eyes appeared darker as he brushed his lips against my ear. I thought he was going to kiss me. He didn't. His breath hit my ear as he spoke. "Unlike you, my dear wife, I'm not fucking anyone on the side." Letting me go, my body went cold as he picked up his black case and car keys, made his way towards the door and left for work.

Hard to believe all those years ago, we were madly in love and inseparable.

CHAPTER TWO

I spent most of the morning in a pissed off mood. How dare he kiss me like that and then accuse me of such things? When the hell did I have time to go out and cheat? He really knew how to get beneath my skin and irk me off.

Dropping the kids off at school, I went in with each of them and helped them put their bags away. I dreaded the day they told me to stay in the car. I loved to see their new artwork and creations. I asked about Noah starting soccer, and his teacher gave me the form to fill out for him to do so. Sad truth but I felt as if I was my happiest here with them.

Once I came home, it was silent and empty.

Mornings were spent cleaning and tidying up. I hung out the load of washing that was put on after I woke, gave the place a vacuum and started working on dinner. A loaf of bread was in the oven to go with tonight's dinner. Brody wouldn't be here, so the kids and I were having bolognese, a usual family favourite. I didn't use jars of sauce. It was true authentic Italian cooking in our home.

The kids often liked helping in the kitchen, Lila mostly as Noah just preferred to lick the bowls and beaters. Usually, by the time Brody did return home from work, I was exhausted from running around. I'd always be on my feet, cleaning up and running errands. I did have my days fairly easy at times, so I couldn't complain too much. I wasn't the one paying the bills. That was Brody, and he never once had asked me to go back to work and help.

He worked long hours, and early on, we had agreed that I would finish work once we started our family and take care of things at home. We didn't want them in and out of childcare or with another family. My mama always offered, and sometimes, I took her up on that. But most of the time, I was the one taking care of them.

Noah and Lila were both eager to change from their school uniforms as I pulled into the driveway of the home. They were unclipping their belts and racing to get in the house first. Clicking my fingers as they raced off, I called out, "Back and get your bags please."

"But mama, can't you carry it?" Noah groaned, turning back with dragging feet.

I laughed, ruffling his hair as I carried the bag of groceries in my other. "You're old enough, and all you have to do is put it in the kitchen for me."

"Yeah, Noah, be a good girl like me," Lila teased, always teasing her older brother.

Noah's frown deepened. "I am a boy."

"You're crying like a girl," she taunted some more.

"Enough. Bags in the kitchen now. Lila, leave him alone. You don't like it when he teased you," I reminded.

God forbid, these two could actually get along for one day without fighting or teasing each other. We took a different route with our parenting and never once smacked. We did have time out for which they had to sit and not move until they were feeling happy again. It worked for us, and the chair was very rarely used.

Heading outside, I grabbed the clothes basket and began to unpeg the dry clothing from the line as the kids rode around on their bikes, chasing each other and racing. Oh, to be a child again with no worries of anything other than losing a race.

They ate their dinner hungrily, making a mess. I could complain about that, but I was just happy they were eating everything given to them. Their father, on the other hand, couldn't cook without setting alarms off. We played hide and seek and then they sleepily went to bed. It was the same every night, a story read then kisses goodnight before I went back to the never ending pile of washing.

I heard Brody coming inside around 10 PM. I was ironing when he walked inside, smelling of booze. "Kids in bed?"

"Yes." I didn't bother to look at him. He'd been drinking, and I just wasn't up for this tonight.

He didn't say anything and just walked away. I heard the fridge door open, then close again. He was in a drinking mood, coming back into the lounge room with a couple beers and putting them on the table in front of the couch.

"Good day at work?" I finally asked, watching as he set the glass and bottle on the coffee table and loosened his black tie.

"Don't pretend like you care," he said, just staring at me as his tie was pulled off and casually tossed on the arm of the chair beside the couch.

My eyes darted up, shaking my head slowly. "You're right. I don't. But seeing as you never ask me how my day is, I thought I'd ask you."

"Don't start, Gabby. I'm not in the mood for a fight tonight," he muttered, rubbing his temples as he took a seat on the couch and lazily stretched out.

I didn't say anything more and continued to iron our clothing. He was watching Law and Order. I took the remote to turn the volume down. "Did you eat anything tonight?"

He didn't answer instead said something completely off topic. "Are you going to show up this time?" he asked, cracking the top of his beer open and lifting a leg up, propping it on the large ottoman.

Sitting the iron down, I began to fold. "What?"

"I asked if you were going to show up this time or not?" he asked, obviously annoyed that he had to repeat himself.

I was completely confused with no idea what it was about. "What the hell are you talking about?" I spat, growing annoyed. "Are you drunk?"

"Your fucking hair appointment? They called me to make sure you were going to turn up unlike the previous. How many times had it been when you cancelled or didn't show?"

My cheeks began to flush red in embarrassment. "Why would they call you for?"

"Why didn't you turn up last time, Gabby?" he asked, and I could see exactly where this was heading.

I had been meaning to get my hair trimmed for quite some time. The last appointment was booked, but Lila was sick at school, and they called me to collect her. With all my rushing around to care for her, I had completely forgotten about the hair appointment. I was extremely annoyed when they called Brody instead, asking why I didn't show, and obviously, today, they had called him to make sure I was going to arrive at my appointment tomorrow that I booked today. I needed to make sure they had my number, not his.

"Brody, you know why I didn't show. Lila was sick. That's all." I was exhausted from fighting and having these petty arguments. "Do you honestly think I'm seeing someone else?"

"Do you think I'm fucking Kate?" he asked, strangely calm.

Kate, the secretary, I hated her, and he knew it. "Are you?"

"Are you?" he mimicked, scoffing. "You seem to think you can throw accusations around. You're diverting the shit you've done to me." Glaring at me, I hated the way he was looking at me. Hatred filled his eyes.

Biting the insides of my cheeks before I completely lost it, I took a deep breath, keeping myself calm. "Was she at dinner tonight with you tonight?" I asked. I hated that I was so jealous of her and more so because she was gorgeous and spending time with him. It killed me that they were working together each day in close proximity.

He didn't speak. He just kept looking at me as he lifted the bottle, taking another mouthful of his beer until he had downed it. Glass on glass, the empty bottle rattled when dropped on the coffee table. "Good night." He then got up, walked away and headed upstairs

Again, I was left to my own inner thoughts. It was silent, and the dread was back in the pit of my stomach. I'd rather we fought at how things were going, at least we argued things we said, instead of these jabs, and petty accusations that kept the other wondering.

I left the pile of folding and turned the TV off. It was late, I was tired, and I couldn't stay down here after what was just said. She had obviously been there at dinner with him. Was it just the two of them? I didn't want to think about it.

I cried myself to sleep that night. My emotions got the best of me. My heart hurt, aching against my chest as I lay in bed in our bedroom. It didn't feel like ours but just a room that we sometimes shared.

Things weren't getting better. I could only wish and hope they would get better, but I just couldn't see a way out from where we were.

Noah and Lila were loud the next morning, running up and down the halls past my room. I woke to their yelling and squealing. My eyes were still stinging from the tears that burned my eyes, the inner thoughts coming back to me. I wanted to lay in bed and not face the day. It wasn't an option.

As I sat up, I heard Brody growling through the walls. "Lila! Noah! I told you both to stop running past the bedroom. Your mother is sleeping."

Like you care, I thought to myself.

"Daddy!" Noah screamed.

"Noah!" Brody grumbled back. "Don't you go in there?"

The bedroom door flew open and slammed into the wall causing me to half jump in fright. Noah came speeding in, jumping up onto the bed and trying to get beneath the covers. "Mama, Lila is trying to bite me!" he squealed.

Oh god, it was too early for this. "Stop that." I covered his mouth with my palm to silence him as I was also making my way out of the bed and into the hall where Lila was still running down.

"Lila," I spoke, motioning for her to come near me.

She halted halfway. "I didn't do it." That's their usual defence line for when they were each in trouble or blaming the other.

"Lila, to your mother now," Brody scolded. His deep voice oozed authority. He stood at the opposite end to me, dressed and ready for work. I hadn't realised how late I'd slept in.

"Daddy, I didn't mean too! I won't do it again, I promise." Her sweet voice came as she dragged her feet towards me.

I bent down to her eye level and sighed. "Sweetheart, if you bite your brother once more, then I'll have to bite you on the arm. I don't care if it hurts, you need to stop it." I wouldn't bite her, but she didn't need to know that.

Her big dark eyes widened. "You have big teeth."

Laughing as I made a biting motion towards her. "Like the big bad wolf."

"So, you better not bite again, or mama will bite you back." Brody was grinning as he walked up behind her, picking her up in a bear hug. "You know better than to bite princess. It's not nice, and Noah is your brother."

She giggled, squirming in his arms. "Daddy, put me down!"

"Are you going to be good?" he asked, holding her up higher as he pretended that he was about to drop her. He was an incredible father to our children, always hands on and caring.

Nodding fast, she giggled some more. "Yes, daddy, I won't bite again."

Setting her on her feet, he walked away, and I smiled, kissing the top of her head. "Go and say sorry to Noah, then come and have some breakfast."

"We've already eaten," Noah pointed out as he slowly emerged from our bedroom. "Dad made breakfast."

The shower didn't seem to help. I wanted to wake up, but the water only seemed to make me want to climb back into bed and sleep the day away. I was tired, and the day hadn't even begun. I noticed the spare bed made already, no trace of him having spent the night in there. The kids never knew that we'd been sleeping apart for almost over a year. On and off, we shared the bed when we had sex or if my parents came to say. We didn't need the unwanted attention drawn to us especially when my sisters or Brody's brother and sister each having happy marriages. We just didn't want to disappoint.

I knew it would all come back to us marrying young and against their wishes. We had been adamant that we were going to be together forever. Why waste time?

"Sleep well?" Brody asked as I walked into the kitchen. "It's almost eight. You never sleep in that long."

I shrugged, tucking a fallen strand of hair behind my ear. "I was tired." I picked up my coffee mug, needing a large glass to keep me awake today. I noticed he was rushing around, wiping down the spilled milk on the countertop. His black suit was the one I had freshly ironed last night and the tie, a navy blue one. I liked the way his hair was done, slicked down with a side part, one side shorter than the other as he had it brushed over neatly. "Are you leaving already?"

"Yes, I have to go and set up for a final proposal. If all goes well, this deal will make the company a lot of money." You would assume he'd be beaming from ear to ear with how enthusiastic he sounds. He wasn't. He just kept his emotions to himself, not sharing or opening up to me about these work deals.

"You could have mentioned something. I would have set my alarm." I actually felt bad that I hadn't been up earlier to help him out. Or that I had no clue what he was talking about. I didn't know, and that guilted me. I was his wife. I should know.

Looking up, he caught my gaze, and my brows slightly dipped as he shook his head. "No, you were tired and obviously needed the sleep," He paused a moment, hesitating. "I heard you crying last night, and—." No. I didn't want him to hear that.

I wanted him to keep talking and to tell me what he was going to say, but Lila ran in holding a brush with a black tie. "Can you do my hair, mama?" she smiled. "Please."

"On the stool." I nodded over towards one of the wooden bar chairs. I turned back to Brody, but whatever he had begun saying was long gone. "Brody," I urged him to continue. I think it was the first time I'd spoken his names in weeks.

He nodded, speaking with his voice lowered as Lila was watching us closely. "We should talk tonight. I'll be home early, and once the children are in bed, we'll talk."

I looked at him. "Okay." This was new. Relief was flooding me as his willingness to want to sit and talk.

He left for work — no kiss, no goodbye, nothing.

Just like yesterday, I took the kids to school and came home to another day of housework. It was never ending. How could two small children make so much mess in such a little time? It drove me mad at times. No one cared because they knew I would eventually clean their toys up. I felt taken for granted by my husband and even my children at times.

I could have taken Brody's approach after stepping on a piece of Lego, threaten to throw the whole lot out if they weren't kept away.

Throwing out yet their father felt so guilty for yelling that he went and brought more.

I was awake with coffee, but my insides were filled with dread as I watched the clock, waiting for Brody to come home so we could discuss things. I knew what I needed to say.

I wanted us to spend more time together and maybe, just maybe try a little harder; each to make an effort, showing one another that we both needed to work on ourselves and towards each other... If only it were that simple.

As much as I wanted to say those things to him, I couldn't.

I was pretty much ready to just give up, and I had a feeling he was too.

CHAPTER THREE

"Dave has met someone else."

She decided this was the best way to inform me. Mid-sip into my double shot cappuccino I held in both hands, I frowned towards Cathy while ignoring the hot burn down my throat. I felt for her, having her marriage end in such a terrible way.

"I'm sorry." I wasn't sure what else I could say. She was clearly having a hard time coping since their marriage had fallen apart.

"It's okay." She managed a weak smile, her dirty blonde hair tucked over one shoulder as she lifted the silver spoon up. "Want some?"

It looked delicious. The food here was always delicious and the coffee, even better. "Yes." I grinned.

"I'll swap you. This is for your almond croissant." She peered over, eying the pastry on my plate.

Laughing, "I change my mind. I'm not giving this up for anything." I really shouldn't be gorging on these. The rolls of my stomach would triple if I didn't stop eating all the crap that I had been consuming of late. "Eat yours and tell me how good it tastes."

We were sitting outside Sweetbrew on George Street, a Patisserie and Espresso Bar that never disappoints. We came here every Wednesday to have our weekly catch up coffee and eat whatever looked tempting and tasty. The weather was too nice to be sitting indoors now that spring had arrived.

The Launceston Mall was close by, a few short minutes' walk to pick up some new school shoes for Noah as his others had worn in the toes. These would be his third pair this year. Cars driving by were rushing. Everyone was always so busy. I thought about taking coffee to Brody and visiting him at work, but after he had taken off so fast this morning, I didn't want to bother.

I had gotten my hair trimmed before meeting Cathy. A good two inches were taken off, thinned out with more choppy layers. I hated the mirrors in the dressers. I don't think anyone truly sees how ugly they are until you're sitting in front of one of those. I couldn't help but just stare at myself in the mirror, trying not to cry as I watched my hair fall down like the way my marriage was.

The smiles, laughter, they were all fake mess, and Brody wasn't happy. I knew he was just as unhappy as I was.

Neither of us had been happy for so long. Was it worth just giving up for? I loved him, but it wasn't the same love we once had. We said it out of habit. "Love you." "Love you too." There was no emotion, no connection to those words. I wanted to smile when I heard it. Instead, I felt nothing. He didn't do a damn thing to make me feel that I was loved.

There was never an "I love you," those three small words that I badly craved to hear.

I was no better. I hadn't said that to him, either.

Watching as Cathy hungrily enjoyed the fruit flan, I couldn't wonder if she was as happy as she appeared. Was she feeling the same as I did? She was a beautiful woman. Her hair had grown out from the curls, and she now kept them straight. Her brown eyes were unhidden from the black glasses she used to wear. I envied her, able to eat and never seeming to gain anything. We remained the best of friends since high school. She had gotten married, then unfortunately divorced, confiding in me that she found out David was having an affair. She packed their three children up and left him, only seeing him twice a week and every other weekend when they did the usual kid swap. I felt bad for both of them, especially their daughters who wanted their parents living in the same house. It became awkward at first when they separated as Brody had been great friends with David. Cathy refused to come visit us until all contact with him had seized. Unbeknown to her, Brody was still played poker with him on Fridays.

Although we were like sisters, I didn't tell her about my marital problems. She had grown up to be quite gossipy and loved to hear juicy stories of the mothers at school when we'd wait for classes to end or morning drop off. Someone's downfall was her knowledge gain, and I couldn't dare spill my deepest, darkest secrets to her. I trusted her, but even I didn't want to be spoken about. Behind our closed doors, our problems stayed unspoken.

Cathy pulled me out of my thoughts as she waved the spoon in front of me. "Did you hear me?"

I hadn't heard a word she had spoken to me. "Sorry, I was thinking about dinner." A lie wouldn't hurt anybody.

"I said Dave had a new girlfriend. It's pretty serious." I could hear the disappointment in her voice.

Reaching over, I rubbed her hand gently. "Cath, he's not worth it. You'll meet someone new, just give it time. You'll find someone who treats you well."

"Like Brody?" She sighed heavily. "I'm sorry. I just swear you got lucky with that man. You won't ever have to know what it feels like to see him dating somebody younger." Her brown eyes glassing over as she began tearing up.

The almond croissant felt lodged in the back of my throat. The pit of my stomach was knotting up as I imagined him and Kate again. The idea of them kissing, or him touching her. Were they making love the way we used to? I was feeling sicker than ever. I couldn't fix my age. We were both only twenty-seven and getting older. Would he go for someone younger and something newer? Then the thoughts of myself came to mind, who would want me?

Just like that, I became determined to kick my arse into gear and lose the weight.

Shaking my head, I steered us away from this. "Let's talk about something else, something less depressing."

It worked. Her lips began curling into a bright smile I knew too well. "You'll never believe who got Botox again."

Walking past Priceline on my way back from getting Noah a new pair of shoes from Red Herrings, I slowly came to a stop. The conversation Cathy and I had been in still played in the back of my mind. I was always saying that I wanted to diet and get fit again. I had been so sporty growing up, wearing bikinis during summer, and enjoying myself. Now, I wouldn't be caught dead wearing one. I walked inside, picking up a black basket and making my way down to the health aisle. My cheeks burned with embarrassment as I held the black box of celebrity slim, extra shakes, and metabolism pills. I was going to do this. I wanted to do this.

Brody had brought me a treadmill years ago after constant complaining about being fat and horrible. He had walked in on me trying a pair of jeans on which weren't going up. I had used it no more than ten times. It's been collecting dust ever since. What a waste of money, just sitting there unused?

Not anymore, no more pasta, no more sugar, I had to cut out the bread dipped into sauces and stop the wine. No, I'd cut back on the wine. A woman needed a glass or two after dealing with fighting children and a moody husband each day.

When Brody came home tonight, I didn't get upset that he hadn't noticed my haircut. I hadn't expected him to, and I wasn't going to bring it up. It would just start another argument, and that was pointless. I was eager to hear what he had to say in regards to the earlier comment.

If he heard me crying, did that mean he felt bad? Or was he just going to tell me to hush it up?

Stripping naked, I weighed and took my measurements, writing them down and hiding the piece of paper away from prying eyes. This was for me. I was doing this for me; to get back into the right head space and feel better about my body and the way I looked. I wanted my old confidence back. Not to live in a shadow of what I had become.

Brody's favourite meal was homemade spaghetti with meatballs, and I made that for him tonight. What would I have to give to sit and devour a bowl of that? The smell was tempting me. The thought of drowning a piece of freshly made Turkish and olive bread into the bowl very much tempted me. Instead, I had a shake and left the kitchen to get the kid's bath ready.

Who the hell drinks dinner at 5 PM and then has nothing until the next morning? I was expecting a deep migraine by the time I woke up.

I took a five-minute rest on the sofa before I got back to it. My eyes were growing heavy. Sleep wanted to welcome me back as I barely slept the previous night. As they were almost closed, I heard a loud banging, followed by Brody yelling out and then another slam. My heart pounding against my chest, I jumped up, more worried that he would attract the attention of the kids who were quietly playing in the toy room. I found him in the pantry, holding his bowl of dinner as he stared angrily at the microwave.

"What are you doing?" I practically yelled. "Do you need to be so loud?"

"It's fucking cold." He dropped the ceramic bowl, heavily inside the microwave and flung the door shut with a hard slap.

Oh, he wasn't cracking the shits with me over this. I gave him a nudge aside with my elbow and pressed start. "It was hot when I had made it hours ago," I pointed out, hissing the words angrily between clenched teeth.

"You know I don't eat until later. It's cold," he growled back, looking flustered.

"Maybe you should eat earlier, then, with us as a family." We never ate together, and I hated it.

His eyes narrowed, raising a brow. "Why not wait until I come home then?"

"Oh, Brody, I am so sorry." My voice was heavy with sarcasm. "I forgot this household revolves around you. From now on, I'll keep the children up late just to ensure you don't ever have to reheat your own food."

His eyes narrowed once again and jaw clenched. "You're a fucking bitch. You know that."

"And you're a fucking bastard," I spat back, turning around and leaving him to figure out his own damn dinner when the timer beeped. "You're welcome."

Unfortunately, name calling wasn't anything new to us. We would often say those things in the heat of the moment, anything to make each other feel worthless and pathetic. Nine times out of ten, it would just make me want to pack my things and leave him. Hell, I knew he wanted to do the same.

The anger was brushed aside once we tucked the children into bed, Lila first, and then Noah who often took the longest to fall asleep. "Mama, can you read me a book?" he asked me as I walked into his room.

Brody was standing and putting the one he had just finished away on the case. "Come on, I just read you two. It's sleeping time."

"It's bedtime, baby. Tomorrow, I'll read you one then," I promised, hating to say no to him

His nose scrunched as I pulled the covers over his shoulders. "I'm not a baby."

Leaning down, I kissed his soft cheek and whispered, "You'll always be my baby."

The lights were turned out, and ten minutes later, both of them were fast asleep. I turned around to see Brody walking towards his office door. So much for talking, I walked behind him and followed through the door.

My hand came up, stopping the door as it almost hit in the face, and I pushed it back open. "Watch it!" I growled, rubbing my hands with a frown.

"Didn't see you there." He shrugged, pulling out his iPhone and sitting behind his desk once again. "Come to yell some more or are you after something?"

My frown deepened as I looked at him incredulously. "Brody, you told me you wanted to talk this morning."

He seemed to think it over, obviously forgotten about it. "Oh. Yeah, it doesn't matter anymore."

"What was it?" I pushed, urging him to go on. "It must have been something."

"Mum, just wanted to come around for dinner, and I was going to ask your thoughts, but I told her no. I have too much work to do. I won't have time. Unless, you want to go around with the kids?" His eyes still focused on his phone.

Nothing, and I mean nothing pissed me off more than when someone was having a conversation with me, and they were playing around on their mobile phone. I found it so rude and disrespectful. Walking behind his deck, I snatched the damn thing out of his hands and looked at the screen.

"Are you fucking kidding me?" He was playing a game. "You'd rather play Candy Crush than listen to me?"

"Calm down, Gabriella." Standing to take the phone back but I took a step away and held it hostage from him. "I was getting out of a game that Noah was playing earlier."

"I'm going to go through your messages, voice mails," I informed him. I knew it was stupid, but I was so angry and jealous. I hated being jealous for no reason. "I can't believe you. Are you that bored with me? *Come si può essere così maleducato, sconsiderato e frustrante allo stesso tempo. Mi sento come buttare questo telefono attraverso una finestra di,* Brody!"

He seemed to look more amused than anything as I spoke my native tongue. Instead of yelling, he sat back down, motioning with his hands for me to go ahead and search. "Go for it. I have nothing to hide. Where is your phone? Actually, since I pay for it, I'll just check the bill." I couldn't believe he just went there. That was low and incredibly hurtful. I worked hard. I just didn't earn a cent from it.

"That's not fair," I said, tossing him phone back to him. "And you didn't answer my question."

Catching it before it fell to the ground, he narrowed his eyes. "You know I refuse to listen when you're yelling." He set the phone down on his desk, looking back up. "What isn't fair is that I come home to all your made up accusations daily. You convince yourself that I'm doing something wrong, therefore, you believe it."

He made me sound crazy. "I thought you wanted to talk about us, not your mother!" My voice was more sad than angry.

All emotion left his face, and he swallowed. I scanned my eyes over his, watching as his Adam's apple bobbing and clicking the pen between his fingers with his thumb. "Do you want to talk about us? I have a lot to say."

"Then, talk to me. I don't like avoiding and ignoring each other." I sighed, sitting on the soft couch beside his desk. What I really wanted to say was I don't want to fight anymore.

Brody stood, walked over to where I sat and joined me. "I don't like it either."

I looked up at him, still mad. "I hate when you're on your phone."

With a yawn, he sat back, strong thighs parting as they stretched out. "I hate when you yell in Italian."

"I'll try not to do that anymore."

Taking my hand in his with a squeeze, he pulled me closer against him. My head rested against his chest, and his fingers played with my hair. It was soothing. The urge to close my eyes and fall asleep were there. "Do you love me?"

"Yes. Do you love me?" My heart began to quicken. I adjusted my body, reaching across his torso and wrapping my arm loosely around his waist with closed eyes. I waited for him to hold me back, but he didn't. I could feel him slipping away slowly even if wasn't going to admit it. I knew I had to try, but so did he.

He was quiet for a moment, "I do." He then asked. "What did you yell at me this time?"

I kept my eyes closed, leaving the part out where I had called him rude, inconsiderate and frustrating. I just said, "That I was going to throw your phone through the window."

He chuckled, a loud laugh that rumbled through his chest and vibrated against my ear. "I'm sure that's all. I know you well enough to know that's not entirely true."

I just laughed, and at this moment, things felt a little better.

I knew better than to get my hopes up. We had this same conversation two months ago, and then months before that. We fought and then made up and fought some more and made up all over again. It was a broken record on repeat, and we were just going around in circles.

Was it bad that we'd both try to change for a few days before slipping back to our new routine of yelling and hating on each other? Of course, it was, but that's how things were now. We weren't the same Brody and Gabriella all those years ago. They were a distant shadow.

I wondered just how long it would last for this time.

CHAPTER FOUR

"Sii può fare meglio, Grabriella!" she told me, scolding loudly and telling me that I could do much better than he could.

I refused to listen. He was the one for me. I knew it. Brody was perfection, and I didn't want better. I just needed him. *"Basta arrivare a conoscerlo, Mama, lui è incredibile."* *I told my mama to get to know him, and she would agree that he was amazing. It didn't go down so well.*

Her nostrils flared, and she pointed a perfectly manicured finger towards me. *"Non è italiano!"*

"I don't care that he isn't Italian!" I yelled back at her and then realising my mistake as my papa raised an eyebrow. My parents didn't like it when I spoke English to them. They always preferred Italian at home. It was confusing at times, hard to remember.

"Grabriella , stai avendo rapporti sessuali con questo ragazzo?"

My cheeks burned flamingo pink as my mama asked if Brody and I were having sexual intercourse. I could have died of embarrassment especially since we were all sitting at the family dining table and eating dinner. My papa's nostrils flared, but he remained silent as mama awaited my answer.

Shaking my head furiously. *"Dio mio! No!"* Staring at my papa for some help, *"Per favore. Basta incontrarlo una volta, vedrete che non è una cattiva persona. Lui non è come gli altri ragazzi."* I may have told my papa that Brody wasn't like all other boys, and if he would just meet him once, he would see that for himself.

My papa set his fork down and rubbed his temples. He had always been handsome, extremely caring and kind but, one was to never cross him. He had a wild temper, and I always locked my bedroom door when he had been having a bad day. *"Gabriella, si sposa quando si è eighteen anni si può rimanere amici con questo ragazzo, ma questo è tutto. Fine della discussion."*

I stared in disbelief. How could he suggest that I just stay friends and marry someone else when I turn eighteen? I didn't reply back, knowing it was the end of discussion. I sat and ate in silence.

Dinner was extremely quiet after the embarrassing conversation. They assumed my little romance would be put to bed and ended in the morning. What they didn't know wouldn't hurt them. I wasn't going to end things just because they were so against us.

I was a typical sixteen-year-old girl with a massive crush on the popular boy. Rebellion was new to me, and he was definitely worth rebelling for.

Facing Brody the next morning was extremely nerve-wracking. What if he broke up with me over it? I didn't want to face him. Petty, I know. He waited for me each morning, my Mama would drop me off to school and leave right away. Today, I knew she was waiting until I walked inside, watching to see if I spoke to this boy she had banned me from seeing. Yes, this morning on the drive to school she laid down the law and banned me from dating. I was to remain pure for my husband on our wedding night... my Italian husband.

My sisters had done that and had my mama as she liked to remind me. Although, they were all married to older men. Brody and I were the same age, but I hadn't even thought about sex yet. It was the furthest thing from my mind. I was only getting used to hand holding.

Keeping my head down as I walked inside, I went to my locker, beginning to put away my books when I felt his arms wrap around my body from behind. It still felt surreal that this was happening. That he liked me back. "Hey you, I must have missed you this morning."

"No." I groaned, blushing hard. "I was maybe avoiding you." I said regretfully as I turned around to face him.

Brody was in his usual T-shirt and shorts, always wearing running shoes. He was athletic to say the least, loved running around with a ball and kicking it on lunch break, in between talking to me. I'd sit and watch him with Cathy, who still couldn't believe Brody and I were the schools new "it" couple.

It wasn't that big of deal. Yes, there were the snarky bitches who predicted he felt sorry for me. I knew better, though. If he was playing me, I'd know.

His dark brows creased as he frowned. "You all right?"

"Yeah, my mother is driving me crazy today." I said, trying not to call her mama. I'd been teased for that last week. Brody punched the boy in the face for it, making him apologise. That was one of his friends. He was extremely protective of me, and I loved it.

He nodded in realisation, "Come in here," he said, cocking his head towards an empty classroom door. He pulled me inside, then closed the door behind us. My back leaning against the wall, he stood in front of me. "You told her?"

I nodded, a growing smile as well as a blush coming over my face. "I did. She's not happy. She was asking questions about you all night. It was awful."

"Like what kind of questions?" he asked, smirking. He knew exactly what.

"If we're having sex, have we kissed and do you have any Italian in you at all?"

He laughed and stepped closer. His fingers were gently placed on my hips and his hold growing stronger. "Hmmm, well that's kind of disappointing. None of those are a yes."

"I'm sorry," I murmured, looking down to the print on his t-shirt.

"It's okay, Gabby. My parents want to meet you. My brother keeps giving me shit about you, though," he admitted,

looking quite embarrassed himself as I looked up and stared into his blue eyes as our gazes were locked.

He told his parents about me. I smiled. "I want to meet your parents if you want me too?"

His smile widened. "I want you too."

I caught him off guard by throwing my arms around his neck and hugging him tightly. When we first began dating, there was no way I was game enough to do this. I would wait until he touched me first, made the first move, and we'd only ever gone to first base, holding hands.

We were about to go to second.

His lips were coming closer to mine and hands sliding up the white fabric of my school top. I felt his fingertips graze over my lower back as he wrapped his arms around me, pulling me in and claiming my lips with his.

It was my first kiss, a kiss which I would always remember.

My heart came to life. Endorphins spread like wildfire throughout my body as I began to kiss him back. He tasted orange-flavoured chewing gum as his tongue slid in, only slowly but taking control of this kiss. I could feel he was just as nervous as I was. My back was now completely pressed to the wall. His body was against mine and a hardness pressed against the lower of my belly. He made no intention of grinding against me or pushing my hands down. That's how I knew that he wasn't playing me for sex.

Our mouths parted. A part of me was relieved I could now breathe. My heart raced, still holding him closely as my eyes began to open.

Instead of saying something sweet, he went for the cheesy line. "You can tell your mama that I just had some Italian in me." He wiggled his brows as he went to come in for another kiss.

Flicking his arm in mock horror, I busted out laughing as he nuzzled his face in the crevice of my neck. "Brody, that's disgusting. She'd literally boil me on the stove or have me sent off to some boarding school."

He laughed, looking back towards me. His words a hopeful whisper. "Come, meet them on Saturday, can you get away?"

"I can say I'm with Cathy. They love her." I had it all planned out in my head. Nothing was going to stop us from being together, not even the threats my parents had made.

One last deep kiss, he cupped my cheek with his hands gently and rested his forehead on mine. "You taste like sugar," he smiled. "I could kiss you for days."

"How about years?" I asked, pecking him quickly as the morning music began to play, signalling the start of homeroom class. I didn't want to leave. I wanted to stay in here with him.

With a smile, he leaned back in and whispered against my mouth, "I want to kiss you forever."

Those were the days, the days I longed for again; to be innocent and completely in love with someone where it came naturally. There was no forcing our feelings. They were just there. Back then, I had been so wildly in love with Brody, not listening to anybody but my heart. I had to wonder if my papa had been right. He wasn't the man for me.

Joining the conversation once again, I smiled listening to Brody's mother talking to us. "What do you think, babe?" Brody asked, his arm half around the lower of my back as he held me closely against his side.

I smiled, looking up at him and could see the hidden anger. His grip tightened on my hip as I took my time in replying and drawing it out just to purposely piss him off. "Sounds good to me. The kids would love it. Brody can take the day off. I'm sure he'd like to take his family to the zoo."

"Wonderful, I would love to see photos." Loraine, Brody's mother, beamed as she started to stand and clear up the dining table. I was about to stand also to help her, but she shook her head, waving me away. "No, dear, you sit and rest." She reached, taking my half-eaten plate with a worried look. "Are you not feeling okay, dear? You've barely eaten anything."

Brody glanced over, noticing as well. "Just tired, that's all," I lied, brushing the questions away.

I had eaten, just not as much as I usually would. The shakes were going strong, refusing to slack off even for one night. I was on the treadmill once I dropped the kids at school and then again after lunch. No one would see me, which was the way I liked it.

Fred, my father-in-law, reached over and took the garlic bread from my plate with a wink. "Too good to waste." Softly laughing in agreement, I just nodded.

We were at his parent's home having dinner. They called during another fight. Brody, in the heat of the moment, barked a yes down the phone, seconds before he hung up and flung the receiver across the room. So now, our home phone was not working and broken.

Noah had been doing some drawing, and of course, it was my fault for not watching him closely enough. I had turned my back when he had decided to take his dad's contract paperwork to do a picture on them. He placed them back, and of course, Brody had no idea until he was in the meeting, finding them covered in superheroes and villains. Livid didn't describe his attitude when he came home. He was ballistic, not at Noah, but at me.

I felt Brody's warm breath against my ear. "Why aren't you eating?"

I turned, leaning in and whispering back. Ignoring his question, I wanted him away from me. "Get your hands off of me."

"Not a chance in hell," he growled back, smiling still but glaring like mad.

Acting, we were almost professionals. No one here had a clue. His sister nor his brother and their families didn't pick up on any of our hidden jabs. Noah and Lila were off playing with their other cousin. Brody's older brother, Scott, was married to Rose, and they had a seven-year-old daughter, Tulip. She was a spoiled pain, and I know I spoil my children, but she was on a whole other level of annoying. She always got her own way. With a mother like hers, it was no wonder. Rose loved to live beyond her means and was very high maintenance.

His sister, Jessie, was the eldest out of the three. She was married to Leon. They had no children. Both workaholics had decided the family life wasn't for them. They were happy to travel and live in the life of luxury. I envied them at times to go off and visit a new part of the world. It was always a dream of mine to travel and see the world.

The conversation soon turned into work, and I sat there silently as each one discussed their achievements. I hated that they couldn't leave the office talk behind. Instead, it was like a competition to see who was earning the most and higher up the rankings.

"Boring you, Gabby?" Rose smiled sweetly. "You wouldn't know what we're talking about, would you?" She was edging me on. I wasn't in the mood, though. "Being home all day, oh, you really do have the life."

I shook my head, smiling back. "Not at all. My days are busy, but I do love being home for my children."

It wasn't a dig. It was just how I felt.

"Oh, bro, you'll have to start cutting back your hours soon, then," Scott added in. His brows gave me a wiggle. "That was aimed at you."

Brody shrugged, leaning in as his lips pressed to the side of my cheek. "I think as long as I bring home the cheque, Gabby is perfectly okay with my hours."

"Yes, because it's all about the money," I mumbled underneath my breath. My husband was the only one to hear me.

Jessie leaned in and laughed. "Gabby, don't be too harsh on him. You have it too good at home. Once Noah and Lila are off at school, you can do as you please."

Oh, yes because I don't do anything at all except sit on my ass and watch TV or eat. I hated that, which is what everyone thought I done. No one ever asks about my day or offers to come help do my housework. No, they all employ cleaners because they're too busy working to do it and then spent their free time shopping, travelling or dining out.

I sounded like a bitter housewife. It wasn't who I wanted to be.

Glancing up at Brody, I waited for him to defend me, to say that he knew I had done more at home than they assumed. He said nothing, simply picking up his drink, taking a mouthful and finally downing the lot.

I shrugged his arm from my back and stood up. He didn't make an effort to keep me near. Walking down to the large living room to find the children, Noah was playing blocks, and Lila had her dolly with her, pretending it was a baby. Tulip was playing on an iPad and hitting her fingers hard against the screen.

I felt a hand against my lower back. Instantly, I stilled. His touch, it still made me feel violently ill instantly. "Scott." I couldn't have moved aside any faster.

"You seem upset. Is everything ok?" he asked, moving in closely again.

Trying to force out a smile, I nodded and wrapping my arms around my chest. I was uncomfortable, wanting him to leave. "I'm okay, just tired."

It was a lie, but I just wanted to be far away from this man as possible. I hated Brody's brother, and he never understood why. He'd call me silly and think that I imagined things. Maybe I was, but maybe I wasn't.

Scott went to say something else but stopped when he noticed Brody walking towards us. "Gabby, we should head off. The kids have school, and I've got another early morning."

This time, I was happy he was starting early. "Sure, sweetheart. I'll just go and say goodbye to your parents." I leaned in, meeting him halfway for a chaste kiss; something for the show because that's how we rolled. Everything was for show. The touches, kisses and loved up names — they were all lies.

Brody was in our room when I walked in taking my earrings out. I stood opposite as he sat on the bed looking at me. We had two good days since our talk in his office, but we were now back to the cold and distant fighting. Nothing lasted in this house. I needed to speak up and voice my opinions.

Tonight, I would make a start on that too. "Your sister upset me tonight."

He looked up, unbuttoning his shirt. "She was teasing. It wasn't an attack on you personally."

"Everyone thinks I do nothing," I said, becoming defensive as I put my earrings on the dresser. "You think I do nothing."

"You take care of things here. Everyone knows that. You were rude to them by what you said. You were rude to me, and I didn't even say anything," he pointed out defensively. "We just happen to enjoy working. I won't change that."

With a sigh, I sat on the side of the bed as he stood up and walked away to his dresser. "I want you to be home more, Brody. You're always at work. You never defend me."

"I need to work, Gabby. I'm too busy to cut the hours back," he sighed heavily, placing his black socks in the laundry basket. "I've been working the same for years. You can't ask me to slack off now, not when I'm so close to landing a huge deal."

I nodded. There was no point arguing anymore over it. "Are you at least going to apologise for how you spoke to me earlier, blaming me over Noah's pictures."

He scoffed and shook his head as he stood in a pair of tight-fitting cotton boxer shorts. "You're kidding, right?" That was a definitive no. "Fine, I'm going to sleep, then." I was exhausted, starving, and just wanted to sleep the hunger away.

"You want to you know?" he asked, leaning against the door frame as I slipped underneath the covers of the bed.

My jaw practically dropped open. He was delusional if he thought I was anywhere close to being in the mood right now. "Are you serious?" I asked, dumbfounded. "Way to make an effort with the romance."

How can I want sex when that's all he ever says? Was it too hard to just come over to me or even grab me, pin me against the wall and just kiss me... kiss me like it was his last breath. I wanted to be held, to be taken and grabbed without hesitation.

He stared, looking lost as if he had no clue what that word even meant. For a minute, I thought he was going to try, put some moves on, but there was nothing and his wall went back up. "I'm going to bed. Night, try not to let Noah touch my work. That could have cost me our client," he said with a final warning.

Would it kill him to touch me or kiss me first? I know I could touch him, but I was too afraid of being rejected to put myself out there. I had done it once before, and it embarrassed me like no tomorrow. "I could use my hand?" I suggested, willing to please him and wanting to please him.

Reaching up, his fingers hit the white switch and turned the light off as he began walking away. I didn't hear the mumble. "Forget it. My hand responds more than you do."

As much as I didn't want to admit it, that really hurt my feelings to a point where I couldn't help but retaliate back. I called out loudly. "The only reason you enjoy it was because you don't have to put in any effort!"

Everything went silent, eerily quiet, and then I heard the slam of the spare room door.

Another lonely night left to my own inner thoughts of self-loathing and silent tears

CHAPTER FIVE

His hips began to move faster, grinding down with each thrust. The orgasm inside was slowly building. My moans were growing as I started bucking my hips, moving to match his pace. Our bodies moved in sync and hips slapped together. My legs tightened around his thighs as my fingers dug into his ass, gripping.

Brody's groan was muffled as his mouth met mine. "You there?" His voice was ragged, breathing shallow as I knew he was struggling to hold off. His mouth pulled away, eyes squinting shut as he grew closer to his own release.

"Almost…" I breathed out, focusing on the pleasure building deep inside the pit of my stomach.

All I needed was a little longer. His pace increased harder, and I wanted to scream. The orgasm was fading, and I could have screamed. Fucking hell, he was racing to the finish line and forgetting about me.

Sensing my frustration, he slowed back down with deeper movements. I felt my eyes begin to roll, and toes curled as I was there. Oh, my God, my core clenching as my legs locked tighter, pulling him in deeper as I came. Moaning, gripping his shoulders, I convulsed around him. His cock drove in faster, drawing out my orgasm as he came. Finally, slowing to a stop where he laid still, his cock pulsing and throbbing inside me.

Our moans were muffled by our lips kissing. His hand went to the side of my cheek, caressing gently. Neither of us was overly loud. The kids down the hall would wake up soon, and our bedroom door wasn't shut. His hand loosened from the hold he had on my hip as he then pulled out. Kneeling with a heavy breath, he stood, flaccid and tugging the condom off as he walked butt naked to the bathroom. When I heard the water running from the shower, I got myself up to get the children ready for school.

This morning, Brody had woken relatively horny, tugging at my pyjama bottoms for some action. I didn't stop him. I should have after he practically called me a "useless lay." He shattered my confidence and hurt me. The next morning, he had come down and apologised, admitting he said it only to hurt me. I forgave him like usual.

My mood was relatively good this morning as I made the kids breakfast. I guess that's what an orgasm could do to you, a rare orgasm but definitely needed.

"Mama, do you like this?" Lila asked me, pointing to a painting she had done at school.

I glanced up, looking at the artwork on the bench as I spread her sandwiches. Smiling, I made my response more exaggerated. "You didn't do that!"

"Yes, I did!" she beamed, looking incredibly proud of herself.

I took the painting and went to put it over on the fridge. "You're so talented. I'm going to put it up here, so I can see it every day."

"I'm going to do a picture for daddy. He can take it to work," she beamed, looking proud.

"He'd love that." I noticed the time and quickly packed her lunch box inside her bag. "Come on, we need to go, or we'll end up late."

When we drove to school, I walked them each in and waved goodbye. Lila came running back over, kissing my cheek as she threw her little arms around my neck for a tight embrace. Nothing could ever feel better than this — the feeling I felt when Lila or Noah coming up on their own to give me a hug or a kiss, even saying they loved it. My heart exploded with more love than I ever imagined. To me, the little things matter. These memories would be cherished until the day I died.

Errands were to be run which I liked to get over and done with as soon as I could. I finished sooner than expected, picking up a soccer ball for Noah to practice with at home before he started playing. I worried he would change his mind as he's never really been big on sports outside of school.

I had been doing shakes for almost two weeks and felt somewhat slightly better about my appearance. I hadn't worn lazy clothes. Instead, I wore a pair of jeans and a black top, slightly more fitting than what was my usual. When I walked past Bento, I finally went in.

I've never been a fan of sushi, but Brody raves on about it. Today, I wanted to try some. Blame it on this morning but things were feeling a little better between us. Yes, we'd barely spoken since the morning sex, but at least, there was no fighting.

The nerves were in my stomach as I walked to his office. It had been so long since I last visited Brody at work, possibly three months, that I thought I was in the wrong building and unable to remember his floor number at first.

This was the first place he worked since finishing up school, never once complaining of hating it. I never really understood just what he did until it was broken down into simple terms for me, and then I realised how important it was and why he worked the way did. He's a broker who sells businesses, looks for cheap deals, and then flips them over, strips out assets, cuts staff to make profitable on paper, and sells them for double, sometimes triple. His charm easily wins over sellers and buyers just as he won me over, years back.

Nerves, mixed with a hint of excitement, filled me as I neared closer. He never asked me to come, but today, I wanted to. I wanted to make this effort for him and show him I was trying.

When the doors opened, my heart was slamming against my chest, a rash threatening to break out as I rubbed the base of my neck and walked the quiet corridor to his office. I began to smile as I heard his deep voice, his laughter a foreign sound rarely heard. I had missed that sound, not realising just how much until now.

As I turned to walk inside his door, I stopped. My smile wiped as my heart slammed into my chest for other reasons.

She was in there, sitting on his desk with her arm up, waving chopsticks around and laughing with him. Her thigh was exposed as she draped a long leg over the other, showing off the top of her lace garters. Wearing a tight fitting black dress with heels so high, she would be almost his height. She was beautiful. Her hair and makeup were done immaculately that I could never pull off an eyeliner like hers.

The sight of the two of them, laughing and sharing lunch didn't make me jealous. It made me feel stupid. I was the pathetic fool for thinking that I was still what he wanted. Diets and shakes, all the running and sweating my fat arse had done, I wasn't going to be like her.

My mind was screaming run, just leave. However, my feet were stuck.

I just focused on him. Unable to hear what they were talking about, he hadn't noticed just how much her eyes were all over him, or that she was sprawled out and offering herself to him. Or did he? He was handsome, a woman's dream. Over six feet tall, dark hair and wore a suit well, this was the typical hot boss fantasy. Her young, high perky breasts and luscious plump lips were the obvious focal point.

What man wouldn't envision those red lips wrapped around their cock?

The part that killed me was he was laughing, something I hadn't seen in so long. I may get the rare intimate side with him, but I would do anything to be the one to make him laugh, even smile.

The jealous wife in me wanted to rip her fucking head off.

As he reached for his drink, lifting his eyes up and about to take a mouthful, he paused. Finally, he noticed I was here in the doorway, watching the two of them share a lovely lunch together. His smile was long gone.

Everything began to play out slowly. Time stood still as I stumbled and fumbled to get away. I shook my head, letting him know not to even bother. My teeth sank into my quivering lower lip. Holding back the tears, I reached out and dropped the plastic bag of sushi into his bin.

"Gabby."

"I need to go." I couldn't stand the sight of them.

"No, wait!" he called out.

Shaking my head, I muttered, "Enjoy lunch."

He was standing, pushing up from his desk and quickly moving on his feet towards me. Kate had jumped up from her position, straightening herself up with flaming red cheeks. I hated her.

I could hear her talking, her voice high as she called out, "Oh, my God, is that your wife?" She was giggling, which angered me even more. It took all my willpower not to walk over and strangle her.

I couldn't have left fast enough. Turning, I walked fast back towards the elevator. My fingers forcefully hit the down arrow, needing to get out of here and away from him. They opened, and I had rushed inside. His panicked face was the last thing my eyes saw as the doors closed.

My phone started ringing, burning in my pocket. I ignored the call. The knot inside my stomach was tugging and hurting. I couldn't cry. I didn't want to cry. I was in shock. He slept with me and then come to work for her.

The phone rang again... and again. Each time, my heart pounded harder, aching with agony. I ignored each call. I didn't reply to his texts. I just blocked him out.

What started out as a great day went downhill quickly. I had no idea how I even managed to smile after that. Picking Noah and Lila up, I was in such a daze. I didn't want them to know anything was up, and I definitely didn't need the gossip from the school ground.

My eyes were tired, aching as I forced myself to stay downstairs. My every being wanted to go to our bedroom and cry to sleep. They were doing their homework and sitting at the counter as I prepared dinner, and I helped in between cutting vegetables.

My eyes were always darting to the clock on the wall by the fridge. Nervous dread weighed in the pit of my stomach. Each minute that passed felt like the timer on a bomb. I didn't want him to come home and hear his excuses if there were going to be any. My mind was made up, and the feeling in my gut told me he was sleeping with her. I just had that feeling something was up.

Noah finished his homework first, jumping down to race off outside so he could beat Lila to the trampoline. I was glad there was no fighting tonight between them. I just couldn't deal with it. Lila went off to her bedroom, playing dolls until dinner was ready.

Assuming Noah was coming back inside, I glanced up ready to tell him not to annoy his sister when I froze. Glancing to and from the clock, I dipped my brows. "It's four."

He was never home before seven.

He walked over towards me, I stayed still, unsure what I wanted to do. Scream? Hit him? Cry? I wanted to do them all. He spoke softly, "You weren't answering my calls."

Of course, I wasn't. My voice caught in my throat as he pulled out a bouquet, big and beautiful wildflowers. Green, yellow and pink, they were filled with so many vivid colours. He hadn't brought me flowers in so long. Any other time, I would have been pleased to receive them... now, not so much.

Immediately, I turned away from him and sat the flowers down on the bench top. I couldn't look at him mainly because I just wanted to cry. These were suck-up flowers and nothing more. "Thank you." It was all I could muster in response.

His arms slipped around my waist, his chest to my back as I felt the warmth of his lips against the base of my neck, murmuring, "I'm sorry."

"It's fine," I lied. It wasn't fine. I was just too defeated to bother. The yelling in me was gone. I didn't have the energy anymore. Trying to relax against him, I just couldn't, and it made things uncomfortable. I shrugged away, his touch burning.

"It's not," he said more for forcefully, taking hold of my elbow and turning me around to face him. My heart pounding as our eyes locked. His glassed over, red-rimmed. "It's damn, well, not okay. I would have lost it if I see what you saw today, Gabby. I would hate to ever see you with another man." Both hands cupped my face tenderly. His thumbs caressing and I think this is the most affectionate he's ever been. "I didn't know you were coming."

"Why would you have known? I was trying to do something new and surprise you." Blinking back the tears, I quickly glanced away as they began to spill once again. "I should have called…" My words were failing me as I began to cry. "I don't want to interrupt you next time."

"There's nothing to interrupt. Nothing is going on with her."

I scoffed. "Don't lie to me. I'm not stupid."

The pads of his thumbs traced inwards and rubbed away the tears. "I never said you were stupid. I called. I left you a voice message, seven actually."

"I deleted them."

His expression was painful as he released my body, stepping backwards and a hand through his hair as he swallowed hard. "I feel like a bastard, Gabby. Jesus, I can't get the way you looked out of my head."

"How do you think I felt?" I couldn't believe he was trying to make this about himself. This was more about easing his own guilty conscious than worrying about me. "Do you have lunch with her every day?" I asked.

"No. Of course not, today was a once off." His voice was becoming frantic, pleading with me to believe him. "You believe me, right?"

"She must be comfortable around you to lay herself out like that. Why didn't you tell her to sit on a chair?" I knew why, and I hated that I finally realised that. He liked it. He liked the attention from other women, and I wasn't giving it to him. I shook my head, "Forget about it, Brody. I don't want to talk about it anymore. I don't want to even speak to you."

"You don't?" He sounded hurt. "I screwed up. I know that now. Tell me what to do. How can I fix this?"

I just stared into the eyes of the man I had fallen madly in love with. "You can't fix it. If I hadn't gone there..."

"Don't go there. Nothing else happened."

I glared, shaking my head with anger. "I don't believe you! How the hell am I meant to believe that? She was all over your desk!"

"I didn't ask her to sit there. Fuck!" he growled back. This time, both hands dragged through his hair as he paced the kitchen. "I'm not fucking her."

"Do you want to?" I didn't want to ask, but I needed to know.

His eyes hardened and glared. "I don't want to fuck anyone else."

"Yeah because our sex life is just so wonderful." I laughed and rolled my eyes as I reached for a tissue. "You don't get it here, and clearly, she's offering for it all. A midday quickie, I don't think we've done that since before we were married."

"Our marriage is based on more than just sex."

I almost asked what marriage. What we have isn't a marriage. Hearing Noah outside, I shook my head. "I'm done talking. I don't want Noah or Lila to hear or see us." I would hate for them to both see this and to hear their parents like this.

He glanced at the door, and Noah came inside with a wide grin. "Dad, you're home!"

Brody bent down, grinning. "Sure am. I thought we could have dinner together and then go outside for a kick of the soccer ball. I hear you're starting on Saturday?" I knew he was just as pleased as I was in regards to Noah playing sports.

"Sure am, dad! Mum got me a new ball. Can I show you it now?" he asked.

With a nod, he stood once again. "I'll wait here for you," he called out, Noah already running off. He began to undo his tie, slipping it off and then rolling the sleeves on his light blue buttoned shirt. "Will you come outside too?"

"I think I just want to go to bed once dinner is done. I'm tired." Half was true; half was a lie. I was tired from crying.

"Am I allowed in the bedroom, too?" he asked quietly. "I just want to hold you."

I bit my lower lip, shrugging. "If you want…"

Turning around, I went back to stirring the food and fought off the tears again as he kept quiet behind me. He was my weakness. To feel his arms around my body and that he wanted to hold me, it was what I wanted. What I have been craving. I also knew this was just him trying to feel less guilty.

Slowly, I heard his footsteps walking up behind me once more, and his arms slid around my waist. A kiss to the top of my head and he stayed like that. "I'm sorry, Gabriella. I've disrespected you. I disrespected our marriage. I won't do it again."

I didn't believe him, and that should have been the first sign.

CHAPTER SIX

"Where is Brody?" Loretta, my sister, asked as she nosily glanced around the large auditorium. "I thought you were coming together."

Leaning in, I spoke quietly wanting to keep this from Noah who was beside me. "Stuck at work again. He's just going to stand in the back when he arrives. He doesn't want to draw attention to himself if he's late." *Lie.*

My other sister, Maria, gave me a pointed look after she and Loretta shared another between the two of them. "He better turn up, this time. He missed the last one." I knew that. The fact that she kept pointing it out bothered me. I loved my sisters and was extremely grateful that they were both here showing their support, but sometimes, they knew how to really tick me off.

It was bad enough that Brody wasn't here but to sit and listen to them complain about him, the same way they had done since we first began dating eleven years ago, it just grew on my nerves.

Brody and I may have kept dating, but when our secret relationship was revealed, my God, I got into trouble, grounded and forbidden to see him. To this day, I had never seen my mama so wild and furious. I never revealed to Brody the full truth about what happened that night especially not about my papa striking me with his belt until I could barely stand straight. I only told him they just grounded me and nothing else. Every day, my sisters would tell me what a plain boy he is, nothing special, and it wouldn't take long for me to find a nice Italian boy to make me forget.

It also didn't take me long to learn how to sneak out of the house without causing the sensor lights to go off. That was my big *screw you* to them all.

Still, they kept their reservations about him, suggesting we weren't the same family as my sisters had with their husbands. They lived the way my mama wanted me to, completely Italian. I was still Italian, but it was mostly with my cooking.

Loretta, my eldest sister, was thirty-six and married to Aldo. He was in his early forties, and they had four children together: Carina, Siena, Luca, and Liliana. My other sister Maria, who is thirty-two, also married an older Italian male, Franco, and they had five children: Alessandra, Gianna and Lia, twins, then Aida, and Roberto.

Then, there were us. We had Noah, and being the first-born male in our family, we were expected to name him after papa. Instead, we chose Noah. They were disappointed. I guess in a way, I felt a little bad for him, but we wanted him to have his own name, and Noah was one we both really liked. Brody chose Lila's name himself. I instantly fell in love with it. We didn't speak Italian, and I wasn't going to force Brody to live a way he wasn't accustomed to. I tried teaching the children a couple words, and the only ones that stuck were Ciao, Per favore, and Si. Now and then, I would try, but they said it was too hard, maybe when they're older, they'd like to learn, but it wasn't something I pushed on them.

"He'll be here," I assured them both but more to myself. I needed him to show up.

Lila loved to dance, so enrolling her in classes seemed the best thing to do. She grasped the routines with ease, and it was a great way for her to socialise with other kids her age. I just hoped Brody hadn't forgotten because she would be heartbroken if she knew the truth. He hadn't made it to a single of her dance performances. She had only been dancing ballet for the past two years, and it was still exciting to her. It was also teaching her patience, a skill she definitely needed to learn and something that her brother wasn't at the moment.

"Mum," Noah moaned. "I want to go home. I'm bored."

"Mum?" Loretta whispered. "My bambinos would never dare call me that."

I gave her a look. It didn't bother me that they went from mummy to mama to mum. "Noah, please don't start. Lila is excited, and we're not leaving." I wasn't in the mood for this right now.

Crossing his arms over his chest, he slumped backwards in his head and huffed. I ignored him, not wanting to make a scene. When the lights dimmed low, I just hoped Brody was standing in the back.

Maria leaned and whispered, "Make sure you call mama. She's missing you."

"If she misses me so much, then she can call me for once." I was sick and tired of being blamed for everything that I'm not doing right. I always called her without fail. Yet if I missed a day, she would overreact and complain to my sisters that I wasn't speaking to her.

Loretta chuckled. "Someone's in a mood. Papa is thinking about retiring. We should do some celebration for him."

"He's sixty-two. I think it's about time he retires." He'd been at the same car dealership since we made the move from Italy to Tasmania. It was due time he resigns and enjoyed his life. "Let me know when the party is. I'll help with whatever I can."

Lila danced beautifully, and of course, Rose and Scott's daughter, Tulip was also up there; front and centre stage. I couldn't help but snicker as she wobbled, her posture off. That's what you get for trying to make your daughter number one, I thought to myself.

As the curtains closed, I couldn't have been anymore prouder of Lila. She'd been nervous, but once they started, those nerves obviously vanished away. Noah also watched with interest, not as bored as he claimed. As I went backstage to collect Lila, my sisters kept an eye on Noah, so he didn't wander off. When we returned, I spotted Brody walked through the doors.

Lila saw him instantly. He was hard to miss. The only one dressed in a sharp black suit with his hair neatly done. She took off with a squeal. "Daddy, did you see me?"

Maria raised a brow as I joined my sisters. "I see he didn't," she pointed out, shaking her head as she put on a fake smile facing him. "Brody, how are you?"

Looking at Maria, he smiled politely. "Well, thank you." He leaned in, kissing my cheek. Pulling away, he lifted up Lila. "I did, sweetheart. You danced so well." She didn't know that he had missed it since she kept talking about her favourite parts with enthusiasm.

My sisters waved us off, and we walked outside. The darkness greeted us as night had fallen and colder than when we had arrived. I rubbed my bare arms, scolding myself for not thinking to pack a jacket. I noticed Rose storming across the car park, Tulip in tow as she stomped behind her. She had been too busy to chat earlier. I wondered why Scott didn't show up but was grateful that he hadn't.

"Can we go now?" Noah groaned. He was by my side, frowning at his father. He knew he hadn't made it either. Kids weren't stupid. They knew what was up.

Brody glanced at Noah, who wouldn't look up him. His hand clung tightly in mine. "Sure."

"Good. I didn't like it," he muttered. "Boring dancing."

"It's called ballet, Noah," Lila corrected, her hands fixing out her light pink tutu as Brody set her back on her feet. "You're so silly sometimes."

Noah reminded me of his father when he rolled his eyes. "Well, I don't care. I don't want to watch that again."

"Be nice. She watched you play soccer," Brody said. "She never complains that you're only kicking a ball."

I looked at him, shaking my head. How would he know? He again never took him to practice after school. It was me, taking him during the windy and sometimes, rainy days, listening to Lila being bored and complaining that she wanted to go home. I'd tell her to go and play on the equipment to distract her until the practice was over. Brody would show up on Saturdays, help coach, and that pissed me off.

The two started racing over to the car. I ignored Brody's apologetic look as I began to follow the kids. "Gabby," he began, stopping when I glared.

"You missed it." I walked past him, unable to say much else.

Jogging a couple steps to catch up, he was soon by my side. "I was on my way out the door, I swear."

"Let me guess, someone else needed you more than your kids did." It was harsh but the truth. I was sick of never being first. The kids deserved to be first for a change.

He sighed heavily. "That's not fair. I'm in charge. I have to help when it's needed," he retorted, pulling open the back door of my black SUV. He'd parked his car beside mine, a black Audi A4 company car that he didn't have to pay for. He leaned inside the car. "Hey, kids, want to go grab an ice cream?"

Of course, when you ask children if they wanted to have sweets, they're going to want one. It was late, just after 9 PM. If it were any other night, I probably would have been okay with it, but I had to be the bad one and say no. "Sorry, you two need to go home; school tomorrow," I reminded, glaring at Brody for even bringing it up. "Don't do that."

"What now?"

"Don't come in late after missing her show and think ice-cream will fix it. You make me the bad one when I have to say no," I said, keeping my voice down low from other parents still lingering around.

Glancing towards Lila in the car, he looked back to me. "She didn't notice I wasn't there."

"Not the point, it's the second concert you missed just like you almost missed something else that was twice as important." I threw their births at him, giving him a guilt trip from down memory lane.

His jaw tensed, and his voice was low and harsh. "Almost; I made it there."

With a whisper, I opened the car door and ready to climb in. "You should have been there from the start."

He rolled his eyes, sighing heavily. "I'll see you at home." And with that, he walked to his car and left me to drive home with tired, complaining kids.

"It's not fair," Noah grumbled. "Dad said we could get ice cream!"

I ignored him, hoping they would fall asleep in the twenty-minute drive home. The entire trip was quiet. The kids luckily passed out on the drive and were still out like a light when Brody pulled up behind me in the driveway.

I couldn't look at him. Anger boiled inside of me as he came down from carrying the kids up to their beds. Everything agitated me. When he walked into the kitchen, I refused to listen to his excuses and repetitive apologies. They were all the same. My heart ached. I just couldn't take this.

"Don't walk away from me when I'm speaking to you!" he snapped harshly.

I kept walking, taking my hot tea into the living room. "Don't speak to me, then. I have nothing to say to you."

"Bullshit, You're being overly dramatic."

That struck a nerve, and I spun around with the teacup in my hands, tempted to throw the hot liquid at him. "Get out of my face. I'm not in the mood tonight," I warned him, gritting my teeth.

"You're never in the mood apparently," he muttered with a scoff. "Only thing you enjoy is a good bitch."

He knew how to push my buttons and pushed he did. I lost it.

Midnight was nearing, and we were still going. The accusations and insults were carelessly hurled around. If one walked away, the other followed, still yelling. I'd been called a nagging bitch who wanted everything for nothing, and he was a bastard who was never here for his family. Our fights very rarely lasted this long, and they definitely weren't as bad. We'd go to bed mad, wake up the next morning, and our fight was never mentioned again.

"You never put this family first, Brody!" I shouted, walking into the living room with him hot on my tail.

"Everything I do is for this family!" he roared, picking up a glass vase filled with fresh garden flowers and threw it across the room. Glass shards shattered down to the floor. "You are always first!"

"If I were first, you wouldn't do things to hurt me like having lunch with your secretary," I spat back. "I bet you're doing it more than what you've told me!" We were back to this.

With a mutter, he groaned rubbing a hand over his face. "Jesus Christ, it was one time, and I admitted that I fucked up. It wasn't anything sexual, and you know it. You get these thoughts into your head, and it infuriates me, Gabby."

"What if I never showed up that day? God, Brody, do you have any idea what that had done to me? How would you like to see another man all over me like that?" It still crushed me to this day, just thinking about it. I was going to say something to her because it was highly inappropriate being at work, and completely disrespectful to his children and me, but why should I do that? He put us in this situation in the first place. This was on him.

"You want that don't you? You want to go out and fuck another man!" he yelled in my face, his breath hot and reeking of whisky. His face was red and jaw hard as he went to yell some more. "You want another dick—"

My hand came up. The loud smack that echoed the room shut him up as my hand connected with his cheek, hard. His eyes watered as his breathing flared up. I had never done that to him before, but I was so angry. I couldn't stop myself. "Don't you ever talk to me that way again?" I said, low and so furious that I was shaking. I regretted hitting him instantly.

Nostrils flaring, he stood taller and wrapped his hand around my wrist, probably worried I was going to hit him again. "Fuck you, Gabriella. Fuck... You!" he said, menacing low and angrily. His tone scared me. I'd never heard him this angry, and it frightened me. "If I were like the men in your family, I'd have hit you back. I should fucking do it. That's how pissed I am right now."

"If you want to hit me, then damn well, hit me," I challenged back, still shaking as I watched his cheek turn redder. The sting in my palm burned, throbbing with agony as I rubbed it.

"I won't ever lay a hand on you, Gabriella." I didn't see how I could slap him and him not slapping me back.

My father and brother-in-laws, they hit my mother and sisters. It was allowed, and they never spoke of it. I had witnessed my father wrapping his hand around my mother's throat and slapping her hard across the face when she spoke back to him. Brody promised me that he never would lay a finger on me, and he had kept that promise.

I should have let it go. I didn't. I needed to know. "Do you want her?" I yelled. I was so angry with him. "Tell me the truth!" I demanded.

Forcing his eyes shut tightly, he shook his head. "No, God, I've never even looked at her that way!"

"I don't trust you," I blurted, but the words felt good to finally say.

He blew out a long hard breath. "Go to bed, Gabby. Otherwise, I'll say something I'll fucking regret."

"Grow some balls and say it. You never talk, and that's what fucks me off with you. You just yell and ignore me. So get it off your chest and damn talk!" I pressed, pushing him against the chest. I'll damn well give him crazy.

"You think I'm the problem? All I listen to at home is you nagging and constantly complaining! I can never do anything right with you!"

I mocked a laugh. "Exactly, you don't do anything right. When was the last time you sat and ate dinner with your children?"

His eyes narrowed. I'd pushed a button. "Are you calling me a bad father?" I remained silent. "You're always quick to judge me but look at you. You don't let them do a lot of shit that they want to do."

"No, I just don't throw toys and ice cream in their faces. I don't want them to grow up like your brother's daughter!" The conversation was soon taking another turn. We would often do this, pick on each other's faults and then bring each other's family into our argument.

Brody closed his mouth. He knew I was right. Sweeping his tongue across his lower lip, he began attacking mine back. "My brother? What about your sisters and your parents? All they did was meddle and take control when they're here."

Rolling my eyes, I scoffed, "Don't be stupid."

"Stupid?" he spat. "I fucking listen to them bitch and complain in damn Italian, and I feel like a fucking idiot because I can't understand any of it!"

"Learn it then! How many times do I say that I would teach you some words? God forbid, you want to do anything with me, though! By the way, I always stand up for you. If they're attacking you, I have never ignored it. Unlike you, you never defend me when I'm being belittled about not working!" I threw my hands up and angrily and turned away.

Brody, of course, needed the final say. "Just because you don't hear it doesn't mean I do not say anything back to them."

"Whatever." I scoffed, not believing him. Turning around, I wiped fallen tears from my eyes. "You just don't care. It's all about you… you and work. If we mattered, you'd be home earlier and putting the children first. I get you have a busy job, but you're missing out on a lot here."

"Don't throw that in my face," he grimly muttered.

My arms crossed over my chest as I sighed heavily. I went to speak when a loud scream startled us both. "Shut up! Shut up! Shut up!" Lila's hot tears streaming down her cheeks as she stood there, clutching her dolly tightly. Noah had an arm around her as he stared at Brody angrily.

I don't think I've ever felt more terrible in my life, to have our two innocent children visibly upset and crying. My heart was in my throat as I couldn't think of the words to say. What could I say to them? There was no escaping this with a simple "Daddy and Mama are just having a little argument." This wasn't little at all. We'd let them down and made them see how bad things were.

"Fuck." I heard Brody whisper from behind me.

"Noah… Lila…" I began, my breathing ragged as I fought back the sobs.

Noah lifted his arm out, holding a piece of paper. As soon as I took it from him, they both ran upstairs. We heard one door slam, and I realised they were in Noah's room together. We terrified them.

I sat down, vision blurred as I uncrumpled the piece of paper. "What docs it say?" Brody asked, walking over and taking a seat beside where I sat.

My heart broke as I read Noah's handwriting; three small words that had the biggest impact on our lives. *Please stop fighting.*

I burst into tears. My heart ached with agony as I passed him the paper and watched as him read it. His expressed immediately went pained and regretful. My guilt was heavy. I was disappointed with myself that they heard us arguing and felt the need to come and ask us to stop. No child should ever have to do that.

Our argument had ended. It was the children who were suffering, and we couldn't keep going on like this anymore. Things needed to change. We both needed to change. I buried my face in my hands, crying with his hand on my lower back, rubbing soothing circles, but it didn't help. Nothing could.

The tears hot, stinging my eyes when I finally spoke, "We can't keep doing this. I can't keep fighting with you."

"I don't want to fight anymore, either," he said quietly, pulling back away. His eyes were on the wooden floorboards as he rested both elbows on each knee.

"They deserve to grow up without parents fighting constantly." I sniffed. "We're not working, and nothing seems to change." It was the same fights and the same petty arguments that would also happen.

Standing up, he walked over to the fireplace and placed both hands on the mantle, gripping the ledge. "I know. I know things need to change." He stood there a moment before coming back to me. Sitting on the coffee table, facing each other, he reached over and took both my hands in his. "I want a divorce."

I was silent. Nothing could have prepared me for what I felt. It was a relief, not desperation to beg him to change his mind. "Me too," I whispered back.

Sitting and just staring at each other, the reality slapped us both hard across the face.

We were done.

CHAPTER SEVEN

I should have felt hurt, but instead, I felt relieved; then, it all began to sink in. Shock and the fear of the unknown washed over me. What happens next? How would it happen? I was a woman who spent my days knowing exactly what I would be doing, and now... I had no damn clue about everything.

"I have nowhere to go," I whispered.

The desperation was now there and banging inside me like a drum, and I realised we were going to be separate. I would have to change my last name. We'd be raising our children in two different homes.

Our children would spend Christmas in two different places, birthdays, and Easter. Oh God, I was going to have an anxiety attack. My hands were shaking, chest heaving and tears spilling out uncontrollably. Was it too late to take my words back? I had never regretted anything so much in my life.

Brody, squeezing tighter, forced my eyes up to meet his. "I'm not going to throw you out. You're the mother of my children. I'll leave. I'll get a hotel or go to mum's."

Panic began to eat me alive. "What? No." I didn't want him to go. "What will people say?"

"I don't care what they say. This is our decision."

I heard him, but it wasn't fully sinking in. My parents would be furious, disgusted that I was shaming the family with a divorce. It would all come back to our teenage years of rushing. I couldn't bear to think about my papa's reaction and his look of disappointment.

I swallowed, licking my dry lips. "Stay," I pleaded, not wanting to see him leave. The kids would be devastated beyond words and would want to go with him.

"Gabby," he pleaded. "We're constantly fighting."

"This is your home. You bought this house. I'll go. I don't want you to leave here." Being in this house without him would be a nightmare.

His blue eyes were glassy as he smiled sadly. "Stay in the guest house. There's no rush for you to leave, and the kids—" pausing, he let my left hand go and reached up to rub his temples. "— Fuck, the kids."

Divorce — it was one thing we never wanted them to go through.

"I know. I feel terrible."

"Don't. We can tell them together," He suggested.

"I don't want to tell them just yet. Let's just wait and figure some things out before we go telling anybody?" It needed it to sink in, and we had so much to discuss still. "We need to have the answers. People will ask, and right now, I don't have any."

With a nod, he looked at me. "I agree."

We were silent for a moment, and then I broke the thick air. "When did you stop loving me?" I asked. I wasn't mad, just sad to know I wasn't what he wanted anymore. I never considered the man I married would fall out of love with me. I guess I hadn't considered feeling this way about him either.

With a sad smile, he shrugged. "I never stopped loving you. I just…"

"You're just not in love with me anymore," I finished the answer for him.

"I'm sorry. Things just became too tough," he sighed, sniffing back his own tears.

I nodded in agreement. "It's okay, Brody. I know what you mean. We fought so much that I began to dread you coming home. I guess some things just aren't meant to be."

He sat there looking as miserable as I felt. His red cheek faded from where I had hit him. "You dreaded me coming home?" He shook his head and took a breath in. "Jesus, hit me right where it hurts, don't you?"

"I'm not trying to hurt you." I pulled my hands from his and set them in my lap. Fumbling with my sleeves, my fingers dug into my palms. My eyes watered even more. "You can't say that you loved coming home. You didn't like the fights that always came."

"It wasn't all bad. I mean, we had some good days, though." He reached forward again, rubbing my thigh with a gentle squeeze. "Didn't we?"

A soft smile pulled at the corners of my lips, and I nodded. "We did; then, I think we just began to have more bad than good. I don't want that anymore, Brody. Our children deserve to grow up without their parents fighting so much. We never did anything as a family, the four of us. That's not fair to them."

"I know," he agreed, and slowly, his hand loosened. Soon, it was gone from my leg.

There was no way that I would be able to fall asleep and Brody, the same, as he retired to his office to work or drink, probably both. Noah was fast asleep in Lila's bed with his arms wrapped around her protectively, and I felt the guilt hitting me harder than ever. I don't want them to live life this way. They deserve so much more than what we were giving them.

Instead of sleeping, I went into our bedroom and began to pack a few of my things. It may have been a rash idea, but there was no way I would be able to sleep after tonight. I felt sick, nauseated. My head throbbed, and heart ached. This was for the best. I just had to keep telling myself that. Our son and daughter deserved better. They deserved parents who were in love with each other. I love him, but like he said… that intense, passionate love wasn't there anymore.

As I pulled out each item of clothing, I cried at the realisation of what was happening. I was going to move into the guest house we had for when my parents came to visit. It may not be ideal, but it was better than the alternative, moving to a hotel and being away from my children.

By the time the sun began to rose, I was coming back from the guest house after putting away some clothing. My hair was still damp from the recent shower but eyes red-rimmed. I was emotionally exhausted. The tears hadn't gone away, but they had died down from what they were. Walking inside quietly, I was surprised to see Brody staring into the fridge, wearing a pair of sweats that hung low, clinging to his ass.

Looking away as he closed the door with a sigh, he seemed surprised to see me in here. "Did you get any sleep?"

I shook my head. "Not really. You?"

"The same, not able to sleep." He walked inside the pantry, appearing seconds later with the waffle maker in his hand and plugging it in. "I'm going to stay home today," he added as I began to prepare breakfast, mixing flour and water. "We need to talk to Noah and Lila about last night," he said, guilt all over his pained expression.

Nodding as I walked to the fridge, taking the eggs and adding them. "Thank you. I think that's a good idea."

Brody didn't leave as I kept whisking, probably harder than I ought to have done, but it distracted me for a moment. My eyes were blurry, chest heaving up and down when he reached over and placed his hand over mine, squeezing to urge me to stop.

"You didn't have to move out of the house through the night, Gab. You could have stayed in our room," he said quietly as I set the bowl back on the bench.

Wiping my eyes with the hem of my white t-shirt, I shook my head. "May as well rip the band-aid off quickly. I didn't want to drag it out." Otherwise, it'd probably never want to leave.

"There is no rush, Gabriella. I mean that." His tone caught my gaze. "I'm not as heartless as you assume."

He was staring right at me, and I couldn't explain the feeling that brewed up inside of me. I'd had expected him to be in a rush to make me leave. I knew it would have to be done, but I was thankful he wasn't pushing for it. I needed to find a job, to look for a new home and I couldn't move out until I was earning money. There was so much to think about and organise. I wanted to be able to provide for our children, to be able to rely on myself and not him or my family.

"I appreciate that, Brody. Thank you," I said softly.

Whispering back, he nodded. "I'll always take care of you."

When the kids came downstairs, it was obvious that they were surprised to see their father standing in the kitchen, not dressed for work. "Daddy!" Lila squealed, running towards him and jumping up his legs.

Brody chuckled and lifted her up. "Hey, pretty girl," he said as he carried her towards the dining table where he set her down. "Mama's making waffles. You want some or not feeling that hungry?" he asked with a wink.

Giggling, she tried tickling him. "I'm very, very, hungry!"

"Oh, like the hungry caterpillar?" I asked, smiling as I brought her a plate, and gave her a kiss on the top of her head. "Eat up. You've got to make room for burgers and ice-cream for dinner tonight."

"We get to have that, really?" she asked.

I nodded. "Of course, you do." It was probably more me feeling guilty about everything we'd put them through. I just wanted to keep the smiles on their precious faces.

"Me too, I want waffles too!" Noah said, rubbing his stomach and sliding in his chair across Lila. "I want waffles too. Big ones."

Chuckling, Brody looked up. "All right, Noah wants a big waffle."

"I think I can manage that. Are you having breakfast?" I asked, glancing at Brody nervously as I poured a drizzle of maple syrup all over Noah's breakfast.

He nodded, joining them at the table. "How can I say no to waffles when you're making them?"

I gave him a soft smile, unable to remember the last time we all sat and ate breakfast together. Why did it have to reach a mention of divorce for it to happen? Maybe, I hoped we would be able to remain friendly after this was done. I would hate to be on bad terms with him. Then again, this could just be like the other times. We would have a raging fight and then be nice to each other the next morning. As long as we weren't fighting in front of the kids, I didn't care.

I sat, sipping my coffee as the kids and Brody ate breakfast. Afterwards, we took the kids into the living room for the dreaded talk we both needed to have with them both. Brody held Lila on his knee as I held Noah to my side. It broke my heart that they had no idea, oblivious to what we were really going through. Relationships are tough, and I prayed they would never have to experience this like Brody and I were going through. I would be crushed to know my babies were unhappy and felt trapped in life that they thought it was impossible to leave.

Clearing his throat, Brody began talking first. "We want you to know that last night, we are extremely sorry that you both had to hear us fighting like that."

"Why do you fight?" Lila asked so innocently.

"Sometimes, mama and daddy fight," he said, looking at me with remorse.

Noah spoke up, "Why?"

"Like you and Lila, we sometimes don't agree, or we get upset and end up yelling at each other," I said trying to put it in a way that they would understand. "It doesn't mean that we hate each other. We shouldn't have yelled especially around you both. We're so sorry that you had to hear it."

Lila looked upwards to her daddy. "Do you like yelling at Mama?"

"No, I should never have spoken to your mama that way," he smiled weakly, kissing the top of her head. "Are you okay, Noah?" he looked over, worried.

"Will you stop fighting?" Noah asked. "I don't like it."

"Yes," he promised. "We're going to work very hard at being nicer to each other." It's a shame that it took this to promise that.

Noah seemed please, standing up and pointing outside. "Can we go outside now? I want to ride my bike."

Reaching over, I wrapped my arms around him and hugged him close. "Of course, you can. Wear your helmet, okay?" I said, letting my arms loose from around his waist. "Only for a little bit. You have school soon."

"I'm going to get my dolly! She wants to ride my bike too," Lila said, jumping down and running towards the stairs to go up to her bedroom. "Noah, don't touch my bike!" she called out bossily.

Brody and I both laughed as Noah yelled out to her. "Like I want to touch your pink bike! I don't want girl germs."

"Doubt he'll be saying that in ten or so years," Brody grinned, shaking his head as he leant back on the couch.

I made a groaning sound, shaking my head. "Please don't remind me how fast they're growing." That was another thing I didn't want to think about. Although this talk and the breakfast had taken my mind off our impending divorce, that was going to happen soon.

The day passed slowly. The kids at school made this day painfully quiet. I barely moved from the couch, laying down and for once, just watching TV. I slept on and off, exhausted from being up all night. I tried cleaning the guest house up, making it feel more at home, but nothing could make it feel less depressing. I took another shower, trying to ease a headache as Brody worked in the office. We hadn't seen each other much since speaking to the kids this morning even for lunch which I skipped to still focus on my shakes. The good thing was the treadmill was in the guest house, and he couldn't see me running. It became my focus. I was more determined than ever to get fitter.

Lila and I baked cookies while Noah and Brody played in the pool and were seeing who could do the biggest splashes. It was a relatively normal day, but I felt incredibly sick with dread for what was to come. When night time came, those nerves were only growing. I barely ate any dinner, and I noticed Brody hadn't either. The kids thought everything was well and good between us.

Almost 9 PM and I just stared out the glass door. Staring at the backyard, I tried talking myself into opening the door and walking across the garden, to the guest house.

"Gabby?" Brody spoke up softly, startling me. I thought he'd gone to bed.

I shook my head if he said anymore, then I'd break down again. "I'm fine." I forced out, my voice strained. The first night would be the hardest. That's what I kept telling myself. It'll get easier.

I could see his reflection standing behind me through the glass. He didn't come near me, just keeping his distance and staring. "Are you okay?"

"Yes." No, I wasn't okay. "You should go to bed."

"I just… uh, good night," he said quietly, making no intention of walking away.

"Good night." I couldn't even muster a smile. "I'll be up before they wake," I said, referring to our children. I didn't want them to know we were sleeping this far apart, just yet.

He was still there, staring at me from behind. I felt anxious and nervous. "Gabriella."

"Yes?" I asked a mere whisper, afraid to know what he wanted.

"I'll go over there. You don't need to do this. Stay in the house." I felt his hand on my shoulder, squeezing with comfort.

Momentarily, my eyes closed. Taking a steady breath, I reached up, covering his hand with mine. "I'm okay," I promised again before I dropped my hand and took a step forward, away from him.

I felt him still standing there in the darkness, watching me. My heart was booming. The sound filled my ears as I put my hand on the silver handle, turning the knob and opening the door. All I could do was walk out the kitchen doors and go to the guest house where I would spend my first night as a separated woman.

And it sucked.

CHAPTER EIGHT

Crouching down low, I felt like a complete idiot as I walked like Pocahontas through the jungle. It's just that I wasn't actually walking through a jungle, just down the side of my parent's home until I reached the barbed wire fence where I could stand, and then taking gigantic steps, I ran to the edge of the driveway.

It hadn't set off the sensor lights once, and I'd been doing this twice a week for the past three weeks to meet up with a certain boy.

Giddiness set upon me as I came to the road and pulled my hooded jumper off my head. Thank goodness, we lived a little out of town. Otherwise, people may just think I was a freak... or tell my parents about my excursions, who in turn, would go bat shit crazy.

Pulling my phone from my bra when I felt it vibrate, I read the text on the glowing screen. "Have you left yet? X"

I replied as fast as I could. "Yes, I'll be there soon. Xoxo"

Soon, I was at the spot we always met up at and spotted him. Wearing a navy hooded jumper himself and a pair of black sweatpants, I smiled and tucked my phone back into my bra. I really should have worn trousers or a jumper with pockets.

Brody stood up from the ground on a small bank down by the lake. We didn't really have anywhere else to go, and this was within walking distance from his house and mine. If it were raining, then we'd have to cancel, and I hated that but we'd text all night long until I passed out. He always waited until I fell asleep.

"Hey," he whispered like someone would hear us.

"Hi yourself," I smiled, biting down on my lower lip as I came to a standstill in front of him.

His arms were instantly wrapped around my lower back, and he pulled me in close. "I'm freaking out that you'll get caught."

I grinned, nodding. "Me too."

"Why are you smiling about it?" he asked, matching my smile.

I shrugged and softly giggled. "I don't know. It's not funny, but you just make me smile. If we get caught, I'm dead. They think I'm over my crush on you."

"Are you?" he asked, raising a brow as he leaned in closer.

Shaking my head, I could never be over my crush on him. "Nope."

"Good, now, come here." Pulling me in closer, his hands slid down to my ass, and he rested them there. "God, I've missed you." Looking down, he raised a brow. "Are those sheep?"

I blushed hard as I glanced down at my pink flannel PJs. "I had to wear them. If they catch me walking back to my room, at least, I'm in my jammies."

He laughed, a beautiful sound that always made me smile and heart pound harder and faster. "Oh god, I love you." Hold on... what? My eyes widened, and he shrugged. "Don't look so surprised. I've loved you since the moment you walked into class."

"You mean that?" I asked, unable to hide the happiness I felt. He nodded, and I could have just burst from excitement. "Oh Brody, I love you too! I'm so madly in love with you."

He smiled and squeezed me tighter. "I don't ever want to be apart from you. I hate that we can't see each other after school."

I ran my hands up his chest and let my arms slide around his neck. "Me too. Least we do get to see each other at school, though."

"Not the same, Gabby," he groaned, slowly nearing his mouth to mine. "I hate that we have to sneak around, but I cannot not see you."

I nodded, knowing what he meant. "Me too."

Our mouths crashed over each other. We were hungry for kisses. I couldn't get enough of him. Needing his skin on

mine, our hands roamed all over each other and bodies slowly
rubbing against one another's. His tongue darted in my mouth,
and he groaned as I matched his pace but still let him take
control.

It had taken me so long to figure out how to breathe
and kiss at the same time. We were now so good that we didn't
need to stop every minute. Embarrassing, I know. Soon, we
were on the grass. Brody's body moved on top of mine as we
kept kissing. His knee nudged my thighs apart to let him in
closer.

My legs wrapped around the backs of his thighs as my
hands roamed his back. He kissed me harder and hips
beginning to push forward created a new pleasure I had only
recently experienced. I had become incredibly embarrassed as
I had moaned when he first did that, and to ease my
embarrassment, he told me he had to stop before he came in his
boxers, which he was extremely close to doing.

We didn't take it any further than just making out that
night. But soon, we would.

You would think things felt easier after being separated
for a couple of weeks. It wasn't. Brody and I were back into the
cheating accusations and jabs towards each other. We made
sure to never fight like we had done that night around the
children again, and we kept that promise.

The sleeping alone wasn't too bad. We'd been apart for
so long that I was used to being in a large bed by myself. It was
the silence that ate me up, going into a small house and being
alone. Nobody could hear me cry each night to sleep. I was also

able to use the treadmill in here; twice a day, I had been running. It took my mind off everything.

If you're wondering if I had gone and done a new makeover to make myself feel better, you're damn right I did. Although it didn't help, at least, I now had clothes that fit my body better than the other clothing I owned. Cathy and I had gone shopping. She didn't know about Brody and I. Nobody did.

How do you tell someone you're getting a divorce? It wasn't that simple especially when we were still yet to tell our children, Noah and Lila.

Brody was back to working constantly, and it was a good thing that I had stayed at the house. He was working early to almost midnight, and the kids were missing him like crazy. Of course, I assumed he was cheating.

As I washed the dishes in the kitchen and began to make Brody's lunch for work, I couldn't help notice that he kept glancing over as he sat and ate with the kids.

"So what's going on today?" he asked.

"I'm going to play with my friends. What about you, Daddy?" Lila asked, sounding so grown up as she sat on his lap and tried to fix his work tie.

"Well, I have work to do, and then tonight, we're going to go out and celebrate," Brody answered, not bothered that Lila's greasy fingers were all over his silk tie like he normally would be.

Lila, being her nosy self, replied, "Mama too?"

I felt so guilty when she asked this. I plastered on a smile and looked over at her. "Of course, sweetie. How about you leave daddy alone and finish your breakfast? Otherwise, you won't get to play with your friends at school."

"I'm finished," Noah said with a mouthful. "I'm going to brush my teeth now."

Watching him walk off after handing me his empty bowl, I glanced at Brody and internally sighed. He always looked so good in a suit. "Your breakfast is ready, and coffee is hot." He met my gaze, and I realised he probably thought I'd be joining them for dinner tonight. I'd just make up some excuse like normal and let them have time together.

Brody stood up, downed his coffee and pushed the bowl of food aside. "I'm not hungry. I've got to go. Can't be late today." I didn't say anything about the food. I didn't care anymore. "I should be home by five."

Normally, I would have said good luck. It just didn't seem appropriate to do right now. "Okay."

Lila watched us like a hawk as we both faked a smile and wrapped our arms around each other. Our mouths met, and although there was still something there, I always blocked it out. We gave each other a kiss goodbye and pulled away.

"See you all later. Have a good day!" He called out, picked up his briefcase and left for work.

I gave Lila a curious look, and she grinned. "You have germs from daddy," she giggled.

Rolling my eyes with a smile, I nodded towards her food, "Eat up, little miss, or I'll come and give you some of my germs that daddy gave me."

When everyone has gone to work and school, I cleaned the house spotless; then, wrote the grocery list. I also searched online for jobs, and apartments. There was nothing unless I wanted to be a check out chick who worked with an on call type of roster. I needed something that would suit the children as well as me.

When I found nothing, I went into town for my usual waxing appointment. There was only one time that I became shy, and it was when the girl waxing me had my legs spread apart and hot wax in her hand.

"The usual?" Avora asked.

I went to say yes, just the usual bikini wax and trim, but instead, other words came out that had me blushing like a tomato. "All of it."

Not that I was extremely hairy down there, I liked to keep myself tidy and trim, but now, I wanted to do something different. Maybe, I was having a midlife crisis with my impending divorce. It was a bad excuse, but I just wanted to change everything about me, not that anyone would be seeing me naked anytime soon.

"Gabby, don't go all embarrassed. I see dozens of vagina's each day. This is like brushing hair. Only, I'm taking it off," she said with a giggle. "Relax, it won't take long."

When she pulled that first strip, I was already regretting my decision. My god, it was painful!

I was sure I was limping as I picked Noah and Lila up from school, still adjusting to new waxing style. It didn't hurt after a while. I was just too numb to feel anything. They were inside playing on the Xbox when I went to find Brody to see if he was still taking them out or not.

Walking down towards the gym, I stood at the door for a moment, watching him flex his strong arms as he lifted the weights. Letting my eyes wander, the heat began to spread, and the desire set in as I struggled to take my eyes from him. Sweat trickled down, his shirt wet. Oh god. Stop it. I had to remember why I was coming in here. Tearing my eyes away, I pushed the door open further making a noise, he looked up and stopped. Setting the weights down on the floor either side of him, he started to walk towards me.

"Noah and Lila want you." My words failed as my breath caught in my throat. "Are you still taking them out? Otherwise, I'll make something," I said, barely able to look at him and still tried to wipe the image of him working out of my mind.

Wiping the sweat from his face with the bottom of his shirt, he answered, "I promised them I would, and I won't break that promise as you broke yours to me." He began to walk past me to leave the room. "All the weight loss and getting back into shape. Is it for him?" he muttered coldly. "Does he satisfy you the way I couldn't?"

I was so fed up with these jabs about another man. They'd been going on for the past week, almost every day. "You're a bastard. How dare you accuse me of screwing someone else?" I hissed, the desire long gone. "If I were getting satisfied, then I wouldn't have been begging you not to come before me. Just because you're now fucking Kate, don't try to blame me!"

He began to laugh. "You're a bitch. I haven't and wouldn't fuck anyone else but you. I'm an honest person and faithful unlike you! That's why you were so quick to move out, isn't it? So you could sneak off to him or have him over. Who is he, Gabby? Who?" With each word, he soon had me pinned against the wall with nothing between us as his body pressed against mine.

"Get off me!" I tried shoving him. Hands flat against his chest, I felt his new muscles. "God, I wish there was someone else just to shut you up! You know there hasn't been anyone else. But if you're so convinced that there is, please, when you find him, let me know as well so I can finally meet the man I'm supposedly having so much sex with." I yelled, gripping his T-shirt and trying to ignore the spreading heat throughout my body caused by him.

I hadn't felt this way since before Lila was born.

He just glared. His eyes narrowed even more while his arms were pressed either side of me as he had me completely trapped. "Yeah? Why get back in shape then? Why get your hair done more often now? It's been coloured darker."

I felt so small and trapped between the wall and him. We rarely touched, and now he was pinning me with his body. His erection pressing into my stomach was something I hadn't expected. God, it aroused me, though. I was starting to go back to the place of want and need.

Shaking my head at him, I sighed. "Is it so bad that I wanted to lose weight? I have been running my ass off each and every day to lose all that extra weight. I hated that I had to lose almost fifteen kilos to start feeling good about myself because you never made me feel that way." Tears were burning my eyes. "You're divorcing me. Who the hell is ever going to want some fat housewife who's too insecure to get naked? I did this for me. I'm doing it to feel good about me."

He sighed, and his face changed from hatred to sorrow. His voice was almost a whisper. "I didn't. You have always looked good to me." With that, he pulled away and left the room, leaving me and my hot tears behind.

I waited until I was able to speak before heading up Noah's room. I walked in and acted as if nothing had happened. "You two, I need you to get dressed. Daddy is taking you out to eat."

"You too, Mama?" Noah asked.

I hated lying to them. "Oh, sweetheart, I've been feeling a little bit sick. I think I'm going to stay home and have an early night. You go and enjoy your time out with daddy, okay?"

I felt like disappointed when I noticed their smiles fading. Placing Noah's clothes on his bed, I turned and left the room before I cried and then went to get Lila's clothing for her to wear.

When I heard the knock on the guest house door, I sighed and got up off the bed. I just wanted to change and go to sleep. Walking to the door, I opened it and noticed Brody standing there in a pair of navy denim jeans and a black top clinging to his body. God, I hated how he had become more handsome over the years.

"Come to search the place for men before you leave?" I asked sarcastically. "I haven't turned on the red light to my brothel just yet."

He just stared at me. "No, I came to see why you weren't coming to dinner. You told them that you were, this morning, and you should come. I sold off a company after almost a year. It's finally a done deal. It's over."

I had no idea he was working on something for so long. I actually felt bad that I knew nothing about his work other than he was incredibly smart and made his bosses a lot of money.

"Do you really want me there? I told them I was feeling unwell," I said, leaning against the door frame.

"You need to eat too." Raising a brow, she gestured to my body. "I finally found the reason you're not eating much, shakes. Gabby, for how long?"

I shrugged, unable to meet his heated gaze. I felt ashamed. "I don't know, two months maybe."

"You're coming to dinner. You need to eat something instead of skipping meals."

"I'm not skipping meals," I pointed out. It wasn't as if I were starving myself. "I just… you wouldn't understand."

"Make me understand then." He walked further into the small kitchenette, shaking his head. "I can't stop thinking about what you said; fat housewife? If you truly believe that's how I have made you feel, I don't blame you for wanting out." Turning, he faced me. "You're fucking sexy. Now, get your ass changed. We're leaving soon."

My cheeks flamed. Fucking sexy? Realising there was no way out of this, I gave in. "Give me ten minutes to change, and I will meet you in the car."

Nodding, he stood up straighter and smiled with triumph. "Good. We'll wait for you in the Audi."

I walked away into the small bathroom. Staring in the mirror, I thought, My God, what a mess I looked. Quickly, I washed my face and picked up some of the make-up I had bought but rarely used. If we were going out to celebrate him, the least I could do was make an effort especially if he was making me join them.

Slipping my legs into a pair of navy blue fitted jeans, I contemplated on changing. I was always in trousers, and it was a nice night out. I bravely dared myself to wear a light grey tee dress that came just above my knees. It was comfortable, casual but not too plain. I then made my way towards the car.

Brody was sitting in the front seat and the kids chatting in the back about where they thought we were going to go. I asked him where he wanted to go, but he just kept staring at me like he was lost in his own little world.

"Daddy, can we get ice cream afterwards, please?" Lila asked excitedly.

"Um, what? Yeah, we can do that, sweetie," he said with a confused look on his face. "So, uh, where do we want to go eat?"

I frowned a little and looked out the window. "That's what I just asked you." If he was going to ignore me, then I didn't really want to be here. "Wherever is fine. You choose since this is to celebrate your successful day at work." I glanced over and gave him a small smile.

He did something that shocked me. He smiled back at me. "Sorry, I didn't hear you ask that." Then, he looked out the front window. "How about pizza? I know a good place."

The kids loved pizza, so they were excited to eat there. I agreed as well.

I had expected to go down to the normal parlour in town, only a ten-minute drive away, but when we began talking about our day and the kids rambling on about theirs, I lost track of time and realised we weren't at the place I had expected.

Brody had driven to the same place, the same small pizzeria that he had taken me to on our first date.

CHAPTER NINE

"I wonder if those booths are still in there." I found myself whispering to no one in particular.

The place still looked exactly the same even down to the sign hanging out the front of the brick building. I was still in a dazed shock that he had driven us here to eat. Of all places, maybe, this was a trip down memory lane.

"I want a cheese pizza," Lila was saying as Noah then told her that wasn't a pizza. "It is!" she grumbled back.

"Is not. You're just eating bread with cheese like a sandwich," Noah retorted. "Except it's hot."

"Please don't argue or no ice cream, remember?" Yes, that soon shut them up.

Looking over towards Brody, our eyes locked, and I couldn't begin to describe the feeling that came across me. Was it nerves? It sure felt like butterflies. It must be nerves. I pushed it away as soon as they came.

He gave me a small smile as he took hold of Lila's hand. "Noah, hold mama's hand please."

His hand wrapped around mine as we walked across the road. Once inside, I realised it wasn't just the outside that hadn't changed. The inside was still the same too: dim, romantic lighting and families eating together. It was a family type of restaurant, and it felt nice to be back, like home.

"I'll go order. You pick out a spot to sit," Brody said as Lila was clinging, stating that she wanted to stay with her dad.

I looked towards Noah. "All right, where do you want to sit?" He could choose. There were a few empty spots available.

Noah was leading me towards the back booth when I felt a hand touch my shoulder. Turning around, it took me a moment to realise it was the man I had once worked for. I was surprised. "Richard, wow, small town."

"Elle?" He was the only man who had never called me Gabby or Gabriella. "Wow, it's great to see you again. You're looking well."

I nodded, not denying the compliment made me feel good about my choice in outfit. "Thank you. Are you here with Trish and the kids?"

"Yes, family night out." He tilted his head in the direction of where his wife and three children sat, already halfway through their meals. "Where are you working now? You must be keeping yourself busy somehow."

"The kids keep me fairly busy for now." I laughed. "Not much life outside school and activities."

"Let me know when you're interested in coming back to work."

I slightly rolled my eyes with a laugh. "It's almost been nine years. You say this every time we run into each other." Way to remind myself how long I haven't been working. Then again, it wasn't like I had taken a vacation.

"No one's ever been able to make my coffee the way you do," he grinned. His brown eyes twinkling with playfulness.

Oh, now, he was just baiting me up. I felt Brody's eyes on us, but I couldn't bring myself to look over at him. Politely smiling at Richard, "Well, of course, they were the best. I slipped in a couple happy pills."

Barking out a laugh, his head tilted back. "I bet you did." Glancing towards Noah, he patted my arm once more. "I see you're out with the family, so I won't keep you. Give me a call if you ever need a job. I'd hire you back in second."

I smiled, giving him a wave goodbye. "I might take you up on that."

Wrapping my arm around Noah, I looked towards where he was looking. "Have you picked out a table?"

Lifting his arm up, he pointed directly towards a small booth. Oh, dear God, please don't let it be that one. He smiled. "I want to sit over there."

Just my luck, he picked out the exact same table his father had chosen over ten years ago.

We walked over, sliding into the deep red booth seats. I glanced towards Lila and Brody as they were heading back over, and I noticed his raised brow, silently asking if I had picked this spot purposely. I shook my head and tilted towards Noah. He had done it all on his own.

Our pizza and drinks were brought over, never one to keep their customers waiting. It smelled the same. The freshly baked dough had my stomach grumbling with hunger. Brody kept giving Richard a glance now and then. He had hated it when I worked for him, always thought he were a sleaze who was trying to nail me. I'd laugh it off and tell Brody that the only one doing any nailing would be him.

He nailed me twice that night.

I'd been trying to avoid it all night, but the urge was there. I wasn't doing it purposely, but out of curiosity, reaching over, I lifted the napkin holder and saw that our initials were still engraved into the piece of wood. Memories flooding back as I remembered that day so clearly like it was yesterday.

Brody, with a cheeky grin, slid closer towards the wall. I hadn't had a clue what he was up to until I spotted the knife. "Brody," I whispered. "You'll get us kicked out."

My parents, finally realising that there was no way they could keep us apart, agreed to let us go out on our first date. I made them drop me off a block away so they couldn't embarrass me with giving him a lecture.

His mum wanted to join us so his older brother drove him here and would take us both home once we'd finished our dinner. We were drawing this out for as long as possible.

Looking up, he rubbed my foot with his underneath the table. "I don't care. When we're old and married, we can bring our kids back here to show them where it all began."

"Kids?" I raised a brow. "You're getting ahead of yourself, aren't you?"

He silently laughed as he tightened his hold on the knife. "Babe, you're the type of girl a boy marries. When we're both eighteen, I'm going to ask you, and you'll say yes."

"How are you so sure?" I asked back, taking a sip of my coke. "I could say no."

Shaking his head, he stood up slightly and leant over the table between us. "Because I know nothing will come between us. I'm going to love you forever." He then kissed me on the lips and sat back down with a grin.

"Me too," I smiled, knowing I couldn't ever stop loving him.

He pushed the knife into the wood and began to carve out the letter B. "Keep watch; otherwise, it's just going to be my initials inside a heart," he chuckled. "And I definitely don't want that!"

I kept my eyes out, kicking him every time I thought someone was coming over, and when he had finished, inside a heart read the letters B.W 4 G.S... and I knew that we'd love each other forever.

"You would have thought they'd replace that." Brody's voice broke me out of my daydream.

I looked up. "I guess so. I still can't believe you did that."

"I'd have done anything for you back then, Gabby," he smiled sadly, as I pushed the napkin holder back in place. It was just too bad some things didn't last the way we had hoped for.

Deciding we needed a change of topic before I burst into tears, or we ended up arguing over something petty, I picked up a piece of garlic bread and tore a piece off. "How about you tell us—?" I said at the same time Brody had spoken, "What did that—?"

Blushing, oh God, was I really blushing? I smiled at just pointed towards him, "You go first."

"I was going to ask what that tosser wanted?" he said, nudging his head towards Richard.

I couldn't help the snort. "Brody." I shook my head. "He could have heard you."

With a shrug, he replied, "He's a sleaze, out with his wife and kids but was all over you."

I almost accused him of being jealous, but I bit my tongue instead. "No. He just asked if I wanted my old job back pretty much."

"You're going back to work?" he asked, looking slightly surprised. "Didn't think you were looking?"

Nodding, why hadn't he realised this? "I'm going to need to go back to work, Brody," I said quietly. "I can't afford not to."

I would never take Brody's money from him especially if I weren't working. I just couldn't be that type of woman. "I know. I just… it just took me by surprise that's all. I hadn't put much thought into it," he said, looking quite annoyed but masked that emotion up quickly. "What were you saying?"

"Oh, right," I had almost forgotten. "Tell me about this deal at work. You sold a company obviously."

He nodded. "I did. We had a meeting at nine, and by half past, he'd signed the paperwork. He was so impressed with my proposal that he agreed to sign over three million in stocks, and I'll have it tripled within the year."

"Wow!" I didn't have any words. He had always been clever with maths. I should know. He did help me study before I had a test. "That's great, Brody."

"It is. He's even offering to throw in a family vacation for John's and my family..." he kept talking and then began to go into the more detailed side of things, and I was actually listening until Noah decided that he was bored.

"Ugh, that sounds boring, dad!"

Brody chuckled. "I know, buddy, tell me about your day at school."

"Yep, we had a rocket launch at school, and mine went off the highest in class! It was so cool. I'm going to make one at home this weekend and let it off in my room."

I laughed, shaking my head. "Oh, I think you should do it outside. It might go through the ceiling, and then you'll have to sleep with a hole in the roof."

"I guess so," he said and thought about it. "I don't want to have rain coming in my bed."

Lila piped up, "Daddy, Mama, I know what I want for my birthday!" she beamed, taking a bite of her cheese pizza. Yes, she got a cheese one. God bless her little heart. It was hard to say no when they smiled so brightly.

Brody and I both raised our brows up, looking down at her. "Oh, yeah? What is that?" I asked.

"Lila, you know I can't get you a unicorn, right?" Brody teased with a grin. "Or a real fairy."

Her birthday was in three weeks, and so far, she had listed off things from a kitten to her own ballerina dancing stage. This child had a vivid imagination. She had watched Peter Pan, and for weeks, she begged and begged us to buy her a real Tinkerbell. She wanted to have a pet mermaid to swim in our pool after watching The Little Mermaid. Then when she asked to grow her hair as long as Rapunzel, I gave up listening. Her choices changed too much to keep up with.

Giggling, she shook her head. "Nope, not that, daddy. It's even better, and my friend has one so I would like one too, please?"

"What is it?" I asked, intrigued by her enthusiasm.

With a big bright smile, she set her food down and beamed brightly at us both. "A little baby sister!"

Being in the middle of taking a mouthful of his coke when Lila had asked that unexpected and startling question, Brody was obviously not prepared for it either and sprayed his drink out of his mouth, directly at me as his began a coughing fit.

Lila just giggled.

Noah rolled his eyes and took another bite of his pizza, completely uninterested.

I just sat there, stunned as I reached for the napkins but found Brody had beaten me to them.

"That was unexpected," he laughed embarrassedly as he reached over to begin patting me down with a handful of napkins scrunched up on his hand. "I'm so sorry."

Wiping the droplets of coke from my bare skin and over the tops my breasts which he hadn't noticed he was patting down now. "It's okay. Honestly, I didn't expect that either."

Pulling back, he genuinely looked remorseful as Lila sat patiently waiting for her answer. "Um, Lila…" This would have been amusing if we weren't divorcing. "I don't know. We just can't give you a sister. It's not something that we can just magically create. We can't do it." Brody glanced up towards me. I knew he felt bad. He would give her the world if he could.

"Why?" she asked, dipping her dark brows down and looking confused.

Oh, God, why did she have to ask me this?

I really had no idea how to answer his. "Because it's something that takes time and a baby wouldn't be here in time for your birthday. Maybe, you could ask for a doll that is like a baby?" I suggested, trying to get her to that idea.

I noticed Brody giving me a soft smile. "Thank you," he whispered, and I returned the smile.

For the remaining of dinner, Lila had seemed to drop the idea of a new baby sister. I could only imagine if she kept wanting one, how she would react when we would need to tell her no. She didn't like not getting her way sometimes. Plus, I already had one of those dolls bought and put aside for her with a pink stroller and little baby clothes. I doubted she'd want a baby sister once she had heard the crying or if came out a boy.

We left the restaurant and began walking towards the ice cream truck near the beach, the kids ahead of us, skipping and seeing who'd get there first.

Brody, beside me, asked, "About what Lila said…"

"Oh, God, talk about random," I grinned, looking over towards him, only to see he was already looking back at me. "She'll forget about it by the morning, anyway."

"Maybe," he said quietly, and I felt his fingertips grazing softly over mine, no holding hands, just a soft touch. "Did you ever think about another one?"

I frowned a moment, a smile breaking out. "Another baby?" I asked, surprised by his question, but I was trying to fight off the blush that was spreading as we bumped hands again.

"Yeah, I mean, they were born so close together, and we never really spoke about it, anymore." He was completely right. We hadn't.

Nodding as I glanced back towards him, "I mean, I guess it's natural for me to want a few. My sisters have big families, and I love babies. When Lila started school, I was really keen for another baby, but you were working a lot, and we fought. It wouldn't have been fair to put that type of pressure on you especially if we weren't really getting along so well. I just couldn't ask you for that."

"You should have told me," he said, and I couldn't tell if he was relieved, mad or upset. "I wouldn't have minded another one…" His words trailed off to a faint whisper.

No more words were said until we walked up to the kids. Brody ordered ice cream for each of us. It was nice to see that he'd remember the flavour that I most loved without having to ask me — coffee bean.

Walking back towards the car, I laughed as Noah came up towards me with chocolate all over his face. "Eww, you, two, need a bath when we get home." I reached into my pocket and wiped his mouth with a napkin, then allowing him to give me a kiss.

"Love you, Mama," he grinned, and I melted on the inside.

Brody and I hadn't had one fight all night, and being honest, it was really nice. It was a relief to see that we could get along. We weren't stressing, and I wasn't getting annoyed by anything. Not even his coke all over my chest had pissed me off.

"I hope they pass out in the car," I said to Brody as we walked towards the car.

"You think that after their ice cream? I bet they're completely wired in the car," he chuckled. Pulling out his remote control button and unlocking the doors, he came to a complete standstill and smiled. "What's the stakes if I lose this bet?" He couldn't be serious. He wanted to bet on this? "How about if I win then you don't cook for a week?"

I was confused. "Don't you mean if you lose?" Did he hate my cooking that much?

"No, if I win," he said seriously. "And if I lose, the same applies."

"Uh, ok. Well, if I win, you can buy me a back massage," I grinned back at him, not sure why I had said that, but a massage sounded pretty darn good right now. "If I lose, then I'll keep on cooking."

Just as we walked around to the door, Brody blocked my view. "Do we have a deal?" he asked, walking closer and holding out his hand.

"Okay, we have a deal," I lifted my hand out, and we shook on it.

It was reminding me of something that we'd have done as teenagers, not adults.

Sitting in the front seat, I clipped up my belt and glanced over my shoulder. That was a fast bet. They were passed out. Brody glanced over too. Our faces near and our lips so close, I could feel his warm breath against my skin. My heart began to beat quicker as his blue eyes locked on mine.

We sat there a moment, just staring. I couldn't break contact, wanting to, but my eyes wouldn't allow it. The nerves were there. Gosh, I was incredibly nervous. It was as if I had forgotten to breathe again... just like our first date.

"Damn, you've got to be kidding me. You won," he grinned, and something twinkled in his eyes. He knew he was going to lose our bet. But why, why would he have chosen not to have me cook for him for the entire week?

We arrived home in complete silence, and Brody carried Noah as I lifted a slightly lighter Lila. They were both out like a light and didn't wake when I had dropped Lila down much harder than intended. She bounced a little and then rolled over still asleep.

"So much for their baths," I sighed, noticing their dirty mouths.

"Do it in the morning. It's Saturday, anyway." Brody was behind me when I turned around to walk out of the bedroom.

We were in the passageway, and just an awkward tension was surrounding us. Maybe, us getting this divorce was a blessing in disguise. If we were not fighting now, then maybe it was just meant to be.

Brody cleared his throat and rubbed the back of his neck. His eyes never met mine as he spoke. "I've got some things to go get ready for tomorrow, work and all."

Just like that, I realised it was all just a show. There was no way that whatever had been going on tonight would remain. "Yeah, I'm pretty tired. Night."

I tried not to show him that I was hurt. I mean, why the hell should I care? Or why should I be hurt? This was him and me. We fought and didn't get along. This is how it would always be, and I wished that it wouldn't.

Going to the guest house, I was barely able to sleep again. My head was pounding like no tomorrow, and the shower didn't help. I slipped into the new red and black lace boxers and revealing camisole top, which I had bought when Cathy begged me to go into Bras N Things. God, I'll never live that down. Although their panties and bras were extremely comfortable, they weren't my usual style. But, hey, I now have a waxed genitals, so I can't really talk. I went inside to the main house, wishing I had changed into something else, but the lights were off and at 3 AM. I doubted Brody would be up.

The glass in my hand as I stood and leaned against the fridge, I waited for the water dispenser to fill my glass up. I wished my migraine away as I swallowed the two pills. I was about to lift the water to my mouth when I heard a noise. Turning, I let out a half scream, the cup in my hand thrown up and tossed at the figure standing in the doorway. My aim was terrible. Glass broke on the floor in front of Brody, and water sprayed over his chest.

"Jesus, can't you remember not to do that?" I said, still trying to catch my breath.

Brody, only in a pair of tight boxer shorts, began walking towards me. He bent down, picking up the few broken shards of glass. He stood so tall before me. His eyes lowered to my body, and I internally groaned as I realised he was staring at the open fabric that revealed my stomach.

"Sorry," he said quite huskily and placed the remains of the glass in the bin. "I just wanted some water. I couldn't sleep."

My lips parted, taking in the black Calvin Klein boxers as he walked closer. I hadn't been aware of how close we were until his body had me pushed back against the fridge.

"Brody," I said, feeling him against my belly. Oh God, he was so hard. I couldn't even try to stop my fingers from tracing over his taut stomach muscles. "You need water?" My voice now was coming out a breathy whisper.

He didn't speak, but I felt him twitch against me. His eyes devoured me with every gaze. He slowly began to lift and slide beneath the thin satin material, caressing my stomach. I never let him touch my stomach. I had always been so ashamed. "Nice PJs, are they new?"

"You bought them for me two weeks ago when I was mad at you," I smiled with a blush. He had pissed me off, and I went shopping with his credit card.

His eyes darted up, and a soft smile appeared. "Hmm, I have excellent taste then. I'll have to buy you things like this more often, or you can do it for me when I piss you off."

I tilted my head to the side, realising that my migraine had started to ease as his other hand came up and cupped my chin. His fingers on my skin kneaded the spot my shoulders and neck. "Feels incredible."

"How about I give you that massage?"

"Oh, God, please…" I moaned, enjoying his fingers on me immensely. The tension in my head faded, and my spine tingled with each touch. I could let him do this for hours. The pleasure was almost unbearable as my eyes closed. Opening again, I realised it wasn't the massage that felt so good. It was him... the sexual tension from today, in the gym, at the restaurant and the walk. I needed more.

Without thinking about it, my hands slipped further down. One cupped his sac and squeezing it while the other began stroking his erection over the fabric of his boxers.

He looked into my eyes, and it matched what I was feeling... lust, desire, need.

Making a growling sound that drove me incredibly wild, his hands were now both cupping my breasts. God, we never did this. I pushed my chest out, urging him to continue. Damn, it felt good. My nipples hardened.

His mouth neared as my hand stroked him still. "Like what you feel?" he whispered, huskily. "I do."

We were staring at each other, looking up at him through heavy hooded eyes, I nodded. "Yes."

Our bodies reacted with primal instinct. Within seconds, our mouths were on each other. Hungry and passionate, Brody's tongue pushed into my mouth, and he kissed me so forcefully that I had to grip him by the waist to keep myself upright. I moaned. Every nerve in my body was on fire that could only be put out by him. Slamming my body back into the fridge, his hands almost enclosed around my throat as he pushed himself into me more. A guttural groan escaped his throat as I pushed back, grinding against him.

We pulled away, breathless and panting hard. Biting my lip, I was craving what we didn't have, and he was too. His hands were all over my body, touching my skin, but still, he was searching my face for permission.

I never demanded what I wanted. I'd do things his way, but now, I wasn't going to be that shy woman. I uttered out two words, which would normally have me blushing like a fool. "Fuck me!"

I needed him... right now.

CHAPTER TEN

We were going to regret this in the morning.

It was clear neither of us was really thinking about what we were about to do. The only parts of our bodies doing any thinking were the parts rubbing against one another. Brody led me upstairs to our room, the room we once shared.

To be more accurate, he carried me like a caveman. Barely letting his mouth free from mine, we kissed our way through the darkness, bumping into walls, giggling and laughing. There were even moans of pleasure as we fooled around, almost like we were two drunk and horny people needing the same thing.

We weren't. We were completely sober.

Brody pushed open our bedroom, or his now, and I noticed the bed still made. He's obviously not been sleeping in here, either. Laying me down, the cold white duvet made me shiver for a slight moment until he was back on me.

This time, without his boxers, his thick length pressed into me. Beads of pre-cum seeped out as I ran my thumb over the tip of him, rubbing it in and lubing him up. My hand wrapped around his swollen head, stroking and squeezing.

"Keep it up, and I'll come faster than we both want," he groaned as he kissed my neck and let his hands wander over my breasts. His attention was then on my erect nipple where he began to lick and suck. Running my hands through his hair until my top was lifted off, I grew shy for a moment.

I hadn't been completely naked in front of him for so long that I worried he wouldn't like what he saw. That thought was gone the moment he went back to devouring my breasts, squeezing hard and grazing as he captured a hard nipple between his teeth.

Crying out, my fingers dragged up and down his back, surely leaving marks. "In me!" My hips bucked. I needed to feel him inside me.

"Wait," he groaned, pulling back a moment. I stilled as he looked further down, licking his lips. "I want you so badly."

"Brody." I bit my lip, moaning again, when his hand rubbed over the silk material as his eyes washed over me hungrily. "You don't have to."

Leaning down, he was inches from my face. "Shhh, just enjoy and don't think," he said and began to kiss down my stomach.

It was so new for us. We never did foreplay, and when I say never, I mean never. I'd given him a hand job here and there when we were sitting in the movie theatre or before we began having sex with each other. Yes, he fingered me in school, but it hurt so bad that it didn't really count.

The new part was that our mouths had never gone down south. It was new and exciting.

As he slid down my bottoms, he stilled, and a sharp intake of breath came out. "Fuck... What did you do?" He was staring right at my newly bare mound, and from the grin, I knew he loved it. Lowering his head, he began to place soft kisses before his tongue darted out and licked my slit.

My legs shivered with anticipation as he inhaled and used two fingers to spread my folds apart. He was staring directly at me, and it made me blush and turned me on. I watched as his head moved forward, and he pressed his nose to my nub while his mouth covered me.

Groaning as he tasted me for the very first time, "Hmm, so sweet."

A couple of different strokes and he'd found his rhythm. I'd also found heaven while still alive.

He began to lick faster and faster, pleasuring me in a way I had never experienced. My body reacted in completely different ways than when we made love. I couldn't stop my hips from rising up and down and grinding into his mouth more. "Brody... oh..." I breathed out. A strong wave of pleasure washed over me and built up to the familiar peak I so rarely got to experience.

My legs were shaking when his fingers entered me. I lost it completely and came so hard. I thought I was going to black out.

Kissing back up my naked body, my hands roamed his chest, and he pressed himself into me. I quivered, still sensitive from his mouth moments ago. Reaching between us, I wanted to taste him, but he flexed into me again.

"I like you bare down there," he said roughly, kissing me.

"I like your mouth down there," I admitted, tasting myself on his lips.

Thrusting deeply inside of me, I cried out as we kept our eyes on each other. He reached for my hands, stretching them above my head and pinning them down. He pulled out completely and plummeted back in, harder.

"Fuck!" he groaned huskily. His pacing increased.

I had no idea who this man on top of me was. He was so sexy, animistic and vocal. He was completely in control, and I loved it! My legs tightened around his as I began to raise my hips up and down and created more friction.

Our mouths were back on each other's, kissing and tasting each other with wanton.

We weren't having sex. There were no Brody and Gabby in bed. It was two completely different people. We were never this way. It wasn't slow and gentle. This was pure fucking, completely driven by desire and raw emotion. There was no desire to stop. We were clutching each other for more, and neither of us seemed to be letting up anytime soon.

My fingers dug into the curve of his ass as I breathed heavily. "Oh... yes, Brody!" I couldn't think straight. I was so damn wet. "Don't stop!"

Our bodies slapped and covered in sweat, the second orgasm building. I was losing my mind. He never lasted this long... never. His mouth was enclosed mine again with a moan, and I made what came out like a whimpering squeal sound as I came, long and hard.

"That's it, baby... fucking take it."

Soon after I came, Brody pumped faster between my wide spread thighs and groaned loudly as he released inside of me, twitching as he filled me with his deep spurts. He didn't move instantly, but when he pulled out and rolled onto his back, he pulled me over towards him and wrapped his arms around my body.

Keeping me close, he didn't go straight to the bathroom. He held me.

I laid there, breathing heavily as my limbs felt too heavy to move, exhausted and incredibly sated. Our sweat-clad bodies, naked and clinging to one another, neither letting go. I rolled my head against the warmth of his chest, feeling his heart beating beneath my ear. It was soothing and calming.

His fingers stroked my bare skin, a tender kiss on my forehead. It wasn't long before I fell asleep, and I oddly felt completely happy.

When my eyes fluttered open the next morning, I was pinned down by a warm body behind me. It didn't take long for me to remember the night we'd shared; the aching between my thighs, a pleasurable reminder of the passionate fucking. Sleep was long gone as my lids flew completely open, and I realised what had happened. My mind was telling me to get out of the bed and leave, but my body wanted to stay wrapped in his arms, and soon, I fell back asleep.

The second time I woke, things were much clearer. He was going to regret it. Did I regret it? No, definitely not. I laid there, watching him sleep and so desperately wanting to reach out, to touch him. The realisation that we were divorcing washed over me. I fought back the dreaded sickness and tears, slowly slid out of bed and picked up my clothing thrown all over the floor. I quickly dressed and tiptoed through the house like I used to sneak out of my parents' home and went to the guest house.

I was afraid we had just really screwed up.

Showering just made me remember the way he touched me. His hands... mouth... cock... how he felt inside me and taking me in a way like no other before. My legs were sore and head confused. I didn't know where things left us; if this was just one of those "get it out of our system break-up" fucks or was it more? Everyone was still asleep. I wrote the grocery list, needing to start the usual Saturday morning groceries. Leaving Brody a note on the fridge, I left and drove to the store.

The entire drive, to and from, I couldn't get one thing off my mind. Other than the throbbing between my thighs, something else was really distracting me.

That was, by far, the best sex we'd ever had.

How was it that it took so long without ever really experiencing each other in a way like this? We would be slow and gentle. Brody was always cautious about hurting me, and I was too damn nervous or shy to think he would be put off with me making a lot of noise. After years, we just fell into the same routine without ever thinking to spice it up with new things.

Of course, now, of all time, it just had to be when we were separated and going through a damn divorce.

Coming back home a couple hours later, I walked inside and heard the kids playing outside. "Where's daddy?" I asked, carrying the last of the bags, which were for myself.

"Working, he's grumpy." Lila pouted. "He said we were too loud and couldn't come inside until you came home."

I wondered what was up with that. Walking down to his office, I pushed the door open. "I'm back. Are you hungry?"

He looked up and smiled as our eyes met. My heart fluttered. "I'm starving, actually," then he pressed a button on the phone. "I'll be down in a second. I have to file these papers."

Shit, I hadn't realised he was on a call. "All right."

I stood, lingering in the doorway, and it hit me. Maybe last night wasn't anything spectacular to him. Was it the itch that needed scratching? He probably needed to come and needed a release for his build-up. I walked away and went back into the kitchen to serve up the burgers and fries.

Calling them, I took their plates to the table. "Noah, Lila, come and eat please!"

Brody came downstairs as the kids came running in and grabbed his plate. "Thanks." He sat down in his usual spot and began to eat but paused, "Thought you weren't meant to cook for me?"

I shrugged. "I bought the food, and it's no big deal. You know I love cooking."

"Yeah, but you hate cooking for me," he said quieter, so the kids wouldn't hear.

Looking back up towards him, I smiled slightly and pointed out, "Only when you don't eat it."

Our eyes stayed on each other for a moment, and then we were looking at the children as they mentioned that they wanted to go back to the pizzeria and get ice cream again.

Brody told them we'd all go again next week. I wondered how long this would keep up or when he wanted to tell people about our impending divorce. We all ate, and I began cleaning up.

The day was too nice to be stuck inside, so the kids were getting their bathers on to go for a play in the pool. Brody was going in with them. I'd prefer to sit and take photos of the three playing together; plus, me in a bikini wasn't on my to-do list today. I just wanted to sit back and enjoy this rare family day we all had for I didn't know when they'd be coming to an end.

As I tied Lila's hair up, I heard a knock on the front door and frowned at Brody. "Are you expecting anyone?" I asked, not mad, just wondering who would be here.

He shrugged. "No, I would have mentioned it."

The kids were already running to the door, and then I heard them yell out. "Grandma! Grandpa!"

Looking up, I caught sight of Brody's parents walking in and looking extremely happy. They were up to something, and I had no clue what. Luckily, Noah and Lila tugged on their hands and led them off somewhere, giving us enough time to sort the kitchen out.

Brody's eyes were wide as he stood up, obviously, not expecting them either. "I'll help you clean."

"No, distract them!" I whisper.

His mother was a complete clean goddess. She loves everything sparkling clean and didn't like smears or fingerprints. I honestly couldn't care if my children were happy, then I was happy. Yes, our home was clean and tidy, but there were times when I'd rather leave the dishes in the sink and go spend time with them.

One of those moments was today, and we were about to go swimming.

Brody grabbed the sauce bottles and went into the pantry to put them away. Soon, I heard him speaking, more to himself than anyone else. "Oh, dear God."

"What?" I asked, glancing over my shoulder as I piled the plates inside the dishwasher.

Eyes flew open as I remembered that my clothing and my new lacy underwear were sitting on the bench in there. Quickly standing, I raced in, thinking the worst, only to find him holding up a pair of black panties.

"Since when did you start to wear these?" he asked, smirking. In light grey sweats, he was rock hard.

CHAPTER ELEVEN

"Put that away before your mother walks in!" I hissed, snatching the material from his hands.

He smirked. "Are you wearing something like that now?"

I rolled my eyes. Blush crept over my cheeks. "I'm not telling you!"

"You, two, come out here. We need to discuss something important," Brody's mother called us.

Humour and playfulness were gone as he pointed towards my black panties scrunched up in my hand. "We need to talk about last night when the kids are asleep as well as why you're suddenly all smooth down there. I have questions, and I want answers."

I would have given him an eye roll if I didn't feel so completely embarrassed. He had a way of doing that, going from happy to pissed in second and bursting the bubble of happiness. "Well, I have questions too. First is how you could last so damn long!"

His jaw ticked but said nothing as he adjusted himself so his erection wasn't noticeable. "Keep it down. She's got ears like a hawk," he muttered, his own blush prominent. He walked out, saying to her, "What are you, two, doing here? You could have called."

"Can't we come visit our grandchildren?" His mother chuckled as I put the panties aside and left the pantry with a fake smile on. "Gabby, is everything okay?" she asked, carefully watching me.

I nodded as she kissed my cheek. "Of course, just putting the sauce away. You know how Brody leaves everything out."

Brody scoffed since I blamed him for the mess and replied, "My lovely wife cooked such a delicious lunch that I was too full to do anything just yet. Oh no, she brought burgers back from the store."

"I couldn't be bothered cooking, you know, after cleaning all morning," I smiled sweetly back towards him as he walked towards me. My eyes told him to keep his fucking hands off me.

His eyes said, not a chance in hell, and he then reached out, wrapping his arm around my waist and leaning in to kiss the side of my head. "After last night, I thought you'd be too exhausted to do anything. You certainly passed out fast." Oh, my God, I could kill him.

My elbow shot out and nudged him hard in his ribs, causing him to make an *oomph* sound. "Sweetheart, don't be crude. Your parents raised you better than that."

"We did," his mother agreed with a smile while his father just looked amused at our back and forth bantering. "Now, kids, please come back in here. Grandma has something to tell you all."

The children ran in and jumped up on a bar stool each. "What is it?" Noah asked excitedly. "Did you buy us a present?"

Fred, Brody's father, pulled out something rolled up from his back pocket. "Now, before you say no, just listen and then answer." Oh no, we were going to be put on the spot somehow. "We've been thinking—"

He spoke too slowly, and Loraine jumped in, cutting him off before he got another word out. "We've been doing some talking and researching. Now, over the third term school holidays, we'd like to take a family vacation. It's our fiftieth wedding anniversary, and we're going to renew our vows. Hamilton Island has an amazing resort, and we're going, all of us, your father and I, you four, your brother and his family, and then your sister and Leon. It's one big family getaway! You two never went away with us anywhere, and the children would love it!" She sounded as if she'd had one too many wines before coming over, that or she was high.

Fred chuckled nervously. "She's already booked it. We've got the house already booked and paid for." Sliding over the brochures, I glanced down to read. Hamilton Island and then the house they had paid for, I almost gasped. This place was not cheap. It didn't help that it looked simply stunning.

"It's big enough for everyone to do their own thing if you wanted a bit of privacy, and Brody, it would mean the world if you came along. We'd love to spend time with our grandchildren." His mother was pulling the heart strings, guilting him like what she did best.

My heart, on the other hand, was racing. They had no idea about our problems or that we were getting a divorce. Why the hell did they just had to drop this in front of Noah and Lila who were eager as hell to go?

The guilt began to consume me because we'd never been anywhere as a family. There were no trips with just the four of us. We never made that kind of time. Our lives were busy. Brody had work, which always came a high first.

"Please!" Noah repeatedly begged as Lila batted her lashes at her father, something that always won him over.

I glanced down at the paperwork, noticing the date. "That's in two weeks." I glanced then at Brody. I had no clue what he was thinking.

He was just staring at them as if they were completely crazy. His eyes met mine, and he sighed. He didn't like being put on the spot any more than I had done. "I don't know. Let me discuss this with my wife, and I also got work. I can't just be up and leave for a holiday that you've sprung on us."

"You're basically the boss. Don't you dare think about cancelling, Brody?" his mother scolded; then, her features softened. "I bet the children would love to swim with dolphins and go on walks through the forests."

I nodded, wishing she'd stop trying to get the children's hopes up this way. "Yes, they probably would, but we need to discuss this still. Brody's work is important, and he can't just leave for eight days, a lot of people rely on him there." Not as much as we relied on him here, but he didn't think we needed him the way work did.

Noah's smile faded fast. "But he always works. We never get to do anything fun!"

"Please, daddy! We'll be good," Lila begged, a pout appearing where he smile once was.

Brody let out an exasperated sigh, running a hand through his still wet hair. "Sweetheart, I will try, but I need to check and make sure things are okay for me to leave work first."

"Can we call you later with our decision?" I asked, not liking their chances of us actually saying yes.

A soft smile appeared, and Loraine nodded. "Of course, you can. How about you talk it over or even Google the resort yourself? There's much more to see on there than this piddly little brochure."

"Thank you. Now, would you like a coffee?" I asked, glad to end that conversation.

"Oh, no, we need to go and talk to your sister. She got another thing coming if she thinks we're going to some high-end fashion show. She won't be needing all those heels and dresses. We're going to the beach, not Paris," she chuckled and kissed the children on the cheek goodbye.

When his parents left, I felt extremely rattled. We couldn't go. It wouldn't be fair for them. The swim in the pool never happened, so I set the kids up in the living room with a bag of popcorn each and some lollies to watch a movie after they'd finally agreed that they'd watch Frozen after Despicable Me. God bless them for actually getting along. I think it was more to do with "being good," so we would allow them to go on this trip.

Walking into the kitchen, I found Brody at the table with his head between his hands. "You look like you could use a strong drink or two." I grabbed a bottle of wine for myself. I'm Italian. I can drink wine at two in the afternoon if I want. It was five somewhere.

He laughed, rubbing his eyes and looking up. "Yeah, but I don't want to drink when we need to talk."

I grabbed a large wine glass, sliding down into the seat across him. This was the dreaded conversation I didn't want to have but was needed. "All right, let's talk."

His hands sat on the table in front of him, and his ring caught my attention. He was wearing it still, a simple gold band. I also hadn't taken mine off yet. I just couldn't.

Waiting until I had finished pouring the glass of red, he began, "Last night. I asked if you were sure you wanted it." I think I should have grabbed the vodka for this kind of talk. "I'm just going to say it. It was the best sex that we've had, obviously. Or is that just the way I see it?"

"No, you're right. It was the best," I agreed. "I don't mean that every other time was awful, though. It's just always rushed." I was partially relieved that he had thought the same as well. "Last night was different." I lifted the glass, about to take a sip but set it down again. "I don't regret it if that's what you're asking."

He then grinned. "That is what I was trying to ask, yes as well." His smile vanished, and he turned serious again. "The waxing? The new undergarments?"

I nodded, not liking where this was going. "What about them?"

"Is there a specific reason that you had done that?" he cocked his head to the side as he swept his thumb over his lip and bit his top teeth down. Memories of his mouth ravishing me flooding back to my core and heating up.

Closing my thighs, I shrugged. "Is there a specific reason as to how you lasted that long, and I doubt you've been rubbing ten out a day?" I lifted my glass again and brought the cool liquid to my mouth. Oh, how I needed this.

My question hit him hard. "I'm not having sex with anyone, Gabriella."

"I brought the underwear for me. Also, the waxing was for me too. I wanted a change." Not to mention, I felt intimidated by that piece of ass he worked with. Why the hell did I care so much? I hated that she was under my skin. "But no, Brody, I'm not having sex with anyone or going out and trying to, either."

Smiling, he nodded. "We'll go on the trip. It's already paid for, and she's not going to take no for an answer. I can't just leave with a shit load of work. I have to shift meetings around and redirect clients." Pushing himself up from his seat, he stood. "I'll need to get a few things from town tomorrow. Was there anything else you want to discuss?"

God, could he have been any more of an ass? I bit down the insides of my cheeks before I called him one and stood up instead. "Nope, nothing at all. Dinner is at six." I couldn't even look at him. Why would I expect anything different? I pushed him away, and this happened. I did this to our marriage. "I've got things to do," I said, taking my laundry from the pantry and walked outside, the bottle of red still firmly held in my grasp.

Screw the wine, I definitely didn't feel like drinking anything except my tears.

Letting the door slam behind me, I practically stomped towards the guest house. I was angry at myself. I wondered if that's how things would be from now on, a quick catch up and back to separate ways. This was what we wanted, though. It was what I agreed to — a divorce.

I was curled up on the sofa in the guesthouse, underneath a soft pink knitted throw blanket. A candle burned which kept my attention as I drank the bottle of red. About to go to bed, I heard a faint knock on the door. So he was knocking now.

Brody stood there, still in his sweats and a long-sleeved shirt. His eyes showed exhaustion and sadness. I moved aside to let him in.

"Is everything okay?" I asked softly. We hadn't spoken at dinner. I purposely ignored him, and he made no intention to speak to me.

Walking to where I sat moments ago, he took a seat with a shrug. I made my way over, unsure how this was going to end up or where it would lead.

He just looked right at me, his eyes intensely watching as I took my seat beside him when he asked, "You hate me, don't you?"

By the sounds of things, it seemed as if we were in for a long night ahead of us.

I hadn't been quite expecting him to ask me that. There was still a gap between us by some distance. I reached over and refilled my glass.

"I don't hate you." I hated we had come to this. "I know I've made you miserable, and I understand why you asked for the divorce."

"How did you give me a reason for the divorce?" he asked baffled. He looked down, shook his head and took the drink from me, taking a mouthful then continuing, "I work too much. That's what did this to us! I put work first."

The alcohol was going to be blamed for my sudden confidence. "You work a lot, but I nagged you. I wanted you home more, but I just didn't understand how busy you are there." I sighed and rubbed my temples as I laid back on the couch. "I stopped trying. My insecurities made me not want sex and when I did…" I took a deep breath as I got this off my chest. "I felt so unattractive. You and I grew apart. All I've done is be a bitch to you." Wiping my tears away, I said quieter, "I've never even thought about cheating on you, Brody."

Looking up, I noticed he was beginning to get tears of his own. "I know, and I hope you know that I never have done that to you. I'm constantly at work. I don't have the time or energy to do that. I would never do that," he said more forcefully. Reaching over, he took my hand in his and brought it to his lips. The simple gesture made my heart swell. "This trip could be good for us, no work, just us and the kids unless you don't want to go," he said, suddenly realising that I may not.

"I want to go," I admitted. I really did want to go. I wanted to have once last shot at this. "Do you hate me?"

Shaking his head, he looked me in the eyes. "I could never hate you, Gabby, never."

"I wouldn't blame you if you did. I hate myself some days," I admitted. I would never want him to hate me, and I couldn't ever hate him. He gave me two beautiful children. "Your mother's crazy, you know, plotting a trip and springing it on us with the kids around. She knew it'd make us go."

The last trip they offered, we said no. The time before that, we also said no and so on. She learned her lesson of calling and asking. If she was to show up in person with the trip already booked and paid, then what choice did we have but to go off on this crazy holiday with them all?

"I'll be working a lot until then, but that's only so we can all go away. You understand that, right?" I could tell he was trying to make me understand, and I needed to lighten up about his job.

Looking towards him, I nodded. "I do. Plus, it's hard not to say yes when those two inside cleaned their rooms and ate all their dinner without complaining. They deserve to at least experience what a family holiday is all about," I said, but my mind couldn't stop wondering what would happen when we came back home.

He smiled. "Yeah, they do. Do you, uh… want to come tomorrow? I understand if you're busy, but I figured you might need a new bikini." I couldn't help but notice his not so subtly raised brow as he asked that.

I scoffed lightly. "Pervert."

He let out a laugh, and it made me smile. I made him laugh. The sound was wonderful. "Can't blame a guy for trying."

"I don't even want to be thinking about a bikini just yet." I was going to wear a bikini in front of them all, including both of my sister-in-laws who were perfection. Something else just hit me. "We're going to be sharing a room."

He nodded. "It's not like we're strangers." My eyes were on his hand as it reached up, moving towards me he ran his fingers through my straightened dark hair. "I like your hair this way. You never wear it out anymore."

I was leaning into the comfort of his palm. "It's easier to tie it up and not have to deal with it," I said softly.

He pulled his hand away all too soon and checked his watch. "Uh, I should go back inside."

"Do you want to see Lila's present?" I asked hesitantly when really, I just wanted him to stay in here for longer.

He nodded, and we got up and walked into the bedroom. I went towards the closet and slid the door open, reaching up, and pulled down a pink box. "I think this might keep her quiet for a while," I smiled, sitting the box down on the bed beside him. "Once she hears just how loud this baby cries, she'll be happy it's just a battery operated doll."

He chuckled. "God, and if this doll is anything like what Lila was as a baby, I think I'll be hiding the batteries."

I sat down on the bed and agreed. "She just wanted attention constantly. I don't think I slept for the first six months with her. Noah was so different as a baby."

"Speaking of babies," he paused and lowered the box in his hand. "I didn't use a condom, and last I knew, you weren't on anything. I came inside of you." Looking at me, he set the box aside and looked up.

"I'm on something. Don't worry, you're safe from that," I said, betting he was relieved I wouldn't end up pregnant to him again. A baby would complicate everything so much more than things were already. "I really should get some sleep, you too. You've got a busy week." I was now nervously glancing around the room.

"Wait," he held up his palm and shook his head, refusing to end the current topic. "You are? Since when?" If I didn't know well enough, I would have said he looked slightly disappointed.

I really didn't want to get into it right now but needed to tell him. "A few months ago, my cramps came back, and they were becoming painful. I started on the pill which has helped a lot."

"Are you okay? I mean, how bad were they?" he asked, looking worried.

"Oh, yeah, it's better now. Nothing to worry about," I assured him and leant back on the bed. "You don't seem as stressed out. Was that account you had been working on really that stressful?" I honestly felt so awful that I didn't support him with work. I just blamed him for never being at home.

He moved closer and nodded. "Yeah, it was a major deal. It has made the company even more successful. John was pretty damn happy, and I feel great that I landed it. Now, it's just getting things ready for him and keeping the money flowing in. Gaining capital, it's going to make him lots of money, like millions, Gabby."

He was talking, and I was hypnotised by him. Completely focused on him but not his words, I vaguely heard him mentioning money, and his boss was extremely happy with him, but I didn't know what I was doing until I pressed my lips against his.

He shut up real soon, kind of startled but kissed back. My tongue glided against his, tasting the sweetness of sugar. We just kissed slowly until I pulled back to catch a breath. "I'm sorry." I blushed. "I shouldn't have done that." What the hell was wrong with me? I kissed him. God, I actually kissed him in the middle of talking. I couldn't stop myself. He was extremely gorgeous when talking about something so passionately.

Brody just stared, probably wondering if that had really just happened or not. Oh, believe me, it did. "If you wanted me to stop talking, you could have asked. But then again, I liked the way you shut me up," he smiled, his blue eyes twinkling. "Don't be sorry. It was nice."

I laughed. "You can talk, I just feel awful that I had complained so much about you always at the office. If I had any idea as to how important that client is, then I wouldn't have made you feel so bad about it."

He nodded, drumming his fingers together. "He is important, but I shouldn't have let my family suffer from not having vacations or not spending time with you three." He sighed and shook his head angrily. "I get that my job pays the bills, but fuck, I could have relaxed a little."

Shocked by his sudden outburst and realisation, I nodded and agreed. "Well, now, you're getting time to finally relax just with your parents and everyone else," I said with a laugh. "I know the kids will love having you around each day," and me too. "We can just deal with the other things when we're back home."

"What about you? Will you like me around every day too?" he asked, placing his hand over the top of mine.

"Yes, and I will too." My heart began to race from his skin on mine. "It's going to be good to get away. Do you remember the last time we actually went somewhere?" I asked, laughing with a groan.

Remembering that we told all our family we were going on our honeymoon and wouldn't have any phone service when really, we were just downtown, staying in a hotel room. Even though it wasn't anything exciting, we had the best time together.

He laughed a full-hearted sound, and my heart almost exploded some more. He hadn't laughed in so long around me. It was almost as if I was experiencing it for the very first time, and that made me incredibly happy. I wanted to hear it more often, to be the one who gives him that sound.

Brody nodded and squeezed my hand. "It was fun although you deserved something better than Chinese or pizza every night."

"I have never complained about our honeymoon. It wasn't like we were wanting to spend our days touring through towns," I said with a wink. We spent most the time naked and in bed, watching cable and eating when we weren't fooling around.

Brody rubbed his chin, grinning. "I know, screw that. We would have ended up lost somewhere, anyway."

This trip down memory lane was going to lead us back somewhere familiar. Sliding my hand from his, I rubbed my

Forgotten Sweethearts |139

thighs down nervously. "I should really get some sleep. Just let me know in the morning when you're ready to leave."

We were getting a divorce. This was just us reminiscing and being sentimental.

Standing up, he looked down at me as I sat still on the bed. My gaze dropped to my hands. "I will do. Night."

He walked out of the room without another word, and I sat there feeling like shit. I hated that we weren't sharing a room. I hated that we weren't together. I hated that we were getting a damn divorce.

After laying on the bed for a while, I thought about what had happened between us, the kiss and how it made my cheeks flame with embarrassment. It broke me to think about him moving on with another woman, touching her the way he used to touch me, even thinking about another woman in my children's lives.

It was drowning me on the inside, but I knew what had to be done. I was trying to ignore it, and it wasn't going to fix itself. This is what was meant to happen next.

Pushing myself from the bed, I went outside and into the main house. I needed another bottle of wine. I almost went up those stairs to find him. But I didn't. I grabbed the red, then walked outside and laid back on a lounge chair by the pool and stared up at the sky as I drank.

As I almost finished off my second glass, I heard a thud coming from inside and assumed one of the kids must be up. I walked into the kitchen and found Brody trying to wrap his hand with a cloth. "Brody, what have you done?" I asked, rushing towards him.

He just laughed. "I hit the bag the wrong way and heard a pop. It's fine. I don't think anything is broken, maybe out of place," he said, looking into my worried eyes. "I'll take that drink now, though."

"You've got to be more careful," I said as I began to re-wrap it tightly. "Go sit outside. I'll make you a drink."

He walked out without a fight, and I went to make his usual scotch on the rocks. Coming out to him, he was in my seat and laid back, looking in pain and uncomfortable. I sat his drink down and sat beside him. "I didn't know you were using the punching bag again. When did you start that?"

That punching bag probably had my face stuck to it many times.

"I, uh, I just started not too long ago. It usually keeps me focused, but I guess it didn't work tonight."

"Why not?" I frowned, then sighed. "It's because of this trip, isn't it? Of course, it is. I know this isn't what you wanted, and it's going to be weird. I mean, being around your family who have no idea about anything that's going on here. I know you don't love me anymore, but we just need to try to make this a good memory for the kids. They're going to suffer when everything changes."

As I finished my rambling, I noticed he was just staring. "It's not the trip. I'm actually excited about it, the time off, spending it with the kids and you. It's just..." he trailed off. "I'm worried about things especially now, and I'm so damn confused."

"What are you confused about?" I asked a mere whisper in the middle of the night.

He sighed, not once looking at me. "Everything, mostly you."

Of course, I knew it was coming. I was probably only adding to all this stress of being here, and I knew what I had to do. It would be hard at first, but there was no point in prolonging this. I mustered up all my courage and strength to tell him. "I'm going to move out after this trip." I looked at him sadly as I awaited his reaction, but there was nothing. "It'll make everything easier, and once we're back, we can tell the kids what's happening then."

"Oh, if that's what you really want," he said sarcastically. Grabbing his glass of alcohol, he swirled it around and let the cubes clink the glass. "I need the fucking bottle," he muttered and downed it.

CHAPTER TWELVE

Of course, this wasn't what I damn well wanted.

He got up and left to grab the bottle from the kitchen. I kept my eyes on my glass, trying to keep my cool. Unfortunately, I held it a little too tight as I finished it off and set it down with a clatter as it fell over. Christ, how many fucking glasses would break this weekend? I thought as I watched it fall to the ground, smashing into tiny shards of glass just as Brody walked back.

Brody looked, about to open his mouth but I shot him a glare that had him shutting it again.

"You think I wanted this?" I asked a seething low hiss as I stood upright. "You think I dreamt of being divorced and having to move out of the home I shared with my husband and children?" My voice became louder as I kept talking. "You have no idea, do you? You just think of yourself and your own feelings, Brody!"

"What does that even fucking mean?" he yelled back, his eyes narrowing.

"When have you ever asked me how my day was?" I said with a yell as I threw my hands in the air. "You never ask me anything about me anymore!"

He looked surprised that I had become so vocal. He must have fucked it out of me last night. "Gabby, lower your damn voice. I won't listen when you're screaming at me."

"Screaming? You're kidding, right?" I scoffed. "It's all right for you to rant and rave about but when I become angry, I have to shut it, so you can have some peace and quiet."

"That isn't what I meant. It's after midnight, and you just sprung that you're moving out on me like it's no fucking problem," he spat back angrily. "Of course, I'm going to be bloody pissed off!"

With a roll of my eyes, I mocked a scowl. "What do you think was going to happen? That we'd live here still, divorced and fucking occasionally?"

"Don't," he snarled low. His finger pointed directly towards my chest. "We didn't just fuck, and you know it. I've never once just fucked you."

Stop saying fucked, I begged in my mind. I wanted to fuck again badly.

I shook my head and began to walk away. "You're drunk. Go to bed, and we'll talk tomorrow. I can't deal with any more of this arguing. I'm tired and exhausted from it, Brody. I hate it!"

"You hate it!" he thundered as I passed him. "I am fucking sick to death of having the same arguments. God, you want me to ask how your day went? I'll do it. I never knew it was such a big deal to you because you've never said anything before! You just complain that you're at home all day doing the same damn things. I'm sorry that you're so unhappy with this family."

Spinning around, I came back towards him. "Of course, you don't think that. Just because my day is the same, doesn't mean I wouldn't appreciate you asking how it was. But no, you just don't give a shit about anything that I do around here."

"That's a lie," he ground out.

Shaking my head, I poked him in the chest. "No, it isn't. You may pay the bills and provide the food that's put on the table, but who is the one who cooks and cleans? Who's the one who makes sure your work shirts are evenly pressed and hung up each morning ready for your day at work? I clean the house, me, not you! You don't even know how to cook toast without setting off the smoke alarms."

"You know I appreciate everything you do around here!" he yelled, getting closer to my face.

My hands were shaking as I scrunched them into fists and tried not to let his size intimidate me. "No, you don't. The only time you have ever helped me clean up is when your mother might be coming around. Other than that, you don't help me here!"

"That's another fucking lie!" He glared. "I help out."

"Yeah. I guess when you're taking care of yourself," I said as tears ran down my cheeks. "You know what would mean the world to me? If maybe when you made yourself a hot drink, you'd make me one too. Would it kill you to tell me I looked pretty?"

He sighed. "How the hell am I meant to know any of that? I can't read your mind."

I crossed my arms over my chest as I leant more on one foot. "Did you read my mind when I walked in on that girl showing off her stockings to you? You came home pretty fast that day; must have known how upset that made me."

"Fuck sake, we're back to this?" he sighed, looking exhausted. "I'm sorry that happened. How many more times can I apologise for it?"

I shook my head. "I don't give a shit anymore, Brody."

"What's that mean?" He asked, his expression changing instantly from anger to worry.

"I'm lonely, Brody. I'm so lonely and have been for years! I need your attention. I damn well needed it." I diverted my eyes as they burned with more tears as I ran a hand through my hair and shook my head.

His mouth snapped shut as he didn't bother with whatever it was he was going to say. I hadn't meant to blurt that out, but in a way, I was glad I did. He needed to know that in his big house, I felt so alone and craved someone to talk to me, to make me feel something other than a house maid.

I couldn't do this anymore. Backing away, I spun on my heels and began to take off.

"Well, you're not the only one, Gabriella!" he roared loudly, and then I heard a loud thud followed by an even louder smashing noise. "I need you too!"

Spinning around with tears hot on my cheeks, my eyes were stuck in horror as Brody held his bleeding fist, our table now had a massive open space where the glass used to fill it.

"What did you do that for?" I practically screamed. "My God, are you insane?"

He was standing there cursing and began to pull out his phone. "Go to bed, Gabby," he muttered.

The wind picked up, and I shivered as the cool air hit my bare legs. "I'll call your sister to come over while I drive you to the ER. I need to change. Stay there or follow me."

He was hot on my tail, and I could only imagine the pain that throbbed in his fist right now. It was probably broken after punching it in the bag and then doing that again to the table. I wouldn't be surprised if he broke a bone or two.

His feet were behind me, and as I reached for the door, he grabbed my elbow and pulled me to face him. His good hand pushed me back into the door, which rattled as his lips came crashing down hard over mine. Kissing me furiously, I could feel his rage as I clutched at his chest. Grasping for anything that I could hold onto, I moaned against his mouth, needing his mouth as our bodies pressed tightly together.

The last of liquor burning in my mouth was gone as I swept my tongue over his. Moaning, he pulled away. "I'm not drunk."

"No?" I breathed out, my lips tingling still from his. "You just punched the table," I said, wanting to push him away but couldn't.

His blue eyes glassed over as he looked down at me. "I'm not drunk, just confused," he said, his eyes darting back down to my lips again.

"Brody, I gave you a way out of that. I wasn't trying to make you confused, just trying to offer a solution," I said and let my head fall back against the wooden door with a soft bang. "What are we doing? Why are we like this when we've never been before?" I asked in a lustful daze.

"I don't know, but I like it." Leaning in closer, he rested his forehead on mine. "This is why I'm confused, Gabby. I can't fucking keep away from you. I hurt my damn hand because all I could see was you in that damn lace, and I've smelled you on my skin all day and tasted you in my mouth. I can't concentrate on anything but you!"

I wish I had known that earlier. It probably would have saved an unwanted argument.

I didn't know what to say. I was stunned and in a good way. He had been thinking about me that was why he hurt himself earlier. The smile was twitching on the corners of my mouth and slowly began to grow.

"I haven't thought about anything except last night either," I whispered, bringing my hands up to cup his strong jawline, leaning forward and placing soft kisses to his mouth, and nipping lightly as my fingers stroked over his skin.

Whispering over my mouth, he kissed me once more tenderly. "I really need to get my hand checked before I pass out."

I had almost forgotten about that, distracted from our small confessions towards each other. I changed into some warm clothes and re-wrapped Brody's hand that was now oozing blood. His sister and her husband came over, asking what happened. I didn't know what to say other than sex gone wrong.

Brody smirked but said nothing. We needed not anyone to know just how bad things could get between us. I didn't want to deal with their help or advice. He and I needed to do this on our own.

At the ER, I went in with him, not caring if he didn't want me by his side. I grinned a little when the nurse raised a brow at him and mentioned anger management classes. That didn't impress the patient one bit, who in turn told her to worry about cleaning up his hand rather than being a shrink.

After his hand was clean, we stayed around until it could be X-rayed and that told us it wasn't broken, but he did need stitches. Thank God, he didn't need any surgery. That would hopefully teach him a lesson not to punch things.

On the way home, Brody was on some pretty strong meds when he asked. "Do you think I need the anger classes?"

I glanced over, shaking my head. "No, it's not like you're punching things all the time." I then smiled. "I would recommend some happy pills, though," I said, turning off on the highway.

He just laughed. "Happy pills? No, I don't need them. I just need to set my priorities straight. That's all." I felt his other hand on my thigh and a gentle squeeze. A small show of affection and it meant more than he would ever know. "Thanks for being with me tonight. It meant a lot that you took me."

The little things meant the most to me.

"It's okay. I just wanted to make sure you were okay, and luckily, it'll be healed in a few weeks." I couldn't help but laugh. "You know, we're going to a place surrounded by water, and then you go and practically break your hand. You're going to get so scolded by your mother when she thinks it's just an attempt at trying to stay home."

His mum was going to lose her shit with him.

Brody laughed, agreeing. "Yeah, she will. I'll call her tomorrow sometime, and it's not broken, just stitches."

"True, Noah will probably be disappointed that it's not in a cast." He would think his dad was pretty awesome then.

Silence filled the car as I drove us through the night back home. "I want to ask you something." He sounded incredibly nervous. He was never nervous. "Can I ask you something, Gabby?"

Pulling into our garage, I parked and took the keys out. "I guess so, what is it?" I wondered, looking up at him.

Swallowing, he ran his fingertips over mine and gently held my hand. "I was just wondering if you'd consider coming back into the house for a few nights?" he asked, glancing up towards me with hope in his eyes.

My heart filled with nerves, and it wasn't nerves of being afraid. It was nerves of, well, being nervous. I nodded slowly as I stuttered like a fool. "I... I... I'll come back inside," even it was for just a few nights.

Brody offered me a heart-warming smile. "Thank you. You need any help getting anything from the guest house?"

Shaking my head, "No, I will wait until your sister leaves, then go get my pyjamas."

"You don't need them." He winked.

"I'm glad to see your humour is still there," I muttered dryly. "I'll be wearing them."

"All right, let's go inside and send them home, so we can get some sleep," he said and pushed open his door.

Jessie and Leon were sitting on the couch, watching TV when we walked in, and she jumped up with a yawn. "I was almost ready to pass out," she said as she tied her light brown hair up in a bun. "Is it broken?" she nodded towards Brody's hand as Leon sat still.

"Nah, luckily," Brody grinned. "Teach us for drinking."

"Well, I'd tell mum if I were you. She'll be pissed if you don't," she scolded teasingly. "Why didn't you just have sex in bed, anyway? The kids could have come out and caught you."

I blushed. Brody shrugged, winking at her. "I take her wherever the urge comes on."

I blushed harder. "Oh, God." He and I both wished.

"Ew, you're a pig!" Jessie shuddered, looking down at Leon. "Come on, babe, I'm tired and have Pilates in the morning."

He stood up and gave us a smile. "Night."

After they had left, we didn't speak much. I just went to grab my pyjamas and hesitated as I went to reach for my usual ones. Placing them back, I grabbed the newer ones, and some clean underwear then went inside the main house. Sitting down on the bed after I had changed into the sleepwear, nothing extremely sexy, just a simple pair of cotton boxers with a thin tank top, I ran my hands over the top of the bed we'd shared for so many years. I flushed as I thought of last night, the lovemaking. I began to feel nervous again. I felt completely shy and wondered if he meant sharing a room again. I hadn't asked him what he meant when he asked me to sleep inside.

Was he in the spare room?

My questions were answered as the door opened, and Brody walked in. Walking into our suite and leaving the door open. He brushed his teeth and then walked back into the room to undress. He'd never been shy or worried about the way he looked, and he didn't have a reason to.

"I haven't been sleeping in here," he said lifting the shirt over his head. "I've been in the spare."

"I was just wondering about where you were sleeping tonight," I said, watching him. I had assumed he was on the other but wasn't sure. "You know, I just assumed being out there was for the best, right?"

He nodded as I stood upright and pulled the duvet back. "I get that. It wasn't like I didn't push that on you, though."

"Sleep in tomorrow. I imagine that your hand is going to be extremely sore."

He began to pull his side of the covers down and stopped. "You want me in here, right?"

Nodding, "I do." Tonight, I just wanted him to be close. "We're going to be sharing a room soon. May as well get used to it."

That was far from my only reason. I wanted to sleep beside him again, to feel the comfort I once felt. He laid on his back, and I rolled to my side. Facing away, I whispered, "Good night, Brody."

He softly spoke back, "Good night, Gabriella."

I wanted to face him. My core was flooding with heat. Trying to fall asleep in such a state of arousal was proving to be difficult. I needed him. I was on edge but somehow, managed to fall asleep.

During the middle of the night, I felt him shifting. I barely slept, too strung up on nerves and excitement. It had felt like the first night we stayed together, completely shy and worrying that I would snore. He'd made me feel so at ease. After talking, it all felt so new again.

When he moved again, I made sure to keep my breathing steady in case he knew I was lying here wide awake. My hip felt a soft pressure of his hand, his body moving and closer to me.

"I'm sorry. I never wanted to hurt you," he whispered, and I felt his lips against my cheek before he pulled away and rolled over.

Silent tears began to roll down from my eyes as I badly wanted to turn around and hold him back. I didn't. I just couldn't even move. I was completely taken off guard by his words, and I fell asleep with them rolling through my mind.

When I woke up the next morning, I felt different. It was probably the best sleep I had in months. I went to get out of bed like I would usually do. But I stopped myself and laid back down. Looking over, Brody was still fast asleep. I couldn't stop stealing glances at him.

Not wanting to wake him, I reached for the book on my bedside table and began to read it. As I was getting on a page, my book knocked forward and almost hit me square in the nose. I let out a little squeak and pushed it away, almost hitting someone.

Brody had rolled over and bumped it with his elbow. Giving me a sleepy smile, "Sorry."

"I almost whacked you," I said with a soft laugh. I didn't make any movements away from him, though, as we lay side by side and facing each other. "Are you sore?" I found myself reaching down to his wrapped hand and gently stroking it.

"Very but I'm a big boy, and can handle it." He grinned, sliding his arm underneath his pillow and watching me. "How did you sleep?"

"I've missed this bed. I forgot how comfortable it is." I also missed you and your sleepy morning voice. I kept that thought to myself. "It's a nice feeling to wake up and see you still in bed," I admitted quietly.

Our eyes locked once more, and I could feel the warmth of his breath against my skin. We were moving closer, and it was unintentional. He went to talk when Noah came bursting through our door and screaming as he jumped up on the bed.

Brody and I both broke apart as Noah tried to hide underneath the covers. "She's going to get me!"

"What?" I asked, sitting up as Lila came charging in the room with her hands on her hips.

"Daddy!" she huffed defensively. "He called me a baby!"

I almost laughed at how adorable she looked while so angry. She definitely had the Italian in her. Noah peeked his head up between us. "She was annoying me."

Brody's head fell back on the pillows, and he yawned. "Can't you, two, get along? Every morning, you're fighting." They sounded like us, always bickering and snapping.

"Exactly, no more hitting, biting or name calling. Otherwise, you're going to have things taken from you," I warned, rubbing my eyes as Noah snuggled up to me. "Will you stop the fighting?"

They both began to giggle, saying together, "Nope."

"Well, at least, you agree on something, but mama is right, no more fighting. If I hear about any hitting or screaming, we won't be going on a holiday." Brody looked up at me, and I had to admit. This really felt nice.

The kids both looked surprised. Lila ran towards the bed. "Daddy, really, we're going?"

"Yes, only if you behave," He warned. I liked that for once. He was the one putting his foot down and warning them not to misbehave.

"Yes!" Noah grinned, getting extremely excited.

Lila beamed. "Come on, Noah. I'm going to jump on your bed if you don't play with me."

He groaned, climbing out of bed in his little Superman underpants. "All right," he gave in.

"Hang on, don't you think you should give your father a kiss and say, thank you?" I asked, watching and chuckling as they raced back over.

"I love you lots and lots. Thank you, daddy!" Lila squeezed Brody around the throat while Noah kissed his shoulder, saying, "You're the best!"

I don't think we'd ever had a morning like this, not in such a long time.

It also stirred something else up inside of me as I lustfully gazed at him. Brody instantly noticed, and soon, his grin turned playful. "See something you want?"

Saying nothing, I quietly climbed out of bed and walked towards the door. I heard the children in Noah's room playing. I closed the door quietly and flicked the lock over. Looking back towards Brody, I nodded and climbed back underneath the covers.

I knew exactly what I wanted, something we hadn't done in a very long time on a weekend. "I want morning sex."

He stared but moved towards me. "You sure?" He wanted it too, judging by the thing poking into my thigh.

I wanted him bad. All I did was nod, and before I could move, he had his lips against mine and kissing me passionately. Growling over my mouth, he hungrily lifted my top up. Our mouths only parted for a slight second when my shirt was lifted and thrown behind him. Rubbing between my thighs, he tugged the elastic on my bottoms down while I pulled his boxer shorts down, kicking them all off with my feet as he moved over the top of me.

Naked, I wrapped my thighs around him. No words were needed as I felt him pressing against my entrance and pushing into the depths of me. Both of us moaning, he began to thrust slow and lazy, which was just right for this moment.

I heard him wince slightly and realised I'd forgotten all about his hand. Raising himself up, he pulled back, and I let out a slight gasp as his arm wrapped around my waist, flipping us over. Reaching up with his good hand, he grasped my breast and began to squeeze lightly, causing me to moan. The pleasure surged straight between my thighs, starting a slow grind as I adjusted to the fullness of his manhood inside me.

This shouldn't be happening again. But it was.

I sat upright more, getting used to the change in position that we hadn't done in an extremely long time. My hands against his chest, he gripped my breast, even more, digging his strong fingers in and raising his hips up and down with a groan. My hair pulled to one side, keeping it out of the way. Breasts bouncing, I leant back, giving him the full view of my body as I rode him.

Crying out loud as his finger came between us, pressing against my clit and rubbing. "Fuck," I groaned, my eyes on his as I rocked back and forth quicker. I wanted to come badly. Jesus, why hasn't he ever done this before?

My mind was lost as I fell forwards. That feeling grew, driving me crazy as I became needier and moving faster and rubbing myself against him. Kissing him through hard pants, I knew my peak was coming, and I moaned loudly as I hit it. "Oh God, you feel so good."

Tugging his hair as I came and pulling on it, his hand came down to my ass and squeezed it. "Not as good as you right now." Lifting my hips up and down, he began fucking me from beneath. His moans were loud. I knew he was close. His eyes shut as he tried holding off.

"Come inside me," I moaned breathlessly.

His eyes forced open, face to chest with my bouncing breasts. "Shit," he groaned and exploded with his own release.

As I caught my breath, I moved off him and fell to my back, staring up at the ceiling and thinking. "I thought the other night... it was just a once... that we were... oh, God, I don't know anything anymore." I trailed, barely making any sense of what I was trying to say to him.

He reached up, and his fingers grazed over my breast. Instantly, goosebumps formed. "I know what you mean... It's different, and I don't know why." Maybe we somehow realised what we're losing. "I certainly enjoyed you on top."

I smiled. "Me too. I liked that." God, I must have been a horrible lay for him, always on my back. It suddenly dampened my mood.

A loud banging on our bedroom door, "What are you doing? Why is the door locked?" Noah asked.

Brody's hand grabbed the covers and pulled them over us quickly, covering out sweaty naked bodies. "What is it?" he asked strained.

"Lila spilt milk everywhere, the cereal too!"

"I was trying to make breakfast!" We all heard from downstairs. Oh, God, the mess was going through my mind. I could only imagine. Last time, it was a dozen eggs smashed all over the floor and took me forever to clean up.

I groaned and got out of bed to put my clothing back on. "She does this every weekend."

He chuckled, pulling his own bottoms on. "Isn't this the reason we bought her a play kitchen?"

"Yes but she likes the real stuff," I chuckled, walking towards the door.

I turned and looked back at him. Was this just sex between us? I wasn't sure. I wanted to kiss him. We'd just had sex again, twice in the same week and that never happens. Whatever this was, I didn't know if I wanted it to stop.

Brody walked towards me, cupped my cheek and placed his lips against mine. Pulling away, he smiled softly. "Let me fix it. You go take a bath. Don't worry about the mess. It'll be cleaned before you come down."

I stood there, shocked. It was a morning full of surprises, and strangely, they kept on coming.

CHAPTER THIRTEEN

Sitting nervously on his double bed, I watched as Brody stood slowly and walked towards his bedroom door, closing it quietly. With a push of his thumb, it was locked. Turning back around and heading over to the stereo, his feet padded on the carpet as he turned the knob to make the music a little more loudly.

"That okay?" he asked quietly, coming back to bed and standing in front of me.

I nodded as he reached down, taking my hands in his and helping me upright. "Yeah."

"You're sure?" he asked, his blue eyes checking for any signs of regret. There was none.

With a nod, I squeezed his hands tightly. "I'm ready. I promise."

We were about to sleep together for the first time.

I was so nervous, but it was what I wanted, what we both wanted to do. I hadn't dared to ask my mama to allow me on the pill. They were still mad about us dating, and there was no way they would allow me to be over here without his parents around. Unbeknown to them, Brody's parents didn't care if we were alone in his room. We always had the door open as we studied together or laughed.

Today, for the first time, we closed the door.

Brody had taken a condom from his brother, Scott's room. We knew this was what we wanted. We'd talked about it, and our kisses were only leading us to do more to each other. This was the next step in our relationship, and being together for almost seven months, I knew he was the one I wanted to be with. I wanted him as my first, and he wanted me as his.

Reaching in his drawer, he pulled out a roll, and I giggled. "Six? You think we're going to go that many times?"

He smirked. "I wish."

"Brody, it's going to hurt," I said, more scared than I wanted to sound as I sat on the bed again. I was sick with nerves. I'd been nervous all week just thinking about this moment.

He shifted on the bed and came closer towards me. "We don't have to. I'm okay with waiting."

I nodded. This is why he was so perfect. I also knew he wasn't going to run straight to his friends and brag. He wasn't that type of boy. "I want to. I want to be with you in every way."

"Me too," he smiled and then came even closer. Our lips against each other, kissing softly as our hands came up and touched one another. Brody lifted my top, pulling it up over

my head. I did the same to him until we were standing in our underwear.

I hadn't seen him naked completely before although I did give him some pleasuring the previous weekend. He was always in clothes, and when Brody fingered me, I always had clothes on too.

We climbed underneath the covers, and I unclipped my bra as he pulled his boxers down then moved to take my panties off. "You're so pretty, Gabby. God, you're fucking hot."

I nervously giggled again. "You are, too."

As he moved over between my thighs, he sat upright and tore open the condom wrapper. I watched eagerly as he slid it down his impressive length, fumbling with nerves until it was rolled out. Spitting on his fingers, he then lowered them between us and gently pushed them inside of me, slow, soothing strokes.

It was an awkward pain, not pleasurable but not enjoyable. I shook my head and pulled his hand away. "Make love to me."

"God, I'm going to blow so fast," he grinned. Coming down on top of me, he kissed me as he positioned himself at my entrance. "I love you so much, Gabby."

Clinging to his arms as he thrust in, I screamed in my mind as he stilled and didn't move. His breathing was extremely ragged and hard. "Are you okay?" I managed to ask. I was so full of him. I could feel every pulse and throb coming from his body. I shifted a little underneath him, and he groaned.

"Yeah, just don't move or this will be over embarrassingly fast. Are you all right?" he asked back, raising

up enough to kiss away my silent tears. I nodded and tightened my grip on his back. My nails were going to be imprinted into his ass.

Our mouths soon met again, and Brody began to move his hips as he found his rhythm. The pain slowly subsiding until it ended all too fast.

Our kissing had done the talking as we lost our virginity together that day.

I did something that I haven't done for an extremely long time. I laid in the large bathtub, filled it with bubble bath and lit a candle; then, soaked until the water began to go cold. I put more hot water in and soaked some more until it was cold again.

As I rubbed body wash into the skin of my smooth leg, I thought about Brody. I'd been thinking about him since he left the bedroom. Things had been so bad for us, for so long. It was strange to feel at peace and not on edge all the time. Usually, I'd just be waiting for another fight, and now, I was hoping there would be no more between us.

I didn't want to fight with him anymore.

After my bath, I pulled on some of my newer clothing. I did my hair, left it with the slight wave that naturally came. Thank God, unlike my mother, I didn't have thick bushy waves. Putting on some makeup, I smacked my lips together, rubbed in the light red gloss, and made my way downstairs.

As I walked downstairs, I got that warm feeling I used to get whenever I looked at him. I couldn't believe that he had cleaned up everything. The kitchen had no sign of a mess that Lila had made and even the kids were quiet.

Entering the kitchen more, I smiled up at him as he was laughing with them. "Wow, thank you. It looks really clean."

"Um, kids, why don't you get your shoes on and go play outside?" He coughed, setting his coffee down, and they ran off chasing after one another. Brody walked towards me. We were close enough to almost touch, and I felt his hands skimming down the curves of my hips. "Are you trying to kill me?" he whispered huskily.

My eyes widened. I shook my head. "Nope, why would I want to do that?"

"I might be overstepping here, but..." Moving in front of me, he ran his eyes down my body, and I internally shivered. "You look absolutely beautiful." He then leant forwards and kissed me lightly. Pulling away all too soon, he leant back and crossed his arms over his chest.

"Are you all over me because I've lost weight?"

He looked hurt that I had asked this, pulling me back against him. "Are you kidding?" I shook my head, letting him answer. "You look great. I'll give that to you, but it has nothing to do with the weight. Now or before, you're sexier than you give yourself credit for."

I nodded, wishing I could believe him. "I'm sorry. I just doubt and over think everything."

"Don't. There's no need to." He pulled me back to him and sighed. "I have breakfast made, but the kids said it tasted like burnt ducks feet. Don't ask me. I didn't even ask them to elaborate that one." He laughed.

"You cooked?" I eyed him curiously. "Well, I'm sure whatever it is you made would have been nice."

He laughed. "You know my cooking sucks. It always has."

"Yeah, that's why you married me. You'd always be fed well," I said with a grin. When my own words sank in, Brody wasn't smiling anymore. He was quiet, and then an awkward silence followed. I glanced at his hand and found the perfect excuse for a subject change. "Did you want me to re-wrap it? It must be throbbing by now."

I couldn't help but still smile on the inside after he called me beautiful, one compliment that would last a lifetime. It definitely wasn't overstepping.

He shook his head. "I don't think it needs re-wrapping. I might just sit for a while. It's fine really."

Noah ran inside, puffing as he caught his breath. "Daddy, did you fall on the table outside? It's broken."

I forgot all about the glass out there. Just great, I didn't want the kids to know what happened. "Noah, keep away from it. Tell Lila to stay away also. I need to clean it up." I glanced over at Brody. "Daddy just tripped, and his hand hit the table." I had no clue what to say, and Brody wasn't giving any answers.

Brody stood back up and sighed. "I'll clean it."

"Don't be ridiculous. Your hand is hurt. I'll do it." The last thing he needed to be doing was cleaning up the glass when he'd already sliced one hand open.

He shook his head. "No, I'm lazy and don't do anything around here. I'll do it."

He didn't think I heard him muttering that as he left the room, and I just stood there, hurt and also annoyed. What the hell was that? And why would he just snap for no reason when we were getting along so well? Was I offering to help with his hand really bother him so much? I was completely confused.

There was a change in the air as Lila walked in. Pouting, she wrapped her arms around my legs for a cuddle. "Daddy's crabby. He told me to get lost."

I snorted a slight laugh, rubbing the top of her dark hair. "Were you annoying him?"

She nodded shyly. "I told him he was silly and that only angry people hit tables. He didn't like that."

"Well, he did it by accident," I said to her, lying through my teeth.

"Mama, what's a divorce?" That stunned me frozen. Her sweet voice could make the easiest of questions seem the toughest. This was a tough one. How do you even begin to explain something so difficult to a child?

Grabbing, the dishcloth, I wiped the bench top, trying to buy myself some time. "Why did you ask that, sweetie?" I asked her.

"Daddy was talking about it. He didn't know I was there, though," she said with a little giggle. "I was hiding."

"Hiding or spying?" I asked, raising a brow at little Miss Sticky Beak.

"Mama, don't change the subject. What is a divorce?" she asked again. I knew she wasn't going to let up about it, either.

With a sigh, I bent down and lifted her up. Sitting her on the kitchen bench top, I couldn't lie to her. "Well, it's something mommies and daddies get when they're not getting along, but only if they're married."

"Why?" she asked.

I smiled sadly. "Sometimes, they're not happy together, and being apart is the best thing for them."

"Daddy said divorce, mama." She smiled.

My heart was pounding so hard against my chest. "What do you mean? What did daddy say?" I couldn't even hide the shock from across my face.

"He said a naughty f-word divorce." She giggled. "He said a bad word, mama."

I nodded, hearing her, but I wasn't paying any more attention. Brody had been speaking about the divorce. I was feeling sick to my stomach, only imagining what was said. Lifting Lila back down, I was shaking as I left her in the kitchen and walked outside to where he was.

"What the hell did you say? Lila just came in asking what a divorce was," I said, my voice shaking with fear.

His eyes grew. "She was out here?"

"Yes, she was spying on you like she always does." I sighed. "What did you say?"

With a shake of his head, he held his hand up. "Don't worry about it. I've cut my finger. I need to go and clean it up."

He had to be kidding. "Okay, walk away as usual, then," I said and walked off. Maybe Lila had just heard wrong. I knew he wouldn't want to call the divorce off. I honestly thought things were going to stay good between us. Maybe I was just wrong.

I went to put away the children's laundry and was almost at Lila's room when I heard her and Brody talking. I stood outside, listening. "What did you hear daddy say, sweetheart?" he asked her.

"Am I going to get in trouble?" she asked back.

I almost laughed at how serious she sounded. "Not if you tell me the truth." Brody was calm.

"I just heard you say something about divorce. Mama said it's for people who don't love each other anymore," she said quietly. "Do you love mama, daddy?"

Holding my breath as he answered her, "Of course, I love your mama. She gave me Noah and you, and I'll always love her for that. Don't worry your little head princess. Daddy isn't going anywhere, all right?"

Backing away, I ducked into Noah's room and closed the door quietly before I broke down into silent sobbing. This was already interfering with them. The one thing I didn't want them to do was to think about yet. He was still going to want this. I thought maybe it would be different but no. I knew it wasn't.

Noah's door flew open, startling me as Brody rushed in. "Gabriella, are you okay? What happened?"

No more beating around the bush.

"What's going on with us?" I asked through a cry. "It's confusing me, and I-I am feeling things." He moved, kneeling between my thighs and took the wet shirt from my hands. "I heard you talking with Lila." I could only whisper that part to him. "How can you say those things... making promises to her?" I sucked in my breath, shaking my head. "You should have just told her the truth that I'm a bitch."

He sighed and wrapped his arms around me. "Don't ever call yourself that again. You're nothing of the sort. I don't know what's going on with us either. I like how things have been with us, and I do not just mean the sex."

"I like how it's been too, Brody." Oh god, it felt so good to get that finally off of my chest. "The past couple weeks have felt like it used to, like how our family should be." Leaning forwards, I wrapped my arms around his waist and hugged him back.

"I know. It's been nice," he said quietly against my forehead, placing a soft kiss. "We have a lot to work on still."

"I know. We're going to go away for a week. I'm afraid that it'll wreck things even more. How are we going to handle things?" I asked, pulling back and sniffing away the tears, but relief flooded me as we both agreed on this.

He shrugged and then smiled sadly. His eyes glossed over. "We just do what we've been doing for the past years. We fake it."

"We fake it," I repeated. "All right then, let's go on this holiday and fake being the perfect couple they all think we were." If only it were that easy. "I don't want to have to fake a happy marriage. We should just have that."

"I know." He agreed, just as solemn. "Let's not think about the divorce right now and take it one day at a time."

We were anything but that. They had no clue, and they wouldn't.

Brody and I were either going to come back from this trip, giving our relationship another shot, or calling it off and ending things for good. I hoped we'd work, but who knows.

You can't always choose the fate you're given.

CHAPTER FOURTEEN

The morning we were meant to leave was a chaotic nightmare. My head felt ready to explode from a pending migraine that wasn't easing up, and the children were dragging their feet to get ready. I could have screamed my lungs out, and they still wouldn't listen. Brody had loaded up the car the night before, and we finally got to sleep at 10 PM. Not to mention, I had a nagging feeling in the back of my mind about forgetting something.

Maybe having three-hour sleep was my problem.

Who thought it was best to get out of bed at 1 AM to catch a flight at 3 AM? Oh, that's right, the two people who booked this trip.

Brody's hand slipped over mine and squeezed my fingers. "Sleep on the plane."

"I hope those two would," I said, nudging towards the kids.

He chuckled and let out another yawn. "I've got the iPad. They'll watch a movie or play games while we get some sleep or at least try to."

I couldn't complain about things between us. We barely spent any time with each other. Brody was working so much that he would only come home to sleep, and then he was back in the office. Yes, it bothered me, but I didn't say a word. If it means he was able to come on this trip, I would suck it up and deal with it. Oh, and no, we hadn't had sex since that morning.

All I knew was that we were trying. We were going to try to make another go of things before we call it quits for good. The weight of the pending divorce had been lifted off my shoulders, and we were both on the same page with that, put it on the back burner and focus on us. We just needed to communicate more than we had done. We needed to express our feelings. No matter if it was something bad, we needed to talk.

"This trip, it'll be good for us," I said to him, but more so to reassure myself that it would be. A positive frame of mind is what will keep me going.

Lifting my hand, Brody brought it to his lips as he gently kissed my hand. "We need this. It'll be good for us, Gabby. We need this." He said again, sounding like he had to tell himself that.

"I know," I said, giving his hand a squeeze back. We really needed it.

Arriving at the airport, we checked our baggage in. I took hold of Lila's hand while Noah walked with Brody. Spotting his family in the cafe, we walked towards them. They were all dressed and looking marvellous in fresh faces and done hair. Here I was, not an ounce of makeup and my hair in a messy bun on the top of my head. I had thought I was just lucky to have dressed in some leggings and a baggy off the shoulder shirt. If it weren't for Brody putting the kids in the car, I'd have been coming here in my PJs still.

"Morning," Jessie beamed. "You, kids, want some breakfast?"

"No," Lila yawned, her hand tugging on mine. "I want a doughnut."

I covered my mouth as I yawned after her. "Really, with sprinkles or just icing?"

"Both," she giggled. "Please?"

Brody chuckled. "All right, come on. You two can get doughnuts and hotdogs before the flight."

"I would have suggested some fruit or yoghurt." Jessie frowned. "Brody, you really should feed them a little healthier."

My husband raised a brow at his sister. They had an "older sister, little brother" syndrome and bickered like crazy when they weren't getting along. "When you have your own children, you can feed them whatever the hell you want."

"Tulip loves her Greek yoghurt and muesli," Rose piped in, pointing that out.

Noah scrunched his nose up. "You're weird, though."

Oh, my God. "Noah!" I whispered, dying of embarrassment. "Don't say that."

He shrugged and tugged his dad's hand. "Can we get a coke?"

"Nice try." Brody shook his head as he laughed, giving Noah's shoulder a soft squeeze. "No way, you can have orange juice or water."

I sat down and pulled out my phone to play words with friends. I needed the distraction. "Babe, can you grab me a coffee?" I asked, unbeknown to me I had just called him babe in front of his entire family.

Looking up, I noticed him smirking at me. "Come for a walk with us. I'll get lost, and we'll miss the flight."

"You better not," his mother warned, glancing up from her newspaper. "Brody, don't you dare wander off? You already damaged your hand punching tables. I won't have you trying to miss the flight on purpose. Work can wait."

I stood up and held in my giggle. "He won't miss the flight. We're only going over there." Pointing towards Krispy Kreme doughnuts, I was going to grab a box for the flight, screw the diet. I was starving for pastry.

Brody slipped his hand around my lower waist, pulling me closer into him, and I tried to control my heart rate. "Did you talk to your mother after she hung up on you?" he asked once we were on our own.

Shaking my head, "No, I didn't call her back. I can't help something that isn't my fault." Sighing, she overreacted.

Mama has been trying to get us to take a family trip to Italy so we can all go back and visit relatives I haven't seen since a child. It's not that I wouldn't love to go, I would, but she wanted me and the children to go without Brody. It all came back to me not marrying an Italian. My sisters were on the call too as they liked the group chat. I felt outnumbered and ganged up on when mama accused me of treating Brody's mother better than how I treat her. Trying to explain, it was useless. She didn't believe me when I said the trip was booked and paid for; she hung up on me.

"Don't worry about her. She'll get over it."

I glanced up at him and nodded. "You're right. She will..." not.

We grabbed our food. I hesitated on whether to eat anything just yet. I'd lost all this weight, and I didn't want to go back to how I looked before. It smelt incredible, but was it worth it? The struggle was real.

Brody leant in and roughly whispered to me, "Eat, or I'll feed you."

Blushing as Scott glanced over, his eyes lingered on me for far too long as I pretended not to notice. "I'm going to eat, I just..." I trailed off, ashamed of what I was thinking. "Are you sure you don't like me more now because I've lost weight?"

When he didn't speak, I knew he was pissed. Standing up, he looked over at his parents. "Watch the kids for us. We're going to grab a couple things for the flight."

"We are?" I asked, looking confused.

"Yes." He nodded and took my hand. Almost pulling me from my chair, "We are."

Walking to the small news agency in the airport, I went to the magazine racks. Brody grabbed a couple bottles of water and some chewing lollies so the kid's ears won't pop. He came over and looked at the magazine I held in my hand.

Blocking my path, he flicked his eyes up at mine. His gaze was strong and dominant. He was angry. "I'm only going to say this once, so listen carefully, and if I hear any more about your weight, so help me God, I will have you bent naked over my knee and your ass red from my palm."

Oh, my God… Was it possible to have an orgasm from words?

His blue eyes were hard to mine, figure intimidating me as he stood tall. "You have never once been unattractive to me. Yes, you were a lot thinner years ago, and that's only due to not having the children yet. I couldn't give a shit how much weight you gained. You're still as beautiful as the day I first laid eyes on you in class. I love seeing your breasts bounce and your thighs touch. I love that you're not afraid to sit and eat bread just for the fucking hell of it. You get me hard a lot more than you'll ever know."

"Brody," I cut in. A woman quickly walked past us. The look said it all. She heard him.

"I'm not done speaking." He overrode me with his tone. "I know that I've put these insecurities in your head. I didn't tell you enough how sexy and beautiful you are. I'm going to try to make that right, but I need you to do something for me."

I waited to make sure it was okay for me to now speak. "What is that?"

"Please don't turn out like my sister or brother's wife. You enjoy food; it's in your heritage, and I have always loved that you're never afraid to eat what you want. I see that today, and I miss it." He came in closer, his hands against my hips and gripping them tightly. "I love your body, even more, today than years ago. Want to know why?" he asked, and I nodded. "Because this body carried our two children. That alone is far more attractive than someone who's a rake like my sister. I promise you. I have never once thought you needed to lose weight. You're not as big as you think you are. Gabby, you don't see yourself the way I see you. You're absolutely breathtaking."

That was probably the one thing I least expected to hear. Smiling, I nodded again and leant into him. My forehead against his lips and he kissed me gently. "I am not sorry for losing the weight because it made me feel more confident, but I will lay off the health kick." I wanted to stay looking nice for him.

We bought some items and made our way back to the others. For Brody to put himself out there and say that to me, it truly meant the world to me. I had always thought of myself as unattractive after having the kids. To know that he was always and still is attracted to me, it was a major confidence boost.

Finding seats on the plane, we were behind everyone else. Noah and Lila were in front of us, sharing a bag of mixed lollies and watching Finding Nemo on the iPad, while Brody and I sat quietly behind them. Both of us fairly exhausted. I was pleasantly welcoming the sleep that wanted to claim my body.

Lying my head against his shoulder, he held my hand and rubbed his fingertips over the top of my skin. I was nervous about flying. I hadn't been on a plane since I was a child. I didn't want to sit by the window. I couldn't look out and not panic about being so far above the ground. Brody was doing his best to calm my nerves.

"Sleep, Gabby, it's okay. You're safe," he whispered soothingly, placing a tender kiss to my temple.

Closing my eyes, I soon drifted off to sleep, and it had never felt better.

When I woke, the plane was still dark. Most people were still asleep. Glancing towards Brody, he was sitting upright with his legs spread, looking uncomfortable but comfortable enough to make the most out of his position. His height was a bastard on tightly spaced spots like planes.

I unclipped my belt and checked the kids. Both were asleep. Good. Hopefully, they slept until we were about to land.

I just sat there, watching Brody and taking in his appearance. Even dressed down, he was extremely handsome. As I kept staring at him, my feelings began to stir inside my core, and his words from earlier played over in my mind.

Soon, I was moving closer and undoing the metal zipper on his navy jeans.

Stirring in his sleep, I slipped my hand inside his zipper and began to rub his growing erection through his boxer shorts. My core heated up as I felt him thickening, growing against my palm. Squeezing and stroking, I wanted him now.

"Gabby," he whispered. "Wha—"

I pressed my lips to his to silence him. I kept my eyes open and whispered over his mouth, "Shhh... tell me if someone's coming..." Biting my lower lip, I pulled back and said even softly, "Besides you."

My hand pulled him out of the pocket in the cotton boxers. I stroked him slowly until he was rock hard and oozing with precum, and then I lowered my head with an eager and welcoming mouth.

"Gabby," he sucked in a sharp intake of breath as my tongue swirled around the top of his head, flicking the ridge with my tongue before engulfing him again. "Holy fuck..." he groaned, fingers through my hair as I began to suck him quicker.

Hearing him moan only wanted to make me suck him deeper. Using my hand to play with his balls, massaging him and stroking him, I felt him pulsing inside of my mouth. A thick stream bursts from his tip, filling my mouth. His fingers now pulling at my hair and holding my head, he jerked his hips upright and thrust more into my mouth as he climaxed.

Swallowing because I most definitely wasn't going to grab a sick bag and spit that into it. I sat up, a small smile twitching on the corners of my mouth as he stared at me lustfully.

"Fuck," was all that he could muster up to say. Once his breathing returned to normal, he fixed his jeans back up and placed his palm against my cheek. "You didn't... did you enjoy it?"

"I liked that," I said honestly. I really enjoyed being able to pleasure him that way without anything in return. Oh God, I hope no one heard or seen what we were doing back here.

Getting some sensation back in his body, Brody pulled me towards him. "Feel free to do that whenever you want." He kissed me, passionate and deeply. Pulling back, he smiled once more. "You're amazing. Fuck, I want to take you in the bathroom, but we'll get caught."

"Maybe on the way back home?" I flirted, biting down on his bottom lip as we kissed some more.

He was beginning to become flustered again. "What's gotten into you? You're... Jesus, I can't even explain what that was or felt like."

With a soft smile, I rested my head against his shoulder and reached down, taking his hand in mine and playing with his fingers. "You just made me feel..." I knew I was blushing. "You made me feel sexy, Brody."

With a kiss on my forehead, he wrapped his arm around me, resting his hand on my hip where he played with the bare skin of my hip. "You are sexy, Gabby, and I'll make you feel like that more often. I promise."

"You're just saying that to get head again," I teased.

I waited for his laughter or the cheeky answer. But it never came. With a soft murmur, he spoke, "No, I should have never stopped making you feel that way."

The kids woke up just before the plane landed, and then we all got off the flight. The hot air and smell of sea water were fresh in the air. Such a gorgeous view to be looking at and it was only beginning to get better.

Brody and I had been extremely cuddly as we boarded another flight to make the short distance to Hamilton Island Airport. Lila wanted to sit with her dad, and Noah wanted to sit beside his grandpa. I was going to sit alone or with Lorraine as I thought until Scott slipped in the seat beside me.

I pushed myself closer towards the window seat and tried my best to ignore him as I listened to Lila and Brody taking behind us.

"Daddy, what can we do on an island?" she asked.

"Swim," Brody replied. He had no clue how to make something sound interesting even the way he said swim

sounded boring and forced. He'd been unaccustomed to not
having to go and do these fun activities. Simply, he didn't
know how to make them sound appealing to children.

"Is there parks or somewhere to play?" I could hear the
frown in her voice.

Smiling, I turned and glanced up at them through the
crease between the chairs. "Sweetheart, you're on an island.
We can play in the sand and search for shells even go for walks
in the deep jungle. Maybe we'll find some animals like on
Madagascar."

"You got the bikini out and ready, Gabby?" Scott
grinned. "Or is Brody forcing you to wear a one piece."

"Watch it," Brody responded, low and demeaning.
"That's my wife you're talking about."

"Chill, baby bro, just asking a question," Scott grinned,
taunting him back.

I sat back in the seat and shrugged. "Don't you have a
wife to annoy?" I asked, wishing he would leave.

He chuckled, and I felt the graze of his fingertips
against my upper thigh, too close to my ass for a brother-in-law
to be touching. "Don't be mean, Gabby. I was just making
conversation."

Shooting him a glare. I wasn't going to make a scene. I
couldn't. "Hey, Lila, do you want to sit with mama so we can
talk more about the jungle?" I asked, my voice slightly high-
pitched. I couldn't handle the touch of him again. I wanted to
scream.

"Yes!" She jumped up. "Uncle Scottie, move please!"

Scott had his eyes on me, smiling as he removed his hand and then stood up. "All right, I'll sit with your big oaf of a father then."

"It's all muscle." Brody grinned, flexing his bicep as Scott sat beside him, poking his brother in the gut. "Yours is just beer and pizza, should lay off that shit." Scott wasn't at all fat. He was strong and lean. Brody just happened to be fitter and tower over him in height.

"Yeah, whatever. We can't all sit around drinking top shelf."

Turning around, I silently giggled as Brody and Scott compared their gym routine.

The flight thankfully ended quickly, and we were on our way to the resort. Noah and Lila were like they usually were on Christmas morning, excited, and happy. It really gave me a warm fuzzy feeling to see them like this again especially after all that we'd put them through.

Arriving at Hamilton Island, everything was absolutely breathtaking.

I felt Brody's hand against mine. My smile grew as our fingers were interlacing. "We can do this," he whispered, and in his words, I heard the promise he was making to me. I just hoped this promise wasn't one that would be broken.

"We can," I promised back.

CHAPTER FIFTEEN

"So which rooms are which?" Jessie asked, grinning as she held out her hand for the key to the guesthouse.

We had the large beach house, a huge lap pool out on the deck that came off the open plan living room. It has a laid back feeling, relaxing.

Fred chuckled, letting out a sigh as he took a seat on the large chair. "Hold on, young lady."

"Well... I'm not staying with you. No offence but we need our privacy." Jessie winked, giving Scott a nudge in the side.

Sitting on the chair, Lila climbed up on my lap, softly yawning. "Mama, I'm tired."

"You can sleep soon, baby," I whispered, kissing her cheek as I played with her dark curls.

Loraine read her information sheet, set it down and looked up, pushing her glasses further up her nose. "Okay, well, Rose, Tulip and Scott, you're all in the room down the hall. Unless Tulip would like to sleep in with the others, Noah and Lila will be sharing a room."

Rose, looking smug, smiled and took them. "Excuse me? No, she'll share with us."

My head fell back against the sofa, resting on the soft, padded cushion. I couldn't see how they were so ungrateful. We were here on holiday, fully paid for, and they had the nerve to complain about it. My gaze drifted outside, staring at the crystal blue marina while they fought over rooms.

"Scott, you and Rose are down the hall. Jessie, I'm sorry, but Brody and Gabriella are in the guesthouse downstairs." Her mouth parted, looking to question her, but Loraine simply held a finger up. "You two don't have children."

"We don't have to." I didn't mind sharing with the kids. I was used to it by now.

She ignored me. "Brody, here's the key. Lila and Noah, you're going to sleep in the second room here with grandma and grandpa. Leon, you and Jessie find the other room."

"Yay!" Lila jumped up. "Grandpa, can we watch TV in the bedroom?"

Fred chuckled as Noah climbed up on his lap. "Only if you don't tell your parents." A boisterous laugh followed him, making me smile.

Jessie looked pissed. "Wait, Brody's getting that one?"

"Jess, it's just a room," Leon said quietly, tugging her hand to calm her down. "Who care's when there's a whole ocean to swim in or the massive infinity pool on the floor below us."

She wasn't having a bar of it. Gesturing herself to us, "We don't have kids. Why should we have to stay in here? They do not even have to share with their children. It's just them on their own."

"Settle down. Look, if you want it, then have it. I honestly don't give a fuck as long as there's bed." Brody was beginning to grow agitated. How the three of them could be related and still be so opposite was amusing.

"Brody," Fred sighed, giving him a pointed look.

"Jessie, Brody works hard, and these two deserve a break on their own," Loraine said firm with a wink as she glanced over. "They haven't been anywhere since their honeymoon, and it's their first trip with us. You had the spa chalet in the snow last year."

"That's hardly my fault," she snorted with an eye roll.

Loraine pushed the keys into my husband's hand. "Jessie, enough, Brody and Gabriella are in this room, and that's that. You and Leon will be so busy exploring the island. I'm sure it won't matter." She placed a kiss on his cheek and diverted her eyes towards mine, giving me another wink.

My stomach almost in my mouth as I realised she knew.

His mother knew about our marital problems. Here, I thought we'd been careful and sneaky; apparently, not as good as we thought we were doing. We walked down the pathway and up the smaller guesthouse where we were going to be spending our nights. The kids weren't at all fazed that they were spending time away from us. I think they were enjoying it. I also knew that they'd be well taken care of and spoilt rotten. His parents loved Noah and Lila.

Brody let out a low whistle as he walked inside. "The parents really outdid themselves. No wonder Jessie wanted this room so bad. The pool's a decent size as well." He nodded towards the infinity pool. The clear blue water made me want to swim in it or drink it. It just looked extremely inviting in this warm weather.

I set my bag on the table in the living room, then walked towards him. "I want a shower." I was sweating and felt so icky. I was also sure that I smelt too.

Brody slid his hands down over my hips. Taking a step forward, our bodies were pressed together. "Now?"

"Yes."

His brows raised up, a smirk appearing. "You want some company?"

My heart pounded once more. With the number of time I panic lately, I was going to have a heart attack. "Brody... we've... it's been." I couldn't even say it.

Getting my point, he nodded, and his smile faded slightly. "I know. It's been a long time since we showered together."

"Before Noah was born; I... I'm nervous," I admitted. Broad daylight, naked and in his view, he was going to see every new curve, bump, and mark on my body. With sex, it was different. He wasn't too focused on my body. He was thinking about something entirely different. It was enthralling and scary all at once.

"Don't be nervous. I've seen you naked plenty of times before," he smiled, grasping me tighter and knocking me off my balance, so I fell against his chest.

I fisted his shirt lightly, beginning to pull it up over his head. "Let's go shower then."

"Really?" he didn't wait for my answer, hands slipping underneath the hem of my shirt and lifting it off my head. I tugged on his jeans and pulled the down. He was hard, pitching a tent in his boxers. Lust in my eyes, I roamed my eyes over him. He pulled the drawstring, and my bottoms were down in a flash. He grinned, then lowered his white, fitted boxers, and I squeezed my thighs together as his erection bobbed while he took a step closer and kissed me lightly.

He was naked, and I was still standing in my bra and panties before him.

Brody, taking a step back, just stared at me. "You know what I find so beautiful? It's these." Stepping forward, he traced a finger over the two faint stretch marks on my lower belly, just almost underneath my hip bone. They were what I had been so embarrassed about. Barely noticeable but if you looked closer, they were there.

"You do?" I asked, glancing down at his finger touching my skin.

Causing me to shiver, he nodded. "You should be proud of them, Gabby. They're from the two children you carried and have protected since they were conceived. Don't ever shy away from that. I love that there's a constant reminder of what we created together."

Tears in my eyes yet again, "You're going to make me cry."

"You're only ever allowed to cry over something good." He chuckled. His hand reached around my back. Flicking the snap, my black bra fell down the floor by my toes. Taking his time, he undressed me slowly.

My back against the tiled shower wall, water sprayed down above us both. His fingers gripping into the curve of my ass, holding tightly, only pleased me more. Our mouths latched, tongues dancing and tasting as I rocked my hips back and forth against him. I think I was going to enjoy these midday showers.

"Brody," I moaned. "Keep doing that." Whatever the hell he was doing, I never wanted it to stop.

He pulled back, slammed my back into the wall harder and removed his hand. My hold on him kept me upright still as his hand cupped my cheeks, one moved to the back of my hair as he held it tightly and brought his mouth closer.

"So perfect," he murmured.

Gasping as he went in faster, biting down on my lower lip and sucking, I whimpered and tilted my head back underneath the hot stream of water. His mouth then latched onto my neck, sucking with a guttural groan as we came together.

Coming down from out high of bliss, we kept our position, placing a kiss on his bare shoulder. I lifted my head and kissed my way to his jaw covered in stubble. "We've got so much to make up for, so much lost time."

He placed a single tender kiss on my forehead and softly spoke, "No, there's no making up, just making new memories. Memories neither of us will want to forget."

New memories, now, that was something I looked forward to. It gave me an ounce of hope that everything wasn't lost after all. I knew we needed to talk still, and us being alone in here gave me a shred of hope that we could sort things out better before we left for home once again.

I laughed, holding him tighter with fear of being dropped as he walked us to the bed. Dropping me down on my ass, he came between my thighs and over my body as he laid against my naked, wet skin. I glanced at the door, worrying his sister or mother may spring a surprise visit on us at any moment. "Someone could come in."

His eyes suddenly darkened as his lips skimmed the soft skin of my neck. Murmuring with each kiss as he met my gaze once more, "There's only one woman who's going to come for me ever."

"I love the way that sounds," I smiled lazily down at him.

My arms were wrapped underneath his, pulling him in closer as he tried climbing away. "Baby, I can't go another round. You've worn me out." He grinned, laying by my side and propping himself up on his elbow, his hand against my belly.

Laughing, I rolled to my side, staring at him. I focused on his eyes. "I think you wore yourself out, Mister. You're the one who wanted to see how fast you could go in the shower without slipping." Reaching up, I traced the bridge of his nose, then the smile faded. "Your mum knows about us."

He looked up and nodded. "I know. She booked the tickets so we would be forced to come together. She got the kids with them and us in this big room. It's all part of her matchmaking."

Trailing a finger over his cheek, I sighed. "I don't want to go home and have things change for us, Brody. This feels nice right now." Just being here, like this with him was what I had craved for so long, an intimacy we hadn't shared in years. I couldn't imagine going back to separate rooms or rare touches.

"I know. I don't know what this is, but I like it."

"What do you mean?" I asked, confusion sweeping over me. "I thought we were trying again?" We'd called off the divorce for fuck sake.

"I just meant that I wasn't sure if this was us, just fucking and having fun." His expression pained. "I didn't—"

Instantly, I wanted to throw up. "Fucking and having fun?"

"That came out wrong."

I scoffed. "No shit."

Pulling my hand back, he reached out taking hold of it again. "I didn't mean to upset you. I just meant whatever happens back home, I want to just live at the moment."

"We need to at least try, both of us." I couldn't stress that enough to him. We both needed to work on our relationship and making it work. "I at least want to try."

"I have something we could try." He released his hold on me, standing by the bed and pointing to the floor in front of him. "After that blowjob on the plane, I want to watch you on your knees sucking my cock."

He had fucked me senseless after I sucked him empty, legs up, bent over the coffee table and ass in the air.

Three hours later, we finally managed to pull clothes on, get dressed and make our way towards the house to find the kids and take them down to the beach. We, unfortunately, ran into Scott and Rose along out way, who by the looks of it were headed to the main resort bar for drinks. I couldn't care less what he was doing, just as long as it wasn't near me.

"Hey, you two, um, have some fun?" Scott chuckled as Rose thumped him in the side with her elbow. "What? Gabby was moaning and all shit. I didn't mean to hear it."

Brody's fingers tightened around my hand, keeping me close. He wasn't impressed but kept his cool. "Have you seen the kids?"

I was actually mortified that he had heard us. I just wondered how long he had been listening to us. Rose just smiled. "Oh, yeah, they're watching TV with dad. Tulip is with them too. We're sneaking off for a couple hours to relish the atmosphere in the bar."

"Fun." I sighed, watching Brody who was having a glaring match with his brother. Tugging on his hand, I urged him to follow. "Come on, kids can watch TV later. I want to go for a walk."

Walking around the corner, Brody pushed me back against the house. Oh, God, his eyes were hard to mine as his lips came closer with a soft whisper. "You should have kept it down." Feeling his fingers grazing just beneath my dress, my bare thigh quivered. "I don't like the idea of my brother hearing you come. Nobody but me will ever get to hear you come."

"Brody…" I needed to tell him. I had to tell him. "I…"

"Oh, there you are." I was cut off by his mother as she came walking towards us, catching us out. "Get off her, young man. We need to talk now."

"Ma," Brody groaned, pulling away. "What is it?"

"Private." She narrowed her eyes and grabbed him by the ear, pulling him down to her level. "Excuse us, Gabby, my son is in a lot of trouble right now. What kind of animal are you? In broad daylight?"

Brody looked bewildered as he ripped her hand from his ear. "Are you fucking crazy?" he snapped.

"Are you?" she retorted back. "Follow me now!"

I smiled, laughing as he was dragged away. "Be a good boy. I'll meet you down on the beach."

Noah and Lila were all too happy to come down for a swim. I sat on the sand, watching them running around and playing. I ran around chasing them, and then they turned to chase me. Lila was laughing. Noah had picked her up and dropped her into the shallow of the water. Her shorts wet, she stood laughing louder as she chased after him.

"I'm going to get you, Noah!" she said, determined and began to chase him.

"You're too slow!" Noah teased back and sprinted off.

"Not too deep!" I called out, laughing and taking another photo of the two of them.

Sitting down again, my legs stretched out and watched them having the time of their lives. I smiled when I heard his deep voice as he sat beside me. "They're obviously having fun."

I nodded. "A lot of fun," I replied. "Everything all right?"

He sighed. "No, not really, Lila must have told mum about the divorce and us fighting. Mum put two and two together and came up with a hundred." He rubbed his thumb over my fingers and squeezed my hand. "She thought I had hurt you badly," he said, and his voice grew darker.

It took me a moment to understand what he meant. Cheating, "Oh," I said quietly.

"I told her I haven't and never would." His voice was deadpan as he wanted me to believe him. I did. "She also planned us to have the bigger room on purpose, wants this to be like a second honeymoon for us."

I smiled with a laugh. "Oh yeah? Did you tell your mum we've already screwed four times already?"

"No, she almost ripped my ear off," he grinned, rubbing his ear where she had been grabbed before.

"I didn't really want anyone to know what's been going on at home. It's still raw, and we got so much to sort. I didn't want your whole family talking about us like we're gossip," meaning his sister and sister-in-law.

He nodded, understanding where I was coming from. "I understand. Mum spoke with Lila and told her not to repeat anything. We'll do that same after they finish running around."

"Okay," I smiled and rested my head against his shoulder as I leant into him.

"You were going to tell me something before she interrupted." He brought up, and I pulled away, looking back to the kids laughing.

Shit. Not here, not while the kids were around. This needed to be spoken about in private. It could go two ways: one, Brody believed me or second being that he didn't believe a word I said about his brother. I hoped he would, but I just couldn't be sure. "Oh, I don't remember, nothing important." I couldn't tell him this now.

Brody, fully clothed in shorts and his shirt thrown off, took the kids, grabbing them both and walking out into the ocean. They were squealing with laughter as he threatened to drop them both in. I couldn't have laughed any harder when he turned his back, and they both went crashing into him. They all went down, soaked with water.

He couldn't have looked any more of a mess, but he was definitely doing things to my heart. Those feelings were stirring up again, coming back to me.

"I lo—" I stopped myself before I blurted something out and ruined everything. "I think they both tricked you into doing that."

He laughed loudly. "I agree. I have sand where sand shouldn't be. I need another shower, and you, two, need a bath."

The kids nodded, and we made our way back to the shore to grab their towels.

"Gabby, don't worry about anyone else, just us, remember?" Brody reminded before we walked back inside the house to shower and bath the sandy, wet kids.

Nodding. "I know, just us." It should be easy to do, focus on the good and leave the bad alone.

"We should go for another walk later, just the four of us," he suggested.

Walking into the bathroom, I turned on the water for the kids. "Do you think we need to see a counsellor? Talk to a professional?" I wanted us to have the best shot at getting past all the hard times that we'd been through.

He closed the door quietly behind him and leant against it. "No, I don't think we do. I think we can do this on our own.

I mean look at how close we're becoming again." He pulled me forwards. I fell into his chest, and the door thudded softly. "If you want to see one, then I'll do it. I'll go to one."

Shaking my head, "I don't want to go back to how things were before. I hated it so much..." I shook away the tears. "The silence and then the fighting. I want to make it work. We will try on our own. If it's not working, we'll see someone." We needed to try on our own again.

"We will. We're going to communicate more. That's where we went wrong. I stopped trying to woo you," he smiled, kissing the top of my forehead.

"Woo me?" I asked, a growing smile.

He nodded, stroking the fallen hair from my face. "I stopped trying to date you. I had you and just stopped. I should bring you flowers every day, write you love letters, and kiss you whenever I have the chance."

"Brody." I fell in love with this man. "I stopped too. It's not just you."

We both stopped trying, and maybe if we hadn't, then we wouldn't be here in this mess of a situation right now. We would be like another happy family instead of having to fake the perfect marriage for his family to see.

CHAPTER SIXTEEN

"Mama, are you and daddy making a baby? Uncle Scott said you were earlier."

There was no way I was prepared for that question as I washed the conditioner from Lila's hair. Brody was in the shower, and Noah sat opposite her with a beard of bubbles. "Brody?" I called out, asking for some help.

He cleared his throat. "Ah... Not right now, I think you two are plenty for us, princess."

I smiled at the thought of another baby. It pleasantly surprised me that he hadn't shot that down although there was no way we'd be having another baby just yet... if ever.

Noah frowned. "How does a baby get in there, anyway? Do you no clothes cuddle with daddy?"

I don't think I had ever heard Brody cut off a shower so fast. I was stunned. Lila went to open her mouth, and I blurted out the first thing that came to my mind. "Stop talking and wash your hair, or we're going home."

The bathroom door opened, Brody's mother walked in, and he grunted as he wrapped the towel around his waist. Luckily, he was behind a frosted shower door that you couldn't see anything from the waist down. His mother had no boundaries.

"I'm naked," he ground out. The kids giggled.

"I gave birth to you. It's nothing I haven't seen before."

He smirked, and I knew exactly what he would be thinking, something dirty about having a much bigger cock than before. "It's a bit messy in here," water, sand and bubbles everywhere.

"Oh, now, this is a picture if only I had the camera. Let me finish washing them up while you both go get ready for dinner." Loraine took over and made herself right at home as Brody shook his head with a grin.

"Thanks." I stood up, watching as she took my place in the bath.

We walked back to our room, and as soon as the door was closed, I spun around to see the blaze on my husband face. We were thinking the exact same thing.

"Naked on top of me?" I basically shouted, raging with fury.

"I'm going to kill Scott if he's telling my kids this. It's not his fucking job to do so!" Shaking his head, his anger subsided as he watched me starting to dress for dinner. "I wouldn't mind naked cuddling until you moaned my name, though," he smirked, pulling me into him. How did we just go from killing to naked cuddling? "Or baby making."

My eyes opened as he said that. I knew he was teasing from what he had heard moments back in the bathroom. Babies were great, but a band-aid baby wasn't going to happen.

Trying to pull away from his grasp, I smiled and shook my head. "Nope, we need to get dressed, and you need to..." and his lips roamed my skin. I forgot what I had been saying to him, letting out a breathless moan instead. "Quickly; has to be, oh God, quick."

My back pinned against the wall. His hands cupped my face as he dove right in and kissed me passionately, growling over my mouth, as he tasted my tongue on his own. "God, you're so incredibly sexy, Gabriella." My name slipped from his breath so easily.

"Brody..." and soon, we were soon lost in each other.

Something smelt delicious in the dining room of the beach house. Everyone was seated at the table as Brody and I entered the room. His mother walked over, holding a baking dish and beaming. "Sit, you two. I made your favourite, Brody."

"You don't even try to hide who your favourite child is," Scott muttered, rolling his eyes at her.

Jessie agreed, seeming happier than earlier, "True. Brody's always going to be her baby boy."

Big mistake mentioning "baby" since Lila's eyes lit up. "Mama and daddy are trying to make me a baby sister. Uncle Scott said they have lots of sex."

I wanted to die as Jessie began to giggle, looking anywhere but us. "Uncle Scott needs to shut his mouth around my kids," Brody said, an underlying of anger in his tone as he spoke staring directly at him with a smile.

Scott winked back. "Where's the fun in that? They asked what you were doing earlier, and well, I couldn't lie to their innocent faces; plus, payback for telling my daughter that I was really a woman."

Oh, Lord, the day Brody had convinced Tulip that her father was really a woman was epic. She believed him, and it took a very long time for Scott to convince her again that her uncle was full of bullshit.

"Please, stop speaking to my children about babies and how they're made." I looked towards Noah and Lila. "When you want to know more about babies, you ask your daddy or me. For now, you eat please."

Brody smirked, but he and Scott hadn't finished bickering. "You deserved that. Stop being a sook and get over it. It was almost five years ago."

I felt Brody's fingers against mine, taking my hand beneath the table and resting it on his lap. Holding tightly, it made me smile. It was something he did at school. Jessie raised her brows at us. "Something is different with you, two," she said, pointing towards us but talking to everyone else. "I can't figure it out, though."

"They're showing affection. It's sickening," Scott muttered.

"Nothing wrong with that," I shot back quietly. It was about time we did it.

His eyes glanced up, and he gave me a smile. "No, nothing wrong with that, at all." Only, I knew the hidden message sent through that reply. It almost made me sick.

"It's because daddy isn't divorcing!" Lila announced.

For crying out loud, did children ever have a filter? This was the last thing we needed to deal with today. Everyone was silent, and just staring; then, Jessie burst into laughter. Brody squeezed my hand as I felt like I could just burst into tears.

Clearing his throat lowly, Brody pointed towards Lila with his finger. "We aren't. Please eat your dinner and stop talking."

Everyone seemed to take the hint in not asking anything about what Lila had blurted. I would speak with her later tonight about keeping everything private. I stared down at the plate of salad. The mood to eat was gone as I pushed some leafy greens around my plate.

His lips hit my ear with a heated whisper, "Eat, or I'll spank." I instantly blushed at the thought.

"Seriously, I'm going to throw up if you don't stop that. It's like watching you in school again," Scott snorted, pushing his cutlery aside. "That was bad enough, lovesick teens."

I was getting so fed up with him. Giving him a kick underneath the table with my foot, he shot me a surprised look, and I glared more. Did he not see that I loathed the sight of him? It was a struggle to even be near him after what had happened. "Just because you were the dork who refused to cut that god awful mullet... No wonder the girls refused to date you."

Brody laughed, not noticing the resentment I held for his brother. "Told you he wanted to be a woman." His hand then moved to my thigh, sliding up and squeezing. I tried not to think about his fingers being so close as they made their way inner.

Loraine laughed as she set her wine glass down, almost spluttering out her red. "Oh, goodness me, I had forgotten all about that. I am still trying to forget about those acid wash skin-tight jeans and muscle tops, my God."

So long was awkward sex and divorce talk, it was all now all about Scott and his punk rock phase during his late teens. After dinner, we took a walk just the four of us down to the beach. The kids had a bucket each as they searched for seashells and crabs.

I wrapped my arm around Brody's waist as he pulled me against his side with his arm around my body. "I could have strangled our daughter tonight." I was laughing.

"Agree with you there. We need to talk to her about talking about our family life with everyone else," he said with a sigh. He pulled me and grabbed my waist. "Gabby..." he began. "I never stopped loving you. I just lost my way."

Was he saying what I think he was about to say? Oh, the hell with it. I was done holding back. If I couldn't say this to my husband, then who the heck could I say it too? "I think I'm falling in love with you all over again."

A smile of relief came across his face. "Me too. It's like seeing you for the first time. I've missed your smile."

"I've just missed you."

"We fell into a routine, Gabby. We became boring, and it was never about us anymore. It was everyone else. We forgot about each other." I had sat and thought about this before. I completely agree. I do agree. We were so set in a routine with sex and everything else. There was never an effort put into it.

I nodded agreeing with him. "I know."

I wouldn't be that woman anymore. I had to show him that I loved him more. I couldn't just expect him to romance the hell out of me. Men need romance too, and I was going to start showing him just how he made me feel. Whether it is lunch every day with him at work or just a romantic dinner at home, I was going to do those little things that I used to do again. It was a two-way street, and if we were both trying, I'm giving this my all.

"I'm sorry about how things were, it'll change. I promise. I will change," he said more determined.

"Mum, Dad, come look at this!" Noah called out.

"It's very disgusting!" Lila added, poking whatever it was with a small stick she picked up.

Wrapping my arms around his neck, I nodded and placed a kiss to his mouth. "Me too. It will change."

The kids looked excited as we walked over. I assumed it would be a crab. Instead, Noah pointed to the remains of a fish. I scrunched my nose as Lila done the same while she drew a circle around it.

Brody then smirked as he stood back up, telling Noah and Lila about fish and a ridiculous story about how it died from jumping out of the water and sunbathing. "I think the kids look tired. It's getting late."

"It's not even nine," I laughed, then gasped with a squeal as I felt his hand on my ass and giving it a naughty pinch. "Ouch!" I spun around, laughing.

"I didn't mean for us to sleep. I'm far from tired." Then his smirk turned playful, and I shook my head backing away. Oh no, he wouldn't. "Run, baby, I'm coming for you," he grinned, rubbing his hands together and getting ready to pounce.

"No! You're so much faster than me. It's not fair," I ran, giggling and squealing at the same time which only slowed me down even more. "Brody, don't you dare?"

"Mama, he's going to get you!" Lila squealed, pointing behind me as her father's heavy footsteps were almost up to my ass. "Faster!"

His arms were wrapped around my waist, pulling me backwards with legs in the air as he lifted me up and then lost his footing. Both of us fell into the sand and laughed incredibly hard. My stomach hurt from the amount of laughing I had been doing while Brody also laid there with a roar of hearty laughter coming from his chest.

Pushing myself up with my hands, I smiled down at him. "You're such a big oaf."

"A what?" he said, brows shooting up as slowly his laughter died down. "Did you just call me an oaf?"

Nodding, "Yep, I sure did. You got a problem with that, big guy?"

He wrapped his arms around me and pulled me back down against his chest, he shook his head grinning. "As long as I'm the only big oaf in your life, then I'll gladly take that name."

Grinning over his lips, my fingers drove through his hair. "Just you, nobody else."

Our mouths met, skimming over one another as he ran both hands through my hair, brushing it out of my face. "Nobody else, just us, baby."

Just us.

CHAPTER SEVENTEEN

"Best way to start the day."

"So you say," I pointed out, my legs still shaking. "Now, that you've finally tasted pussy, I might say you're addicted."

"Addicted to yours."

Pushing myself back up from the bed, I shook my head, walking up to him still naked, and kissed his mouth which was still glistening wet. Tasting myself on his tongue, I pulled away. "How about some actual breakfast?"

"We're on holiday," he said. I raised a brow at him, waiting for another answer. "But I do miss your food."

My heart warmed and not because I was still in a post-orgasm phase. "I'll make you breakfast." I smiled, not bothered at all, as I kissed his cheek and began dressing. I stopped halfway because of the loud, piercing scream coming from the main house.

Brody frowned, rushing to pull his shirt on. "Was that Lila?"

It took a moment to register her sobbing. With that, we were both running up to the house, Brody taking two steps at a time until he was inside. I wasn't far behind him.

Running into her bedroom, she was standing in the middle of her room crying. "She said you left us here," she sobbed, even more, taking a leap forward and clinging to my legs.

"We'd never leave you. Who said that?" Brody asked, kneeling beside us and rubbing his palm soothingly against her back.

Noah coming forward, he crossed his arms over his chest. "Aunt Rose said if Lila didn't eat her breakfast, then you were going to leave her here. It's shit food, dad. We don't like it!"

Brody sighed. "Don't say that word, and I will take care of your aunt."

Standing up, he was pissed. With a glower, he stormed off down the hallway, and soon, we could hear his hot-headed temper directed towards her. "Don't you ever and, I mean, ever speak to my children that way. You have her in bloody tears!"

"Relax, Brody, I just told her if she didn't eat, she couldn't leave the table. How was I meant to know that she would scream like that?" Rose sighed, "If you let them stay with other people, then they wouldn't be so demanding for only their mother's cooking! They're too spoilt," she replied to him.

I walked in to witness Brody tossing out the bowl of muesli. No wonder they wouldn't eat it. "Uh, Rose, please don't feed them that again. They're children. If they want bacon, eggs or pancakes, that's fine with us."

"Oh, I forgot. You're Italian, so it's normal to eat two or five croissants for breakfast, probably smothered in butter and jam."

Whoa, that was much uncalled for. "Um, that's not really Italian," I pointed out. "And five? Really?"

I shook my head as everyone began to leave the room. It was just Scott and me since Brody took our children to our room for breakfast before we took a walk and then came back for a swim.

I returned to their room. On my knees, I went through the mess of a suitcase as I looked for Noah's swimming shorts.

"Enjoying the holiday?" Scott asked, startling me. He was there, smirking and leaning against the wall.

"Leave me alone," I warned, my words low and harsh as I balled my fingers into my fist. "I mean it."

Chuckling, he shook his head as I stood to leave, blocking my path. "We're practically related. We're family. I can't do that."

"I'm going to tell him. He has a right to know." This secret was killing me. Brody needed to know the truth about his brother.

Scott's eyes narrowed and shut the door behind him. "If you open that mouth of yours, look out. He'll never look at you the same again. Remember that he's going to look at you and be so hurt. You lied to him for so long."

Guilt ate me away. I hated him. "Go away from me. I mean it!"

Hiding my tears, I stormed off and tried not to cry as I walked back to the others. All I could think about was whether Brody would hate me or would he be able to understand that I was too ashamed to tell him the truth about his brother and me.

As soon as I walked in the room, Brody pulled me against his chest, and I hadn't felt guiltier in my life. Instead of saying anything, I wrapped my arms around his body and held him back just as tight. As soon as this trip was over, I was going to tell him the truth about what happened between his brother and I even if it were nine years ago.

On our fifth day, we were on the deck as the kids swam in the pool, sunbathing while the men drank and talked about sports and finance. Work, of course, had slipped in, unable to stay away for too long.

"I honestly feel like Italian," Jessie spoke, peering over her Cosmo magazine as she sunbathed on a lounge chair. I knew she was looking at me, but I didn't say anything. "Yeah, I seriously want to eat that for dinner."

I kept quiet as I braided Lila's hair, probably pulling too roughly as her head tilted back with a jerk. "Ouch, that hurt."

Whispering, "Sorry, baby," I leant forward; kissing her soft locks then went back to doing her hair.

It had been a long day. After the other morning with arguing and the kids fighting, I was exhausted, and lying around, doing nothing was so different for me. Brody was only in a pair of board shorts and looking edible as he tilted his head back and swigged on a beer. Oh, God, he was really driving me wild lately. I struggled to keep my hand off of his strong body, those biceps and hard stomach.

"Do they serve that on the menu?" Loraine asked Jessie. "Or is it in the restaurant?"

Rose, rolling onto her back, looked towards me just as Lila ran off and jumped into the pool. "I think it's your turn to cook, anyway."

I had no problem with cooking. It's the way she said it as if I was just here doing nothing. Loraine waved her hand through the air, brushing Rose off. "Oh, don't be ridiculous. Gabby cooked all week long. I would never ask her to serve dinner for everyone."

"She doesn't work. She has the time to plan out dinner recipes all day long, anyway," Rose interjected. "I know she loves cooking. The kids would love spaghetti bolognese."

Ouch. Did they really think all I did each day were sit on my ass and look up recipes? They were having a conversation about me while I was still here, yet they couldn't even ask if I minded. Maybe I didn't want to cook. It's not like I threw dinner party's each week for dozens of people.

"She makes Italian food for Brody all the time, though. It's not fair," Jessie pouted. "I am really craving Cannoli and fresh bread."

"Oh, don't forget tiramisu..." Rose sat up, pulling the strapless top of her black one piece. "Wait, let's get a pen and paper and see what the men want. That'll be easy for you to go and shop."

Loraine offered me a soft smile which I returned. I lay down further on my back and pulled the shades over my eyes. Turning my head so I was able to keep an eye on the children swimming, I let the silent tears roll down my cheek while the others all went on saying what they wanted to eat. Everyone said something different like it was going to be a piece of cake to make eight main dishes and three others for the children. I should have spoken up instead of biting my cheeks, but I was too polite to make a scene and carry on about cooking for the people who paid for us to be here.

I was only in a sundress so I didn't need to change into anything as I sat in the kitchen going over the list of dishes. It ranged from Steak Florentine to Bruschetta to Risotto and then Roasted pears with prosciutto, not even I cooked half of this at home. Did they just think because I was Italian that I knew how to cook everything?

I know the old school recipes, ones handed down from generation to generation, not goddamn Veal saltimbocca. I, however, did smile when I read someone's choice as spaghetti and meatballs. Brody really made it easy to cook for. Serve him that with fresh garlic bread and he'd think it was the best damn dinner he's ever eaten.

The sliding door opened, and the devil himself walked in. "What's going on?"

"You know, about to go shopping," I couldn't help myself when I gave an eye roll.

"Oh yeah, you want some help ordering it?" he asked, going over the list and letting out a low whistle. "Geez, I don't even know what half of this is. You won't be able to carry this back, get them to drop it up here once they've cooked it."

He had no clue. It was a cure. "Darling, who do you think is making all of this?"

His blue eyes widened and narrowed with annoyance. "You're not cooking for anyone, Gabriella." Snatching the piece of paper, he scanned his eyes over the list, reading. Then he scrunched up the list and tossed it into the sink. "You're not fucking cooking anything like this. You're on holiday."

"And I'm the only one who doesn't earn any money! I don't get to have a say. I'm basically freeloading you," I blurted in a huff. "How can I refuse to do this when all of you work, and I just..." stay home and look after the children? I take care of the house, but that was never made important or considered a job.

Brody looked as if I had slapped him across the face. "Freeloading? Is that what you think you are?" Shaking his head, he walked to the door and stepped outside. With his back to me and body facing his sister and Rose, "Who told Gabby that she was cooking tonight?"

There was silence.

"Don't make me ask again. I know it was either you two." He shook his head and scoffed. "You're all going to buy your own dinner. I'm taking my wife out, and I won't have you telling her she had to cook all that ridiculous food just because she isn't working. It would have taken her all day."

"What are you talking about? We're ordering dinner." Fred frowned, looking over at the girls. "Aren't we?"

"No, dad. Just because my wife is Italian doesn't mean she's catering for everyone." Brody walked back inside and closed the sliding door before his sister and Rose ran in.

I hated this. I got up to leave. The door opened again, and Rose spoke, "Gabriella, if you didn't want to cook, then you could have said something rather than tattle tailing."

"Rose," Jessie said quietly. "I don't think you should—
"

She did choose not to listen. "I am so sick of this. I can't sit around and listen to you all praise her for doing nothing. She doesn't work. She just stays home and drowns herself in a packet of chips and tub of salsa," Rose pointed towards me. "We all know Brody is too good for you. You're taking advantage of him. You're just a stuck-up bitch who fucks everyone who opens their wallets for you. You stay home, don't work, what do you do when the kids are at school? Nothing! You don't have to do anything." There was no stopping her. The wine had gone to her head, and she was unleashing hell onto me as my husband stood there saying nothing. Jessie was backing away as Rose kept going, "No wonder you're divorcing her. You can do better."

Brody's jaw hardened, frowning with a deep glare. He remained silent. I shot him a look. "Thanks for the support!" I hissed and pushed a finger into Rose's chest. "You think all I do is sit on my fat ass all day?" I asked, not caring who the hell heard me. I was so done with all of this every damn day. "We don't hire a maid or a cleaner or whatever the hell it's called. I am that person. I don't go out because I don't have the time between cleaning, cooking and taking care of our children. I have an hour to myself at most each day. I'm up at six and ironing suits, then getting the kids ready for school. I take them to school. I come home, and I clean. I don't spend all day searching recipes. The food is sorted a week beforehand when I do groceries. Just because I am not working doesn't mean I don't have a job."

"You're not leaving for work. How dare you judge me for bringing a paycheck home?" She pushed me back, and I was ready to unleash hell even more.

"Puttana!" I spat angrily at her.

Brody laughed so loud, and Scott glared at him. He tried covering it up with a cough, not expecting me to call her a whore.

"What did you just say to me?" she shrieked. "She said something horrible! Look that word up."

Rolling my eyes, I shook my head. "Just so you know, I am not useless and lazy just because I am a stay at home mother. I'm many things, and none is lazy!"

"Like what?" She just couldn't leave it alone, could she? "You have it easy. Admit it!"

My temper was reaching boiling point. I was so angry and pissed that Scott was allowing her to speak to me this way. She was walking around as if she were the Queen Almighty.

"Gabby, come on," Brody reached out, taking my hand, but I shrugged him off. "She's not worth it."

By now, I was so mad that I could no longer give a shit about them. They were never going to get it. They all worked. Their daughter was in childcare, and just because Brody worked, didn't make him superior to me. We were equals.

"I'll tell you what I am," I smiled. "I'm a CEO of the household. I have Masters and PhD in patience. I am also a family law enforcer. I'm a dolly doctor and a hairstylist who specialises in pigtails and wiggly clients. I'm in the search and rescue for small plastic pieces, not forgetting that I am also a fast food chef. I work in the department of make-believe, often digging around underneath beds as we go searing for lost treasure. Also, I am a sleep scientist. I do mostly work night shifts, though. What else?" I tapped my chin pretending to think. "Oh yes, I am a personal chauffeur, expert driver and birthday party planner. My favourite is tantrum and toy hostage negotiator. Oh, and lastly, I'm the mother fucking chief monster hunter!"

By now, everyone was holding their breaths as I let loose on this woman. How dare she speak to me in such a way? Brody was the first to crack, followed his parents and Leon as they burst into a heavy fit of laughter. Rose stood, cheeks flaming red with the embarrassment of just getting her ass owned and handed to her on a silver platter.

"Mama said a bad word," Noah's voice giggled behind me.

I smiled down at him, and my bad mood was suddenly gone. "Yes, I did baby. Come on, let's go for a swim." I also aimed that towards Rose as she had told the kids to not get Tulip's hair wet.

Turning around, I heard Brody speaking to his brother as I took the kids and began to walk away. "Your wife needs to leave, or both of you go stay elsewhere."

We all made our way down the trail, and I sighed when I felt his hand on the small of my back. "I told mum not to bother us. We'll spend the day together, just the four of us. I'll take the kids out on jet skis or something," he said, pulling me close and kissing the top of my head.

I smiled, slipping my arm around his waist. "I'm glad that even though things were bad with us, our children turned out the way they are."

"Me too," he smiled back. "We have you to thank for that, though. You're a great mother, Gabby, and I honestly can't wait to have more with you."

"More?" I asked, unable to hide my surprise as I cocked my head back, looking up at him. I brought him to a stop and wrapped my arms tighter around his back, bringing him in close. "I thought you were teasing about babies."

Just when we were about to begin kissing, there were little groaning noises. "Eww, girl germs!" Noah said.

Lila began to sing, skipping ahead. "Mama and daddy, kissing in a tree…"

"Lila," Brody laughed. "We're not in a tree."

"Dad, you don't play pretend!" she whined, which made me laugh.

Brody just smiled. With a laugh, he pecked my nose. "All right, we'll work on more when they aren't around. Let's go for a swim, and you're getting in too." He did not answer my questions but obviously decided for me.

Sitting on the bottom step of our pool, Lila and I watched as the two boys swam around and tried doing handstands in the water. She moved around and wrapped her small arms around my neck as I swam out into the water with her clinging to me.

We spent most the day in the pool or down on the beach, lazing around in the sun and having a blast with the four of us. Brody and I were acting as if we were teenagers again, enjoying the moments and not taking anything too seriously. It was really feeling easy to slip back to how things were before. There were still those little nerves and flutters in the tummy whenever I caught him looking at me.

After the swim, we went for a walk to the putt-putt golf, and I sucked badly, losing. The boys won.

We decided to have something to eat in the café there. We were hungry. They got a plate of fish and chips, and Brody and I shared a bowl of hot chips, only because my husband was serious about taking me out for dinner later tonight.

"What do I wear?" I asked, looking through the suitcase for anything remotely nice.

"Something easy to take off," he replied and began talking to someone else. "What are you doing here?"

"I feel awful," Jessie said quietly. "I never meant to hurt Gabby's feelings. I came to apologise to her."

"It's fine," I said, not knowing what else to say.

"No, it's not," she said with a sigh. "We're sisters, and I don't ever want you to hate me like you do Rose. Seeing her taking things that far, it was a slap in the face. I am really sorry. Leon even came under me for how I've been acting."

If Leon brought things up to her, then I guess she really was sorry. "Thank you." It meant a lot that she was able to apologise to me. It was big of her to do so.

Leon then stepped inside and handed Brody a beer. "Let's sit out there while these two girls talk," he chuckled.

I realised this was a set up to get Brody out of the room. "What's going on?" I asked after Brody was out of sight.

She began pushing me towards the bathroom. "Now, Brody is taking you out for dinner. I guess you need something to wear, and I have the perfect outfit for you." Holding up a bag and a pair of heels, she winked. "Let's make my brother jealous with how gorgeous you're going to look. He won't like any other man staring at you, and that's exactly what's going to happen tonight!"

"I can't do that," I said staring at myself in the mirror. "Your clothes won't fit me."

Her hands on my hips from behind, he pulled in my top to bring out the curves. "Of course, you will." She started as she met my eyes in the mirror. "He needs his ass kicked for flirting around with the office tart, and this is your perfect payback. He's going to regret the day he ever let that thing sit on his desk, flash her legs and underwear."

"How do you know that?" I asked, hating that I had almost forgotten about that, and now, my jealousy was back out as an image of the two of them flashed through my mind.

Raising a brow, she smiled. "He told me about it. Now, you're going to show him that he's not the only one others look at. You're going to make him feel the way you did that day. I guarantee he will cut his own balls off before ever doing that again."

Oh, she was naughty and an evil genius.

CHAPTER EIGHTEEN

My husband wasn't impressed.

The entire walk, he barely said two words to me, and it was because of the dress I had on. His hand was on mine and tugged me in the direction we were heading. We were almost the same height now that I was wearing a pair of black heels that looked like they could poke holes through someone's foot if I stepped on them accidentally.

The dress was a shock to fit into. Jessie had picked out a winner, and I was to go out embarrassed at first. I begged her to choose something a little less revealing, but she insisted that this was the one. It was just covering my ass.

When Brody had taken one look, his eyes widened, and he told me to take it off.

Hence, he was ignoring me and in a shitty mood. I didn't take it off.

"I'll go get us a table," he muttered and began walking off.

Leaving me alone in the bar, I was ready to turn around and walk out. Was it that hard for him to take me out on a date and make me feel sexy for once? He was in a navy suit, looking absolutely gorgeous. I wanted to feel worthy enough to stand by his side. Did he not see that all I wanted was to fit in and be like the women he worked with every day?

I wanted to dress up. I can't even remember the last time that I was able to wear heels, to wear a dress above my thighs or even have my hair curled. It was all so new, and I felt young and happy. Him angry wasn't helping my confidence.

All I felt right now was ridiculous and embarrassed.

Deciding that I no longer wanted to be standing around like a fool. I walked towards the bar and took a seat on a stool. Ordering a drink, I felt a presence behind me and assumed it was Brody. Until he sat beside me, I realised it wasn't my husband at all.

"If you were my wife, I wouldn't have left you alone for a second," the man, looking in his mid-forties, smiled. I couldn't say he was hideous. He was very handsome. He also wasn't Brody; therefore, I wasn't even remotely attracted to him.

"Is that some pickup line to see if I'm married?" I asked, a smile appearing as I took my drink from the bartender. "Because, I am."

The man smiled again and laughed. "I figured you would be. Can't be too sure."

"Can't be too sure about what?" Brody's smooth voice entered our conversation as he placed his arm possessively around my waist. The grip was hard and hurting.

Smiling or trying to keep my smile, I answered, "Just that I am married."

"Of course, you're married. I'd be a fool to not marry you," Brody replied, a look of annoyance in his eyes.

The gentleman beside me grinned. "Lucky man," he then stood up and walked away. "Have a lovely evening."

If I thought Brody's mood couldn't get any worse, I was wrong. Pissed was an understatement. He said not another word as we walked out onto the terrace that overlooked the gorgeous Hamilton Island water. It was stunning tonight.

"Why are you in such a bad mood?" I asked him with a sigh after our main course was brought.

He looked up and shrugged. "I'm not."

"Brody, that's a blatant lie. You're pissed off. You have been since I came out in this dress," I accused quietly.

The phone beside him began to vibrate for the fifth time tonight, and I was getting sick of it. Before he was able to set his fork down, I reached over and snatched it with my hand. The vibrating in my hand stopped.

"Who's calling?" I asked, noticing the number wasn't saved in his phone. A voicemail message came through, and I dialled 101.

"Leave it, probably just work," he said, trying to take the phone back.

I pulled it to towards my ear and listened to whoever was calling. All I could do was give him a disappointed look as I heard her drunk giggling voice between words.

"Brody... um, I kind of need you to come get me... I'm so drunk and horny... I know you're married but... oh, God, I'm going to throw up..."

I just looked at the screen as I deleted the call. I calmly began searching his call logs and found that she'd been calling him all hours of the night and day. He hadn't said a word to me about this, and I had no clue if he had been speaking to her while I wasn't around or when I was asleep.

"It's not..." I shot him a glare. "All right, I can't do anything about it while I am here. I will handle her once I am back in the office."

"Do you want to fuck her?" I asked, point blank.

"Jesus, keep your voice down, will you?" he growled back. "No, of course, I don't."

I thought about calling her back and having him tell her that. I put the phone in my purse and closed it. "I want to go home."

"All right, I'll get the check." He went to wave his hand towards a waiter, but I grabbed his wrist gently and lowered it down.

"No, Brody, I want to leave this place. I don't want to be here anymore." I needed to make that clear. "It's beginning to turn into fighting every day. After Rose and Scott, I just don't want to be here anymore."

"What about Scott?" he asked, then frowned. "The kids love it here. It's not fair on them to just up and leave. Rose is the one who needs to leave."

"Why didn't you tell me about these phone calls?" I asked, not angry but curious. "We were meant to be open and honest with each other more."

"I didn't want to upset you. I haven't spoken to her. I ignored the calls, Gabby." Taking a moment for my words to sink in, he shook his head. "No, we're not leaving because you're pissed about some phone call. I told you that I would sort it out."

"Well, why would I want to be here? It's plain and simple. When we're alone, we just can't get along. It's been great. But for us to go out and eat somewhere, it just doesn't work," I said quietly. Maybe we were just wrapped up in trying so hard or faking it so much that we hadn't noticed we were faking it. "I want to go, get out of these obviously hideous clothes and just go to bed."

"You don't look hideous, Gabby," he said softly. "Quite the opposite."

With a shrug, I mostly spoke to myself, "You haven't told me I looked pretty all night, Brody. I feel like you prefer it when I'm weak and self-conscious in public. You like everyone to look at you and then wonder why I think someone as attractive as you would be with someone like me. I think you hate that you finally see that I'm desirable to other men? Or is that impossible too?"

"Watch your words," he gritted out low. "I'm sitting over here with a stiff cock that hasn't gone down since we left our room. I'm angry as fuck because you're so beautiful, and I almost let you go. To top it off, the way you smiled earlier at another man, I haven't seen that smile on you in years." Clenching his jaw, he shook his head. "So yeah, I'm pretty fucking mad, not at you but myself."

"I was just being polite, Brody. I wasn't flirting with him," I said softly. "He asked if I was married, and I said that I was."

"You're not for someone else to look at. You are mine, Gabriella. I won't sit smiling as another man buys you another drink in front of me," he warns lowly.

Shaking my head, smiling but I was annoyed. "You ate lunch with another woman. I don't think you have the right to say anything on the matter. Oh, and you brought me that drink as you'll see when the bill comes."

"You are my wife," he ground out.

"Yes, I am. But you are also my husband, and if you don't want me with another man, you better get it through your head that you're off limits also. She has your personal number. How am I to know what's going on there?"

"You need to not worry about her. It's not like I went to a bar, got drunk, then went and fucked her."

His words hurt. The pain in my chest, I was beyond upset. "That's disgusting, Brody. I can't even..." I stopped myself from saying any more. Tonight wasn't going how I had envisioned it to be. It was going badly.

Smirking, he leant back in his chair and picked up the glass of whisky. Bringing it to his lips, he paused. "You need to realise one thing," he said with a grim smile. "You belong to me."

"Belong? I'm not a piece of property, Brody," I murmured, running a fingertip over the rim of the martini glass. "You think that just because I belong to you that I will not talk to another man? I've never told you to stay away from other women."

"It's always been implied," he said, then took a mouthful. "You sure that rule still stands after everything that happened with Kate?"

I shook my head. He was pushing me on purpose to get a response even her name made me want to scream. He was going to know one thing, and I wasn't kidding around. "You touch her, and I will walk out with our children. I will take everything you own and make you regret it."

"We have an agreement. You belong to me." Before I protest, he raised a finger up. "And I belong to you."

"I need to…" I smiled, upset but wouldn't let him know how much this conversation was starting to hurt me. Placing my napkin on the table, I looked away from him. "Excuse me."

I caught the confusion, "Gabby," he said quietly. "I didn't mean to upset you."

"Fuck you." Giving him his phone back, I shoved it against his chest. "Well, you have. I was looking forward to tonight. Maybe I wanted you to look at me and rip my dress off but obviously not." I bit my lip. "You can be such an ass when you drink, sometimes," I muttered softly.

Standing up before he could object, I rushed towards the ladies' room and thankfully, it was empty. Blowing out a deep breath, I fanned my face and tried to keep the tears from escaping and ruining my makeup. I just needed a moment to myself.

This woman was going to get a rude wake-up call when I got back to the city.

Startled when the door opened, I glanced up through the mirror. I went to apologise until I saw Brody walking in and closed the door behind himself, twisting the silver lock between his thumb and forefinger.

"You can't be in here," I said, trying to make myself sound normal. "I won't be long."

He looked up, his navy suit jacket slowly being shrugged off and tossed on the counter top beside me. The look of hunger and starvation was apparent in his eyes, as he stood tall behind me. I notice him loosening his tie and then beginning to unbutton his crisp white shirt.

A hand on my hips, he shuffled himself even closer. Pressed against my bottom, I felt the thickness pushing into me. His other hand, at the small of my waist, slowly felt its way up my spine and explored my body, inch by inch travelling up the curve of my hip towards my breast. He stopped for a moment. He brushed all my hair to one side and then resumed his delicate touching. He slid his hand down and around the front of my dress, directing into the open material and gropes me with a firm cup of my breast.

A groan escaped his throat as his lips skim the bare skin on the nape of my neck. With his tender kisses, my nipples were erect even more into his soft palm. The touching turned rushed and forceful as he pulls the top down, letting my breasts out. Nipping at my skin, he then bent me forward with a forceful push and bunches my dress up at the hem. My ass was exposed to him as he pulled the black lace until they rip.

Shoving my scrunched up panties into his pocket, he met my eyes in the mirror and mouthed three little words, "I love you."

He pushed my thighs even more apart with his knees, nudging them open with his body, fingers raking my inner thighs, clawing at my soft skin, and he thrusts in deeply. Grasping my hips desperately, he dug his fingers in and not letting me go as I keep forward. Anticipation thrilled me as I drench in fear yet excitement at being caught as Brody began to increase his pace too hard.

Fucking me... Taking me... Using me...

Owning me

CHAPTER NINETEEN

"You need to apologise right now."

My eyes looked upwards to see whom Brody was talking to. I had a mouthful, almost choking on my lettuce as the waitress was blushing a beet red. Oh, no, my husband's tone was pissed.

"I..." the poor girl stuttered. "I'm sorry."

Brody then directed his eyes to me and pointed his finger towards me. "Apologise to my wife, not to me but her." By now, he had caught the attention of everyone else at our table. By everyone, I mean myself and our children and also a couple of diners near us.

What on earth was going on?

"I... I'm sorry. I didn't mean to."

Brody scoffed and handed a white piece of paper back to her. "You think by writing your number on the tab that I would call you? You can tell your manager that I'm not paying for lunch. The service is disgusting. I'm out with my wife and children, and you do something so idiotic? No, I refuse to give you anything."

She nodded and scurried along. Bursting into tears, she ran through the doors of the kitchen. I sat there confused by what had just happened, but I was also in awe of him and how he had done that, considering that I had been too preoccupied cutting up Lila's piece of chicken to notice her giving my husband her number.

"Brody," I began. I didn't know what to say.

He reached over and kissed my cheek. "You need to see. That's it's only you, no one else, just you."

A soft smile met him as I leant forwards and kissed him back. "Thank you." Pulling away, I had another question. "Does that often happen when you're out with clients?"

"I honestly don't pay attention. If there's a number there, then I ignore it and hand the check back to them. What about you? Do you not notice the men salivating over you?" He smirked, gesturing toward the men at the bar.

I hadn't even noticed. Wow, I don't notice much. "I don't know. I rarely go anywhere other than the school or supermarket." I leant in again and kissed him. "If you feel like picking up a girl at a bar, then I'm up for some role play."

"Kinky little thing you are. Who knew?" He kissed me. "I'd rather pick you up right now!"

"No need to pick me up especially when you've already got me," I smiled once more and met his lips again for another sweet kiss.

"Ew, please stop kissing! It's gross, and you're embarrassing us." Noah groaned as he shoved a spoon of ice cream into his mouth.

Brody laughed. Just to annoy Noah, he leant in and gave me a bigger smack on the lips with his mouth. "He says that now," he said into the kiss and pulled away. "Are you both enjoying the food?"

Both kids gave their dad a thumbs up, and I sat back with a smile. "I think we've got the best kids ever, so well behaved and not fighting at all. Hopefully, they're this good back home."

Brody nodded in agreement, giving my thumb a squeeze as he kept his voice low. "I think it's mostly because we're not fighting. They're happy because we're happier than usual."

Smiling sadly, he was spot on. "I know. I want to keep it this way."

We left the restaurant, and true to Brody's word, he refused to pay a cent for the meal. The waitress was then blasted in front of us. I felt awful, but at the same time, it was her own fault. Walking the kids back to the beach house, I stopped Brody on the way.

Giving me an odd look of confusion, "Yes?"

I grinned, placing the palms of my hands against his chest. "Go change into something warm and meet us down with your parents. I have something for you."

"What are you up to?" he asked curiously.

Shaking my head from side to side, "Oh, no, you don't. It's a secret, baby. Go change."

I helped the kids get into their swimmers so they could have one last swim with grandpa before bedtime. I then walked into the kitchen; ignoring Rose's burning glares. His mum had done as I asked her to do and helped me with a large picnic basket full of seafood; fresh fruit and wine which were already down on the beach waiting for us.

"Thank you again for this," I said smiling as I hugged her. "I hope he'll like it."

She hugged me back and kissed my cheek. "Don't you worry about that? He's going to love it. I know my son loves being romanced every now and then."

I giggled softly. She was right. I used to do things like this all the time and was going to start that again. I heard the back door open and pulled away from her. "Brody, you ready?"

"What are you up to?" he asked, wrapping his arms around my waist and kissing my forehead. "I thought we were going to have an early night, and you know."

"Brody, you better not be crude!" Loraine scolded, popping her head around the corner. "I raised you better than that."

"Ma, seriously?" he groaned. "Stop eavesdropping and go take a nap or something old people do."

With the look on her face, safe to say, we left extremely quickly after he said that to her. Of course, he was only kidding around, and she knew that. Making our way down towards the beach, I spotted where we were spending the evening alone.

Pointing towards it, I watched as he took it all in. "Really, babe?"

"Yeah," I smiled.

"Now, this looks like a lot of fun!" he winked, giving my bum a pat as he walked ahead and inspected it closer.

The teepee was gorgeous, just like the brochure I had looked at yesterday, but it was better in real life, cushions galore lanterns pegged into the sand, cuddled up with the throw rugs and watch the ocean as we ate our dinner.

Climbing in after him, he stretched out and grinned. "We, sleeping out here?"

"Would you like to spend the night? Either that or we can go back to our suite," I smiled, taking off my sandals and wiggling my toes, only to be pulled and rolled on top of the man's body beside me.

With a giggle, he squeezed me tightly. "I like the way you think." Lifting his head, he kissed me and pulled back, resting his head against the cushions. "It's going to be a perfect night, baby."

Better than the previous one where we had fought during dinner and screwed in the bathroom for dessert, Brody mouthing those three words, I couldn't bring it up. I didn't want to because the fantasy of what I wanted him to say could have just been him mouthing something else and my mind thinking it was I love you.

Getting back on my side of the cushion, I ran my finger over the teal fabric. "You know, last night was our first dinner alone in seven years."

As his eyes met mine, I noticed his smile fading fast. "I know. Last night, well, it wasn't a very good date. Tonight will be better, and I promise to have dinner alone with you more."

"I look forward to 'us' time." Lifting my leg over his, I felt like a teenager again, only to be pulled back on Brody's lap like sitting together at lunch time, me on his lap as we sat outside with our friends.

Grabbing the picnic basket, Brody leant forward and took an inhale of the food. "This smells like mum's cooking," he grinned, kissing my cheek. "I wonder what you have in here."

I shrugged, pretending that I had no clue. "Hmmm, you'll have to tell me."

He pulled out the sushi first and a look of surprised crossed him. "Gabby, do you even like this?"

Smiling as I took the roll from his hand, "I'll soon find out, but you said you did. I wanted you to know that I listen to things, Brody, and if you like something, then I want to be able to eat it with you."

Long live the sushi rolls tossed into his office bin. Part of me wished that I had shoved them somewhere under Kate's desk so they'd be rotting away for her to never find, only to smell.

Pushing the food towards his mouth, he opened up and took a bite. Moaning, he grinned, "Hmmm, so good. Your turn, open up, beautiful."

I shook my head to object, but he had taken the sushi and put a piece into my mouth for me to try. It wasn't the best thing I had eaten, but like sucking him off, I'd get used to it. Kidding, I loved doing that to him.

Finishing the food in my mouth, I leant in with a whisper, "You're turning me on." Who knew feeding someone could be so erotic?

His mouth met mine. "That's the point."

Kissing me harder, he laid me down on the soft cloud of pillows and began stripping my body naked. Once we were both fully undressed, his hands held my hips as he pulled me on top of him. He was so ready.

I began to kiss down his chest. My tongue left a wet trail as I teased his nipples, biting lightly and then working my way down further. There was no need to rush this. We had all night. He needed to know, just how loved he was.

Wrapping my hand around his length, I began I gently stroke. His moans were growing as my tongue stuck out and swirled around his silky head, sucking and licking in the drops of pre-cum that began to leak out.

"My God... Gabby." He moaned, my eyes darted up to find him looking at me with hunger.

Growing harder in my hand, I began to continue my assault on him, teasing and bringing him a bliss of satisfaction until he was grabbing my head and thrusting his deep spurts down my throat with a guttural groan.

Panting, he had me on my back and his tongue on me. My God, his mouth was kissing all over my body, up to my inner thighs and stopped against my bud. "Damn, you smell intoxicating," he grunted as his tongue began flicking back and forth before increasing his pace.

My body bucked underneath him, grinding my hips up into his face as I rocked back and forth. "Don't stop," I begged, fisting whatever I could get my hands on. "Shit." Another moan as I neared, "Brody... Oh, yes!" I screamed as came. I whimpered as I exploded into his mouth when his tongue buried deep inside of me. Thrusting in and out, my orgasm heightened, and I was pulling his hair, pushing him away but also bringing him in closer.

He was on his knees and hands underneath my ass, squeezing as I kept coming. I was begging him to fuck me.

His mouth moved from my neck to collarbone as he slid in deeply. Staring with deep and slow thrusts, he couldn't hold back. He was pounding me, holding my legs and grasping my thighs as he rocked back and forth. Pulling me on top of him, he fell to his back. My fingers dug into his chest, setting the pace as I rode him hard.

His brows dipped down low, frowning almost as he stared into my eyes. "You like it like that?" I growled out.

A slap on my ass, his hands grasped my flesh and helped me move up and down his slick cock faster. "You know, I do."

Moaning, I almost came. He grinned and let my breast free from his grasp. With a coy smile, I slid off him and turned around. Sitting on him reverse, I laid my back against his chest, and he pushed in. His hands wrapped around my thighs, almost pulling me backwards as he began to pound in and out deeply.

"I'm going to blow. Shit!" he grunted, trying to slow.

"No, rub me," I moaned, grinding down into him.

His hand traced down one thigh, and I held it up as he gave a pulsing slap of his hand to my clitoris. Sending me over the edge for a final time, he blew deep inside of me. My legs were shaking as I tried to catch my breath.

I didn't want to move, and I don't think he had the energy to, either. I laid there, smiling with a soft laugh. "Do you remember the first time we slept together? I still think your mum knew what we were doing up in your room that day."

The vibrations of his chest tickled my body as he laughed. "Everyone knew what we were up to! God, after you left the next morning at breakfast, all mum did was glare. Dad was smirking, and Scott was wiggling his damn brows while Jessie ignored me. Those looks said it all." He brushed a piece of my hair away and kissed my bare shoulder. "I was so nervous that day, but I'm getting better, yeah?"

"I had no idea that they knew. It wasn't like we didn't know each other, though. I'm just glad your music was on to block out our awkwardness and thank God, you didn't move to the pace of AD/DC," I smiled and tilted my head to see him better. "You've always been good, just now, things are really good. We have some pretty amazing sex."

Smiling back, he nodded. "I have never hated having sex with you, Gabby, but yeah, let's keep having some amazing sex."

Moving, he laid on top of me and kissed me passionately. Our bodies were sweaty and in need of a shower. I really hoped that no one had decided to take a stroll along the beach. Otherwise, they'd have gotten quite a show from us.

Pulling away, only for a moment, he skimmed his lips to mine and ran his fingers down the curve of my breast. "I'm really sorry for the past years."

Reaching between us, I began stroking him hard again. "Me too, I took so much out on you, and it wasn't fair."

"I can take the blame. I deserved it. You were never treated with respect." He began to kiss me again, groaning as he kept getting harder. "I want you bent over, baby."

I grinned, kneeling forwards on all fours as he teased me. "I hope no one is outside."

"If they are, then they'll be getting a free show." He then slapped my ass again harder. "Oh, God, I love your ass," he said as he entered me and began a delicious pace.

Moaning, my eyes flew open as I felt his thumb somewhere it had never ever wandered to before. "Wha—?" I squeaked, buckling forwards. As much as I wanted to hate it, I damn well couldn't. It not only made everything feel so much more intense, but I came so hard that Brody had to hold me into him before I fell forward completely.

With a final thrust, he came and pounded faster. "Oh God, that was so hot. Did... you enjoy it?" His final words came out very hesitant and wary.

I couldn't speak right away. I just nodded, laying on my stomach until my legs finally stopped trembling. "It was intense. What made you do that?"

I caught his smirk. "I don't know. Just wanted to see your reaction and thought maybe down the road we could try anal if you're okay with it."

How the hell could he ask me that so calmly? I never had once thought or wanted to try that. I didn't want to make him feel embarrassed for bringing it up, so I just smiled. "Uh, let's stick to the finger first, then talk more about the other thing when we're home." There would be no anal. "But, that was incredible."

He laughed, "Fair enough. If I do something that you don't like, then you tell me, right?" I could see he was trying so hard not to screw this up.

I nodded, rolling to my back and grazing my hand up his thigh. "Of course, and you do the same too."

We took a naked swim in the ocean, ate most of the food, and both of us got drunk by swigging out the wine bottle. Our bodies became reconnected with each other as we acted like two horny teenagers who only had one night to spend together. It felt so real, and I could feel us connecting ever more. Our bond was growing stronger.

The next morning, the water woke me up, and the smell of sea salt only brought a smile to my face as I lay, curled against Brody's side and his strong, tanned arms wrapped around me.

A soft whisper escaped his throat, and I heard it perfectly this time. "I love you."

"I love you. I love these mornings with you, just us and in your arms." Everything about it was perfect.

He sleepily opened his eyes and kissed my nose. His voice laced with sleep. "We need to get back to the kids. Speaking of which, when are you going to stop your pill?"

"Soon-ish," I said, luckily my voice was low and husky from sleep because he would have been able to tell I was literally shitting myself over that question.

It hadn't even occurred to me or let alone clicked into my mind until now. I finally figured out what I didn't pack. That with all the sex we were having, I hadn't taken my pill this entire trip.

CHAPTER TWENTY

We walked into the kitchen where the family just happened to all be. Brody first got over to the kids as they sat up eating a massive plate of bacon, eggs and pancakes. They get so spoilt by their grandparents. I couldn't help but notice Tulip eating scrambled egg whites. That poor child.

"Nice evening." Scott's smooth voice came up behind me. I nodded, almost paling.

"It was, thanks." The kids luckily had come at me for hugs, so I moved closer to them and away from him.

"Perfect evening," Brody corrected, smiling as he took a seat. "Food looks good, mum."

"Are you saying it doesn't normally?" Loraine raised a brow as she kissed the top of her son's head, setting a plate of eggs, bacon, pancakes and fruit down in front of him. "Eat up.

I'm sure you need fuel after, hopefully, making me another grandbaby last night."

Oh, my God, the look on Brody's face was priceless.

He laughed after a moment while my face was still red from embarrassment.

"From what it sounds like, they've been working on that since getting here," Scott chimed in, taking the seat opposite Brody at the large outdoor dining table.

He was getting on my nerves. Sitting down on Brody's lap, his hands immediately snaked around my waist, placing a kiss to my shoulder blade.

"I am a little worried that you're a Peeping Tom, though, been standing at our door with your ear pressed against it or hiding in the bushes with your hand down your pants?" I said the last part low enough so Loraine or Fred would not hear, not that they could with Brody and Jessie's hysterical laughter that followed.

Scott's eyes narrowed, not amused one bit. "Why the hell would I want to listen to my brother lasting less than ten seconds?"

"He doesn't, so maybe you can ask him for some tips if you're in need of them, probably help your bad mood," I winked, enjoying that I was pissing him off.

"I swear you, two, fight more like brother and sister than he and I fight like brother and brother," Brody pointed out.

"Maybe because you've barely been around with all your working," Scott spat back underneath his breath. "For anyone of us."

I felt Brody tense against my body, and I slowly slid into the chair beside him. He sighed and shook his head.

"That's not fair, and you know it. I neglected certain people, but I was still around."

"Daddy never eats breakfast with us. Mama gets really, really angry, and she, one time, threw the bowl of food at the wall." Lila giggled. "It's cause daddy has a whore."

Christ, the kids heard everything. Lesson well and truly learnt.

Brody's head snapped up faster than an elastic band. "You said that? In front of them?" He wasn't yelling, but his tone was urgent and upset. "I can't believe you really thought that I had someone on the side. All I damn had time for was work."

Cringing as I kept my voice down, luckily, his parents were outside on the deck. Unfortunately, his brother was still opposite us. "I… How was I meant to know she was listening? I was mad, and you were rushing off. I'm sorry, but I was upset, and you had just accused me of screwing the neighbour."

Brody shook his head. "He was looking at you all the time. He still does."

"Doesn't mean I was on my back for him," I said back to him through gritted teeth. "You made it sound like I was the neighbourhood tramp."

Scott snickered, and Brody shot him a heated glare. "Fuck off."

"Never said a word." Scott grinned back, taking a sip of hot coffee.

I took the hint to leave. It had immediately become awkward, and the way Brody was now, chewing his food, put me off being near him. Pushing myself up from the table. I looked over at the kids. "You two come get dressed."

"But we're still eating," Noah whined. "I haven't finished my drink."

Lila nodded. "We're going to the beach. Grandma said we can build sandcastles."

"Sit and eat," Brody sighed. "You haven't had breakfast."

"I'm not hungry, and I refuse to sit beside you when you're eating your food like an animal," I muttered and walked off.

I couldn't sit there across from Scott and listen to him snickering about our problems. He'd be getting off at the thought, loving the fact that his mother's favourite son wasn't doing so well at home with his wife.

His presence was behind me, and I tried to avoid him for as long as I could while doing a load of the kid's laundry. Cleaning wasn't taking anything off my mind at all. Everything just seemed to be building up.

Us fighting, the kids, no birth control, Scott — I was going to snap and lose it soon.

Turning around after I closed the front loader door. I slumped against the machine. "I'm sorry. I know that I shouldn't have said what I said about another woman in front of the kids. I didn't know she was there."

Brody sighed, walking in the laundry and closing the door. "Do you want us to work?"

Looking into his eyes, I nodded. "Yes, I do."

"Gabby, we're going to fight. But we can't run after every one of them. I'm just shocked she said that, but I will get over it. Don't ever think you're the one in the wrong because we're in this mess because of me."

"Do you really think a baby would be good for us now?" I did want another, but I was completely terrified it would be too much of a strain on our relationship.

He sighed again and pushed me against the machine. "If you don't want another, then I am okay with that. But we don't have much more time." Kissing my forehead tenderly, "I don't like seeing you upset, but we need to sit the kids down and talk to them. They need to know."

Slightly confused, I pulled away. "What do you mean we don't have much more time?"

He laughed, a grin breaking out over his handsome face. "We are getting older, baby."

Old — I hated that word. "We aren't even thirty, yet. You may be older, but I am not," I said looking at his chest. My gaze drifted lower, and with a sudden yank, his sweats and boxers were down around his thighs.

He stood there, smirking. "The door isn't locked, baby."

"Real quick," I smiled, kissing and nipping at his jaw as I pulled my own shorts down.

He stopped me, grasped my arms tightly and lifted me up onto the washing machine. Sliding my panties to the side, he entered me swiftly and kissed me hungrily. "Real quick, that's something I can do."

I tried not to giggle at his joke about never lasting long before. I loved how long he lasted, obviously not before. But now, it was good timing, and I didn't care if I got off or not. I just wanted him buried deep inside of me, feeling him take me roughly.

"Give it to me hard," I moaned, wrapping my thighs around his hips and leaning back.

The vibrations of the machine were something new, definitely pleasurable as it brought my orgasm closer. The bouncing had me moaning into the crook of his neck, biting down to muffle my moans as I began to come. I was clinging to him and clawing his bare arms when the door pushed open, and then I was clawing for another reason.

Scott stood there, staring directly at me.

Expecting Brody to yell, he turned his head slightly and nodded at the door. His cock pulsing inside of me as he held me in place, covering my body with his and reaching to slam the door. "You mind? Not finished yet."

The door slammed, and I didn't know whether to laugh or cry. I was horrified. "I haven't taken the pill since we came here," I blurted out instead.

He stilled inside of me and looked down. "You fell pregnant on the pill with Noah. I think you're going to leave here pregnant," he said and gave my thigh a smack as he started his pacing back up. "Such a bad, naughty girl. But fuck, I love you."

I stayed in the laundry room, finishing up with what I had been doing in the first place. With a stupid grin on my face, I stared out the window dazed and somewhat giddy. We were having a lot of sex, crazy and spur of the moment. He was driving me insane. I just wanted to grab him and rip his clothes off as often as possible. With the wet linen in the basket, I left to hang them out while Brody had gone to shower.

As I was pegging the last shirt, Brody walked up behind me and gave my ass a slap.

"Why didn't you stop when he walked in?"

"I was so close. Be fucked if I stopped." He tapped my nose as I turned around. His hair was still damp and brushed over, and he was shirtless. How was I meant to control myself when he looked like this? "Now, talking about surprises, let's talk about that thing you did with your mouth after I blew."

Blushing, I took off, up the path, and he chased after me. Laughing the entire way to our room, I left Brody down at the beach and went down to the main house again. This time, I took the light sun dress off as I lay out and tanned with Rose and Jessie. I wanted to work on my tan, and if they were in bikinis, then there was no way I should be ashamed of the way I looked. Brody made me feel beautiful, and I didn't want to be afraid any longer.

"You and Brody seem to be taking a lot of parent time together. I am exhausted just by watching how often you're sneaking off," Jessie smirked, glancing at me over her thick black sunglasses.

I smiled. "He's not working. It's really nice having him around again."

Loraine walked over, handing us girls a cocktail, a special homemade mix, which often had people drunk by the second glass. I only stuck to one. Loving the heat against my skin, I laid back and listened to them talking about a girl's night out, which we were all in for.

Lila and Noah took a shower after their swim, and I found myself back on the floor cleaning up the wet clothes thrown around the room as well as the fresh laundry that was also tossed about. Brody walked in, sat down on the bed and folded a pair of Noah's boxers back up. "Scott just told me something very interesting."

My heart stopped, almost. "Oh?" I asked, thinking shit he knew.

"Rose has been cheating on him. He hasn't told mum or dad, but he's going to move out once we're home again."

Whoa, I hadn't expected that at all.

"Oh," I said quietly. "Why is she here then?" I mean, I hated that he was cheated on, but he wasn't exactly innocent in things either.

"Free trip, she wants the money, and that's it." Brody picked up a shirt and went to hang it up. "I guess they had a field day at breakfast after what Lila said. I also made it very clear to mum that neither of us, have and would never cheat."

"No, we wouldn't," I smiled. "I can't even look at another man that way."

Pulling me to him as I stood up, he tucked a strand of my hair behind my ear. "I know, and I wouldn't do that to you either. Rose, however, does hate you. I don't understand why. Guess, she's just jealous."

"How did he find out about her?" I asked, quietly.

Shaking his head, "Tulip told him that mummy was wrestling with a man naked in bed. When he came home sick, he walked in and found them fucking the day before we left for the trip. He's pissed, and I guess she's not really giving a shit what he thinks. It's been going on for almost a year he said. She's still with the guy."

That was harsh. I felt bad for him, only a little bad.

"I want two more babies."

His eyes opened wider. "Two? I was thinking one, but two would be great," he smiled. "We'll try for two."

"If we had one, then that would need a little friend to play with," I smiled. "Oh, and all our lovemaking is making your sister tired."

Brody grinned. "Yeah, Scott said with all the sex we're having, he can't see how either of us has time to cheat." Of course, he'd say that.

"You know, your mother is expecting us to give her some exciting news at Christmas time," I said, wiggling my brows. I didn't think we'd be pregnant in a few months' time. But, we'd just have to wait and see.

"Lila may be getting her birthday wish after all," Brody groaned. "She's going to be eight. Damn, time has flown by. It feels like yesterday you were pregnant and carrying Noah around on your hip."

"That's what I got for telling you I wanted another baby six months after he was born," I laughed. "I was so clucky and sad that he was growing up too fast."

He was going to get sentimental on me. "You were beautiful pregnant. All right, before I start to feel really old, let's get these kids to the waterfall."

The kids, unfortunately, invited Scott who had been drinking too many of Loraine's cocktails, and Tulip just wanted to colour in. Rose was passed out on the couch, and Brody's parents had taken an afternoon nap. None of us wanted to go near that bedroom, as we were sure nap meant afternoon delight. Jessie and Leon were going windsurfing, well, Leon was. Jessie was getting her tan on as she watched.

"Come on, I want to go," I called out as Lila went to find her sandals.

"Hang on, mama!" she bellowed back.

I slumped the beach bag on the kitchen table and went to help her when I hear Brody and Scott in a heated argument. Hiding behind the door, I listened in like any curious and normal person would do.

"You need to stop it. Don't make me warn you again," Brody snarled low. I watched him giving Scott a slight push through the crease of the door. My mind ran a thousand possible scenarios of what had happened to make them argue like this.

"What?" Scott smirked. "Who knew that underneath those clothes was a tight body like that? You may have married her, but you've neglected her for years. As far as I can tell, it's game on. Sorry, little bro, but she's up for grabs after that fight during breakfast."

A laugh escaped Brody's throat. "Scott, we're having another baby. She is mine, my wife. Fuck off and find someone else."

"Pregnant and drinking? Nice try, you may want her knocked up, but it's only so she's stuck with you. She won't be able to leave if she has a reason to stay. You're both trying to work things out." He smirked. "Who do you think was around when you weren't? You took her for granted, and I'll be there to pick the pieces up after this trip is over."

Fuck, Scott was starting shit up that didn't need to be brought up here.

"If you're fucking serious, you better fuck off now." I watched as Brody stepped closer, grabbing his brother by the throat with his hand as he slammed his back against the wall. "Let me tell you something, bro! It's not just me. She wants it just as bad, and you better believe that she isn't going anywhere but with me," He snarled low, giving his body another shove before letting him go. "You're sick in the head if you think it's all right to make a move on your brother's wife."

Quietly rushing back into the kitchen, I looked up when Brody walked in, completely pissed. His face was murderous, and I didn't blame him.

"Brody," I began. Oh, shit, I was a bundle of nerves. "I have to tell you something."

His eyes glowered on mine as he walked towards me. "Pantry now!"

CHAPTER TWENTY-ONE

My cheeks flushed pink, breathing ragged and legs jelly like.

I blushed hard as Brody and I stumbled out of the pantry. Doing my hair up while Brody fixed his shorts, I noticed his shirt on backwards, inside out. Trying a fake cough, nodding and making eyes at the tag, it clicked, and he went back into the pantry to fix himself up.

God, could we have been any more obvious?

Fred startled me as I looked up to see him, sitting at the table with an empty cup. "Gabriella, enjoying the holiday?"

"I am."

"Great to hear. So, what have you been doing besides my son?"

Oh, God, I was definitely blushing now. He just heard us having wild, angry and possessive sex.

"Um, you know, swimming, tanning, and exploring the island." I tried my best to keep calm, ignoring his teasing smile and remarks about the constant shagging.

Fred laughed, standing up with his mug. "Now, I can finally make coffee." He eyed Brody who came back out again, making his own drink. "Your mother is eager for a grandchild."

"She has three already," Brody pointed out.

"Very well, I hope you cleaned up whatever was dropped in there, and son…" Leaning in closer, his voice gruff, "That's no way to speak to the mother of your children."

Oh, good Lord, I turned around, absolutely mortified as I buried my face into my palms.

Brody pulled me into the pantry. His only intention was to fuck me. I wanted to talk about what had happened out there with Scott. He refused to listen and wanted to vent through sex. There were things I needed to come clean and explained. I was told to shut up, get on my knees and suck it. "Bend over. I'm going to shatter your pelvis by the time I'm finished…" and last but not least, "Come with me, now!"

As my nether regions ached from the constant pounding, my heart, too, ached with guilt.

We were back to where we used to be, and I was going to make sure I worked hard to keep us feeling like this. I didn't want to go home and be strangers living together again. I wanted to feel loved and make him feel loved. We were falling back into a deep love we once shared, and I didn't want this feeling of happiness to disappear again.

Looking back at Brody, I smiled. We needed to talk, but he just didn't want to.

With a kiss, he walked away and over to Jessie who was eating a platter of fruit. I could hear parts of their conversation without even trying to listen. Brody's father too, he wasn't showing it as he kept talking about his boat back home and wanting to go out on a fishing trip later this afternoon.

Making my way outside, Brody smiled, kept talking, and then the subject changed. "Has Scott said anything to you about Gabby?"

"Not really, I mean he mentioned how good she's looking after losing weight, which you know—" Jessie glanced over at me. "You didn't need to do. You were gorgeous before. Anyway, he just goes on about what a good mother she is. Why? Afraid they're going to run off into the sunset and turn lovers?"

If only she had heard their last conversation…

Brody looked at her. "I'm not jealous!" he defended, a little too hasty. "Gabby has always looked beautiful, anyway." With a sigh, he put his head in his hands. "He's really fucking with my head. He said he's going to come in and pick up the pieces especially after this morning. I honestly think he wants her like really wants her." Brody looked up, and I could see he was worried. He didn't need to be. I was with him. Shaking his head angrily, he scoffed. "He damn well told me, 'Game on!'"

"Brody," I said, sitting beside him, reaching over and resting my hand on his thigh with a gentle squeeze. "Don't listen to him." He raised a brow, and I let it slip. "I overheard. He's a pig for what he said to you."

"Gabby is right. His own marriage is falling apart, and he thinks he can also come in and destroy yours. He's just messing with you," Jessie said and looked over towards me. "She loves you, and all she does is care for you and your children. You have nothing to worry about unless..." She pressed quietly. "Was things that bad?"

I was quiet as Brody nodded. His expression was solemn. "It was bad. We were in a bad place. All I did was work, and we were fighting so much that divorce seemed like the only option. Neither of us wants that."

"We don't." I squeezed his thigh. Divorce wasn't an option anymore.

Jessie smiled. "Well, I'm glad. Uh-oh, your competition is coming over. Let the games begin," she giggled, rolling her eyes.

"All right, I'm going to get the kids ready. They're waiting for us," I said, standing up.

Making my way past Scott, his hand reached out and took hold of my elbow and in front of Brody, leaned in. "You know you've got a beautiful smile. Shame the man you married doesn't make you smile that way."

"Scott, that's inappropriate," I was actually a bit fearful. He wasn't acting sane. Glancing towards Brody, I begged him with my eyes for him to come and help get his brother away from me.

Brody was immediately by my side. "Hey beautiful, you ready?" he asked and kissed my cheek. "Or do you want to go back into the pantry and make love again?"

Oh, he was edging his brother, and it was working. If only looks could kill...

"Make love? I thought it was a hard fuck." Giggling, I shook my head. "I want to go swimming like we planned on doing."

Scott winked. "Great, I'm ready, and Gabby, you better jump off a rock with me. Don't worry, I'll hold you."

"Get your fucking eyes off her. There's no way in hell your hands will be on her!" Brody was in his face, shoving him against the sliding door. "I'm serious. Stop this shit, or I will kick your fucking ass."

Scott held his hands up in defence. "Relax, baby bro, I'm just winding you up." He smirked. "You may be in this sick honeymoon phase again, but I guarantee she won't be around when she finds out about the hot secretary working late night with you." He glanced towards me as my heart began pounding hard. "Yeah, bet you didn't know that he's with her almost every night."

All colour drained from my face. "What?" I felt as if I'd been sucker punched.

"That's right. While you're at home with the kids, he's at work, eating dinner with her." Scott shoved Brody in the chest. "You want me to continue about everything else?" he threatened.

Brody's fist was pulled back and slammed into Scott's stomach with a swift punch. Scott groaned, bending forwards with a loud cough. I was frozen to the spot, unable to move as I had felt Jessie by my side and her hand in mine, pulling me down the side of the house. I wanted to stay. Someone should be breaking this up.

"Come on, let them sort this out," she whispered softly.

"Why is he doing this?" This made no sense. Rose and his daughter were both still here. Why would Scott do something right in front of her, in front of his whole family?

I looked over at Jessie as I shook my head. "I..." I damn well knew, and Brody needed to listen to me instead of using sex as an excuse for everything. I had things to say, and he wasn't hearing them. Shaking my head, I kept quiet and went to get the kids ready to take them for a swim. The last thing they needed was to see their father and uncle having it out by the pool.

Jessie didn't answer me. She instead tried distracting me by helping me with the kids.

Brody met Noah, Lila and me down at the waterfall. He didn't look the slightest bit injured until he was up close. A light bruise formed on his jaw line from copping a punch. He dove into the water and swam towards us. Noah was up, on his back not for long as Brody lifted him up, and dropped him in the water with a loud laugh.

The kids were looking at the colourful pebbles in the shallow part of the waterfall when Brody came up behind me. "Let's take them out tonight, just us and the kids."

"Yeah?" I asked, turning in his arms. "That would be nice." Dinner with him and the kids was perfect. Lifting my hand, I gently ran my fingers over his jaw, and he hissed softly. "Are you okay?"

"Let's not talk about him anymore. He and I are done for the rest of this trip," he spoke back, entire mood tense and angry. "I don't want you around him alone, Gabby. I mean it. Something isn't right with him, and I don't know what's going on. But, I will find out."

Nodding as I stood up and reached for a towel to dry off. "I know, baby. I know." There was more to this than he let on, and it was worrying me.

Glancing down at the menu, I sighed, as I had no idea what I wanted to eat. Being told by my two small children to hurry up and order was a little funny since it had usually been me to hurry them along. I would have ordered much quicker if Brody was here with us.

The moment Scott walked in with Tulip and took a seat at our table, I knew something was off. Brody never broke his promises, and if he promised to join us for dinner, then he would. We left him to take a business call back at the house, and I told him that I would just meet him in the restaurant. Everything was fine, going as planned. But, that was almost an hour ago, and the kids were getting antsy, not to mention Scott being a pain in my ass as he kept saying Brody was still on a phone call as he left. Rose had taken too many cocktails and was passed out the sofa, according to Tulip who wasn't the slightest bit fazed that her mother wasn't around.

Putting the menu back down, I shook my head. "I think we should go back to the house, just to make sure daddy hasn't gotten lost."

"He's a big boy, Gabby," Scott muttered underneath his breath. "You know what he's like when he's working. You honestly think that it's different now?"

"That was before," I ground out through clenched teeth. "You're causing trouble. Stop it."

He smirked, and I almost slapped him. "I'd never make you cry. This could be our family."

"You're my brother-in-law. That's all you'll be," I smiled, trying not to draw attention from the kids.

I felt a foot rubbing against mine underneath the table and stilled. "I still think about that night." The memories and panic set in. "It's always on my mind. You are always…"

"Don't!" I warned and stood up. "Noah, please hold Lila's hand. We're leaving."

"We haven't eaten!" She pouted. "I'm starving."

I didn't listen to her as I rushed out of there before I stabbed a steak knife into Scott's eyeballs. He was pushing it and bringing up shit that I'd rather forget. Almost nine years of not thinking about that night, and now, it was all coming back to my face. Brody needed to talk to me, and I was doing it as soon as I seen him. I don't care who's in the room. I have to tell him

"Where is Brody?" I asked.

"He's on the phone." Jessie frowned, looking concerned. "Why?"

"He was meant to meet us for dinner." I shook my head, rolling my eyes with a sigh. "Can you watch the kids, please?"

She nodded and immediately got up to make them a snack until I could sort their dinner out. I went downstairs and to our guest house. Nearing the door, I heard him speak on the phone. About to push open the door, I stopped when I heard Kate's name come from his mouth with an exasperating sigh.

"Kate, please," Brody muttered. "I'm on holidays."

Deciding I had had enough of this and her useless calls, I walked in. He immediately stood up and stared at me as he held the phone to his ear. I reached out and took it from him with a snatch. The phone against my ear, I could hear her breathy voice, asking him to leave his wife and come fuck her against his office window.

My rage consumed me. "This is Brody's wife. Fuck off and don't call him again!"

I hung up, almost throwing the phone across the room but instead, decided to be the prying wife and went through his texts. Her number at the top of the list with pictures of lingerie and detailed messaged on how she was going to rock his world.

"You have no idea what you've just done."

I looked up, surprised by how annoyed he sounded. Narrowing my eyes, I held the phone. "What the hell is this?"

"It means nothing. I haven't replied to her."

"For all I know!" I yelled, wanting to smash the phone. "She sends you her pussy, and you tell me I'm overreacting. Yet your brother makes a pass at me, and you tell me never to be alone with him!"

He took a step forward. I stepped back. "Gabby, there is nothing going on with her."

"You should have told her to stop!" My eyes were burning on the rim of tears as I put his phone down on the table. "You have no respect for me at all."

"I do."

"Bullshit. I believed you once before when you said lunch was a once off. I won't be so stupid this time. You should have reported her or told her to stop. You haven't, and that tells me so much, Brody." I sat on the edge of the bed, shaking my head. "You left the kids and me at dinner tonight. Scott showed up with Tulip."

"So you had dinner with him?" he scoffed, "And you have the nerve to fucking get pissy at me."

I looked at him, hurt that he could turn things around so quickly. "I can't believe you."

"Dinner!" Lorraine called out from outside, talk about great timing.

"Tell her I've gone to sleep," I muttered, not wanting to be around him right now. The photos of Kate's body were vivid in my mind. "You didn't even delete the texts. Is that why you're so horny, fucking me because you imagine it's her?"

"Shut up." He glared. "Don't be so fucking stupid."

I looked at him. "Don't talk to me like that again."

Pushing past him and tears in my eyes, I walked outside and stared up at the sky. The sun began to set with a warm breeze. I inhaled, wanting to calm myself before I face everyone. Inside, it wasn't much better as everyone gathered around.

Brody and I barely spoke to each other. The tension between us was thicker than ever. Scott came back with Tulip and sent her off to find Rose for dinner.

Everything seemed fine as his mother and father came over to kiss the kids good night. Brody, by now, had a few beers when he stood up, laughing as he walked towards Scott.

Confusion was seeping in. Why was he laughing?

Leon had jumped up to stop him, but it was too late. Brody walked up to his brother, and it finally sunk in as he threw a fist into his jaw with enough force to send a six-foot man falling to his ass. He then scuffed his collar, pulled him up with a harsh yank and snarled, "Fuck you!" before hitting him again and again.

CHAPTER TWENTY-TWO

Brody had been eerily silent.

Sitting on the plane, he was staring at his tablet and reading through emails. I just sat beside him, resting my head against his shoulder, saying nothing, just wanting to be close to him.

The rest of our trip was far from amazing. After the boys had brawled on the floor, which left Scott with an almost broken nose and two black eyes, we booked tickets to leave the next morning, just the four of us. His mother was less than impressed but being there was only going to cause more havoc they didn't deserve, not for their wedding anniversary. We would miss their vow renewal, a sure reason to never be asked back for another holiday.

Brody turned off his screen and wrapped his arm around my shoulder. Placing a kiss at the top of my forehead, he murmured, "I'm sorry."

"Don't be sorry. It's not your fault." It wasn't his at all.

Shaking his head, he glanced towards our two kids in the seats across from us. "They're pretty upset that we left."

"They'll get over it. We can take a few days at home. Do something fun there," I suggested. Although it was awful to see their disappointed faces, they were too little to understand the full extent of everything going on around them.

Scott was out of control. Brody let his fury pound into him repeatedly, and when Scott had muttered something underneath his breath as he went to walk away, Brody was back into him worse than ever. He wouldn't tell me what was said, but I could imagine it wasn't good.

Sliding my hand over his thigh, I gave it a squeeze. "Can I ask you something?"

"Depends on what it is," he eyed me with curiosity and then smiled softly. His blue eyes closing and dark lashes fanned the tops of his cheeks. "Ask me."

"Brody," I asked quietly. "Before, whenever we made love, you were always so quiet. How come?"

"Wasn't expecting that." He didn't smile, just kept his eyes closed until he let out a long sigh and then opened them. "Because I was trying to focus on lasting longer. We'd rarely have sex, and you always felt so good that I was just ready to come right away. I guess I was shy to be more vocal and let you know how good you felt. So I would hold you tightly and yell in my head about how much I loved you while trying not to come."

That actually explained a lot. "That's kind of romantic."

"I wanted to savour those moments. They were rare, but I never wanted them to end." Okay, that was very romantic but, at the same time, sad that we rarely made love.

"I love you," I smiled. I hadn't brought up the Kate subject again even if I wanted to.

He chuckled quietly, a grin spreading over his soft pink lips. "Also, because I had no idea what I was doing half the time. We'd always gone slowly. I should have asked how you liked it instead of being so selfish. I still have no clue what I'm doing."

"Me either."

He smiled, reaching up and caressing my cheek. "If I could go back, I still would never have fucked around with other girls like my mates had done. I'm honestly relieved that we've only ever been with each other. It makes it better, we can learn together."

"We are learning," I smiled, leaning into his palm and relishing the love I felt from him. "It's been amazing."

After arriving home, the kids, Brody and I piled into our bed and put on a movie. Lila was pretending to be the doctor so she would check her daddy's temperature every so often and then tell him he needed to rest. I'd fallen asleep on and off, and when I woke for the final time, Brody was just lying there staring at the ceiling. The kids between us were fast asleep.

"You okay?" I asked, whispering, so I didn't wake them.

He kept his eyes to the ceiling but nodded. "Yeah, I'm just worried about Scott. Putting it nicely, he has lost his fucking mind."

"Brody…"

"He told me that he knew you weren't on your pill, said he was going to fuck you, and asked how I felt about having a new niece or nephew."

I felt sick instantly. Bile rose in my throat as the thought disgusted me. "You didn't hit him hard enough."

Brody scoffed. "I hit him pretty hard. He looks like a panda."

With a smile, I laughed. "You have no idea how sexy you look when angry and in a fight."

"Did you think I was sexy when I used to yell at you?" he asked, rolling onto his side and resting his hand over mine that was snuggled around both of the kid's little bodies.

Just the thought of all our yelling put a damper on things. "I used to cry to sleep every night."

"I know." Admitting that shocked me a little. I hadn't expected him to hear. "I'd stand outside the door and listen to you. It made me feel like such a pathetic bastard. I've been a shitty husband and absent father."

His fingers stroked my skin. I blinked back the tears. "We both were horrible to each other, not just your fault."

"Do you think he's mentally unwell?" As angry as he was with Scott, I could see he was more concerned beneath the pissed exterior.

I hadn't thought much of it. He sure had something, though. "Maybe he's just angry about him and Rose. That's possibly why he's this way. Wants to destroy your marriage as well?" Then again, why not go after Jessie and Leon?

His hand tightened around mine with a squeeze. "I don't want you alone with him... ever."

"You do know that nothing would ever happen between him and me? I wouldn't do that to you. Please don't ever worry about his threats. He's just throwing a tantrum."

"This isn't like him," he said softly as Noah stirred in his sleep. "Something needs to be done before he harms himself or anyone else."

He was right. Something needed to be done. "Has Kate called you today?"

It was a change in topic but a fair one. "No. I think you scared her off."

"Good." My smile triumphed. "I wish you were cuddling me right now."

Brody sat up more, leaning over the kids whispered huskily, "I need to be inside you. I want you."

With a smirk, he was climbing over and laying between my thighs. The kid's right beside us, sound asleep. My god, this was so not going to be happening. The bulge in his boxers could go away. It wasn't getting out and getting in anywhere.

Shaking my head as he began kissing down my neck, "No, Definitely not."

"Bathroom? Please?" he groaned, sucking at my neck as he flexed his hips against me.

Rolling my eyes and slipping my hands down into the band of his boxers, I grabbed his taut ass. "Spare room?"

"Deal."

It never happened as we soon heard little voices giggling. They awoke again, sitting up to watch more of the movie. "Eww, Gross!"

"Very gross." I winked and wrapped my arms around my husband as he was still on top of me. He flexed against me, kissed my neck as he slid underneath the covers and cuddled me from behind. "Brody, no."

"Why not?" he smirked against my skin as he kept placing kisses on my bare shoulder.

I giggled, squirming away as he tickled me. "Because they're like right beside us." I couldn't fool around with them right there.

Pushing my bum against his groin, I heard his sharp intake of breath. "Send them to bed. You could pull me off."

"Nope, you'll have to wait," I smiled, glancing over my shoulder at him. "I'll make up for it tomorrow."

As Lila began to talk about her birthday next week, he gave up on his conquest and just wrapped his arms around my waist and kissed my shoulder. My eyes grew heavy until I passed out.

When it came time for Lila's birthday a week later, she was one hell of a mood. The last thing I felt like was a party. I'd been tired all week from catching up on housework and cooking. Her friends were here for a good part of the morning until they left, and it was just family now. She was angry and agitated. Mostly tired, from being up since 5 AM. The good thing was that she loved her new doll. The bad, she threw it in the pool during a tantrum.

Brody came over and shook his head. "You don't get another one. You can go to your room!"

"No!" she yelled back. "Get me the doll!"

"I beg your pardon?" I asked, shocked as she threw her hand on her hips and frowned.

Noah was too busy stuffing his face with chips and cake to notice her tantrum. Lila began to walk away, but Brody grabbed hold of her arm and pulled her to face him. "Watch your tone. Don't speak to your mother that way!"

"Let me go!" she yelled. Her face was red with anger.

Letting her go, he pointed towards the back door. "Get to your room. I won't have you acting like a spoilt brat in my house. Stay up there until you're in a better mood. Otherwise, put your pyjamas on and get to bed now!" He growled, not loud but loud enough to catch the attention of his parents and my sisters.

They were waiting for him to strike her, which he would never do.

My father walked over with a chuckle and shook his head disappointedly. "I bambini, avete bisogno di un cuore tenero e una mano ferma, Gabriella."

I raised a brow at my father. "Papa, Brody does have a soft heart and a firm hand, but he would never hit our children." Of course, I spoke back to him in Italian.

"Perché no?"

"Why not? Giovanni, I won't ever hit my children," Brody spoke, coming up behind us. "Lila's just loaded up on sugar, plus she was up early."

Too damn excited to sleep and now she was over tired, letting the world take the wrath of her meltdowns as she refused to go to sleep and wanted to show us all that she was another year older and the boss on her day.

My Papa sighed. "It won't hurt them, Brody. Gabriella, I wish you would raise your children better than this. You don't see your sister's Bambini carrying on."

"Papa," I warned. "Stop it. Brody and I are doing things our way. Back off a bit."

"Gabriella, guardare la tua bocca!" my father growled, glaring. I had to laugh as he thought he could tell me to watch my mouth.

Part of me wanted to take the bait and bite back at him. My dear hubby beat me to it. "You moved here, must have liked something about the country otherwise you wouldn't have left Italy," Brody smirked, bringing his beer to his lips. "There's nothing wrong with my parenting skills."

"Abbastanza!"

Swallowing hard, Brody shook his head and took a step closer to my papa. "Enough? Listen, mate, if you don't like it then get out of my house."

"Okay. It's time for cake!" I blurted out, needing a distraction before the two men went head to head. "I'll go get Lila."

Rushing off inside the house, I ran the steps two at a time and went into her room. She was sitting on her bed, wearing her nightie and playing with a Barbie doll. Her eyes were big and watering as she looked up and tossed them aside. Noticing me, she'd flung herself underneath the covers and hid in her bed.

"Lila," I said with a smile, taking a seat on the edge of her bed where I pulled the covers down and looked at her sad face. "What's wrong?"

"Nothing," she squeaked. "Daddy scared me."

I fought the laugh. "Daddy is very upset. You have been really rude to him today, and he's sad that you don't like your presents."

"Mama," she sat up and then kneeled in front of me. "When you have a baby, I won't be the littlest anymore, will I?"

Oh, boy, "No, sweetie, but that doesn't matter. You're always going to be my little girl."

"Well, I changed my mind. I don't want a baby sister anymore."

"You don't?" I asked curiously, knowing Brody was entering the room, as I smelt his aftershave.

Shaking her head, "Nope, I decided that I want to be the littlest all the time now. I'm too small, and babies are too loud. I don't want a baby sister or brother."

Brody took a spot on the other side of her bed and sat down. He was looking a ton of mixed emotions. "You know, that's for mama and me to decide, right? Just because you don't want something doesn't mean we will listen."

"If you love me, then you won't have another baby," she challenged and growing more upset. "I have Noah, and that's heaps for me."

Maybe if we weren't actively trying for another baby, it could be put off and talked about, not that I was going to let our eight-year-old daughter tell us when we could and couldn't add to our family, but I had a feeling when the time came. She was going to be one, very unhappy camper.

Brody, shaking his head, let out a loud sigh, stood up and nodded. "Come on, let's go and blow your candles."

Jumping off the bed and running off, I leant against his chest and tilted my head back. "She's being a bitch of a thing today."

He smirked, skimming his hands down over my ass and pulling me against him with a squeeze. "I can't wait for her to go to bed and we can, *not,* make a baby."

I laughed with a groan. "Oh, I can't wait." Then another thought hit me. "You know we still have to get through the teenage years yet."

With a groan, he said how I felt. "Fuck."

CHAPTER TWENTY-THREE

The next few months began to fly by, and soon, we were heading into October. The weather was getting warmer, and the thrill of Christmas was looming closer. I absolutely loved this time of year when the children were getting ready to go on the end of school holidays and when summer began to come on. This summer, I was not going to hide out in oversized clothing, and I was definitely going to swim in the pool.

There was still the dreaded secret that I had been keeping from Brody, and it was eating my insides. I was afraid to tell him. Once it was done, it would be out there, and Scott would know I said something. I was so humiliated and afraid of it getting out that I had always just assumed keeping it locked away in secret would be the best thing.

Brody was going to be more than hurt, and with things being so good between us, I just kept putting it off.

Scott, however, kept calling my phone. I ignored him each time, as I didn't have anything to say to him. I'd tell Brody about the calls, but he would dismiss them and said he would handle it. I had no idea if he did handle it, but it was getting to the point of being called all hours of the night. He'd never leave a message. He would just hang up and an hour later, call again.

I was taking action into my own hands.

Of course, Brody and I weren't perfect, and there were those small fights and sometimes big ones, but we never went to bed angry. We made a promise to talk it out, let the other person speak and listen to what they had to say. It was like our own therapy. Truly, I just didn't want to ever go back to how things were with us.

We had screwed up with just agreeing to give up before getting to the root of our problems, and that was not talking.

Slicing up the apple, I put the pieces into Lila's school lunch box and grabbed a handful of grapes for Noah as Brody entered the kitchen. He kissed each of the children's heads and then made his way over. I smiled up at him.

"Morning." His deep voice sent a shiver throughout me.

"Morning, are you having coffee here or at work?" with the bitch who he still hasn't fired yet. I, however, was being calm and not mentioning her name to him even if it really pissed me off and upset me.

"I'll have one now. You were up early, everything okay?" he asked, grabbing an apple and tossing it in the air.

"Course, why wouldn't it be?" I asked, glancing up and snatching the apple before he caught it again.

Shrugging, he ran his tongue over his lower lip. "You were up early and were pretty restless all night."

My heart began to beat faster as I looked away before he could tell that I was lying to his face. "I had a headache and just trying to decide what we're doing for Christmas. Mama called and wanted us to go there, but then, your parents wanted us to go to theirs. It's just trying to figure something out without upsetting the other."

"You're so considerate, Gabby," he smiled and checked his Rolex. "Shit, I actually need to head off, got a meeting, but I will see you later, okay?"

"Sure." I leant in as I stood up on my toes, and I kissed him as he met me halfway. "I love you."

"Love you too, baby. See you later." Kissing me again, he waved goodbye to the kids and left hastily.

I wouldn't deny that he rushed to work bothered me. But there were no more late evenings, and we had made a point to sit and have family dinner each week. He had also made it to Lila's dancing and Noah's soccer games. Things were improving. Little steps were what counted.

I heard the back door open not even twenty minutes later as I was doing Lila's hair. Brody came storming inside the house. "Where is my other case?" he bellowed out.

The kids froze, as did I. "Brody?"

"Who else would it fucking be?" he snapped, a loud bang, and I looked up when I saw him entering the living room. "You!" He pointed directly towards Lila angrily. "What have I told you?"

She stiffened up. I knew something was wrong.

"What?" Dread filled me.

"Oh, nothing, I just opened up my briefcase, only to find it full of pink glitter and coloured gel shit all over the contracts and paperwork that I needed for this meeting! I'm going to be fucking late now. Thanks to this shit!"

"Brody," I tried calming him. "She's..." I had no idea how to get out or try cover up for this one. Part of me just wanted to laugh.

"No, don't, Gabriella. I don't want to hear it. Where did you put my other case?" he stood up, storming off.

Lila then burst into tears as Noah sat quietly, building his Lego and looking ready to cry himself. Nothing pulled my heart more than seeing my two babies upset and teary eyed. "Wait here, please."

Practically sprinting up the stairs, I found him in his office going through each cabinet furiously, searching and throwing everything around. Mess and paperwork were strewn all over his desk. "Calm down, please."

Spinning around, he narrowed his eyes on mine. "Calm down? Do you have any idea what this could cost me?" He shook his head. "Of course, you don't. You're not out working!"

He was venting. I tried not to take it personally but screw that. "What the hell did you just say to me?"

"Nothing," he muttered and walked away from me.

Marching after him, I gave his back a shove. "Turn around and say it to my face. Don't you dare come in here all hot and wild about something that isn't my fault?"

"You should have been watching her!"

"I'm sorry that I can't be all over the house." I threw my hands up. May as well take what he had to give.

He glared. "How many times have I told them not to go into my office?"

"Stop yelling. You're scaring them," I pleaded, giving him my own glare back. "Screaming isn't going to solve anything."

"I don't have time for this. I'll see you tonight," he muttered, and I swore I heard him add, "or not."

Maybe he was about to have a mid-life crisis.

Our fight lasted until he stormed off, and it was far from resolved. Lila wouldn't tell me why she had done it. Noah didn't really give a crap about any of it, too busy playing his Nintendo DS in the car to listen to me scolding her about getting into the office and drawing all over his paperwork.

Hopefully, he would be calm when he came home tonight... if ever he came home.

Panic rushed through me as I sat in the car, staring at the building and counting down the time until it was time for me to go inside. Stepping outside as the clock hit 10:45 AM on my watch. I locked the car door and put the keys inside my black leather handbag. Running a hand through my hair, I forced a smile and made my way down the stone footpath.

Looking up, there he stood. I wasn't going to deny that he was handsome, not that I was paying too much attention to his looks. He'd been my doctor since the first pregnancy. "Steven." I smiled, greeting him nervously.

"Gabriella, you're here early, or am I late?" he smiled, his light blue eyes twinkling as he held the front door of the brick building open. "Come in, don't worry. You'll relax once we're inside and you're on the bed."

I raised a brow. "You make it sound sordid."

He laughed, holding the door open for me. "I apologise. I'm an obstetrician. It's nothing uncommon for me to have women on my work bed."

"If I didn't know you so well, I'd be looking for a new OB," I pointed out.

Taking a deep breath, I blew it out slowly and then took a step forward with shaky legs into the building. After this morning's fight, I was suddenly anxious and wondering if this was the right thing for us. A baby had been talked about for months, but the way he blew up at the kids, I couldn't imagine he would be in the paternal mood tonight. Oh, well, it's a bit too late for that now. I had taken a home test, and it came up positive.

Steven confirmed that I was six weeks along, and I was excited but utterly terrified.

The flutter of the tiny heartbeat on screen made it more real. A baby was in my stomach, growing. Lila wasn't going to be the youngest anymore, and I could only hope she grew to love her brother or sister. I had a photo printed out to show Brody and booked my next appointment for another follow-up.

When I walked into the house two hours later, I wanted to burst into tears at the sight of him leaning against the bar. "Brody? I didn't know you were home."

"Why would you? All I do is work, remember?" he muttered, and then I noticed the alcohol in his glass. He was drinking.

Setting my bag and car keys on the bench, I frowned. "The meeting didn't go well?" I asked, treading carefully.

"Like you give a shit about anything I do."

"Don't say that. I don't want to fight with you," I said, walking over to him and went running my hands up and down his back to massage him. "Let me rub your shoulders?"

He shook his head and moved away from me. "Did you fuck him?" he asked.

My heart almost stopped. I think my throat closed over. "What?"

His eyes burned into mine. "I asked if you fucked him."

"Who?" I was completely confused.

Shaking his head, he slammed his fist against the table, and everything rattled. "You lied to me this morning. Think I wouldn't use the app on your phone and track you?"

"Brody." I felt sick as well as betrayed. He followed me? God. "Let me explain."

"No, I don't want to hear another one of your lies, Gabriella!" he spat, looking at me with hatred. "I know where you were, and I don't need to talk about it. Nothing you can say right now will fix this."

I was confused. He had this all wrong. "Listen to me."

He scoffed quietly. It wasn't until I noticed his eyes weren't red from the alcohol, but from his tears. "I spoke to Scott yesterday."

My stomach dropped. "What about?" I asked, not wanting to know.

When he looked at me, I knew that he knew. "Do you really need me to tell you," He stated, staring at me with hatred in his eyes. "You should have told me."

"I wanted to!" He had to have believed that. "I wanted to. I was going to."

"But you never did!" he thundered. "You fucking didn't! You've made a fool out of me."

Wiping my own eyes, I blinked back the tears. "Please, I thought you wouldn't understand."

"Understand what? That my wife is a whore." He turned, refilling his glass again. "I can't stand the sight of you right now. That's how much you hurt me."

His words slapped me. "What did you just say to me?"

"So you and my brother, huh? You sure had me fooled. You had everyone fooled."

I was either really stupid, or he was having a stroke. "I don't know what you're talking about. How have I fooled everyone?"

"You put up the Saint act and have everyone thinking you're a loving wife and mother when really, I have no idea who you even are anymore," he muttered, swallowing a mouthful.

Staring at him, I thought maybe he was just having a bad day. Turned out, he was just pissed at me. Scott had gotten to him and told him what I should have done years ago. Instead, I fucked up by keeping this from him, and now, I needed to fix it.

"Brody, let me explain things. I can make this right."
I'd do whatever it took to fix this.

Tossing back his scotch and swallowing hard, he
breathed out two words I had never expected to hear today.
"Get out."

My eyes were already watering, vision blurring and
heart beginning to race with panic. "No, please don't do this!"

Shrugging off his black jacket, he laid it neatly over the
back of the dining table chair. He began to leave for the door
but stopped. "I won't repeat myself. Pack a bag and get out of
my house."

"Why?" My feet chased after him before he could walk
away and lock himself in his office like always. "Tell me why.
You can't throw me out! What about the kids? I won't leave
them."

He stopped, turning around, and walked back. Stalking
back was more like it. The glare he gave sent a shiver
throughout my body. He wasn't fooling around. This was real,
and it was serious, more serious than the last time divorce had
been brought up. Brody just narrowed his eyes with a cold
menacing glare. "You can still see them. I'm not that much of a
bastard. You, on the other hand, I don't want to see you unless
it's with my lawyer."

"Brody, please, I thought things were getting better."

He just stared, and his features softened. But his once
warm, caring eyes were now cold. "Things change and I finally
realised that trying to fix us was nothing but a mistake."

CHAPTER TWENTY-FOUR

"And how much a week is this?" I asked, glancing around the small three-bedroom apartment. It was nothing compared to the home I had been living in. It was nice, but it was cramped and old. The windows rattled as a gust of wind blew from the outside.

The realtor smiled as she checked her clipboard and looked back up towards me. "It's three fifty a week."

I almost fell to the floor in shock. "I'm sorry, what? I'd rather buy a house than pay that much a week in rent, not happening."

I needed to find somewhere soon and fast. I was so sick of staying in a hotel courtesy of my soon to be ex-husband, eating Chinese or Thai most nights. I was living off a takeaway. Fuck the diet. I was depressed and in need of carbs. Pregnancy cravings kicked in too. I was hungry all the time.

She clicked her tongue and blushed slightly. "Oh, I'm sorry. I just thought…" That I could afford this place considering who I was married to as she knew. Newsflash, I was separated. No, I definitely couldn't afford it at all.

"That's okay. Can you call me if something cheaper comes up? I honestly don't want to be paying this much." It's not worth it. I should drain our joint account. No, he knew I'd only ever do that if he cheated on me. He'd be broke within a second.

Walking back to the hotel of dread, that's what I had called it since moving in, it was all I felt once I walked into that small room and slumped down on the bed. The pillow had seen more tears than a tub full of water.

Brody wasn't speaking to me. The kids had hated me. They thought I had abandoned them, and that killed me. I would never do such a thing. When Brody sent me custody arrangement papers three days after being kicked out, I wanted to curl up into a ball and scream the pain away. I had actually screamed into my pillow as I cried over and over.

I thought about calling up Richard and seeing if the offer to come back to work was still on the table, but I would only end up disappointing him when I had to finish again. Maternity leave wouldn't be welcomed with open arms after being away for so long. I needed something to provide for the children on my own without relying on Brody. He didn't want me, so I had to stop wanting him. Only, I didn't want him. I needed him.

Going to visit the children didn't go so well.

Lorraine was staying there, helping. She would throw daggers my way, giving me the evil glare as she'd called out to them. Brody refused to speak to me, and all I could hear was him yelling at the kids, as they wouldn't come down. I wasn't allowed back in our house.

Instead, I had to stand outside like a stranger while Noah and Lila told their father how much wanted to come live with me. I wished I could take them, but I had nowhere to go, and there was no way they were going to see the hotel. I was trying to settle somewhere before picking them up. I would go to their school and see them each morning. Lila sobbed every time, and it broke my heart into a million pieces.

She told me how angry Brody was, that he was so mean and always yelling at them. They were eating takeout pizza every night, and he didn't know how to do her hair the same way I did it. I'd redo it for her and tell her how much I loved her.

Noah was just angry and didn't say much. They were hurting because of us.

Trying to sleep the day away, to forget about the pain I had caused, I rolled over when I heard my phone beeping, I checked the message — *Friday. My office. Sign.*

Did he really feel nothing towards me? He wouldn't let me explain anything. There was so much to tell him. Stupid me should have done it weeks ago. No, I should have done it when it first happened.

This whole mess could have been avoided. I tried telling him the day he told me to get out. I screamed, crying as I chased him. He told me to get the fuck away from him before he really lost it, in other words before he hit me. I'd never seen him so wild before. He was angry, but he could be brought down and calmed. This time, there was no calming.

We were meeting at Brody's office to settle the arrangement for the children. He wanted it over and done with quickly, and the fight in me was going. I couldn't deal with this. If we weren't meant to be, then we weren't meant to be. But, I was convinced we were.

Entering the large building, I took the elevator and rode to the top floor. Walking out, I spotted her giving me a smirk as I strode past her. I tried to look nice, but who was I kidding? I was feeling anything but putting on a nice dress to show him what he's losing. Instead, I opted for black leggings and a long thin, white tank with a grey knit over that. The top covered the slight bump I had begun to show.

"You need to have an appointment," she smiled too sweetly. "Miss."

I shot her a look. "Fuck off," I warned, not in the mood for this tart's drama today. No, today, this bitch was going to meet my fist or foot, whichever lashed out quicker.

"Gabby!" he snapped, stopping me before I could lash out. "Office. Now!"

I didn't miss her smirk as I turned and stared at the man who was growling my name with a glare.

Brody looked as I felt, like hell. He was unshaven and black suit crinkled. His hair was not even brushed. It was as if he had just rolled out of bed and rocked off to work after having scotch for breakfast. He looked like shit, but damn me if he wasn't the most handsome man in my eyes. He still took my breath away. Taking a seat, I forced my eyes away from him. It broke my heart too much to see what I had cost myself.

"Let's get this over with," he finally muttered, taking a seat opposite me.

His lawyer, intimidating as he oozed power and confidence, began speaking first, "My client wishes to advise Miss Orecchio that her current lovers are not to be around their children." Nice touch on going with my maiden name, he was here to hurt me. The part about the lovers rattled me like there was anyone in my life right now or would there ever be.

Brody had so gratefully considered hiring a lawyer for me. Clearing his throat as he began his own list of demands, I had nothing I wanted except my children. I wouldn't give them up without a fight, but I wouldn't dare take them from him. It would be a shared arrangement. I ignored half of what was being said, unable to really care. I just stared at Brody, wishing he would look at me. He didn't. "My client wishes to make a couple of adjustments, nothing major but it is unnegotiable."

Brody's brows raised. "And what are they? More money?" he asked. Each word dripped with sarcasm.

The power suit beside him cut him off. "I don't know what else you would want since against my wishes; your client is getting a rather large sum of money. My client has been more than generous."

"Paying me off won't work." I rolled my eyes, sick of this mediation already. He glared.

"As you're aware by now, your brother's sexual harassment has landed him with a restraining order. After the first attack, the judge ruled in her favour, and we wish to keep Lila and Noah away from him while this is in place." Brody's head snapped up. His eyes were a mixed confusion of shock and rage. "The photographs he has threatened her with must be handed over immediately. Otherwise, my client is advised to take further action that I have advised. It doesn't matter how long ago the assault happened. She was still a minor."

"What?" Brody asked, confused. "Photographs? Assault."

This is what I got for keeping secrets. I brought this on myself.

When I looked up, his lawyer was pushing over the paperwork and a pen. "All right, we will consider what you've said, but we're here to sort the children out, not bring up the past. Brody is handing over full custody of Noah and Lila to Gabriella. He will continue to support them with whatever their needs are."

"That's what we need to amend."

"What she doesn't want them?" His lawyer cut in, rolling his eyes.

I narrowed my eyes. "Don't be a dick!" I spat, having enough of his smart ass comments.

Brody glared. "Gabriella."

I shot him a look, warning him to keep pissing me off. "No, I want to make an adjustment. Although you want to give me full custody, I think we should have shared. I don't have a name yet, but we need to add that on also or are you planning on ignoring the baby as well?"

"Baby?" he now looked completely lost. "Wait. I don't understand. You were…"

"No, not were, I am." Tears began to form in my eyes. I looked at him. "That's where you followed me that day after tracking my phone. I get that you're pissed about me seeing a doctor before telling you, and I am truly sorry. But, I had to be sure before I got all excited and told you that I was pregnant. Well, congratulations, daddy, I am pregnant!"

"We'll need a DNA test," his lawyer muttered grimly.

"Avrete bisogno di un test del DNA per il momento ho finito con stronzo!" I hissed back. His eyes were directly on me, angry as I told him that they would need to do a DNA test on him once I finish with his body.

"Excuse me?" his face calm, and I was convinced this wasn't the first time he had been threatened.

"I'm going to be sick." Morning sickness had to hit me this moment, and I was jumping up from the table. Running out the doors with a rush, my hand over my mouth, I raced into the nearest bathroom before I hurled all over the table. I didn't let the tears stop either.

On my knees, crying, I gripped the toilet bowl to stop shaking.

The bathroom door flung open, and his thunderous voice echoed, ringing in my ears. "Everyone, except my wife, get the fuck out now!"

I hadn't realised there were others in here until their heels were scampering away at record speed.

"This is the women's bathroom," I said, taking in a steady breath when I was sure the vomit had finished. "Don't worry; I'll be off your property soon." I sniffled and then threw up again.

Instead of leaving, he just stood there. I could see his black leather shoes standing in front of the stall as I turned to face the door. He wasn't going anywhere. "Gabby," he said, almost soft that I didn't hear it.

"Don't." I sat here on my knees, crying. It was a wreck. I didn't have the fight in me anymore. The tears slowly subsided. My eyes were red and stinging. Opening the stall door, I ignored him by walking to the sink, turning the cold water tap on and tilting my head down so I could get a mouthful and rinse the acidic taste from my mouth. Standing up straighter, I looked at his blurred reflection behind me. "What?"

"I'm sorry. I didn't let you explain," he said quietly.

"It's not all your fault," I said quietly. "Actually, yes, it is your fault. You didn't give me a chance."

He hesitated before taking a step forward and then stopped. "I don't want this. I want you."

"Jesus, hell, are you kidding me with this shit?" I snapped, unable to hide the laugh. "You are so up and down with emotions. I thought I was emotional, but Christ, Brody, you are fucking bipolar with everything."

He nodded. "I know."

"You said the same thing months ago, and I believed you. You threw me out of our home and banned me from coming back. Our kids think I'm a wicked bitch who doesn't want to live with them, and your mother hates me." I turned to look at him. "I've been living in a hotel and pregnant because I thought you didn't want this baby!" Before I could stop myself, I balled my hands into fists and hit him, hard against his chest. "You never let me explain, and I should have pushed." I hit again, each word hurting as my eyes spilled with tears. "You made me think that you didn't love me."

He stood there, taking what I was giving, and then wrapped his arms around my body and held me tightly. "I deserve it and more. I should have let you speak, I shouldn't have assumed you were cheating on me, but I was scared. Damn it, I was so fucking terrified that you had enough of me after I called you a bad mother, and I thought you slept with someone else. Scott told me you slept with him years ago. He said Lila wasn't mine. Then when I saw you with the—"

"You saw me with Steven, who delivered our babies." I looked up at him, confused. "He's a gynaecologist in private practice. I thought you knew about the baby and was mad I hadn't told you. That's what I thought."

"I could never be mad at a baby, our baby." He reached up and stroked my cheek gently. "I love you, and I always will. Now, you need to tell me what my brother has done. I promise I won't get mad or yell. I need you to tell me."

Shaking my head, I began to remove my hands from his biceps. "Not here, um, the hotel. Come to the hotel?"

"Now?" he asked in a low murmur.

"Yes, we need to lay everything out, talk and don't stop talking until everything is resolved. No more secrets, there are things I want to tell you about Scott and my father. We need to be honest, and if we can't then..." I sadly looked at him. "Then we're never going to make it."

"I know. I know." He ran his hands through his hair, and the next thing I knew, his fist was in the stall door. "Fucking Christ!" he bellowed. "I could have lost you over a communication issue! This divorce is off the table!"

Least, we agreed on one thing. Brody went back into the conference room. He was going to let our legal representatives know that we were going to talk privately before signing anything again. I went to the hotel to wait for him.

This time, I was going to open up Pandora's Box, and nothing was getting left out.

CHAPTER TWENTY-FIVE

Opening the white door after he knocked twice, I leant against it and looked up at Brody, who stood there with sweat against his forehead. He was nervous. This was a "make it or break it" conversation. I had worried that he would change his mind and not show up.

"My lawyer just called. Can't imagine yours would be too happy with you right now." I smiled as I pushed the door all the way open for him to come inside.

Striding in as he gave the buttons on his black suit jacket a tug open, he shrugged. "He's still getting paid. He'll shut his mouth if he wants to continue working for me."

Taking a seat on the bed since there wasn't a couch in here, I leant back on my hands as I watched him take off his jacket and then loosen his tie. Reaching into his pocket, I noticed a rolled of film of white papers. "What's that?"

Unfolding them, he tossed them to the bed beside me. "It's a custody agreement with a clause for divorce. If you feel like this isn't going to work, sign them, and when we can file, you'll get everything."

"No, we are going to talk, and if we both can't get along, then we'll both sign them. I can't live this way anymore." He wasn't going to make me the bad one. "We both fucked up."

Sinking to his knees, he kneeled in front of me and let his hands begin to wander up my thighs and toward the hem of my top. I watched as he slowly and hesitantly raised the top until my stomach was revealed to him. His warm hand began to move over my tanned belly, and he rested it there. His ring was still on his finger which hadn't gone unnoticed. I kept silent. My breathing increased rapidly as I watched him. Moving closer, he placed his soft lips on my skin and gave a tender kiss.

"I need you to be here this time. I was struggling with you working so much and me at home with him. Don't get me wrong. I loved it, but sometimes, I wished you were there to help a little more. I felt like a single parent at times," I admitted, not to make him feel bad but to let him know that I just needed him to help me and make me feel like I could count on him.

My fingers found their way through his dark hair as he rocked back on his knees and looked up towards me. "I will be there, this time, every appointment, every scan, and when you want to buy something for the baby, I will be there with you."

He had no idea what that meant to me, considering he hadn't done much of that with the other two. "What about when I'm in labour?" I asked, swallowing the lump in my throat. "You can't show up at the last second again."

"You go into labour, and I won't leave your side. I promise you." His voice was much firmer. "I'll take a month off work if you want."

"You said that before," I said in a scared whisper.

He looked at me, eyes narrowing. "I promise. I will be there."

With Noah, Brody arrived at the hospital an hour before I pushed our son out, and then with Lila, I was being set up to push when he finally came in. His excuses were work meetings. It was the start of a not so happy future together.

With a nod, I let my hands fall from his head, and he stood up. "We need to talk. I don't know if you want to go first, but I need to get everything off my chest that's been bothering me for so long."

"Okay, so do I."

"No yelling or fighting?" I needed to make sure that didn't happen.

"None, you go first. I will sit and listen to everything you have to say," he said, taking a spot on the bed beside me. "I want to know more about the shower and when we were younger."

Taking a deep breath, I wasn't holding back; otherwise, I would lose my nerve.

I shook my head, needing to. "Nine years ago, just before I fell pregnant with Lila, I was in the shower, and... you let him stay with us for that week." Realisation began to sink in as he said nothing. "You were at work, and I didn't notice until it was too late. He had been filming me in the shower and taking photographs." It felt so good to finally admit. "He tried to grab me, but I pushed him away and ran into Noah's room, locking the door until he passed out and you came home," I remembered everything so clearly like it was yesterday. "He was so angry, and he kept telling me that no one would believe me especially you."

He cut in. "He's right."

"What?"

Sighing heavily, he reached over and took my hand in his. "Gabby, I'm not proud to say this, but I know I was a jerk back then. I was working, always thinking of work, and if my brother, who was also my best mate at the time, told me you came onto him, I probably would have believed him."

"I know," I paused a moment. "He moved out the next day, and over the years, he has kept making sexual comments about my weight and body. When he sat beside me on the plane, he felt me up."

He growled loudly. "Fuck, I am going to kill him! What else?" Brody asked, his voice harsh.

Fighting the tears as the memory clear as day played in my mind; I dropped my gaze, so ashamed of myself. "He was drunk. You were out with your dad, and I had come to visit on a Sunday. Scott grabbed me. He tried to push me to my knees, but I kicked him and—"

"That's why he spent all day on the couch with an ice pack. You told me you were shopping with your mother," he finished, shaking his head. "Why didn't you tell me?"

I shrugged, rubbing the base of my neck. "He said no one would have believed me. I wasn't emotionally stable enough to deal with it, Brody." I was too emotionally unstable to ever say a word about it. No one would believe the housewife. He said Brody would assume I was just a bored housewife and his brother would never betray him. His words rang loudly in my ears and still did to this day. I wished I had been strong enough to come clean back then when I was younger.

"There's more," I added timidly.

"I don't know if I can take more after this." He paled, pacing the small hotel room.

"Hear me out first." After he nodded, I kept talking. "This happened so long ago, but I feel as if it needs to be said. When we first began dating, my parent's warned me to keep away from you, they told me I wasn't allowed to date someone who wasn't Italian or anybody until I was eighteen. My mother, she caught us kissing at the school and told my father. He hit me because of it."

"I'm sorry?" he frowned. "What do you mean he hit you?"

Nodding, I felt tears spring to my eyes. "That's why I couldn't compete in the swimming carnival. I was covered in bruises and so embarrassed."

"No... no... no..." he said over and over again, shaking his head as if he couldn't believe it. He sat down beside me, his head in his hands. "You were beaten because of me? Fuck, what if they had caught us sneaking around at night or that you weren't a virgin when we married? I'd knocked you up a month before the wedding!"

Kneeling up, tears running down my cheeks, I straddled his lap and cupped his cheeks. "Brody, that's over and done with. Please, it was never your fault."

"He hit you. You... You should have broken up with me." He sounded as if I had knocked the wind clean out of him. "What else? Just talk; otherwise, I'm going to lose it."

"I'm sorry for not telling you about Scott or the baby. I know that I should have done." I know there was nothing I could do or say to show him just how truly sorry I was for hiding that from him. "You hurt me so many times when you make comments about me not earning money. It really hurts me. I feel as if you don't think what I do at home is that big of a deal, I work hard to have a nice home for us, and sometimes, it never feels enough." My hands fell, and I played with his tie. "I'm sorry."

He looked up with glassy eyes and just nodded. "I know you are."

"I have some questions, which I need to be answered by you."

"Okay, ask away." He seemed a bit wary of what I was asking.

"Why did you kick me out? Brody, God, that broke my heart so much. You knew I couldn't take the kids with me."

"I didn't want to look at you and see what I was throwing away." Licking his lips, he closed his eyes and blinked away more tears. "To see you crying, it breaks my heart, Gabby. When you were screaming in the bedroom after I told you to get out, I was in the office, crying, because I regretted everything. Why do you think I was giving you everything? If I couldn't have you, then I didn't want anything."

"You followed me? I don't understand why. I mean we were in such a good place— the holiday, and then staying that way when we came home. I'm pregnant, and we're back to this. It's exactly what I didn't want. I don't know what I had done to make you feel that way."

"I was going to surprise you, come home early and try to cook you dinner. I'd put the app on your phone to try to figure out when you'd be on your way home, and then I noticed you weren't where you said you were. Paranoia got the best of me especially after what Scott had tried to convince me previously. I didn't want to believe it. Every day, I worry that you're going to realise just how better you deserve, and I'm scared that you'll take the kids and leave me."

"No, never," I said, completely panicked. I wouldn't take them and leave him.

Blowing a hard breath out, he blinked back his tears. "Baby, I…"

"You don't trust me, do you?" It had to be it. "You never take my side with your family sometimes, and it really hurts me. Every day, I have fought for you, for us, and nothing that my parents will say could change the way I feel about you." I didn't realise just how hard I was gripping him until I looked at my hands scrunching his. "I take your side. I wished you would have my back."

He nodded, taking my face in his hand with possession. "I'm sorry. I'll do better and try harder."

"Why is Kate still working for you?" I blurted out. I needed to know about this, or it would destroy me with jealousy.

"That day you turned up to work with lunch. There's more to the story than I have let on…"

BRODY

Her ass perched on my glass desk; I rolled my eyes with a sigh as I leant back and smiled. "Kate." I kept my voice calm even though I wanted nothing more than to flick her off my desk with the chopsticks she was waving around.

"Brody." The purr of her voice made me sick.

"No, listen to me," I began, "You can hit on me all you like, but you're nothing but a pathetic, desperate woman who's never going to get that chance."

Clicking her long manicured nails in front of my eyes, she shook her head. "Come on, you can't be serious. I mean, you're married but..."

"But what? I'm married. End of story."

She didn't, and I realised I was about to endure a long hour with her. She's taken the incentive to buy me lunch and then invite herself to join me. Her laughter rang like a cat hissing at a dog. Trying my best to ignore her, I faked a smile so the man I work for won't fire me for blowing up at his daughter.

The worse secretary by far, she couldn't even keep her grades above decent in college. I don't know why Paul thought it would be a great idea to give me an assistant. I didn't need one. I knew how to answer the phone, and I could take my own calls, get my own coffee. I was more than capable of buying my own lunch. She was more of a nuisance, but the man was close to retirement, and I needed to suck it up, land as many contracts and make him as much money as possible until he left.

I had to sit and listen to her go on and on about a club she was going to. Seven more months, I thought to myself.

Seven months and she will be somebody else's problem. Until then, if I wanted to move up to a higher position, I had to grin and bear it and pretend to be enjoying her company when I'd rather drill a nail into my skull or watch paint dry. When that time was up, and he was gone, be fucked if I wasn't firing her. She was the first thing I looked forward to changing.

She'd come in here thinking I hadn't just witnessed her hitching up the dark skirt. Did she assume that my cock would thicken at the sight of her stockings? I wasn't a fan of them. I did, however, love my wife's long tanned legs and her bare thigh even in a pair of pyjama boxers. Gabriella trying not to be sexy was incredibly sexy.

"What do you think?" she asked with a giggle. I hated that sound.

Clearing my throat, I grabbed the water and began to unscrew the lid. "About what?" I wasn't paying attention. I didn't even pretend to.

"We could take a working holiday, you know. If you need to travel, maybe I could go with you." Her brows wiggled, and I almost spat out my drink.

"Like fuck, we will be," I laughed. Hearing a noise, my eyes snapped up, and my heart dropped. "Fuck," I muttered to myself. I was a dead man.

"Who's that?" Kate snorted. "Does she work in the mail room or canteen?"

"My wife." That shut her up.

For the rest of my life, I would never forget the look on my wife's face as she stared at me. She'd been mad before, upset too. But that was nothing compared to right now. She was hurt, and I caused this. She closed the doors on me before I could get to the elevator, and then I ran back to my office, dialling her number, and it went to voicemail.

Kate was strolling out of my office, leaning against the frame. "She mad at you?"

"I had to convince her not to kick your ass, which she'd do in a heartbeat if I let her," I said low, striding past her and tossing her noodles in the bin. "Lunch is over. I have work to do."

"But..." she whined. "I wasn't finished eating."

"Tough shit, get out." Oh, I could be an ass to her. If I grinned and looked happy, then on the security footage, it would never be shown that I was truly telling her off, which I did multiple times.

With a wink, she sundered back to her desk. "All right, big boy, work hard. Let me know if you fancy a blow job."

Apparently, Kate just considered this as playing hard to get.

I wouldn't mind one but not by her.

I couldn't work. I sat there until I felt sick with guilt. I got up and went to find her favourite flowers. It hit me even harder when I realised I had no damn clue what type of flowers she liked.

She deserved more than I was giving her. I didn't deserve her. She deserved someone who would listen to her, who would be there when she needed, and I was far from that man. I had hurt her too many times to forgive, and now, as I sat staring into my wife's dark, almost black eyes, I realised just what I was going to lose if I didn't make some changes.

"Brody," Gabby said quietly. "I wish you would have told me. It explains so much."

"Tell you what? That the big boss had me by the balls, and there's not much I can do about it unless I quit." I scoffed, squeezing her hand. "There's no way I won't provide for our family, and now, we're adding to it."

She sucked in a breath as she cried against my chest while I stroked her hair. "Can't you report her for harassment?"

I smiled, wishing I could. "Do you know what happened to the last man who reported her? He was fired without benefits and had his name tarnished. She's lethal. I have a couple more months left. After that, she'll be gone."

"Did you ask her about the phone calls?" she asked.

"The one where you told her to fuck off?" I smirked. "Oh yeah, she was pissed about that." I had to laugh at the look on her face when she found out I had taken a holiday without her.

Gabriella rolled her eyes. "Not that one, I meant the million she called when we were on holidays."

"No, I didn't bring it up. Ignoring her is working the best for me. Otherwise, I'd end up fired, and after being there for so long, I don't want that."

I found it hard to take my eyes off of her. She was always so beautiful. With a smile, she shrugged as if she was shy.

"Okay, my turn to listen to you," she said

Nodding, I sat with my back against the wall. "I'm not going to lie. You have hurt me with this information about Scott. I wished you would have told me, but at the same time, I know why you didn't. You feared him and being in such a broken place, there was no way you had the confidence I had taken away from you. You were emotionally fucked up, and I wasn't there to help you on the other side. You kept silent and suffered quietly."

"I…" she began.

"No, let me keep talking," I paused, pulling her closer to me. "To know that you were beaten also hurts because I feel responsible for everything that's gone wrong. I took unnecessary shit out on you, and you didn't deserve that. God, I would ignore you and for what? No fucking reason. I belittled you. I damn well emotionally abused you, Gabby. I turned into a money hungry cockhead, and you still stuck with me."

She could always make excuses for me. Deep down, I turned into a man I never wanted to be.

"When I asked for a divorce, I wasn't thinking. I just said it, and you agreed. Damn, I was stunned because I never thought you would agree. I expected you to beg me, and you never did. You were strong and only began to grow stronger."

Smiling, as she kept silent, I caressed her cheek and rubbed her tears with my thumb.

"Did you know that night in the kitchen, I was looking at you for the first time again, and I couldn't get enough of you? I only began boxing to stop myself from jerking off so much. You would always cover up, and I loved your body no matter if you had gained weight or lost it. You're always sexy in my eyes." There was nothing about her that I didn't love.

She smiled, and that's a sight I loved to see. "Will you finally tell me how you really hurt your hand?"

"I was distracted, imagining you naked and lost concentration," I smirked.

A soft laugh escaped her throat. "I didn't expect that. Wow!" She was all right. Her body shifted, and she looked up at me. Her dark eyes brightened by the film of water that I seemed to constantly put there. "We need to talk about the pink glitter glue."

"Firstly, I do trust you." I needed her to know that. She never gave me any reason to falter my trust in her. "And the situation with the glitter and glue, I admit, I overreacted, but she wasn't listening to me. I had told her, three times the evening before. She knew not to go into my office, and still, she did it. I am well aware of exploding on her and also you. You didn't deserve to be yelled at."

"I don't know what to do anymore, Brody. There comes the point where it's easier to just give up than keep fighting for something that might not work."

My hold tightened as hot tears burned my eyes. "I don't want to give up. Please don't give up on us."

"Do you mean that? I don't know if I can keep going. I mean who's to say you're not going to throw me out in a month when I do something to piss you off?" she asked. I had been waiting for that question.

"I won't kick you out, and I'm sorry I had ever done that. Please, I need you to trust me that you'll believe it when I say, I won't tell you to leave or ask for a divorce ever again," I stated firmly, I realised what a mistake I had made. Every day without her in that house, it was torture. I needed her, possibly more than she needed me.

"Your family hates me," she finally said.

"Does it matter what they think?" I asked.

"Yes," she nodded. "Of course, it does."

"I hated every minute of every hour that you were away. On the other hand, it made me see things from your perspective. Being at home, the kids screaming, cleaning, cooking and basically taking care of everything there, I took you for granted. Never did I see just how hard you're working at home." No way could I do what she did every day. "I'll never forgive myself for hurting you, but I am serious. I want you back."

I was going to do anything and everything to get her back.

"Brody, I'm afraid," she whispered.

I looked at her, seeing the hesitation in her eyes. Bringing my mouth down to hers, I whispered as I kissed her lightly, "Me too."

"We're going to really have to work at this. No going to bed angry and I mean that."

"No more secrets," I added. I was still deciding what the hell I was going to do with the news about Scott. I was ready to put him six-foot under for touching my wife. My blood boiled as I remembered the photographs.

"It won't be easy, and I don't know if I can trust you completely. I'm always going to be worrying and wondering if you're going to ask for another divorce. I would never cheat on you."

I knew that now. "I know." I was fucking lucky that she hadn't pissed me off. "We'll earn it back with each other."

She never gave herself enough credit. She was a bombshell. Men looked at her with desire, and she never noticed. Thank God. Maybe if she did, then she'd be inclined to piss me off and go for someone more decent who would treat her better.

"Cathy, she cheated on David, not the other way around," I admitted, letting my own secrets come to life.

Seeming surprised by this, her dark brows dipped in confusion. "What?"

"She told you that he left her, but he was the one who walked in on her and another man. I didn't want to tell you. She's your best friend." Her friend should have told her. I hated Cathy with a passion for fucking David and their daughters over.

Gabby let out a sob. "See, everyone's just lying and cheating. I don't want a divorce, Brody. I can't do that to Noah or Lila. They're so angry at us already, and we're only just going to hurt them even more."

"I won't ever ask you for another divorce." I shifted on the bed, so she was underneath me, and I placed my hand back against her flat tummy, fingers fanning out as I caressed where our baby was being kept safe. "I will, however, ask you to marry me again."

CHAPTER TWENTY-SIX

He couldn't be serious. "What?" I laughed a little as he sat up and pulled me by the hand so I was sitting on the edge of the bed. "You're not serious." There was no way until he dropped down to one bended knee.

"I've never been more serious about anything, Gabriella. Will you marry me again? Let me show you just how much I love you and what you mean to me," he asked and reached taking my left hand. His finger traced the small ring he'd given me many years ago. "Baby, we were young, and with the so many odds against us, I want nothing more than to do this again and make sure we never go backwards. I promise you that I will work every day to keep you in love with me."

"Brody." I didn't know what to say. I was a blubbering mess. Was this like the baby? Thinking that could be a good idea. But when I looked at him, I couldn't want anything more than him for the rest of my life. "Of course, I will!" I'd be stupid not to give this a hundred fifty percent. "No mention of divorce ever, I mean it. It's not an option, off the table and never back on again."

I waited for him to take the paperwork and toss it in the bin. Instead, he slid off my engagement and wedding band. I expected him to slide them back on. Instead, he moved them to my right hand and put them on the opposite finger. Pausing, he placed a kiss on the top of my palm and let my hand go. Holding up a finger as I continued to watch him, he reached into the black suit pant pocket and pulled out something — another ring. As I looked down at it, my eyes filled with water.

"I will agree to all of that. Now, Gabriella Whittaker, will you marry me again?" he asked, sliding the beautiful and delicate rose gold teardrop diamond ring onto my wedding finger.

This new one was huge. "It's gorgeous." Lifting my hand, I inspected it closer and took it back off. He stayed, kneeling as I looked on the inside of the band and frowned slightly. "Is that?"

"The date I first fell in love with you, your first day of school."

This was the single most precious thing he had ever done for me — to take the time and do something random and completely unexpected. It just showed me how much thought he had taken into designing a new ring for me.

Sliding the ring back on, I reached up and cupped his cheeks. "Brody, this is beautiful. I mean, I loved my rings before, but this is wow. I love it."

"You deserve it, baby," he whispered and began to stand up. Only, he didn't.

He came at me slowly and lowered me backwards down to the bed. His touch was gentle and tender. "No more secrets," he whispered against my collarbone, and he began kissing me.

Nodding, I closed my eyes and breathed out. "No more assumptions."

"We'll talk to each other."

"About everything." Our eyes were locked, and I lifted my head to capture a kiss.

My eyes opened when I felt his smile over my mouth. "If your cute butt is itchy, I want to know about it."

I couldn't stop myself from giggling as I broke away from his mouth with laughter. "That's never going to happen."

"Better," he looked up and winked at me. "I mean it, sharing everything. We need to get back there."

"I do have an itch," I said a little lower, raising my brow. My voice changed from amused to desire. "It's a certain itch, which only someone can stop if you know what I mean."

His eyes twinkled. "Hmm, does this itch need me to undress you?"

"We both need to be completely naked," I smiled, wrapping my hand around his dark grey tie and pulling him down so my mouth was just against his. "Undress, baby!"

Letting out a loud laugh, he jumped up and unbuttoned his shirt fast. His slacks were pulled down with his boxers. My husband was hard and ready to go. Another squeal escaped my throat as he pulled my legs apart and reached up underneath my bum. Grabbing the black material, he tugged my leggings off in record speed.

Before he came back towards me, he stopped and admired me from down on the bed. His eyes came back up to mine when he smiled. "I love you, Gabriella, so much."

He climbed up over my body, my legs wrapping around his thighs automatically and locking him in. I grazed my fingertips up over his shoulders and wrapped my arms around his neck. "I love you, too."

Our mouths passionately indulged in each other. Our sweat-clad bodies tangled underneath the white sheets. Hands rarely left each other's skin. We were making love to music; making passionate and slow love, none of the hard, newfound sex that we had been doing so much. We went back to basics, and it felt better than ever. We were consummating the start of something new, a new beginning of our life, a new life that had been created together.

My hand was outstretched above my head, and fingers entwined with him as his pace increased. Our bodies were so connected and in sync with each other, feeding off each other's moans and groaning until we were at the peak together and climaxed with one another. My eyes never left his and vice versa. The intensity brought tears to my eyes and the love I felt right now was unbelievable, and it didn't take long for Brody's eyes to also water. Our mouths met again even hungrier with desire.

I felt our connection blossoming and becoming stronger after we bared our souls and confessed our secrets. We could finally take that weight off our shoulders and not have any worry. We could truly focus on the future.

As scared as I was, I was eager for it.

Knowing that Brody and I was both on the same page, it was a huge relief of happiness. For better or for worse, we hopefully had just gone through the worst and was going back to the better.

"Tell me about the restraining order. When did that happen?" Brody asked after a few moments of comfortable silence, propping himself on his side and walking his fingertips over the curve of my breast exposed to him.

"When we came home, he was calling at first and would call up to ten times a night. I ignored him and then he started to text me."

"What did they say?" he murmured, listening to me closely.

Even if I didn't want to talk about this, I realised that I needed to. Part of my problem before was that I was scared of upsetting him or hurting his feelings. He needed to know these things, and even if it wasn't good, he still had every right to know. "That he wanted me. If I didn't answer his calls, then he would put my photographs online. I spoke to the lawyer when you sent him my way, and he helped get a restraining order."

"I will kill him." He looked completely serious.

Placing a peck on his shoulder, I shook my head. "No, you won't. He's your brother, and you'll just beat him up."

With a sigh, he nodded back. "I should kill him."

"Just promise me that you won't let him in our home?" I asked quietly. "I don't trust him."

Lips skimming down to mine, he nodded. "I promise, baby."

I looked up, and our gazes locked. He was already pulling up to straddle my waist, hard and ready to go again. Our need for one another was becoming completely intense, and it was nowhere near sated.

Brody had called his mother, asking her to collect Noah and Lila from school. We weren't ready to leave and ended up ordering Chinese and getting back into bed naked to eat it. Both of us wanted to stay here until we were ready to go back home, united and sure of everything.

If there was an ounce of doubt, then we weren't leaving this room.

Sitting up, I leant forwards as he brought over a piece of honey chicken towards my mouth between his chopsticks. This was the best dinner we had yet.

"Yum," I grinned, licking my lips.

With a grin, he winked. "You are."

"Such a flirt," I laughed and met him in the middle for a kiss. Yeah, best dinner ever.

We finished and ended up lying in bed at opposite ends. His hand ran down and up my smooth skin when I asked. "How much do the kids hate me?"

"They don't hate you. They hate me," he corrected. "Noah's angry and Lila…" Blowing out a breath, "Well, she's playing up pretty bad and won't listen to a word I say."

"This affected them badly," I said quietly. I hated that we did this to them. "We're going to need to talk with them, sit them down and just really talk. They need to know that we're not splitting up."

He laid there a moment, running his hands through his hair as he let out a yawn. "It's my fault. I can take that blame. I know throwing you out was a dick move, and it affected them badly. I'm going to feel like shit every day about that, Gabby."

Sitting up, I moved towards him and straddled his bare lap. His hands automatically went to my hips where he drew circles with his thumbs. "Don't, please, I don't want to be one of those couples who dwell on the past. Yes, you hurt me so much, and I didn't deserve to be thrown out. But by saying that, I can see your side of things. You thought I was cheating, you had become insecure with my feelings towards you."

He wasn't going to take the full blown blame. It was me too.

"How far along are we?" he asked, his hands now sliding to my tummy. "I'm so happy about the baby. I think I almost passed out in the office when you said you were pregnant."

Looking down at him, I rested my hands on his wrists. "Not the best way to tell you but we're around eleven weeks. It scared me. I was happy but frightened. I didn't want another baby if I couldn't be with you," I admitted. Not that I would ever do anything to change that but it would have just been awful not to be together. "I think the night you attacked me in the kitchen was when this happened."

"I was so hard staring at your ass bent over," he groaned. "I'm hard now."

"I know you were, and now, I can feel how hard you are."

Sitting up, he wrapped his arms around me tightly. "You are so beautiful, and I promise that things will change with work."

"What do you mean?" I asked, tangling my fingers in his hair.

"I have worked so hard for almost ten years, and I sacrificed my family for that. You waited for me, and I missed so much dance concerts, sports games and almost the births of our children. Gabby, I'm not missing anything more."

"Brody, what are you saying? You can't quit work."

He chuckled, placing a kiss to the valley between my breasts. "No, because then we'd be broke, and we need money to pay bills unless you want to move in with my mother."

"Not happening."

He laughed, his Adam's apple bobbing as he swallowed. "No, I mean that from now on, it's nine till five. But I can do most my work from home. Maybe once a week or twice, I'll go into the office and do what needs to be done."

"You can do that?" I asked, my heart racing at the excitement of him doing all of this for us.

"I don't give a shit what they think. I've made them a lot of money. If they wish for me to continue doing that, then I will be taking time off. No work on weekends, either." He was completely serious.

He was so sexy when he talked this way. I was lifting my hips up and sinking into his hot flesh faster than ever. I didn't move; just stared into his eyes so deeply that I was sure our souls were talking. "You have no idea how long I have been waiting to hear you say those words to me. It's... Oh, God; I am so happy right now."

He was going to put us first. It was all I have ever wanted.

Brody's lips parted as his eyes rolled. Deep, shallow breaths, I began to move up and against him. Now was not the time for slow. I needed him badly. His fingers dug into the flesh of my ass as I ground against him. "Shit! Fuck! Slow!" He moaned louder, falling to his back with a groan. "Oh, God!"

CHAPTER TWENTY-SEVEN

Nervousness filled me as I drove behind Brody. We were going back to the house, and I hoped Noah and Lila would forgive us for how we've been acting. Selfish is what we were, but not anymore. They were going to see that their dad, and I were a united front. We were both committed hard to making this work.

We'd had one look at the custody paperwork after finally dragging our asses out of bed and dressed. They were now in the bottom of a bin and torn into tiny little pieces.

Pulling into our driveway, I parked the Jeep as Brody parked his Audi beside me. He got out and came around to the door, helping me out. I could have managed, but I didn't say no. I liked him helping me. Grabbing my suitcase, we walked towards the front door, and I felt nervous.

"The house is a mess. I'm sorry. I really fell to shit after I made you leave."

Offering him a smile, "It's okay. I know cleaning isn't your strongest point. It's only mess. It's not important."

If the house wasn't trashed, then the kids weren't having fun. I may have loved a clean home, but I loved happy children even more.

He was right, though. The house was trashed. Clothing was strewn about. Dirt over the floor from their shoes went to show just how much I actually did around here. Hopefully, he appreciated me all that more. I kept the home tidy, and it felt good to see that he finally realised that I work too. Just that, I don't get paid for it.

I was so anxious as I stepped inside. The noise that rocketed through the house was terribly loud. Noticing Brody's mother Loraine, she looked exhausted as she called out. "Brody, are you back? I cannot keep up with them and their fighting. They won't listen when I tell them bedtime!"

I felt awful that we'd put this on her. Her eyes widened as she noticed me walking inside with him and so did the kids. Their screaming had stopped, and they were running towards me.

"Mama!" Lila's scream came out as she threw her arms around my waist, almost sending me backwards on my bum.

Brody quickly spoke up, "Careful of your mama's stomach." They ignored him even though he didn't let the hurt show. I knew it hurt him.

The look on his mother's face was priceless. She had caught onto his slip. "You're?"

"Yes, we are," I smiled, loving that I was pregnant again.

Giving Noah and Lila both a kiss on their cheeks, I smiled, "Give daddy a kiss and say hello, please. You both know that we always give him cuddles and kisses when he comes home from work."

Noah glared, and Lila crossed her arms over her chest shaking her head. "No."

"Well, go to your room then," I shrugged, standing back up. "And go straight to bed please."

Within seconds, they were giving their father a cuddle and kiss. This was going to be tough, and I didn't expect them to forgive us and be happy. All we could do was show them that things are going to change, for the better.

Brody mouthed a thank you to me, and I smiled. Bending down to Noah, he looked from him to Lila. "I'm sorry that I haven't been a very good daddy these few weeks," he said and hugged them. "I do love you both, so much, and I love your mama."

Lila was the first to speak as Loraine had made herself scarce. "Is mama staying with us again? I don't want her to go."

I smiled. "I'm not going anywhere, baby. We're all going to sit and talk, but maybe before we do that, can you help put all those toys away on the floor? We have a surprise for you both."

"What kind of surprise?" Noah asked, a grin growing, as he looked curious.

"One that is very exciting!" I said with great enthusiasm.

They raced off, and Brody's hand went to my lower back as we walked into the kitchen. I ignored the pile of pizza boxes on the counter. He wasn't lying. He really did go to shit while I was away. With a smile, I sat up on the bar stool as he turned the coffeemaker on.

A voice spoke to us, and I waited for her to yell. "So, you're pregnant?"

"Yes, Gabby is pregnant," Brody said, confirming the news as he came around to me from behind. "She's moving back in here."

Loraine looked at us both and was cut off from speaking as the front door slammed.

"Baby bro! I got booze. We're celebrating your new single status. Good on you for getting that car back too!" his sister called out and came to a sudden stop when she entered the kitchen holding a bottle of Jack Daniels and another of vodka. "Brody, what's going on?"

Brody hardened his jaw. "Do you mind coming and making an entrance like that?"

Jessie set the alcohol on the table, glancing towards me confused. "Umm."

"I got to keep the car luckily." Teasing her seemed easier than getting mad. I just couldn't be bothered with any more fighting.

"I thought," she began.

"You thought wrong. Gabby and I have talked. I blamed her for a lot of untrue things—"

His mum cut him off sharply. "You mean you accused her."

Brody was silent a moment before nodding. "Yes. I will take full responsibility for that. I accused her when it wasn't true."

"Oh, well, you're a dick then, aren't you?" Jessie winked, coming over and giving me a kiss on the cheek. "It's not too late to leave him you know. I'm sure there are men out there who don't overreact."

I laughed, leaning against Brody's side. "Well, it kinda is." She raised a brow, and I grinned big "We're kind of having another baby."

"Oh, my God! You're pregnant!" she almost screamed, grabbing him for a tight hug as she squeezed his top half. "I knew it! You were having so much sex on that holiday."

"Shut your voice," muttered Brody, flushing red with embarrassment. "Not everyone needs to know about that shit."

"That shit knocked your wife up." You'd expect Jessie to have said that. Instead, it was Loraine. She had all three of us shocked. "Now, you, two, better not have any more of this divorce nonsense going on again. You need to make it work, considering your brother has gone haywire, and Rose is just as crazy."

Brody's smile had faded almost instantly. "Speaking of him." With a grim expression, he continued to fill them in on everything that had happened. I felt awful for putting them in this position, but like him, they had the right to know as well.

Loraine looked sombre as she nodded sadly. "Well, I understand. I am quite disappointed in your brother and his behaviour. I think we all are."

"Yeah, he's on drugs or something," Jessie added. "Anyway, tell me more about the baby. When is she due?"

"She?" I laughed. "Could be a he."

"I hope they are twins," Lorraine added. "Maybe next time."

I looked over at the empty pizza boxes once his mother and sister had finished their drinks and took the hint to leave. "So you really did eat a lot of takeouts." I hated that we'd been apart for a stupid reason. "Are we going to tell the children that we were going to divorce? They're so angry at us."

Brody leant his body against the counter and pinched the bridge of his nose. "I think we should explain the truth. It will be hard, but I think that they deserve that." Pushing himself up, he walked towards me and cupped my cheeks, leaning in and placing a kiss on my forehead.

I leant into him, relishing the closeness. "I agree. We'll be fine. We'll get back to that place we were at."

"It'll be better," he smiled. "When is your next appointment?"

"In a couple of weeks, I forgot what was involved with having a baby. It feels like my first pregnancy with all the sickness," I smiled. "Can you come to the next appointment?" I asked hopefully.

He pulled away slightly and looked down at me. "I told you, I wouldn't miss any of them. It's practically my company. I can do whatever the hell I want." His smile turned to worry. "Is there anything you can do for the sickness?"

"You mean besides drinking tca and eating dry toast? Not really, it's meant to help, but nothing eases it." I slid my hands up and wrapped them around his neck. "I think you should take me into your office one day and bend me over your desk."

A laugh escaped his throat. "How did you get from morning sickness to quickies on the desk?" He chuckled. "I think now I'm going to be working at home more. That's definitely possible."

I pushed up on my tippy toes and brought my mouth closer to his. "I love you."

"Love you too, baby," he smiled, closing the distance between us.

"All done!" Noah called out, interrupting and ending the kiss all too soon.

"All right, let's go and sit on the couch." This was going to be hard, but I couldn't put it off any longer.

The four of us sat on the couch. Brody moved and took a seat on the coffee table in front of us and began to speak first. It felt so familiar like we had been here before. We had been when he promised them he wouldn't leave. "Everything has been really messy lately, one big misunderstanding."

"You said Mama didn't want us. That's why she wasn't here." I tried not to let Lila's word hurt me. I picked her up and sat her down on my knee.

"I was angry when I said that," Brody said quietly, explaining to them in the short G-rated version of what had gone on, and I think it was good we could talk to them about things instead of keeping them curious and in the dark.

"What's our surprise?" Noah asked, getting to their main point. I realised they were over talking about us and wanted to get to them.

Looking towards him, I was pleased that they seemed to be taking this well. "Well, your daddy and I, we're going to have another baby. There's a baby growing inside my belly right now."

Brody leant over and kissed me. "Yes, you two are getting a brother or sister."

"Brother!" Noah grinned.

Lila shook her head. "No, it's a sister!"

After the debate of what the baby was, we went into the kitchen, and I was going to make us some dinner until I realised there was no food in the pantry. It was bare and sad to look at. Brody looked embarrassed at how he'd slacked off, but I didn't make a fuss over it. His cheeks reddened as he ran a hand through his hair.

I just grinned. "We need groceries badly," I said as I closed the fridge door. I felt pretty bad about how they had not been eating well. "Did you want to go and get groceries, maybe pick up dinner on the way home?"

"I like that idea," he said. "I feel like shit for not taking care of the household when you were gone."

Putting my hand on his jean-clad thigh, we drove into town to a Coles shop. "We should take them to the snow before the baby comes. They'd love it down there."

"Just us?" he asked, glancing over. "That would be preferred than going away with my family again or yours." Ah, my lovely parents who I had been avoiding like the plague, I just didn't want to tell them about all out problems and give them a reason to say I told you so.

"Yeah, just us," I smiled back, leaning over in my seat and towards his. "You still make my heart race."

A soft groan escaped his throat. "As do you. If you're not careful, I'll pull over right here and fuck you."

Rubbing towards the middle, I grinned. "Too bad those two are in the back, or we'd definitely be pulling over."

He groaned again. "You're killing me, my love." Glancing once more, "Thank you, Gabby."

"For what?" I asked, bringing my hand back to his thigh. I felt really happy right now.

"This, for everything, for taking me back again and giving us the chance we need but I promise you that we will get through this. We'll get it right this time." He placed his hand over mine and held it. "I love you."

"I love you too, and we will get through this. We've been together too long to just throw it away."

Once we'd gone and brought enough food to keep us feed for the week, we picked up some fish and chips and then made our way home. The kids surprisingly were good on the way home, at the store and at the house. They didn't complain nor did they act out in public. I thought it was ridiculous that Brody hadn't actually been able to buy groceries for such a long time, and he was amazing at what food was out. We had a lot of junk foods that was going to keep me tempted to snack on when those cravings hit.

Clearing the plates, I reached for Brody's. "I promise, tomorrow I will cook a roast." I was craving vegetables so bad. "And, now, I think we should get these two into bed and go to bed yourself."

"I agree. You, two, it's bed time," Brody said standing up.

They both just looked at him.

Their moods have changed, and they were still upset. It was understandable. Walking towards them as Brody took the plates from me; I sat on the chair next to Noah. "Please go and say good night to daddy; then, I will come and read you both a book."

When they didn't move, I just looked at Brody. "I'll put them to bed. Why don't you go run us a hot bath?"

He nodded with a sad smile. "All right." Kissing their heads, he then left.

Talking to both kids separately, I think I may have gotten through to them that this wasn't their father's fault. Coming into our bathroom, I sighed and began undressing as I watched Brody who was already in the bathtub, leaning back with his eyes shut.

"I don't like that Noah is swearing, and Little Miss Attitude is going to have those dolls taken away if she keeps her act up," I said pulling a sock off, balancing myself on the wall.

He just sighed. "It's my fault. I'm sorry. I didn't do anything after kicking you out but sit and have a pity party. They won't listen to me at all."

Sinking into the water once naked, I laid down with my back to his chest. "They are mad, yes. They don't really understand. They just think you hurt me and wouldn't let me come back."

He reached forward, wrapping his arms around my body and resting his hands on my stomach. "I was beyond upset, and I have put myself in your place. I was a mess just like you were. I couldn't eat. I just felt numb. Even work was getting messed up."

"You thought I was leaving you. I would have been hurt if you didn't go through some kind of breakdown. I can't imagine what you felt, but I will never leave you or hurt you." I brought my hands up to his. "You took everyone's blame, and that wasn't fair." He never let his mother or sister blame me once. He didn't have to do that.

I felt his lips against the nape of my neck, his warm breath hitting my skin. "It was because I chose to not let you explain. I deserve it all."

"I should have made you listen. Try harder," I said quietly. "I couldn't tell my parents about us."

I could feel his smile slowly breaking out. "I don't blame you. That's a conversation I'd never want to have." Then his body relaxed as he sighed heavily. "The kids, I'm sure they told you that I yelled at them a lot. I was a bastard."

Well, it didn't surprise me that they were so mad at him. "They said you were mean. I tried talking and explaining things." I remembered him saying he'd spent a lot of that time drunk. "Did you, go out drinking?" I hated to even think of him in a bar, and sad.

"No. Never. I stayed in the home office. I even slept there too. I deserve it, I deserve it all." he said and held me close. "I am truly sorry, baby."

"I know." And I did know it. He had shown me just how sorry he was. "Your mum isn't getting twins by the way."

"Oh?" he chuckled.

My eyes closed as I relaxed in the hot bath of water. I loved baths. "Three is going to be a handful."

"But he or she is going to need a friend as you pointed out," he reminded.

I had forgotten about saying that. "Maybe, let's just see how this one goes."

My eyes flew open as he his hand began to wander down lower from my belly and between my thighs as his voice turned husky and cock grew stiff. "Oh, baby, after this one, I'm definitely putting another in you."

If only he knew just how much that turned me on.

CHAPTER TWENTY-EIGHT

I felt as if my eyes were glued shut. I was completely exhausted.

We had spent a good part of the night going over a new challenge, the thirty days of sex. Leon had sent him a text with the link last night, and Brody was eager as hell for it. I, on the other hand, was befuddled; thirty days? Really?

The ground rules for our thirty days of sex challenge. It wasn't just in-and-out basic sex, no. It was quickies — sex in the kitchen, laundry sex, keep your clothes on sex, normal sex, outside sex, naughty outfit sex, fantasy sex, blindfolded sex. It was going to be thirty days of having sex. Rain, hail or shine, or in our case, fighting, kids, morning sickness or late nights, we were going to do it. 2 AM or 2 PM; we were both attempting to do this challenge. I gave it a week before we're calling for a night off.

After all the talk about it, I fell asleep before Brody got lucky.

"What are they doing?" Brody groaned, half asleep with his arm covering his face.

I yawned into the pillow as I listened to the kids screaming and fighting. "No idea." Lifting my head, I groaned when their fighting wasn't dying down. It wasn't even 5 AM. Looking back towards him, I whispered, "Stay in bed, it's early." I kissed him on the arm and got out of bed.

Pulling on some boxer shorts and a tank top, I threw on a jumper and slid my feet into my purple slippers as I grabbed a hair tie while walking towards the stairs. Doing my hair in a messy bun as I walked into the kitchen just in time to watch as a bag of rice bubbles burst open, and little white puffs went spraying everywhere.

"Look what you've done, Lila!" Noah yelled shoving his sister.

Lila, frowning back, tried kicking him in the leg. "You did it, Noah!"

"Enough!" I snapped. It was too early for this. Pointing towards the pantry door, "Noah get there and face the door!" I then looked at Lila and pointed to the wall behind the dining table. "And, you, get over there!"

"But," she wailed, stomping her foot.

"No, don't even think of moving or speaking. You both know hitting isn't tolerated in this house, and you've made such a mess! Sit and shut it." Like I said, I was tired and now moody with pregnancy hormones.

Brody walked into the kitchen just as I scooped up the last of the cereal with my palms. The floor was clean. They could eat it still. Maybe it would teach them a lesson for fighting. Noah glanced over his shoulder and quickly looked away when Brody looked at him. Lila was still being silent and not uttering a peep.

Dusting my hands, I stood back up with the container. "Morning, you hungry?"

"Coffee first, baby. Kids giving you a hard time?" he asked, looking back at them.

"Yeah, they're in a fun mood," I muttered and made them bowls of cereal. "You both, come and have your breakfast now. What would you like on your sandwiches?" I asked, grabbing the loaf of bread.

Noah, propping himself up on the bar stool, grabbed the spoon and shoved it into his cereal. "Dad, let us order lunch every day. I don't want boring sandwiches."

Brody mouthed sorry and set his coffee down. "Look, Noah, your mum is making your lunch for school. Either tell her what you'd like to eat or go without."

"Don't care," he mumbled. I hated that he was acting like this.

Lila was still in a foul mood also. "We have a school fair. I have to take the food to Mrs. Pratt for Friday."

I did a double glance at the calendar and held my tongue. "That's tomorrow, sweetheart. You should have mentioned this last night while we were shopping." Now, I was going to have to race into town, cook like crazy and drop it off when I picked them up today. Ugh, this wasn't a good start today.

Her remark was well heard. "You weren't here."

"She was last night, and you never mentioned it to me. So, I don't think you'll have anything to take now," Brody said, obviously growing tired of their sarcasm towards us.

Smiling at her, I wasn't going to let them know how tired I was starting to get. "It's okay. I'll talk to your teacher and see what I have to make." I then whispered to Brody, rubbing my temple, "Hopefully, things are better by next week."

He just sighed, leaning against the counter with his dark grey sweats hung low on his hip. "It needs to go back now. You don't deserve to be spoken or treated this way by them." Picking up his coffee, he shook his head and walked out the back door onto the porch.

Getting the kids ready for school was something I strangely missed. It was weird how something so boring and repetitive could be missed. Brushing Lila's hair, she sat still and quietly. Noah was reading his home reader to me when I finished doing her side braid.

"Mama, can I have my hair straight?" she asked.

"Maybe when you're older, I like your hair this way." I smiled. She was too pretty to have a flat iron through those gorgeous curls of hers. "Go give Daddy a kiss goodbye."

Grabbing the car keys, they ran back in and took their school bags. "We kissed him, but he was on the phone," Lila informed me and looked at the floor.

I guess it was a start. "Okay, let's go." They took off, and I peeked my head through the sliding door. "Taking them to school."

He looked up and covered the mouthpiece. "Okay, love you. Drive careful."

Dropping the children off, I went to the store and grabbed a few extra things to bake a cake and a couple slices for the fair tomorrow. Heading back home, I felt queasy and nauseated. By the time I walked into the house, that sick feeling was gone. Between cooking and tidying up, I knew my last hurdle was going to be washing the clothes. Walking into the laundry, I almost closed the door again.

"Why don't we have a maid?" I groaned, staring at the floor covered in dirty clothing and the basket with clothes spilling out. "Oh, that's right. We do. I was the maid."

Bending forwards as I sorted out the whites from colours and the towels from delicates, I felt a set of hands on my hips and a bump into my behind. "So delicious," a husky voice murmured.

"You want some of this?" I asked, wiggling against him as I held onto the basket of clothing in front of me.

"You know I do, baby." Skimming his hand down, he roamed it over my lower back and gave another cheeky thrust.

Jumping up, I spun around and wrapped my arms up around his neck. Pulling him in towards me, "The kids kissed you goodbye, right?" I asked, having a feeling that maybe they lied to me about it.

Ignoring my question, his hand slowly lowered and spun me back around, pushing the top half of my body forward again, reaching down under and rubbing me between my leggings. "I want you like this, seeing you fell asleep before I could put the moves on you last night."

Groaning, I nodded, unable to hold in my moan as he began to peel my bottoms off. I spread my legs apart. "Well then, who am I to deny my husband what he wants?"

Reaching behind my body, I began to rub him over his sweats and stroke his willing hardness. When he pulled away, I assumed it was only to pull himself free, not expecting his wet, soft tongue licking me up and down.

"I love your taste," he groaned making me wetter. His tongue pushed inside my core, thumb rubbing my hardened bud as he brought me to a quick climax. Still shaking when he stood, his bottoms hit the floor, and he slammed in hard.

That first thrust was always the best, pounding relentlessly inside me until I couldn't keep the moans down. The vibrations added to our pleasure. I ran my fingers through his hair as I pushed into him, locking my feet around his back.

"You're so hot!" I cried out. He was gorgeous.

Smirking as he pulled me closer, his thrusts grew rapid and needy. "You're so fucking beautiful!" With another slam, he groaned. "I could come so easily right now."

With his words, they could make me come so easily. "I love watching you get off." It was true. He looked so sexy as he came. The eyes growing serious and rolling with parted lips as he inhaled and exhaled in deep, shallow breaths, his body stilled and pushed further in. My hands held his ass as I dug my fingers into his taut flesh. Leaning back, my breast exposed and bounced through the white tank top that was half falling off. I was going to come.

With a groan, he felt me tightening around him like a fist, and he joined me in amazing bliss. Our eyes locked and bodies clinging for dear life to one another as we came together.

"Can we cross laundry sex off our list?" I asked, wondering if we could shuffle the days around.

A laugh escaped his throat. "Not a chance in hell, baby, it doesn't count yet. We'll be back in this room soon."

"I love you," I smiled as he pulled out, bending and grabbing a towel to clean the semen that was running out of me. "You didn't answer before. Did the kids kiss you goodbye?"

Not saying anything until he cleaned me up and tossed the towel in the dirty pile, "Lila did. Noah just waved and walked away." He must have noticed the hurt in my eyes. "It's okay. I don't want to force him," he said and pulled me against his chest.

"I'm sorry. I thought that they both did. They wouldn't let me kiss them goodbye. They didn't even want me walking them to class like normal," I said sadly. "I hope things get better soon. I don't like this silent treatment they're giving us."

"They will. It'll take some time, and I'm sure they wanted to."

"I don't know. It's just hurtful to see them so angry. They're mad because of us."

"I know," he said quietly. He smiled as if he had a grand idea. "Let's do it. Let's go to the snow today after school." I checked the forecast earlier, and it's expected to snow over the weekend.

My brows dipped in confusion, mostly surprised. "It's a three-hour drive. Won't it be too late once we get down there?" I asked. It was snowing at Cradle, but it was also far from home.

"No, let's go stay there for a while; the four of us, taking our own mini holiday." Chuckling as his hand rested on my stomach, "I mean five of us."

He couldn't be serious? Oh, but he was. The way he was grinning, he was planning it all out in his mind. I began to feel excited myself. "We can do that. Of course, we can. I'll pack our clothes, and we can leave after getting the kids from school." My smile turned to a serious stare. "Can you do this, you know, getting away from work?"

"My family needs this. We need this." Bending down, he kissed me just as the machine came to a stop. "I'll hire someone to clean while we're gone. Don't worry about anything. Let's go pack."

I came back into the house once I put the kid's bags into the boot of the SUV and took the cooking out. At least, I was able to have that done and over with. Walking into the living room, I sat on the couch with a yawn when Brody walked in holding my phone.

"Your phone was ringing." There was a hesitant pause. "I answered it."

"Who was it?" I asked, patting the spot on the couch beside me for him. It didn't bother me the slightest that he picked it up. I had nothing to hide.

Taking a seat beside me, his arm lifted up, resting it on the couch, and he turned to face me. "Realtor; she said she found you a two bedroom. That's the only one available in your price range. She asked me if you were able to up your limit."

Blushing, this was so embarrassing. I was unable to afford a decent home on my own. "What did you tell her?"

"I gave her a new limit and then hung up on her," he grinned with a laugh. "She won't be calling back again."

I could only imagine what he had told her. "Thank you."

"You wouldn't have been without a home. If things went through, I would have bought you one myself if you refused to take this one." Placing a kiss to my temple, he held me tighter. "Let's not worry about that, all right?"

This was the side of Brody that I fell in love with, so caring and compassionate towards others, well, most the time. There was the odd exemption that I didn't mind if he was rude to. Say, if he wanted to tell Kate to screw off, then I would more than happily allow that.

"Are we bribing them with this trip?" I asked as we drove to the school. I had called and made up a slight fib that we needed to leave for a family emergency, and the kids would be missing two days of school.

"Nope, we are showing them that we are a family," he replied without hesitation as he pulled into the school parking lot. "Yes, a little but this is how things will be from now on, a family and doing things rather than nothing."

"I can't wait to tell them." Leaning over, I kissed him on the mouth. "You want to come get them with me or wait here?"

"I'll wait here. I'm sure it would be better."

Nodding, I went in and picked Lila up first. Her teacher, unfortunately, pulled me aside to talk about something she had mentioned today, and I was completely mortified with what was assumed of me. Brody was going to flip out once he found out. Noah was quiet, but he did hold my hand as we walked back to the car.

Walking back to the car, I couldn't even look at Lila as I sat and done my belt up.

Brody noticed, of course, and looked in the back seat for the kids. "Is everything, all right?" he asked low and carefully.

Shaking my head, I tried blinking the annoying tears away. "Your daughter is quite the story teller, telling her teacher that dad drinks a lot and gets very angry and that her mother left because she was sick of having to look after them." Scoffing, I looked towards him. "Luckily, the teacher didn't believe a word of it since she knows us."

His eyes widened. "Christ," he muttered and started the car back up. "You're going to end up grounded soon. Noah, I hear you lied to your mother this morning, and Lila, what you told your teacher was wrong. You don't lie." Swallowing, I knew he was trying to compose himself. "Looks like you both won't be having any fun this weekend if you're going to play up."

"Where are we going?" Noah asked.

"Be quiet, Noah," Lila mouthed. "Mama, where are we going?"

"I think you both need to start being a little more polite." Turning in my seat, I looked at them both. "You're children, not adults. Cut the back chatting. If either of you lies again, be rude or argue, then there will be no Santa Claus, Easter bunny or birthdays!" Empty threats but they always worked. Raising my voice to let them know that they weren't controlling us with their acting out, I let them know we were still in charge and in control. "We're going to the snow, and we're going to have fun!"

CHAPTER TWENTY-NINE

"I hate you!"

If your child has ever said that to you, then you know the kind of heartbreak I am feeling right now. Lila, in a bad mood, decided to lash out and say the one thing I'd never want to hear again all because I told her to zip her lips and have a nap.

The car brakes came on, and Brody was pulling onto the side of the road. His face was red with anger as he glared at his daughter. "Apologize to your mother now!" he yelled at her, not too loudly but enough to let her know she'd gone too far.

"No," she challenged back.

"It's fine. Let's just keep going," I said quietly. I didn't want to argue with them anymore.

Shaking his head, he looked back at Lila. "You're grounded until you apologize to your mother, who does everything for you!" He then turned in his seat and started the car back up and pulling onto the road.

Trying to distract him, I reached over and squeezed his hand. "This place has an open fireplace," I whispered, thinking of how romantic that could be.

He grinned. "As long as we are all together, then I don't care what it has."

The drive seemed to pass by quickly. The snow was thick and covered the road as we got to the retreat. The kids were also tired and cranky as they refused to nap on the drive. That was the first thing they were going to do.

"Would you like a nap before we go and have dinner?" I asked Noah as I helped him through the snow.

He nodded sleepily. "Yes, please."

I helped him into the bunk bed and kissed his forehead. "Love you, baby," I whispered and left the room, walking out to the living room and staring through the large open glass windows the snow falling from the sky. "This is gorgeous here. We should move." I'd love to live in the cold, snowy weather, but I did love the summer weather by the beach back home.

"If you're serious, we'll move," Brody said, coming up behind me.

Shaking my head with a laugh, "No, I love our home. But maybe, we could come back and stay again. It's just so peaceful to be here, and it's really our first family holiday with the five of us," I reminded, turning to face him and pushing my flat tummy against his as he came up to me.

"We'll come back." He brought his arms around my back and pulled me against his chest. "I don't know what to do with the kids. Lila was so rude on the drive here. I wanted to turn around and take her home."

Scrunching my face up, I tilted back and looked at him. "I know. She is getting a mouth on her. It's pushing my patience."

"I refuse to have our children walk all over us. Yes, we threw their lives around, but we've raised them to respect others and what they're doing isn't right."

Letting out a yawn, I began to walk backwards and peel up my shirt. Glancing over my shoulder towards the room we were sleeping in, I grinned back at Brody. "This bed looks so big and comfortable. Enjoy the couch stud."

Tossing my shirt at him, he caught it as he begun stalking towards me. "Oh, really? Is that how it's going to be?" He then came to me and tackled me down onto the bed with a laugh.

The kids were sleeping. We had our door closed, and neither of us was really in the mood to go to sleep. A little fun under the covers never hurt anybody, and we were back in that lustful honeymoon phase.

Unfortunately, it was also easy to forget that we were in a much smaller cabin and not a huge house like our home. As I raised my hips up one final time, I bit into his shoulder as I began to come, but also at that exact same time, there were footsteps nearing the bedroom door with chitter chatter.

"Kids... Quick..." I breathed out. My orgasm had vanished. I wanted to scream.

Seeming to get my point, Brody was already coming. His body stilled as he came and left. Literally, he blew and pulled out quickly to jump up and grab his boxers and jeans. "That was close," he panted, pulling his shirt on over his head.

I just stared on edge and frustrated. "Umm?"

He smirked, half-heartedly laughing. "I'll get them, and I'll fix you up later."

I giggled as I lay there utterly exhausted and wondered how I would find the energy to dress and go out there. The motivation kicked up a notch or ten once I heard Lila speaking up.

"What was that noise coming from your room?"

Brody looked stuck for words as I walked out and smiled. "TV was on. We fell asleep to it," I said, hoping she believed that. She did. "Hungry or thirsty? I'm very thirsty."

Brody just smirked. "Yeah, I'm both."

Noah sat on the couch and looked at me as I sat opposite him. "I'm hungry, mum."

"You're always hungry. You know, when daddy was in school, one night, he ate three pizzas to himself. He was so sick the next day." I laughed. "Grandma got so mad when he threw up all over her couch."

Noah began laughing as I reminisced about those days. "I must eat like him then."

"Yeah, but the pizza was pretty good, and your mother barely ate anything." Brody winked. "Lila, are you hungry?" he asked, trying to pull her into our conversation, but she just sat there silently.

Correcting him, I waved a finger at him. "I was too shy to eat around you." Running my hand through her curls, "You must be starving?"

"I'm not eating anymore," she said as a matter of fact.

Two could play at this game. "You know, if you're not going to eat, then you can't go for a swim in the pool. That's going to be boring watching all of us swimming and having fun."

And finally, with a soft mumble, she gave in. "I might be a little bit hungry then."

"Restaurant or order in?" Brody asked, "We could walk down there in the snow."

"Well, I think that would be fun. Let's go out," I smiled, staring to stand again. "Lila, you want to come get ready with me?" I suggested.

I hoped she was going to say yes, and she did but just not to me. "I want daddy."

Brody noticed my smile slightly fading. "Sweetie, go with mama and help her pick out something pretty to wear."

Unfortunately, she shook her head and wouldn't look at me. It really almost broke my heart that she hated me so much. Not letting her see the hurt, I stood up and put on a smile. "It's okay. I won't be long, you just…" I couldn't even finish talking to her. With a sigh, I looked towards her and Noah. "I love you both."

Closing the bedroom door, I leant back against it and could hear their conversation quite easily.

"Kids, we're on a family holiday, and I know we're confusing you a lot lately, but we're trying to have a good time. We want you to see how much we love you both, and that I love your mother dearly. Please don't be rude to her." Brody was trying to hide the desperation in his voice, but he wasn't hiding it as well as I knew he wanted it to be.

"Mama's grumpy."

"Dad yells louder, and you don't hate him."

"Shut up, Noah. You're stupid!"

"Dad, she said a bad word!"

It was never ending.

"Mama is upset that you told your teacher lies about us, Lila. She loves you just like I do, but you need to tell her sorry for what you said in the car and apologise to your brother for calling him stupid. We don't tease or bully each other." Brody made it clear. His voice held authority over them. I could scream, and they wouldn't listen. But when his dominance came, though, they listened.

Lila listened, being his little girl. She was always his little girl. "Sorry, Noah." I didn't miss the next, clear as day, question that had me almost snorting with a laugh. "Dad, if mama is having a baby, will the baby love her? And how did it get into her tummy?"

"Yes, of course, the baby will love her, Lila," Brody replied with exasperation. "And I put the baby in there."

After my shower, I walked out of the bedroom feeling awake and refreshed. Doing my top up, I smiled as Noah sat on the carpet playing with his cars. "I love the baby already. Can it be a boy? I want a brother to play cars with."

"I want a baby too! Can I have one daddy?" Lila piped up.

"Glad you love the baby, Noah," Brody yawned, noticing me in the room. He looked relieved. "No, I'm sorry,

Lila. That's not how it works, and when you're married, then you can think about babies; not a moment before then."

Hopefully, it would be once they're well into the thirties, so I didn't have anything to worry about; not that that's how things worked for us. If only my parents knew our truth, I would have been shunned for sure. It was only relief that we could pass it off as a honeymoon baby, and I went into labour early.

Sitting on the couch with the kid's fresh change of clothes, I smiled, "Go shower. I'll dress these two."

Brody went to shower, and I sat back after dressing the kids. I pulled out my phone and noticed a missed called from my Mama. I hesitated in calling her back. I had missed four weeks of phone calls from her. My sisters wanted to know why, and I could only text them back. If I had heard their voices, I would have broken down, and my heart couldn't take the verbal lashings if they knew about the divorce. She never left a voicemail, and with a sigh, I went over to the kitchen and called her back.

On the fourth ring, my Papa answered, "Buona sera."

"You're meant to say good evening in English on the phone, Papa," I lightly scolded, a smile on my face. "It could have been someone else."

He chuckled. "Ah, Gabriella, Ciao."

"Papa, ciao."

"Your mama is very worried about you, not calling her back," he said.

I almost rolled my eyes. "I'm sorry. I've been very busy."

He went back to speaking with Italian. "Hai tua madre preoccupata. Quello che ti ha tenuto occupato?"

"The kids; and mama knew Brody and I went on a holiday, papa. It would have been rude spending hours on the phone," I pointed out. "And if I remember, she made it clear she was very angry about us doing so."

"Tua madre è fuori in questo momento. Io sono lei chiamare. Vi suggerisco di che rispondere, Gabriella," he threatened.

"I can't promise I will pick up. My reception is bad here." It wasn't my fault she was out. "Oh, umm, so we're having a baby. I'm pregnant." I thought I would add that in, so he was forced to tell mama.

"Sei incinta? Capisco." Quiet a moment, he sighed heavily. "Dove sei?"

"Brody and I have taken the kids to the snow for a long weekend." It was such a relief he'd rather ask where we were than to congratulate me on the pregnancy.

"Un'altra vacanza che vedo," he accused. He was growing impatient. "You will answer when I call."

"Not a holiday, a getaway." I rolled my eyes as Lila began to pull at my leg, whining to leave. "Good night, Papa."

"Ciao." He hung up.

Looking down at Lila, my patience was lowering for her antics today. "Stop that. You're being silly."

She dropped her lip. "I want to go."

"We're waiting for Noah and Dad, then we can leave." I sighed, sitting on the bench. I'd love a glass of red about now. She was pulling at my shirt still, ignoring me. "Stop it. I'll ground you."

"You already grounded me." She rolled her eyes with a glare back. This little girl had my temper and desire to not back down in a fight. The feisty Italian side of her was coming out.

It was getting out of hand, and maybe, food would help. "Babe, I'm hungry, and it's getting dark."

Brody walked out of the room, freshly shaven. I smiled. My mood instantly picked up. He grabbed the cabin key and his wallet. "Let's go."

The kids ended up running in front of us and picking up the snow, throwing it at each other and squealing as the coldness went down their shirts. Snuggling against Brody's side, I sucked in the cold air. "It's freezing."

Smiling down at me, he chuckled. "We could snuggle, naked?"

"You wish," I nudged him with my head against his shoulder. "I called my papa. I even told him I'm pregnant. He reacted the same."

"Ah, so he ignored it." He sighed. "The call didn't go too well I take it."

I groaned with frustration. "No, they're not happy the least. My mama is very pissed. Lila is also pissed. She's being very bratty and ignoring me."

"I was tempted to order in. Her attitude is killing me." He placed a kiss against the side of my head. "Let's try ignoring her next time she carries on. She's doing it for attention."

Lucky for us, there weren't many people dining out. We got a table near the glass windows so we could watch the snow falling. I told them we could go out and build a snowman

tomorrow, which had Noah's eyes lighting up. The snowman
talk turned into a plan to have a snowball fight, boys against
girls, which would be something fun to do together.

This trip was about bonding together as a family. It
wasn't just about Brody and I getting back on track, but it was
about the kids seeing how much we loved them and wanted us
all to be happy. I wanted them to know that things were going
to be different for the better.

No more fighting or midnight screaming matches, it
was all about being a happy family and getting through it if
times ever became tough again.

Dinner had been going so well. The food was
incredible. Noah was drinking hot chocolate and had
marshmallows stuck to his lips which he was trying to lick off.
Brody laughed, pulling his phone out and taking photos of us,
something that he hadn't done in forever. Normally, I took the
family pics.

"Can we get in the big spa?" Noah asked. Brody had
booked the spa cabin for us.

I smiled, "You, three, can, but I can't. The baby would
overcook." Noah just looked confused. I didn't bother
elaborating. "Lila, would you like to get in the spa tomorrow?"

"Fuck off!"

It was clear as day. Others glanced over
uncomfortably, giving us judgemental looks. My cheeks were
burning and not from the fireplace. Noah looked at her big
wide eyes, knowing she was in major trouble. Brody and I both
stared at each other in horror. Had she really just said that?

Reacting the only way, I knew how. I stood up grabbed
her by the arm and wrapped my fingers around her. "I'm sorry.

You and Noah stay and finish your drinks," I said with a hushed hiss. "I'm taking her to the cabin."

"Do you want me to take her?" Brody asked, standing. "We can all head back now."

"No, don't." Glancing towards Noah, "He doesn't need to leave because she's being a brat."

Lila had her feet firmly on the carpet, and I realised she was about to throw one at me. Without another word, I bent down and picked her up. She kicked and screamed, but I didn't say a word as I carried her naughty ass out of the restaurant and made the walk back to the cabin in the snow.

I was so embarrassed and completely mortified.

Dropping her to the bed, I was so angry at her. "You have really upset me!" I began ranting at her. "You embarrassed your father and brother! You know that's wrong, and you know better than this Lila!" I yelled. "You won't come out of this bedroom. Go to sleep before I really lose my patience with you!"

I went to tuck her in after undressing her and putting some warm pyjamas on. She let me do that, but once it was time to get her into the actual bed, it was beginning to prove tough. She was fighting me all the way.

"Stop it!" I snapped, trying to get a hold of her. "Lila, I'm warning you!"

"No, go away!" she screamed back, sobbing. "Get away!"

In the midst of flinging her arms into my chest and almost slapping me across the face, her legs drew back then plunged into my stomach. I stumbled backwards with a wince, and without thinking or meaning to, my hand had come down on her thigh with a firm hard slap.

Holding her breath, she rolled onto her stomach and clutched at her leg where I hit her. She began to cry hysterically. She sounded as if I had beaten her. I left her in the room like that, throwing one hell of a tantrum.

Closing the door behind myself, still in shock while sliding to the floor on my bottom, I broke down crying, as I couldn't believe what I had done.

I had just smacked her.

CHAPTER THIRTY

When Brody and Noah walked back inside the cabin, I was still on the floor by her door sobbing. Lila was thrashing around the room. Her screams hadn't subsided as I wished they were. She would have to tire out soon. Hopefully, it didn't take much longer.

"Baby?" Brody came over, dropping to my level. "Are you all right?"

"I hit her," I admitted through tears. "I didn't mean to. She just kicked me in the stomach, and I reacted on instinct."

He looked confused. His eyes lowered to my stomach. "Do you feel okay? You should go and lay down."

"Didn't you hear me? I hit her." I had done the one thing we both agreed to never do. "I feel okay. If there's any pain, I will tell you, but I'm fine." I didn't want to make this a big deal.

Bashing on the door as I still slumped against it, Lila was at it again, screaming and pounding her little hands into the wooden board.

Brody leant forwards and pounded his own fist into the door. "Knock it off now before I come in and give you something to really cry about!" His voice was loud, thunderous as his anger had gotten the best of him.

Her screaming stopped with an instant. I knew he would never lay a hand on her, but she didn't.

Helping me up and offering to carry me to the couch, I declined since it was only a ten step walk, and that would be lazy of me. Noah walked over, laying by side. "We had ice cream and brought you some back, too."

"Oh, really? Was it good?" I asked, smiling as he could be sweet at the best of times. "I can't wait to try some."

"It was!" he grinned. As I picked up the small tub of strawberry ice cream, he added on. "The girl who gave it to us gave dad love eyes."

I raised a brow, smirking. "Oh, really?" I smiled at Brody. "Well, your dad is pretty handsome, isn't he?"

Brody shook his head, laughing. "You're both crazy. No more sugar for you two."

"Ah, sure, try to deny it by changing the subject." I poked my tongue out, licking the spoon.

Noah fell asleep not long later, and we continued to watch the movie he had chosen. I wasn't paying much attention, just worrying over Lila and what was going through her mind. She must be so confused. They both probably were. Brody carried Noah to bed as the credits rolled and came back to sit with me, bringing my legs up over his.

"You're quiet. What's going through your mind?" he asked, massaging gently.

"I feel awful for hitting her. I feel like I've just gone to my papa's level," I admitted.

Shaking his head at me, he moved and shifted us both around so I was laid on his body as his fingers stroked through my hair. "Gabby, you didn't beat her or purposely strike her. You hit on reflex. If that had been me and she kicked me in the balls, I probably would have done the same thing. You didn't do anything wrong."

"Then why do I feel so guilty about it?" I asked with a whisper.

Responding instantly, he said without hesitation. "Because you're such a good mother, that's why," he said quieter. "I think you should get checked out still, though? I've felt one of her kicks, and while they're not that hard to me, on you, it may do some damage."

"No, I'm okay," I promised. "I just want to lay here."

Kissing my head, he sighed and gave in. "You tell me, and we'll go straight to the doctors if something is feeling wrong."

"We're on a trip, and I hate this. It was meant to be a happy time for us." I sighed, placing my hand over my stomach. "I thought maybe this baby could be something exciting for them."

"Do you think she feels left out?" he suggested. "Possibly the reason for her acting this way. Whatever it is, she's acting like Tulip."

Laying there, I thought about it. It could well be the reason, but we had never shown favouritism between the children. They were both loved the same and treated the same. Listening to the sound of his heartbeat, I closed my eyes slowly and spoke softly, "Tomorrow will be a better day."

I must have fallen asleep. When I woke the next morning, I was nice, warm and snuggled up against Brody as his arms were wrapped around my body, holding me closely against his front.

His eyes remained shut, but he still smiled as he spoke, "You're staring."

"You're too pretty not to stare at," I said leaning in to give him a kiss. "Extremely gorgeous."

"Handsome," he corrected as he finally opened his eyes and kissed me as he rolled me onto my back with a big bear hug. "You're the pretty one."

A sleepy smile and I gave him a squeeze back. "I love you."

Lifting his head, he looked into my eyes and began to lower his mouth with a whisper, "I love you more, baby."

Getting out of bed while Brody went to the bathroom, I needed food before morning sickness kicked into gear and had me throwing up. The kids were still both asleep. I kissed them both then went back into the kitchen. Turning on the plastic kettle in the small kitchen, I yawned and looked into the fridge for something to make. Good thing, we were smart enough to bring our own food as there was nothing except those tiny little pods of milk and a jug of water in the fridge.

Dunking the tea bag into the hot water, I yawned and slid myself onto the couch, tucking my feet up underneath my bottom as I stared out at the beautiful snowing view. Brody had definitely gotten us a great chalet here. The kids, hopefully, woke up in a great mood and were excited to spend the weekend playing in the snow, and then maybe going to the spa and plunge pool. That's if everything goes well; funny how you have these ideas of how things could play out in your mind and then they turned completely opposite to that, like dinner last night.

Brody walked out with his hair wet and messy and a towel wrapped around his waist, and the thing that distracted me wasn't the bulge but the way he looked. He was so strong, and it was strange to see how much his appearance has changed from the tall, lanky boy at school to the strong, well-built man he had become now.

"Gabby?" he asked, causing me to look up and meet his sight.

"Yeah?" I asked coyly.

Grinning, he shook his head. "Stop eating me with your eyes. I asked if you packed my boxers. I can't find them."

"In the side, right part, I think," I answered with a blush as I smiled. "Sorry, you're just really nice to look at. Can't help it if my man's sexy."

Going back into the bedroom to change, he laughed. I yawned and snuggled down on the couch when a creak filled the room. Looking up, Lila's head was popping out of their bedroom. She noticed me, and within seconds her eyes went wide, and she disappeared with a quick shut of the door.

This wasn't how I wanted her to feel, scared.

Brody also noticed as he gave me a confused look and went to walk into the bedroom, but I shook my head, getting up from the couch and motioning him that I would speak with her. I wanted to get down and find out what was going on with our daughter. How she had been acting, it wasn't her. She was more mature than this version which had been greeting us this past couple of days.

"Lila?" I whispered as I walked quietly into the bedroom. "Please don't hide."

I pulled the covers down when I sat beside her on the single bed. Her big beautiful eyes watered as she stared up at me. It broke my heart to see her so sad looking.

"I'm sorry, mama."

Her voice was so soft and pure. I felt the honest remorse from her as she began to silently cry, and my heart bled with tears as I leant down and wrapped my arms around her tiny frame. "I know, baby girl, so am I." More than she would ever know, I was so sorry for all of this. "I love you so much, Lila, you and Noah both."

Her arms clung around my neck with tightness and desperation. "I love you."

We stayed like that for some time until I climbed into the bed with her and just held her. She was my daughter, and I would do whatever it took to help her and try to understand her better. When her sobs had died down, I finally asked. "What you said at dinner last night was very naughty. Why would you say that?"

She was quiet for a moment, and I know she was afraid to tell me the truth.

"Aunty Cathy told her to say it."

The voice that answered me wasn't Lila's. It was Noah's sleepy one instead.

Turning my head, I frowned, as I was extremely confused. "How do you know that?" And more importantly, why wasn't this brought to my attention earlier?

"Lila told me before I went to sleep. She said Aunty Cathy told her to say it to you, and that she would be in trouble if she didn't," Noah replied as Brody now stood at the door with a toothbrush in his mouth. He, too, looked confused.

"When did she say that?" Brody asked through a mouthful of paste.

At his grossest, he still made my heart flutter.

"She told me to say it when you came back home. That it would make you leave again because she told us you didn't really love Noah or me. She said you had another family and didn't want us anymore," Lila said quietly, her voice shaky with nerves and tremor.

I assumed that maybe it could be Scott or even Rose. Not in my wildest dreams would I have suspected my best friend. Luckily, I had been lying down; otherwise, that news may have just knocked me off my toes. That little *cagna* aka bitch; I was stunned beyond belief that my best friend had filled my daughter's mind with such lies. Cathy and I hadn't spoken as much lately, and I knew I was too wrapped up in my family life to be going out for our weekly coffee dates. Being in the hotel, I knew if Brody were the one dropping the kids off at school, then Cathy would know something was up. She'd suss it out by asking the kids, and they didn't have a filter. They knew how to tell the truth. I was guessing they had told her that I was no longer living at home, and daddy and mama were fighting.

Cathy has always been the biggest gossip around. I've always known that, and now, I also know that she's been gossiping about me. It was a slap in the face. Sitting up, I pulled Lila closer. "Is that why you've been so naughty? Did she tell you to do that?" I asked as Noah climbed out of his bed and joined us on ours.

Brody also, after spitting out his paste, came, sat and pulled Noah onto his lap. "You're not in trouble, Lila. We just want to understand better."

"She said you would send me away if I didn't do it," Lila spoke again, clearly becoming more upset.

"Bloody oath," Brody muttered under his breath. "No, Lila, that's not true at all."

Kissing her tangled up hair, I just cuddled her. "Baby, you never have to do that. All you have to do is be a little sister to Noah and a big sister to your new brother or sister. If Cathy comes up to you, and says anything like that again, I want you to tell her no and then you tell me right away. Okay?"

"I didn't mean to be bad. I thought you would send me away," she said softly again.

Shaking my head as I clung tightly to her, "No, baby, never, we'd never send you away because your daddy and I love you so much."

"We love you both like crazy," Brody grinned and held his hands out for Lila to come and hug him.

Climbing over to her father, she jumped onto his lap and squeezed him tightly with a hug. Noah pulled a face as his sister hugged him also. Brody and I did share a look with each other, though, and we were both going to be having a talk with Cathy.

I wanted to find what the hell had been said and why she would fill our daughters head with such garbage.

After breakfast, we all got dressed and rugged up in warm weather clothing. Taking a walk, we went to Dove Lake, which the kids loved. They were spotting possums and even wombats waddling through the snow. There were snow fights, and then they tried making snow angels. Brody even got down on his back as I snapped photographs of the three of them flapping on a blanket of fresh snow.

We had a fun snow fight near our chalet, and the boys won. It wasn't fair since they were faster at gathering the snow than we were. It ended with Brody slipping over and falling flat on his ass, and the kids jumped all over him.

CHAPTER THIRTY-ONE

Walking back down the stairs, I caught Lila's voice as I entered the kitchen. "What is it?" she asked, peering into the bowl of food that Brody placed in front of her.

"Dinner," he replied, blinking. "I just said it was."

Noah frowned also. "Yeah, but no offence, dad, it looks weird."

"Well, I had no idea what I was doing." Brody kept his cool and just turned to me. "Did you enjoy your swim?"

Smiling, I did indeed. "It was nice. It's also nice that you cooked for us all." Pausing a moment, I covered my mouth. "Excuse me, I feel..." Yeah, no time for any more words, I was up and running to the bathroom, where the bile in my throat rose and burned as I threw up.

I could hear Noah's curious questions. "What's wrong with mama?"

"Sometimes, she gets sick because of the baby. But she is fine, and the baby is fine. It's normal," Brody replied he was getting better at explaining things to them when they wanted to know something.

"Will she throw up the baby?" Lila asked. I almost laughed but instead, threw up again.

Brody just laughed. "No, she won't throw the baby up."

Walking back into the kitchen where they all were sitting, Brody came over to me, his hands against the lower of my back. "Are you okay?" He had been everything he promised, caring and very involved with the pregnancy.

"Yes, I'm good. So, what did you cook?" I raised a brow, trying to peer over his shoulder.

He blocked my view, wincing as he said the words. "Spaghetti with packet pasta."

"Oh, you're a naughty man," I laughed loudly. "That's okay. We only came home a few hours ago. I think the fact you cooked dinner is extremely sexy."

"Yeah?" he lowered his voice and eyed me cautiously. "I think two certain kids need to go to bed, so I can lock myself in a room with their mama for some sexy time."

My insides squirmed with delight and desire. "I love the way you think." I wiggled my brows.

We all sat down to eat. The kids finally picked up their forks and dug in. After unpacking the rest of our bags and walking into an extremely clean laundry, we made our way up to our room, and I undressed. Sitting on the edge of bed, I watched as Brody knelt before me. His hands ran up my ankles and the inner of my thighs, massaging my skin ever so gently and placing kisses along the insoles of my heels. I ran my fingertips through his hair and tugged.

Standing up and taking a step backwards, he slowly undressed. I watched, taking everything in and anticipating his next move. Taking me by surprise, I gasped when he took himself in his hand. "Do you like watching me stroke myself, baby?"

My lips parted, and I grew even wetter between the thighs. "Yes." It was all I could whisper. "I need you."

Smirking, he nodded back at the bed. "Why don't you get comfy and enjoy yourself a little more?"

Holy fuck! It would be unbelievably hot if we were to come together by not touching each other.

I was so nervous to lay down on the bed, and part my thighs for him. I was exposed and had never touched myself this way. I had no idea what to do or how he wanted me to touch myself. I just relaxed into the large fluffy pillows underneath my back and began rubbing myself in slow circles. My other hand skimmed up over my skin and cupped my breast. The sight of him stroking his hot length made me so wet.

Brody let out a groan. "God, baby, that's so hot. Slide your fingers inside yourself. Tell me how wet you are. I want to hear it," he growled at me with a command. His eyes did not once leave mine as he walked to the edge of the bed and pumped himself with a swivelling fist.

"Does this count as a thirty-day challenge?" I asked as I slid two fingers in deep to my knuckles. I gasped. I was in such a daze. Matching his pace, I lifted my hips and began grinding into my palm. "Brody... oh, God."

Picking his own pace up, he groaned again, squeezing the head of his engorged cock and his fist jerking faster. "I'm close, baby. Are you? I want to come together. Fuck," he moaned, hissing through parting lips. "Fuck, you're so fucking sexy like this."

"Mmm," I bit down on my lower lip, a moan boiling up inside as I clenched and pushed out around my fingers. As soon as the first stream of thick silky cum shot onto my belly, I came instantly and fingered myself harder. "Fuck, yes! God, I want you so bad right now!" I cried out, needing him inside me.

He was up, on the bed before my orgasm could fully die down, and slammed into me, hard. Over and over, he was hard again and making me come once more. His mouth slammed against mine. Digging my heels into his ass, I clawed at his back. I was going to come again. I never whimpered before, and now, I was crying, whimpering and screaming with a desperate need for him to give it to me as hard as he could.

When I finally woke the next morning, I was woken by soft kisses against the bare skin of my belly. Looking down, Brody was running his hands over my little bump that had only begun to appear.

"Morning," I whispered, my voice full of sleep.

His husky voice replied to me, "When does the kicking start again?"

"Few weeks yet, eager much?"

Laughing as he kissed his way up my stomach, chest and placing a kiss to my lips, he nodded. "I am very eager to have this baby grown and out. I'm not that patient as you may know."

"You're never patient." Smiling, "Hungry?"

"Yes." The look told me. He wasn't hungry for food.

Later that afternoon was when the nerves really began to set in. Cathy would be here within the hour. As far as she knew, we were just having come catch up drinks. Except, she had no idea I was pregnant and was going to dig for answers.

Cathy brought a bottle of red with her. I grabbed the platter of fruit, crackers and cheese and made my way out onto the back deck where the sun was beginning to set. I warned Brody to keep his distance and just let us girls have a bit of a catch up first.

"So, what's new?" she asked while pouring us both a glass of bubbly. "Haven't caught up in so long."

"Not a lot, you know. We just got back from Cradle Mountain. It was so nice down there." My fondest memory was riding Brody's face the night before we came home.

Lifting her glass to her red lips, she smiled. "Oh, I bet it was lovely to get away."

Almost an hour later, my friend hasn't realised that my glass was still full; and she was onto her third. I noticed her eyes were locked behind me as Brody made an appearance. Raising a brow at the glass in front of me, he picked it up and tipped it back into the glass bottle. Cathy didn't look pleased judging from her scowl.

Waving him off, "She can't drink now? That's a bit rich coming from you."

"Well, since he's such a possessive, controlling cunt, then I guess it isn't rich at all."

Spluttering her mouthful, she coughed "Excuse me?"

"You heard me right. The funniest thing happened. I was at school, and a friend came over, asking how things were.

We began chatting and soon enough, she tells me that she overheard a rumour that she thought I should be aware of." My voice was calm as I watched it sink in. "You told people that Brody is so possessive and controlling, that I don't have access to any money. And that the only reason I am still with him is because he's giving me such a lavish life that I refuse to give up." I was more than disgusted to hear this, humiliated that people had possibly believed her and thought this about us.

Right away, she was on the defensive. "How could you say this? You're willing to throw away a friendship over lies... It doesn't explain why you're not allowed a drink. Since when do you say no to wine?"

"She's pregnant. She won't be drinking." Brody's words were sharp and clear.

Cathy snorted with a laugh. "What? How?"

"Fucking. How else?" Okay, the way he was talking was incredibly hot but a little disturbing.

"Okay, that's gross. So, what are you two back together now?" she asked, raising both brows.

"We never left each other," I smiled, sitting up straighter and placing a hand against my stomach. "We're pregnant, and the kids are so thrilled about it, which brings me to my next question. why are you talking to my children and encouraging them to cuss at us?"

When Cathy lied, she would lick her lips twice, exactly what she did right now. "Huh?"

"Don't lie to me. I am sick of your lies, and I cannot believe what you made David look different than he ought to be. You told me that he cheated. It was you!" I was becoming angrier by the second and not in the mood for anyone else's bullshit.

"Yes, he caught me fucking another man," she muttered, not seeming bothered at all. "I didn't want to tell you and have you look down on me."

"I'm hurt that you would even think that. If you had told me, maybe spoken to me like a friend, I would have understood!" My voice was raising, like hell, I would understand. It soon registered in my mind — the looks, always asking about him and meddling with our family, eager for me to move out and be on my own. "You're in love with my husband," I barely whispered out.

"Oh, don't look surprised, the wog arrives in town and snags herself the hottest guy in school. I got it in your head that he was interested in you and even told his friends about your crush on him in hopes that they'd tease you. Who knew, he actually liked you back," she muttered, flashing me a grin. "Don't look so shocked."

As she said everything, that wasn't what my mind was still caught on but the racial slur that came from her mouth, the wog. I felt as if she slapped me across the face.

Looking at Brody, it was obvious that he noticed it too. With a dark look, he raised his arm and pointed towards the door. "Get out." His tone sent shivers down my spine.

"Excuse me?"

"I said get the fuck out," he warned once more. "I refuse to hit a woman, but I am about to lose my fucking shit with you. Get out you vile piece of filth. You are not welcome in this home again or anywhere else near my wife for that matter."

Stumbling, she lost her footing but still managed to throw herself into the cab at the end of our driveway. I couldn't believe she had done such a thing. It was disgusting and a complete letdown. My best friend was really just like the others who made fun of me behind my back and like all the other times... my husband stood up for me.

I was in the sitting room when Brody walked back in and stood in front of me as I sat and stretched out by the fire. "I never knew what you saw in me back then. Sometimes, I still don't."

"I saw you, and that's all I needed, the woman you were and the woman you now are. You are beautiful on the inside, and out."

With a smile, I looked up at him. "You're still so romantic. Maybe you can start with those love letters again?"

"You know how adorable you can be." He bent down on his knees in front of me. "I'm sorry about Cathy. Who knew she was a jealous old cow?"

"She was in love with you," I reminded. "Still is."

"I don't love her. You know that you're the only woman I have ever loved and will love."

CHAPTER THIRTY-TWO

I wanted passionate lovemaking.

I wanted to be kissed all over.

I wanted to be held until I fell asleep warmly in his arms and wake up the same way.

I wanted to be bent me over his desk and have him claim my ass with his seed.

Being horny while pregnant had its advantages. It took me to a whole new level of seduction, and right now, I was standing in his office at 11 AM while he stared hungrily at me. Licking his lower lip, his eyes roamed from my fuck me heels to the red lipstick I wore for him to smear off around his cock.

Undoing the tie on my long woollen coat, I let it fall open and revealed my curvy and pregnant body to him. My breasts swollen and full, mound freshly waxed and the burgeoning bump begging his hands to caress my soft skin. He gulped and stood up from behind his large glass desk.

"Kiss me." It was a simple request, but with much more meaning; that made him know that I needed to feel him right now.

His eyes darted to the window and flickered back to mine as he loosened the black tie around his neck. "Gabby," he said low, taking a step towards me. "I will fuck you if I kiss you right now."

"That's the point."

A smirk washed over his face, and he grinned. "Close the door."

"You want me to turn around, naked?" I faked innocence as I bit my lower lip.

Taking low, slow strides, his arms reached up, and fingers grazed against my pink nipple and twisted, rolling my flesh between his thumb and forefinger. Moaning softly, I whimpered when his touch left me. He walked further behind me, and I heard the click of the door and a lock flicking over.

Hands reached the top of the coat and peeled it slowly off my shoulders. "So sexy," he murmured as his lips began kissing in a row down the curve of my neck and shoulder. "Sweet tasting."

"You should taste elsewhere," I said with a moan, rolling my head to the side.

"Later; need you now."

The clink of his belt and thump of his pants as they hit the floor, my body pushed forward and legs kicked open. Brody, with a swift and precise movement, was inside me and erratically thrust with need.

Doing the final button up on his crisp white shirt, Brody gave me a lazy smirk. "I want to come home. Wait an hour, and I'll be done?"

Music to my ears, I slipped into the jeans I had brought with me because I wasn't a woman walking around without anything on. I brought an extra bag and tossed it on the floor before he noticed. Although, he did speak to me without looking up and asking if I had come to suck his dick.

One woman kept popping her head in every five seconds to ask if Mr. Whittaker wanted anything or needed her assistance. He would sigh and tell her no then she'd leave. Coming back with a cup of coffee and a snide remark about needing to use the gym or to even to brag about a hot date, she went on. I think she was trying to make him jealous, but it wasn't working. He didn't drink the coffee or ask about her dates.

I was able to see what he was like when he really worked, listen to the calls with other businessmen or arranging meetings. He was fascinating, brilliant even.

Standing up with a yawn, I stretched out and picked up my handbag. "I'll meet you at the elevator, need to use the bathroom."

"Still leaking?" He cocked a brow as he peered over the computer screen.

"No," I laughed, "that's disgusting."

"I fucked you twice, just making a point."

Case closed; I needed to use the bathroom and not to wipe out what he blew in there. My bladder was full, and a baby was growing. It was one thing I hated about being pregnant.

As I passed her desk, I heard her snicker under her breath. "Leaving so soon?"

Stopping, I backtracked up to her desk and gave her a smile. "Yeah, Brody wants to go pick out some furniture for the baby's room, you know, since we had sex over and over again until his third child was growing in my stomach."

"There are three babies in you?" she asked, wide-eyed.

Oh, my God... really? "No, just one, but it will be our third."

It was petty, but she was young and acted as if everything should be brought to her on a gold and diamond platter. She brought this bitch side out in me.

"You're? Really?" she asked, a scowl on her gorgeous face. It actually made her seem so much uglier.

My hands slid to the front of my stomach. "Yeah, we're pregnant. It's a wonderful thing." I left her there to sit and mull over that thought.

On my way back from the ladies' and where Brody and I had realised, we weren't over each other, an elder gentleman almost bumped into me as he walked out of the men's room. With a steady hand on my back, he smiled in realisation. "Oh, Gabriella, I didn't see you there."

"It's okay," I smiled and then realised who it was wearing a navy suit. "Oh, hi, just going to meet Brody at the elevator."

Brody's boss, Mr Paul Ward, the man who couldn't believe his little, beautiful daughter wasn't seducing married men. Glancing around, I made sure Brody wasn't on his way towards the elevator just yet, as I gathered the courage I needed to do this.

I had confronted Cathy. I could do this next.

"Can I have a quick word?" I asked, tilting my head towards the empty lunchroom.

Eyeing me with his greying brows, he nodded. "Of course, what can I help you about? If it has to do with your husband's hours, I'm sorry that I can't help with that. He chooses his own time."

My heart was pumping a thousand miles an hour as I shook my head, closing the yellow door once he'd entered the room and followed him in. God, I hated confrontation. "Actually, it's about Kate."

"Oh?" he seemed surprised.

"I'm not trying to start up anything. But to be honest, I'm pretty pissed off." I held my ground and sounded strong, not letting a six-foot man intimidate me with his ageing gaze. You could see that he oozed power and was a man to always get his own way. This could blow up in my face and backfire or go amazingly well. I hoped for the best. With a deep, steady breath, I finally spoke, "Brody won't say anything because he doesn't want to jeopardise his place in the company, but I can't sit back and ignore it any longer."

His eyes turned to little slits of almonds, and his polite demeanour was gone. "I would watch your tone if I were you. I don't take kindly to threats, Gabriella." He was now an evil snake. Damn, I hadn't even said anything bad yet.

Laughing, I crossed my arms over my chest. "She calls him on the weekend more than once, leaving drunken voice mails of being able to come and blow his mind if he's up for it if you get my drift. I suggest you make it stop."

"I don't believe that," he sighed about to stand as he waved me off. "Kate doesn't speak that way."

"You will listen to me because I am pregnant. I am hormonal, and I am ten seconds away from throwing that daughter of yours through the top-floor window." Being pregnant was such a great excuse for anything. No one really denied me much of anything. That or they didn't want to risk the chance of upsetting me and being responsible for the tears flowing down my cheeks.

"Gab—"

"Do not interrupt me while I am speaking. It's incredibly rude! You make it stop because if she offers to fuck him again, I will come in here and deal with it myself. He doesn't need a fuck from her. He gets that from me, his wife, and I would appreciate it if you would make her respect the fact that he's married." I was shaking so bad, angry and tearing into him.

Sighing he swiped his thumb over his lower lip and spoke, "I cannot control your husband's extra hour activities. It's clear to me that you're jealous, and as a pregnant woman, you may be insecure about your appearance."

I gasped a loud snort of laughter. "You... you think he's screwing her? She repulses him. She's harassing him, and it needs to end now." When he looked more amused, that pushed me. "Actually, don't worry about it. I have the text messages and photographs, the ones of her in disgustingly trashy lingerie. Selfies, they call them, it's not just her face but her whole damn body along with graphic words. He saves them. Well, I made him do it for legal reasons. Instead of bringing it to your attention, which you have dismissed without

a damn care, I'm going to take my balls and head on over to T
& Gull. You know who they are since they've done legal work
for you in the past. I have a friend there, and he owes me a
favour for picking his daughter up from school on occasion.
They will take this as sexual harassment and then go after you
as his employer for not doing a damn thing about it. They
would ruin you!"

"Are you threatening me?" he asked, bewildered with a
slamming fist against the table. The force was so sudden it
made me jump slightly.

Gripping my fingers into the leather chair, I leant
forward and smiled, speaking low and slowly for him to
understand. "You're damn fucking right I am. Take that whore
out of my husband's office, or you'll be in your grave and still
dealing with all the litigation and trial dates, not to mention,
being broke after you're sued."

"Now, there's no need to do that. I'm sure... no, I'm
positive it will be fixed by the end of the day today."

"Good, also, my husband deserves a raise, and by raise,
I mean a big fucking promotion for all the work he's doing
while you're sitting on your ass and being blown by the
secretary you think no one notices."

His eyes were glowering and face turning even redder.
The vein pulsing in his neck was increasing. "I am a married
man. You have no right, no right at all, to accuse me of such
ludicrous behaviour!"

"The apple doesn't fall far from the tree. You must be
so proud of Kate, taking after you." Rolling my eyes, I headed
for the door. I tossed the old man a glance, remembering the
day Brody had come home and told me about sitting in a

meeting for two hours while she was under there doing God knows what. "Your desk isn't to the floor. Her grey heels are always poking out."

"Gabrielle," he said with a grumble. I turned back and looked at him, almost bursting into laughter as he uttered words that were probably the most humiliating things for him to ask me. "Don't tell my wife."

Needless to say, I walked out of that lunchroom with a victory smile on my face.

Making my way towards the elevator, Brody was there and waiting. A blank stare covered his face as he leant in and placed a kiss on my cheek. "You have no idea how much I love you."

I wondered if he would still love me, knowing what I had just said to the man he was working for.

"Come on, I want to go look at baby clothing." Baby shopping makes everything better.

When the metal doors dinged shut. My back was pinned hard against the wall from the force of his heavy body against mine. His eyes devoured me, fingers through my hair and erection pulsing against me.

"What?" I breathed out and confused by this sudden charge of dominance from him.

"You know..." Brody smirked with a gorgeous smile. "L'intero ufficio appena sentito che strappare il signor Ward un nuovo stronzo." He sounded so smooth and fluent but husky and manly. Listening to him speak in Italian was like the sweetest of chocolate melting against my tongue and down my throat.

I was too speechless from the sheer shock that my husband had just spoke full blown Italian to me to realise that he'd just told me the entire floor of offices had heard me tearing their boss a new asshole.

All that I could say came out as a breathy moan. "Oh, baby, talk dirty to me all the time."

CHAPTER THIRTY-THREE

Yawning as I held the large hot mug of coffee clasped between my palms, I looked over at Noah and Lila who were eagerly and patiently waiting until their father walked into the room before they were allowed to start opening Christmas gifts.

"Now?" Lila asked, yawning once more.

They'd woken us up at 6 AM, too eager to sleep. They also decided to come and jump in the bed with us until Brody told them if they sat by the tree very quietly, they would get to open gifts before our family arrived. Hot on their heels and off they went, Brody jumped on top of me and put the Christmas cheer on my face with a Good Morning, Merry Christmas fuck.

Walking into the living room, the colourful glow of the Christmas lights lit up the room and almost blinding me because of how early it was. "So," he began as he set his drink on the table and walked over to the kids. "I think mama should open her present first, seeing that she's the most beautiful woman in the room."

Melting my heart with more love, "Aww, you're so sweet."

The doorbell sounded, and Brody stood again. Going to answer the door, he was there for a good couple of minutes before coming back into the living room, giving me a look and shaking his head in anger.

"Wait here," I whispered and followed him into the kitchen. "What happened?"

"Scott just showed up," he said quietly. "Dropping off a Christmas gift."

I hesitated before I asked, "What was it?"

Reaching into his back pocket, he held out a photograph and then another. "Oh, God," I gasped and snatched it from him. "He... just gave them over?"

"Yes."

"What did you say? Did he say anything?" I whispered, unable to talk louder.

Brody flexed his hand out and shook his head. "I reintroduced my fist to his face and told him I had nothing more to say at this point. He mentioned something about rehab, but honestly, I am too mad at him right now. If he's getting help for the addiction of pills, then great. He won't be allowed back until he's made amends with you and until you feel safe around him again."

That made me feel a little better.

"Dad," Noah grumbled. "Hurry up!"

Laughing as we were given our cue to go back to the kids, I sat on the couch and my husband on the floor. Brody just reached under the tree and pulled out three gifts, one with a card attached to it and crawled over towards where I sat. Lowering his head, he placed a kiss to my bump and then a sweet kiss landed on my lips. "Merry Christmas, baby."

"Merry Christmas," I smiled. "I love you."

"I love you more." He took the first small box and held it up to me. "Open it. Leave the card for last."

The kids enthusiastically watched as I pulled apart the red and silver paper until I was staring down at my first gift, a new camera. I couldn't wipe the smile from my face. He knew I wanted to get a new one before the baby came in four months.

"Thank you."

He smiled as I leant forwards and kissed him once more. We may have shared many Christmases together before, but today was different. It was our first one here in our home. Usually, we went to our parents, either for lunch and then the other for dinner. Not this year, Brody told me that he wanted to stay here, and he'd love it if I would cook lunch.

Our parents were on the fence, and he told them that they were invited, but he wasn't bothered if they turned up or not. It was our day, a new beginning and new traditions.

Setting aside the camera, I picked up the second which was a larger memory card, and then I went for the smaller box, a Pandora bangle with five small charms and an infinity symbol to remind me of how much Brody loves me. There were letters B, N, L and a small heart with a light blue diamond since we were now expecting another baby boy.

"It's perfect," I said as I began to swell with tears.

"I'll add another letter when we decide on the name," he grinned and passed over the envelope. "Just read it and then let it sink in before you react," he said slightly sceptical.

"What have you done?" I asked, using my nail to peel open the top of sealed envelope.

"You'll see."

After unfolding the A4 sheet of paper, I read line after line and stared at the small photograph right down the very bottom. Looking up at him, he was busy concentrating on my expression which was confusion.

"I thought you told the realtor to go away," I said after a moment.

"No, I gave her a new limit, remember? Then I told her to go and find us something better, bigger and new," he corrected. "I just let you assume, so my surprise wasn't spoiled."

My mind was going crazy. "You bought us a new house?" I couldn't contain the grin. "That's why you've been so resistant in setting up the nursery."

Brody nodded, and I was soon throwing my arms tightly around his neck as the kids excitedly reached for their presents. "I wanted something where we could have a clean state in. This house has some great memories, but they aren't good ones, Gabby. They're mostly fighting and us in separate rooms. You always tell me that you love this house, but I can see and feel how cold it is."

"You're right."

He looked relieved that I was supporting him in this. "You sure?"

"Yes. This house is exactly what you've just described. It doesn't feel like our home anymore. It's riddled with bad memories, and we started fresh again, I've wanted to move since we got back from our trip to the snow." We'd been on the same page about that.

More presents were handed out, and the kids finally dug into theirs until wrapping paper was strewn across the room in all directions. Toys were unwrapped, pulled from their boxes and each was being played with. Brody opened his gifts. The typical shoes, socks and clothes were there. I stepped it up this year, bought him a new wedding band, something more modern, and suited him better than the plain gold ring. This one had a message on the inside, the date I had fallen in love with him, the same as mine. Then, I had taken the photo he took of the two of us in the snow and had it printed black and white, enlarged and framed for our wall.

"It's going to my desk," he smiled, leaning in and tenderly placing his lips to mine.

In the kitchen, that's when the heat started to kick in and test my patience. Brody had asked me last week what I wanted to cook for lunch. I wasn't sure what to make for the family, but he cut me off and closed the recipe book. Looking me in the eye, he shook his head and spoke again, asking me, what I wanted to make.

Well, being hungry, I wanted to eat everything.

That led me to today, where we had more pastries than I could look at — sweet, and savoury, fruit and cheese platters, salads, cold meat and absolutely no baked vegetables at all. Christmas in Australia, with the hot sun and gorgeous day, we were having lots of fruits, and I even made my first Pavlova.

When my mama looked in the fridge, she was blowing steam up my ass for not making traditional Christmas food. Brody was acting as a translator for Lila, who kept asking what that meant every time something had been said. My mama still refused to speak English to anyone. It was also funny that she hadn't noticed my husband had become fluent in Italian and could understand our conversations better than ever.

All those times I had scolded him for sitting on his phone, he's really been learning Italian and was going to surprise me. He learnt all the dirty words first, and it made sex so much hotter when he would whisper in my ear in detail how he was going to fuck me.

I was standing here, a stupid grin on my face, just thinking about it as my mama and sisters were snapping their fingers and spitting out demands.

"Le patate sono di troppo morbido. Ecco, lascia fare a me." They continue on complaining how the potatoes were too soft.

"Gabriella, dov'è le carote?"

"Daddy, do they have to speak in a funny language?" Lila asked, propping herself up on the dining table.

Chuckling, he kissed the top of her head and smiled, "I know. Don't worry. You don't need to understand what they're saying, baby."

"Speaking of babies," Papa spoke up. "Any ideas on what you may call him?"

Brody was still extremely pissed about my dad spanking me to keep me away from him, but he didn't let it show. I felt his hand on my lap, shaking my head. "No, not really, we'll leave it for a surprise until he's born."

"I think Rylan is a pretty cool name," Jessie winked. "Or even Zed."

My mama almost snorted on her wine as my sisters looked mortified along with her. "Lo spero che non sei serio. Il nome del tuo bambino dovrebbe avere un significato, non un nome moderno assurda" she scolded: I shall hope you're not serious. Your child's name should have meaning, not some absurd modern name

"Of course, we'll have a name that means something, right, babe?" I asked, watching his hand now rubbing over my stomach.

He eyed me curiously but nodded. "Yes, our son will have a meaningful name."

Mama seemed to relax as she smiled, "Grazie, Brody."

He just smirked and winked. "You're welcome." I waited for it, and soon, he spoke again just to taunt her, "Zed, I actually don't mind that."

Loraine just smiled, sitting down beside Fred. "You still have some time to decide all of that. Whatever the name, we'll love him all the same."

"Tipico. Vergogna sul nome ancora una volta. *Typical. Shame on the name once again.*" Rude, and to say it so menacingly low with eyes darting over towards me."

Clearing his throat and slowly but calmly standing upright, "Penso che tu sei quello che ha portato la vergogna. A differenza di te, la mia casa è mia, e mia moglie di. Il tutto è deciso da noi: i nomi, come sono cresciuti e il fatto che non li batte. Noi cazzo, ma non così male come avete fatto. Non mi piace il modo in cui viviamo? Beh, sapete dove la porta è, si prega di lasciare e prendere la vostra negatività con voi. *I think you're the one who has brought shame. Unlike you, my house is mine and my wife's. Everything is decided by us: names, how they'll grow up, and the fact, we do not beat them. We fuck up but not as badly as you have done. Don't like how we live? Well, you know where the door is. Please, leave and take your negativity with you."*

I couldn't be prouder of him right now. To stand up to my parents this way in front of our whole family and say what he needed to say in Italian, I was just staring in awe. His parents looked like he had grown a second head but knew what he had just done.

Standing up beside him, I just wanted us to be a united front. We had each other's backs. "Let's go."

"What?" he asked. "Where? Oh yeah? Kids... come on; we're going for a drive."

My mama, who had been ready to fire back at Brody, snapped her mouth back open. "Hai intenzione di lasciare i vostri ospiti? Come maleducato!"

"Yes, we're going to leave our guests, and no, it's not rude. I'm done with you being rude. He is my husband, the father of my children, and I love him. You will not be welcome here if you cannot get your nose out of the air. You're coming off as a..." Well, there was only one word to describe it. "A bitch!"

My Papa glared. "Gabriella! Come ti permetti."

Waving my hand through the air at them, I wasn't listening. "In our home, we speak English. Our children haven't learned Italian, and maybe, when they're older, they will choose to. But in our home, we talk English and without raising voices. We speak kindly. Now, please stay and eat.

There is so much food. Eat and enjoy. If you'll excuse us, we're going to take a look at our new home. I want to see my Christmas present."

"You're leaving?" My sister, Loretta, asked with a gasp. "We haven't eaten dessert."

Slipping my fingers between his, I looked up lovingly towards my husband. "I want to see our new home."

"As you wish," Brody smiled. "Please, everyone, stay and enjoy the food my wife has cooked. We'll be back later, no doubt needing your help in moving to our new house as I think someone is going to want to move tonight once she sees the place." He not so subtly pointed towards me.

"Don't blame me. You're just as eager." I laughed, pulling him along as the kids ran to put their shoes on. "We'll be back!"

Leon grinned, raising his beer. "See you soon."

Before I left, I looked over at everyone and noticed all of their mixed emotions. The four people who seemed to understand were Brody's family. None of mine did, and that saddened me. At the end of the day, this had shown me who was my real family and who wouldn't support us.

The man beside me was my life, and the children beside us were our future. We would be together through it all — good, bad and the amazing.

CHAPTER THIRTY-FOUR

"My ass is huge." At eight months pregnant, I was over it.

Tilting his head to the side and checking out my ass, I turned. Brody winked, came up and roamed his hands over with a squeeze. "Your ass is amazing." He went back to his desk, opening up a recent email.

"That's extremely…" I clicked my tongue, as I couldn't find the word I was looking for. When I found it, I grinned. "You're a pervert."

Laughing and pushing his files aside, he reached up for my hand, stroking his thumb over my palm. "Sit on daddy's lap and let me make you feel better."

"Brody, stop it." I laughed even more, fighting his pull. "You do know that doesn't turn me on at all."

"Sure, it doesn't," he smirked, letting my hand fall as he rubbed my burgeoning bump as our little baby began to kick. "I love feeling these. Only four weeks left."

"I'm nervous," I admitted. I was afraid I wouldn't have a clue how to do it all again. Lila was almost nine, and Noah, nearly ten. They were far from babies. I couldn't even remember how to make a swaddle wrap. "What if I screw things up?"

"You won't, baby. You're an amazing mother."

With a smile, I stood up and walked towards the door of his office. "I'm going to lie down by the fire. It's gorgeous in there."

The new house, it was our home. Everything felt so much homier, and the kids loved having more room outside to play around in. We had a trampoline, and Brody even built them a cubby house. Inside was modern and warm. I think I mostly loved that we hadn't had a screaming match with each other.

Laying on the floor in complete darkness with nothing but the warm glow of the fire, I felt strangely happy. Everything was done, the kids were asleep, and it wasn't even 8 PM. I had nothing to do except lie around and enjoy these last few weeks of pregnancy. As I stretched my arms out, my hands brushed against a set of feet covered in socks. Startled, I jumped up quickly, groaning when the baby kicked hard. "I hate when you creep up like that."

He didn't speak, to begin with. His voice was soft and erotically tender. "You make this room gorgeous, pregnant and fucking perfect."

"Brody." I tilted my head back, arching to get a better look at him.

He walked around and knelt down beside me, hovering above my body as his free hand skimmed up and down my stomach and dipping into the cotton fabric of my pyjama bottoms which were his since mine didn't fit too well anymore.

Fingers teased me and taunted me. "Tell me what you want."

"You." It was automatic. He was all I ever wanted.

Pulling his hand out, he slipped a finger into his mouth, slowly sucking my arousal and tasting me with lust. Then, he was talking as if he hadn't been fingering me. "Tonight was fun. I kicked all your asses twice."

I smiled, stretching out like a kitten and trying not to eye roll as he continued bragging about winning. "It was fun."

Tonight, we'd taken Noah and Lila ten-pin bowling. Brody had won both rounds and offered to buy the kids a happy meal, to cheer them up. They suggested a mc flurry, and he agreed.

Brody's lips against my neck and smiling, he began to kiss me there. His warm breath was against my skin. "The night's not over yet."

"No?" I asked, tilting my head to give him better access. "Are you going to make love to me by the fire?"

"Is that what you want, baby?"

"Hmmm," softly I moaned as his lips latched on. "I want you to make love to me."

Pulling me up onto his lap, his hands was roaming all over my ass and squeezing. "I love you so much, Gabby." His mouth was kissing me while his one hand found its way through my hair, tugging a little.

Kissing each other passionately, I found the bottom of his shirt and lifted it up over his head as I started to undress him. I touched him so no area of skin went untouched. The need to feel him closely was driven by emotions of wanton desire.

He growled as my hand grasped his length. "Baby, let's take this slow."

"Sorry," I tried slowing down. Instead, grinding against him as my hands gripped his shoulders tightly. Slow was the last thing I wanted.

"That's it, baby, nice and slow. If you behave, then I'll make sure you enjoy everything I do."

Soaking from his words, I ground myself deeper against him and ran my fingers up and through his hair. "You feel so good." As I neared the end of my pregnancy, I had been incredibly turned on by anything — the sight of Brody, naked or if he was sitting at his desk with his glasses on as he typed. Even when he let out a manly burp, it all drove me wild. He did ask me if I'd allow him a time out... I just laughed at him and continued to push him down on the bed. There was no way I wouldn't jump on him.

Sliding down my panties, he moved his body between my thighs and kissed over my stomach, down towards my thighs and slipping his fingers inside me with a moan.

As his fingers assaulted me, a distant thought of the past popped into my head while I writhed and bucked my hips underneath him. "Do you remember when you fingered me at school behind the trees?"

"I remember every moment with you," he grinned and pumped his fingers faster. "What about it?"

Breathing picking up, I groaned softly. "Just how... how nervous you were and always asking if I were okay." Clenching around him, my eyes blurred as my orgasm hit hard. Crying out until it began to die down, I caught my breath and smiled towards him. "Although, back then, you didn't make me come much."

His brows dipped slightly, and he looked confused. "I didn't make you come back them?"

Pulling his fingers out before I could answer, they were shoved into my mouth, and his mouth was on my wet core, licking and sucking hungrily. My thighs automatically wrapped around his neck while sucking his fingers. I bit down, moaning as I vaguely remembered his question. "Not always."

"You faked it?"

I was so close. "No, I got there close a lot of times." Reaching down as he moved, allowing me access to his swollen dick and stroked him. "I faked it. I didn't want you feeling bad."

He bit down on my swollen pink lips and pulled away as I let out a painful yelp. "You faked them?" he asked, upset.

Oh, shit.

"Did you just bite me?" I winced, looking dazed as I sat up on elbows. "Not all of them." I wasn't making things any better.

"It hurts worse knowing this after so long." He pulled away completely and just stared at the fire.

"I'm sorry. You know our sex life wasn't that good. I didn't mean it in a bad way. It's just that I almost got there a few times, but I couldn't get off every time. Not since that night in the kitchen, I haven't faked anything. I just didn't tell you if I came or not." I felt like shit that he had thought he'd gotten me off each time. And I wished I kept my big fat mouth shut.

His eyes narrowed in on me. He shook his head angrily. "Don't ever fake with me, Gabby. This whole time, I thought..." Stopping himself as he sighed, "I thought I was pleasing you, as much as you had done to me."

Reaching out to touch him, I didn't want him to think I didn't enjoy sex with him. I did. "No, baby. I promise that it still felt amazing. Just because I didn't have an orgasm doesn't mean that I didn't enjoy it." My hand rubbed his thigh soothingly. "I'm sorry. I just always thought you may have known."

"Well, I can't damn tell if you're faking it or not," he said frustrated. "For all I know, you just faked it then."

"I haven't..." I said, sitting up and reaching for my bottoms and panties again. "I'm sorry."

He watched as I dressed and took a good few minutes to get myself up off the floor. "Can you see what I'm upset? I mean I get why you may have done it, but it still hurts, Gabby."

"I know it hurts you," I said quietly, holding my tears. "I feel really awful about how I told you. I wasn't thinking."

"My tongue was inside you. I know you weren't thinking," he shot back.

Blushing at his words, I chewed my lower lip for a moment, giving him my best puppy dog eyes. "I really am sorry. Please, don't be mad at me."

"Come here," he said, reaching and pulling me to him. He held me and placed a kiss underneath my lobe as I sat on his lap. "I love you, Gabriella. Just please, don't fake them again."

I felt awful even after he insisted on carrying me to bed. I just wanted to sleep and not see that hurt look on his face anymore. It stung when he tucked me into bed and then left the room, claiming to go and get a drink before he got into bed with me. I rolled to my side and snuggled under the covers. I wasn't going to make a bigger deal out of this. Although it was a hurtful truth that had been revealed, I wasn't going to say it was an argument.

Arguing was us yelling and not talking things through, and we hadn't done that for so long. We talked about things. If there was something bothering us, then we spoke about it and worked out our differences to make things better again.

It was going well for us so far. So much for our night of loving passion or so I thought until a shadow appeared at the door. Brody stood there, watching me silently and then speaking. "Gabby, I need some help."

Sitting up worried, my mind raced when I thought he was hurt somehow. "What's wrong?"

Smirking at me, "I have this problem, and it's not going down. I think you need to come and help me out."

My eyes travelled down to where he was looking at, his rock hard cock.

"Well, I think I could help you out." I patted the empty spot beside me. "Come over and let me take a closer look."

He sat down, and when I went to touch, he reached out and slapped a palm around my wrist. "Oh, no, you don't," he said huskily with dominance. "In ginocchio, mentre I fotto la bocca. *On your knees, while I fuck your mouth.*"

The next afternoon, Lila and I were in the kitchen making sugar cookies. She mixed the pink icing while I cut and placed them in the oven. She had first been a little upset that our baby wasn't going to be a sister for her. She came around when I asked her to come and help me decorate the baby's room.

They both were heavily involved with the pending arrival of a brother. I didn't want them to feel left out in the slightest way at all.

"Almost done?" I asked, peering over into the bowl she held tightly.

"This pink looks really pretty, mama," she smiled back. "When can I ice?"

"Not yet, they need to cool down for a bit."

I went to the sink and rinsed my hands underneath the warm water to clean them up. When I looked up, she was over next to my iPod and turning the song up, Taylor Swift, of course, not that I put her on there. I hadn't the clue who she was, but this song was definitely catchy.

Grabbing Lila by the hands, we began to dance in the kitchen.

Twirling around as I held my tummy while Lila was prancing about, I looked up and caught the eyes of my amused husband. Blushing immediately, the thing about being happy, I was able to be silly and feel carefree again without the worry of my family being embarrassed by me.

With a grin, I shuffled towards him with my old school dancing and began to sing to him. "I never miss a beat," I turned, bumping my hips against his. "I'm lightning on my feet. And that's what they don't see, mmm-mmm. That's what they don't see, mmm-mmm." Lila was giggling, and Brody just watched me. "I'm dancing on my own, dancing on my own. I make the moves up as I go, moves up as I go. And that's what they don't know, mmm-mmm."

With my final words, I pointed towards him and motioned with my fingers for him to come at me. "And to the fella over there with the hella good hair, won't you come on over, baby? We can shake, shake, shake."

That was enough to have Brody in front of me and dancing also, laughing, singing and being absolutely young and crazy in love. This was what it was all about, and I finally understood that. This was happiness.

Brody and I both stopped dancing when our feet felt something wet. First instinct was, "Oh, God, I wet myself!" Laughing hard as I assumed my bladder had just been danced into giving way, I was then going from laughing and into a panic.

Tears immediately rolled down my cheeks. "My water broke!" I said through hot salty tears.

"What?" Brody's smile faded instantly, and he was looking at me as if he had just seen a ghost. "Now?" Panic was starting to set in.

"Now! I... Noah! Lila!" I screamed out, panicking as I was far from organised. Hell, I was still baking cookies. "I need to finish..." I said as the oven timer went off. "I can't just leave them."

Brody was in front of me, shaking his head. "You want to what? Finish cooking? No, we're going to the hospital, and you're going to give birth to our son." He started looking around, unsure what to do. "Um, Noah, get the iPad. You're going to grandma and grandpas."

My mind was going crazy, but I was glad he was here to help me through it. With a smile, I reached up and cupped his cheeks. My tears of panic turned to tears of joy and excitement. "Brody…" Blowing out a steady breath as Lila was calling up Loraine, I just smiled. "We're going to have a baby soon."

"Yes, sweetheart, we are."

Two hours and thirty-two minutes later, I gave birth to our son. And Brody hadn't left my side once.

CHAPTER THIRTY-FIVE

BRODY

Tuscany was such an incredible and gorgeous place.

My wife gave me that description less than ten minutes ago. In my own opinion, it was all right. I was pretty simple to please. Give me a glass of scotch and my wife in bed naked, then I was a fucking happy man.

Hearing Noah's grumble behind me, I couldn't help but chuckle. "What's wrong, buddy?"

"When does the baby stop crying? He's so loud!"

Lila giggled from her room as she dressed. "He's a baby. Babies cry, Noah."

"Indeed, they do. You used to cry a lot," I reminded him although he wouldn't remember being that small. I did, it was before things with Gabby went sour.

"But he cries all the time."

"Yes, he's hungry, and your mother is feeding him. You don't like that sound?" I asked, cocking a brow at my son. He was almost a spitting image of myself when I was younger. He'd gotten his mother's good looks and my incredible charm.

Shaking his head, he frowned. Oh, he got the frown from me too, as Gabby liked to point out. "Please make him stop!"

A few seconds later, the noise had died down, and my cock twitched at the thought of my wife's full breast out and exposed. I had given up that in exchange for letting our son fed. They'd be mine again when the kids were asleep.

"Noah, you better finish eating. Aren't you leaving soon?" I asked, glancing at the watch on my wrist.

Was it so bad that I was eager as fuck for Gabby's parents to take our children for a walk and then go back to their suite for most of the day? No, I was damn looking forward to putting that do not disturb sign out on the hotel room door and making the most of our time together.

"You need any help?" I called out, still looking at the sun rising on the vineyard. Why did kids need to wake up so early?

Her soft laugh sang through the air. I instantly smiled. "Unless you've grown boobs and they're full of milk, I think it's best you keep away. Go and put the bottles in the bag for mama, please."

After the birth of Wyatt, we were in a new-born bliss for a good fourteen months until Gabby announced as she rode my dick that I'd gotten her pregnant once more with our now six-month-old son, Milo. Unfortunately, that was the only time

I had blown before her since making sure she was always taken care of first.

I had a new rule. Fingers and tongue were used on her before my cock went in unless I don't have time to mess around with foreplay like when I took her in the bathroom on the plane while her parents watched our sleeping children or if she was sucking me off. I never said no to her mouth.

Back on track, Wyatt and then Milo were both mama's boys. Wyatt was running around now and pulling Lila's hair, payback for all the teasing she used to do to Noah. The older kids as much as they got sick of their little brothers, I was glad we hadn't had any other children after them. The age distance was good. Lila doted her little brothers. I did catch her dressing Wyatt up in a dress and glittery shoes once. He wasn't complaining, so we let them be.

My wife was a superhero at home. I was a prick for not noticing the amount of work she could do around the place and still have time to tend to everyone's needs. I appreciated her all the more.

When Wyatt was born, so small at seven pounds and with barely any dark hair on his head, I wept like a fucking baby. This is what I could have lost. Seeing how well Gabby went through labour even after she almost broke my hands by squeezing so damn hard, I knew we would be back in there soon again. When Milo entered the world, screaming with his mother's loud lungs, I felt the same way again. Call me stupid but I wanted to be back in there and going through all of it over again.

Lila still wanted a little sister after all.

It would be our anniversary soon, and I had learnt it was the simple things that pleased my wife like taking her for dinner to the same place we had gone on our first date, the pizzeria. The table was pre-booked, and I planned to spoil her that day; then, love her all night, provided our sons slept.

Her parents had finally come around. There was no complaint of the names we chose for our sons. There were lots and lots of tears. After I had finally stood up to my wife at Christmas that day, they hadn't interfered again. Maybe my parents said something I didn't know, and I don't want to. Things were good. That's why we were on this holiday with them even if it were an "I'm sorry for treating you both like shit for the past fifteen years" holiday. Least, it wasn't my pockets that were dug into and paying the ridiculous amount for this fucking awesome suite.

It was wonderful to sit and listen to absolutely nothing but silence. Francesca and Giovanni had taken our brood of four for the day. They all went willingly and excitedly, as they mostly wanted to learn how to squash grapes.

I caught Lila two weeks ago, standing in our kitchen and jumping up and down on the kitchen floor. When I asked what she was doing, she smiled and replied practising her squashing. Yes, it was a fucking mess of red and green grapes all over the tiled flooring.

I know you are wondering about Scott. He and I are slowly on speaking terms, but it's not like before. He's my brother, yes. But he also hurt my wife in the worst possible way, and for that, he could never be forgiven. He wasn't allowed in our home, not until Gabby stopped shaking at the sight of him.

Someone who shook at the sight of Gabby was my boss who had his ass handed to him. She bluffed her way through that conversation with messages and photographs I hadn't seen before. The voice mails were there, but that's about all of it. Kate was fired and escorted that evening. How do I know? I was sent the footage from another employer on the floor.

Sitting at the dining table, I was only in a pair of boxer shorts and wet hair from my recent shower. A feast of food that I would never be able to eat was spread out before me. I would eat something only to keep my energy up.

A low cough came from the door, I smirked as I looked up, and Gabby flashed her thigh to me, making my cock swell with need. Soon, baby, I'd have you very soon. A glimmer from her new ring sparkled, and a rainbow pattern was against the wall as she moved her fingers back and forth. I married that woman again, and I would continue to propose every time she had any doubts about how I felt about her.

We only remarried three months after Milo, and there was nobody to witness it other than our children. We married the way we wanted to marry in the first place, together and simple.

"Brody," she began. "Are you busy?"

Flicking page after page through a newspaper that wasn't interesting me, I thought I'd tease her for a moment before giving her what I knew she wanted. "Can I help you?"

"Brody, my parents took the children for a walk," she smiled, biting down her full lower lip. "Do you know what that means?"

In my eyes, she was the most beautiful woman alive. Standing there before me, she wore her long hair tussled and cascading down her back and the silk robe exposing the slightest of cleavage her olive skin offered me to see. Without a hint of make-up, my wife was the most beautiful woman alive. In my eyes, there was nothing to compare her to.

She was like the Tuscan sun, and I found it hard to ever look away from her.

Lowering my eyes once more, I spoke quietly and trying to hide the smile. "No."

"No?" she asked with a frustrated tone. "I want you, Brody." God, I loved it when she begged.

Putting a finger mid-air, I cut her off from saying anymore and then met her eyes with my loving gaze, a smile with a soft but still stern voice. "Gabriella, I'm going to finish reading this paper, and then I'm going to finish off breakfast and get naked with you again; no calls, no interruptions. The day is just ours."

As our life would always be together.

THE END

Can't get enough of Gabby and Brody?
Make sure you sign up for the author's blog
to find out more about them!

Get these two bonus chapters and
more freebies when you sign up at
http://melissa-
bender.awesomeauthors.org/!

Here is a sample from another story you may enjoy:

CHAPTER 1

THE BEGINNING

Olivia Ford's POV

I glared at my oldest brother Nate and crossed my arms. "Nate! Please get out of my room. Right... Now!"

Nate just stared at me with a smirk on his face as he leaned onto the doorframe. "I will but only after you hear me out."

I scowled and had to hold back the overwhelming urge to throw something at him. "Fine. What do you want to talk about? I have a flight tomorrow morning, and I need to pack."

Nate raised an eyebrow and grinned. "I know, and I'm telling you, you better not have any funny ideas while you're in London. No hooking up, no drugs and no booze."

I frowned and narrowed my eyes. Who does my oldest brother think he is? And, surely, he knows me well enough that I would never do drugs. I felt the urge to throw at him a pillow. Or maybe a purse...

"Nate, seriously. I'm an adult. Treat me as such. Also, please get out of my room," I repeated impatiently and watched as my oldest brother roll his eyes at me. At that moment, I felt like I was a kid again.

Nate made a face and shrugged casually as he leaned against the door frame of my room. "I'm not leaving until you agree to my rules." He gave me a bright mocking grin as he sang his words out and his eyes glinting with amusement.

I sighed exasperatedly and crossed my arms. "Okay. Yes, get out." I pointed to the door, and Nate gave me a smirk before his face softened as he watched me packing my stuff into the little black suitcase on my bed.

"I don't even see why you're working as an air stewardess of all things. You can work at the family company or something."

This topic was an ongoing conversation for the past two years of my life. You can say that my family was very wealthy, and I am an heiress. However, I didn't really want to depend on my family's wealth for a living nor did I want to work in the family business. I wanted a job of my own. I felt that being an air stewardess allowed me to earn my own income and allowed me to travel a little. It was one of my dreams to travel around the world.

As I packed my small black suitcase, my second older sister, Elena, entered my room and knocked, alerting me to her presence. Giving her a distracted smile as she sat on my bed, I asked, "Hey Ellie, do you need anything?"

She shook her head, and her dark hair bounced on her back as she smiled, "No, I just wanted to ask you if you remembered what's going on this Thursday?"

I frowned and slowly shook my head as I tried to remember any events that would be taking place on said date. "Nope. Sorry, nothing rings a bell."

Ellie grinned before prompting. "My engagement party will be held on this Thursday!"

My eyes widened. Good god, I had completely forgotten about it. "Oh god, I completely forgot about it. Ellie, I'm so sorry." I apologised and bit my lip as I turned to face her.

"It's alright, but you will be there, right? You're my sister, and I want you to be there." Ellie hugged me and grinned.

I nodded, "Definitely. I'll be there, and I'll be back on Wednesday." I reassured her before stopping as I realised something. "Wait a minute, why are you so chirpy about it?" I questioned suspiciously. I had a hunch that Ellie was up to something. She was never good at hiding or keeping things a secret.

Ellie bit her lip and averted her eyes, "Uh. Nothing. It's just that Scott has a younger brother who is only one year older than you and—"

"No. Absolutely, not. I'm not interested in blind dates. Not with guys you and Lily are trying to set me up; not even Scott's younger brother," I said and narrowed my eyes at Ellie. At least, she had the decency to be embarrassed. I saw her expressions changed — from embarrassment to disbelief and finally, annoyance.

"Am I that obvious?"

"Yes. It's pretty clear. At least, try to be less obvious about it like Lily. I don't see why you and Lily have to keep setting me up."

Ellie crossed her arms defensively as she sniffed, obviously miffed, that I had seen through her act. "It gets lonely if you're single. All Lily, mum and I want is just to see you happy," she said.

"I know. It's just that I'm happy as I am now."

She hugged me and grinned. "Okay. As long as you're happy, but Scott's younger brother is really, really hot."

I rolled my eyes and zipped my suitcase. "I'm not interested Ellie."

I could sense that Ellie was pouting but sighed as she responded, "Alright. Anyway, Mom called to tell me to ask you to come down for dinner."

I nodded and pushed my blonde hair back. "Okay. I'll be down in a second; I just have to pack some last few items. You can go first."

Ellie stood up from my bed. "Okay. Be quick." With that, she walked out of my room.

As I headed down for dinner, I could hear my brothers yelling in the living room. I rolled my eyes. Even though I was the youngest in the family of six children, my brothers never seemed to grow up.

"Whoop! Score! Ha! Take that you bloody losers!"

"What the fuck, Nate? I'm so going to get you for this!"

"Jake, Go get Tristan!"

I ignored them and walked to the dining room, where my oldest sister Lily was with her husband, Parker, and their two children, Phillip, and Penny. Ellie was there already, sitting next to mom and dad. I took the vacant chair beside my father.

"Just to double check, everyone in this family will be home for Ellie and Scott's engagement party, right?" My mom questioned as she glanced at all of us for confirmation. Lily and

Parker said yes while I simply gave a nod. On the other hand, all three of my brothers yelled, "Hell yes."

"Language!" I snickered inwardly at my mom's narrowed gaze towards my brothers.

"Of course, we have to. We'll be here to see if Scott has any second thoughts and stuff." I tried not to laugh at Ellie's horrified expression at Nathaniel's announcement.

"Mom! You've got to do something! Please!" She begged while shooting evil stares at our brothers.

"You boys are going to interrogate Scott on Thursday?" My dad asked with his eyebrows raised.

"Yeah. All three of us." Nathaniel grinned. Tristan cleared his throat, and Nathaniel sighed before grumbling out. "Two of us."

My dad wrapped an arm around my mom's waist and said cheerily, "Well! I'll join you."

Ellie shook her head, and her shoulders slumped in defeat. "I thought that you approved of Scott!"

My dad grinned. "Yeah, I did, but he may jilt you at the altar. And, no daughter of mine will go through that." At this statement, I was really thankful that I didn't have a boyfriend. Lily started laughing while I tried not to laugh at Ellie's horrified face.

"Dad!" Ellie glared at dad while my brothers smirked smugly at her.

"So Liv, you don't have a boyfriend right?" I glanced up at Jake, Nathaniel's twin and spooned some soup into my mouth.

"No. I'm not interested in having one."

"Good, you're still twenty-three. No rush." My dad butted in as he ate.

"Great. There goes my chance of getting eloped," I replied dryly.

I watched in satisfaction as Nathaniel tensed. "You're getting eloped?"

I shook my head in frustration. "No! It's called sarcasm. God, you're stupid."

Jake glared at me mockingly. "Not funny Liv."

Rolling my eyes at them, I started to eat and hoped that dinner would pass soon. Being the youngest in the family sucked. Lily was the oldest in the family while Nathaniel and Jacob — also known as Jake — were twins. They were followed soon after by my sister Ellie, and finally, another twin, Tristan and me.

It really was not a walk in the park to be the youngest in the family.

Drake Henderson's POV

"Okay, Drake, I have something really important to say, and I need you to listen to me." I glanced up curiously at my older brother Scott and slid my phone into my pocket.

"Okay, you're scaring me. What is it?" I grinned as my older brother rolled his eyes at me.

"I'm engaged."

"And?" I raised an eyebrow and commented dryly.

Scott frowned. "Yeah, that's it. I'm engaged. Why aren't you freaking out?"

I smirked in response. My brother thought that he was being sneaky with his girlfriend who I have yet to meet. But, honestly, was I born yesterday?

"I knew you had a secret girlfriend all along, and well, to hear that you're engaged is not that big of a deal. I mean, sure, I'm annoyed that you didn't tell me or let me meet her, but it's your choice."

Scott grimaced, most probably sulking that he wasn't that good at keeping secrets before smiling at me. "Alright, whatever. Yes, I have a girlfriend who is now my fiancée. I'm sorry for not telling you. You're bound to mess it up somehow."

I shot him a scowl; it was nice to know that my own brother had such little faith in me. "Thanks for your everlasting confidence in me, brother."

"It's true, and you know it. Anyway, her name is Elena Ford, and we've been together for three years." Scott grinned before shoving a playful punch in my arm.

I blinked and shrugged before replying, "Okay. When can I meet her?"

Scott beamed, happy that I was taking his *not-so-secret* news easily without making a fuss.

"This Thursday, her parents would be throwing an engagement party for us at their family home. You can go, right? Seeing that the only family member I have is you. Mom is in Hawaii, and Dad is in Scotland."

"Yeah, yeah, sure. What's the dress code?"

Scott shrugged. "Really fancy. Wear a suit with a bow tie."

"That fancy with so much fuss? Why not elope? Surely that is easier."

"I don't have a death wish! She has three brothers that all play football. The eldest used to be in the army. So, you can imagine their size." Scott gave me a pointed look, and I snorted, already imagining the image of three tall, muscular guys pounding my older brother for eloping with their sister.

"Three brothers? That's a lot. Does she have any other siblings? Also, you're only twenty-seven. You don't have to get married this early you know."

Scott sighed before frowning at me. "Look, I love her, and nothing you say or do can change that. Yes, Ellie has two sisters, an older one and a younger one."

"You're hopeless, but it's your death wish." I shook my head and shrugged. It doesn't mean that because I didn't share my brother's idea of commitment, I was going to discourage him about it.

Scott narrowed his eyes at me before exhaling heavily. "Whatever, man, it's my life. Not yours. Also, do remember to wear a bow tie. Aren't you going to pack your bags? You're leaving tomorrow morning aren't you?"

"Yeah, I already did. The groupies in London are worth a second look, you know?"

Feeling a disapproving stare at me, I looked up to see Scott looking at me with exasperation. "One day, some girl is gonna knock your world off its axis, and you're gonna see that being a man-whore is not that appealing."

I shook my head and smirked. "Sure. She can try, but I like the way my life is now."

Scott simply shook his head as head and went back to his room.

If you enjoyed this sample then look for **Bad For Me** on Amazon!

Other books you might enjoy:

Married to the Bad Boy
Letty Scott
Available on Amazon!

Other books you might enjoy:

One Friday Night
Miss Yvy
Available on Amazon!

Introducing the Characters Magazine App

Download the app to get the free issues of interviews from famous fiction characters and find your next favorite book!

iTunes: bit.ly/CharactersApple
Google Play: bit.ly/CharactersAndroid

Acknowledgements

WATTPAD. Thank you so much, without this website I would have never taken the daunting step and posted my first ever story. I was hooked right from the very start! It started as a hobby, and is now my addiction.

BLVNP. You truly are ninjas!! The incredible work that your team has gone through with this exciting adventure. Le-an Lai, you blew my mind with your very first email! I am forever blessed that you decided to take this chance on me. AJ, I feel sorry for what you had to read in each chapter LOL. Thank you for your hard work in making this book just right, you rock! The team of editors, and everyone else who helped make this dream come true, I love you all!

MEL. My lightsaber partner in stopping crime! Thank you for the wonderful friendship. The daily banter, hysterical laughter and our silly dance moves. For being there and reminding me that I've got this and the book is going to be totally awesome!

NETTY. Thank you nan, for always believing in me from the very start! Your excitement and eagerness pushed me to continue. No one was happier for me than you were.

MUM. There's a bottle of wine for you in my fridge!! I'm not sorry for all the daily phone calls, as I know you secretly love it! Thank you for always being there, and telling me I can achieve anything I want if I set my mind to it.

AUNTY SANDRA. My second mum. If I ever needed a pick me up, all I had to do was call you. Thank you for always encouraging me and being here for me. It means more to me than you'll ever know.

KIKI & LOLO. You both must be super annoyed with me by now, going on and on about this book.. but hey, that's what sisters are for! I promise to keep annoying you! I love you both!

MITCHELL. I'm sorry for the many laptops you have had to buy me when I grew frustrated, and they somehow stopped working.. ha! Sorry for the days that I spent completely engrossed in my writing, not paying attention to you. I am grateful that you have allowed me to follow my dreams, and helped with making this happen. Thank you for your unconditional love and support. I love you millions!

MY READERS. Thank you! Without you, this wouldn't be possible! I have gained so many of you, and will be forever thankful that you choose to read my stories. I have so much more instore for you all, this is definitely just the beginning.

Sweetly, Melissa. xo

Special Thanks To:

Laeticia
Ilona
Chloe gleeson
Lisa Anne Gorman
Sophie Mcbeth
Samantha C.
Jennifer Perez
Chrissy Y.
Underneath_Waters

Author's Note

Hey there!

Thank you so much for reading Forgotten Sweethearts! I can't express how grateful I am for reading something that was once just a thought inside my head.

I'd love to hear from you! Please feel free to email me at melissa_bender@awesomeauthors.org and sign up at http://melissa-bender.awesomeauthors.org/ for freebies!

One last thing: I'd love to hear your thoughts on the book. Please leave a review on Amazon or Goodreads because I just love reading your comments and getting to know YOU!

Whether that review is good or bad, I'd still love to hear it!

Can't wait to hear from you!

Melissa Bender

About the Author

I'm wife to a FIFO miner. Mother of three. Passionate foodie, and a vivid dreamer. Living in a small beach town in the lovely Tasmania. I spend my time between home and down at the beach… making memories, and capturing the moments.

When I'm not glued to my laptop, I'm either in the kitchen creating recipes, cooking, or having a Netflix binge session. Often, I find myself drifting off into the world of make believe, getting lost inside the stories I write.. I write because it's my passion. I want to create a world for my readers to get lost in.. For them to swoon, and fall in love the way I do with each character made.. Oh, and I love starbursts!

Sweetly, Melissa xx

60527648R00252

Made in the USA
Lexington, KY
10 February 2017